SEVEN
DEADLY
THORNS

SEVEN DEADLY THORNS

AMBER HAMILTON

BLOOMSBURY

LONDON OXFORD NEW YORK NEW DELHI SYDNEY

BLOOMSBURY YA
Bloomsbury Publishing Plc
50 Bedford Square, London WC1B 3DP, UK
Bloomsbury Publishing Ireland Limited
29 Earlsfort Terrace, Dublin 2, D02 AY28, Ireland

BLOOMSBURY, BLOOMSBURY YA and the Diana logo
are trademarks of Bloomsbury Publishing Plc

First published in the United States of America in 2025 by Bloomsbury YA
First published in Great Britain in 2025 by Bloomsbury Publishing Plc

A catalogue record for this book is available from the British Library

ISBN: HB: 978-1-5266-8030-3; Export PB: 978-1-5266-8029-7;
Export TPB: 978-1-0372-0090-8; eBook: 978-1-5266-8028-0

4 6 8 10 9 7 5 3

Typeset by Westchester Publishing Services

Printed and bound in India by Thomson Press India Ltd

To find out more about our authors and books visit www.bloomsbury.com and sign up for our newsletters
For product safety related questions contact productsafety@bloomsbury.com

For sale in the Indian subcontinent only

To the villains
Because we're all wicked
in someone else's fairytale

PRONUNCIATION GUIDE

Viola: *veye-OH-luh*

Roze: *ROHZ* (like rose)

Meiga: MAY-guh

Vandenberghe: *VAN-den-berg*

Aragoa: *AIR-uh-GOH-uh*

Castelle: *cast-EL*

Roquelart: *ROHK-el-ar*

Borges: *BOR-hes*

Alexandre: *al-ex-AN-der*

León: *lee-ON*

THE FIRST
DEADLY THORN

Once upon a time, in the winter of war, when the flakes of ash fell like feathers from the bloody sky, the Queen sat in her garden, and from the pitch-black earth burst roses like lesions.

She wept for the death of her kingdom in her garden of roses and ash and pricked her finger on a rose thorn, and three drops of blood fell upon the earth.

Scarlet blood sunk beneath the soil, and she thought to herself, "If only I had a child as dire as ash, as perilous as blood, and as nightmarish as my roses."

Soon after she had a baby boy. He was sprouted, not born, from the ground where her blood was spilled, and he was as wicked and cursed a thing as the soil that birthed him, with hair as white as ash, a mouth red as blood, and a heart as black as death.

He was called Roze and was viler than any in the Kingdom.

CHAPTER ONE

Prince Pompous, His Royal Heinousness, Roze Roquelart, has shredded my last nerve.

I don't hate easily, but after years of enduring him—the way he flaunts his wealth and status, his bullying, the cruel sneer on his lips—Saints, I *hate* him. And I don't feel the least bit guilty about it. He deserves every drop of my contempt.

Today, for example, he's torturing some poor freshman in the Commons, a space that once upon a time was filled with the aroma of freshly cut grass and golden sunshine. That was before I was born. Now, it's as gray and grim as the rest of the castle—a compact dirt floor and a glass ceiling arching overhead to keep the deadly Mists, the curse of our Kingdom, from reaching the students of Vandenberghe Academy.

Roze has forced his victim to sit astride the statue of a griffin at the center of the Commons, where the student now wails the school song at the top of his lungs, completely naked except for his socks. Around the griffin and its disgraced rider, students howl with laughter. The poor boy's face is rose red, and he's shivering in the winter cold that seeps through the enclosure.

And no one is doing *anything*. Students litter the Commons, leaning against the stone of the castle in groups, sitting on benches with open textbooks, or crowding around the griffin to laugh at the freshman.

I sigh and look down at Saint Waffles, my pet gargoyle, sitting at attention at my feet. Sweet little thing. Cerise, my best friend, says he looks like a dirty dish towel, but I think he's adorable—wrinkled from claw to nubby tail, two little tusks poking up over his sagging lips, matching horns jutting from between his ears, and bat-like wings tucked onto his back. "No one is going to stop him," I tell Waffles. "He's their Prince. The Queen terrifies them."

Waffles blinks at me.

"If I don't do something, no one else will."

Waffles snorts like he knows what I'm thinking of doing and he doesn't approve. But I have to do it. I know the sting of being outcast all too well to let it happen to someone else when I have the power to stop it.

The freshman's voice cracks, and a chorus of laughter breaks out. I've had enough. I charge into the Commons, shouldering my way through the crowd, Waffles at my heels.

"Stop it!" I shout over the noise. "Let him down this instant!"

I halt just before the dais where Prince Roze stands, towering over me. He freezes when he spots me, and his face twists into a scowl. His lifeless eyes focus on me in a way that makes him look more like a portrait than an actual human being.

No, that's not right. He's more like a statue, cold and gray and lifeless. Irises the color of shattered glass. Hair like snow-white ash. Every angle of his face is sharp and perfect—so beautiful that he's difficult to look at—like he's cut from marble by a particularly disturbed sculptor.

His hands are covered in those black gloves he always wears. He slides one into the pocket of his trousers. In the other, he's holding a bright red apple. In the leached light of the Commons, it looks like the only living thing around.

Those damn apples. Such an obnoxiously simple way the Prince shoves his wealth and status in all our faces.

The Mists came nearly two decades ago, clouds of ravenous poison sent by our enemy kingdom Castelle to destroy us, killing all life in their path—plant, animal, and human. They forced the whole Kingdom to cage itself inside the castle, shoved together like the seeds of a pomegranate. All that's left of the once expansive orchards of the Aragoan countryside is a

4

small apple grove left in the royals' private courtyard, caged in glass and for their use and theirs alone. In the autumn, I rarely see Roze without a beautiful ripe apple in his gloved hand, red as blood. It's disgusting.

He takes a languid bite as he watches me.

"*Sinclair.*" He says my last name slowly, savoring each syllable. Roze is known for his unpleasantness, but he hates *me* with blistering particularity—probably because I'm the only one who refuses to tolerate his awfulness. "No 'Good morning, Your Royal Highness'?"

I close my eyes, breathing deeply. That old familiar darkness lurks in the back of my mind, but I've had plenty of practice keeping it in check.

Calm.

Control.

I am the paragon of composure, and it'll be a dark day in the sun when I let the likes of Roze Roquelart break me.

My shadows only come when anger, fear, or even unchecked joy rise too high. But that hasn't been an issue in a long time. I learned self-control at a young age, as one must when the consequence of being a *meiga,* a wielder of magic, is death. And if my emotions have been a little more . . . *difficult* to contain lately? Well, I'm eighteen, aren't I? This is my last year at Vandenberghe—there are enormous academic and social pressures, and I have the added headache of being a prefect, which means policing the delinquent behavior of our dear, beloved Prince.

"Let him go, and give him back his clothes, or I'll report you to the dean," I say coolly.

The corner of Roze's mouth bends cruelly. "Come now, Sinclair, it's just a bit of fun. A good old-fashioned hazing. He doesn't mind, isn't that right, um—" He turns to the boy.

"Johnson," the boy mutters miserably.

Prince Roze snorts, glancing down at his naked body, and the surrounding students snigger. "Who doesn't love a little irony, eh, Sinclair?"

I glare up at him. "Let. Him. Go. *Now.*" I keep the command in my voice, but my breathing is turning uneven. I can feel the itch at the ends of my fingertips—my shadows begging to be set free.

The Prince's face flickers from casual amusement to sharp cruelty. My heart pounds as I stare into his unblinking eyes.

Calm.

Composure.

I will not let him affect me.

Roze leaps down from his spot on the dais—right in front of me. He's in my space now, a tower of arrogance. He takes another bite of his apple. Crisp, sweet-smelling flecks of apple flesh sprinkle my cheeks, and I flinch.

He swallows, and his neck bobs where a tattoo of a death's-head hawk moth spreads its peculiarly patterned wings. It's one of only two things about his appearance that are slightly lifelike. The other is the single earring of a black rose he wears in his left ear—a narcissistic reference to his name, I suppose. But these symbols of life, the moth and the rose, contrasted with his emotionless eyes and the coldness of his features, only make him look more like a corpse.

"Why do you do this, Sinclair? Why do you make it your personal mission to be such an utter killjoy?"

I tilt my chin up at him. "You think I'm a killjoy. I think you're a slimy, entitled ass. Regardless, you're breaking the rules."

"Rules," he mutters, eyes roving over my face. "Don't pretend you care about rules. You care about control. Just admit it, Sinclair. You're such a bore, you wouldn't know fun if it stripped naked and danced around in front of you. It's pathetic. You can't have fun yourself, so you spoil mine."

Bore. Pathetic. The words sear me, and my chest clenches. For just a fraction of a second, I feel a ribbon of shadow slip free from a finger. In less than a breath, I have my breathing under control, and my hand hidden in my skirt . . . but I catch the Prince's eyes flash to my hand and then back up to my face.

I almost think he saw something, but his expression doesn't change a bit. I quickly pull his attention back to the argument. "Believe me, *Your Highness*, there's little I could do to add to your spoiling."

Students chuckle behind us, and Roze's frown turns brutal. He drops the apple on the ground, half eaten, and I wince at the wastefulness.

"You're supposed to be some sort of genius, Sinclair, but you don't have much sense if you think you can speak to me like that."

He takes another step closer, leaning in, his perfectly bowed lips sneering at me. Then he brings his mouth close to my ear. I can feel his cool breath on my cheek, smell the aroma of spice, winter, and apple juice on him. Gooseflesh travels down my arms, and I clench my fists in my skirt.

In a voice so low only I can hear, he whispers, "You ought to be more careful. Especially now that I know what you are." And then he breathes the final word that sets my blood on fire. *"Witch."*

The last dregs of my self-restraint slip through my fingers.

I punch him.

CHAPTER TWO

"Viola!" Someone shouts my name, but I barely hear it over the ringing in my ears.

Prince Roze is splayed on the ground, staring up at me, utterly shocked, while Waffles attacks his pant leg, growling and drooling. Blood trickles from his nose—proof that he is at least *somewhat* human, I suppose. I should be horrified at what I've done. But I'm not. In fact, I feel damn good.

My knuckles burn where they've contacted his face, and I don't even see the crowd around me—only Roze's furious eyes, silver and sharp as bayonets. I don't hear the shouting—only the sound of my pounding heart as I stretch my fingers, feeling my shadows pushing at their boundaries as the Prince stares up at me.

A hand grips my shoulder, and I blink, snapping out of it. My vision clears. The shadows dissipate.

"Vi, are you all right?"

I turn, and Cerise is looking at me with her brows shoved together in half rage, half concern as she takes in the scene, particularly the royal sprawled on the ground and my heaving breaths. I'm not surprised that she's checking on *me*, not on him, even though he's the one on the ground. Roze has endeared himself to no one. Cerise on the other hand is the sort of person willing to go to war for those she cares about. She can be rather hotheaded that way.

"I'm fine," I reassure her. If I don't, I know she'll do a lot worse than punch the Prince.

"What's going on?"

A boy with wire-rimmed glasses and smartly combed auburn hair shoves his way through the crowd, and a wave of relief hits me—Kole. He's a prefect and one of the only other people who won't let Roze's antics fly. Except . . . I've just punched Roze, which means *I* am now the one deserving punishment.

The crowd parts for him, and as Kole glances between the Prince and me, I hate how I must look to him. I'm shaking—I have none of the cool calm that I long for. I open my mouth to explain, but he cuts me off.

"All right," Kole says, turning to the crowds. "Back inside, all of you! And someone give Johnson his clothes back."

A few students giggle as the crowds begin to filter out.

"Get off me, you little monster," Roze growls, kicking Waffles aside and shoving himself to his feet. He rounds on me. "You—"

Kole stops him with a hand to the Prince's chest. My breath catches as Roze freezes, staring down at the hand. He looks up, lethally slow.

Kole drops his hand and clears his throat. "Apologies, Your Highness."

I hate that he's cowering before Roze. *This* is the problem. We are all beholden to him simply because of his family name.

Roze does what he pleases. To whomever he pleases. The absolute prick.

"Are we good?" he snarls at Kole.

Kole frowns and nods stiffly.

Roze's eyes flash to mine, and there's a promise in them—this isn't over. He straightens the lapels of his school jacket and struts off. I take small satisfaction when I see him pull a handkerchief from his pocket to stop his bleeding nose. He makes it twenty feet before Waffles chases after him with a tiny, ferocious roar, and Roze nearly sprints from the Commons. I have to bite my lip to keep from laughing.

When his back is turned, Cerise sends the Prince a rude gesture.

"Did I really see you hit him, Viola?" Kole asks.

"He deserved it," Cerise mumbles.

I sigh, turning back to him and hating the look of disappointment in his peat-green eyes. "Yes, but he was bullying that boy."

"Johnson?"

My mouth twitches at the name—Saints, I know I shouldn't find it funny. Kole raises his eyebrows.

"Sorry," I mutter.

"Viola." His mouth is creased with concern. "I thought better of you. Brawling in the Commons?"

"I know," I say.

"She wasn't *brawling*," Cerise cuts in.

"I'm going to have to report this to the dean. You realize that, right?" says Kole.

A stone drops in my gut, but still I say, "I understand."

Cerise's jaw drops. "Come on, Belcamp. You know how the Prince is to her. So she snapped *one time*—"

He shakes his head. "It's no excuse. You know you can't stoop to his level." He looks at me, his expression genuinely sorry. "How will it look if I don't report you after half the school saw you hit the *Prince*? Of all the people to pick a fight with . . ." He pauses for a long moment. "I'm sorry. Really, I am."

I nod, wrapping my arms around myself. Kole raises a hand, as though to put it on my shoulder, but then he drops it, as though he's changed his mind. And now I am colder than ever.

"I'll see you both at dinner." He hurries off, presumably to inform the dean that I've assaulted a member of the royal family.

I watch Kole go—his lean figure, the smart crop of his auburn hair. After that display, how far have I fallen from grace in his eyes?

What a fine day this is shaping up to be.

"I think Roze saw my shadows," I whisper to Cerise. "Maybe . . . I'm not sure. He called me a witch. That's why I hit him. I was . . . I don't know. Scared."

The true terror of what just happened hits me. Several weeks ago, our King died rather suddenly, and since then, the Queen seems to be expressing her grief through a renewed zeal for exposing and punishing *meigas*—*Traitors! Heretics! A plague of debauchery!* So the Queen and her minions call us, stirring up suspicion, turning neighbor against neighbor. The public executions that result are a convenient distraction from issues that are apparently of less concern to the Crown, like the dwindling food supply.

There's little to eat in a kingdom where we can only consume what can be grown and bred inside these castle walls. For those of us who are not a part of the gentry, it means a daily diet of oat pottage, mushroom tea, and root vegetables.

Hunger turns people desperate. Poverty turns them mutinous. The Queen knows this and turns their attention toward heretics like me to keep their eyes off her. I'll be condemned to the gallows if anyone so much as suspects I *might* be a *meiga*.

And now . . . Roze could know. Of all people in the Kingdom, the one person who hates me beyond restraint or reason could know my secret, the one person with the power to *do something* with that sensitive information. *Shit.*

Cerise comes close and rests her head on my shoulder.

"There's nothing wrong with your magic," she says quietly.

"It doesn't matter."

"It *does* matter. You couldn't help—"

I glare at her. She gives me a sheepish look. "Sorry."

Cerise doesn't understand. She has no clue what it's like for your whole life to ride on keeping a secret. I was born with shadows in my bones, and they have brought me nothing but misery. If I could produce even a tongue of flame instead of shadow, it would at least help me read after dark. Keep me warm. Light a candle. But what can shadows do? These slivers of night do nothing but force me into hiding, corner me into a life of fear.

But I can't be frustrated with Cerise. She's the only person I've ever trusted enough to tell her about the darkness inside me—the only person I've let get close enough. I can't say why exactly I knew I could trust Cerise after everyone else had proven themselves untrustworthy. Even my parents abandoned me when they learned what I was. Not Cerise. Never Cerise.

She gives me a gentle pat on the shoulder. "Come on," she says, grabbing my elbow. "Let's get you a cup of tea."

She leads me out of the Commons, and as she does, I force myself not to look at the thing lurking in my peripheral vision.

In a high window of Berlaise House, overlooking the Commons, the wispy gray ghost of a little boy peers through the casement windows, grim eyes set on me. And he's crying.

———

The day only gets worse.

The atmosphere in Vandenberghe has been tense and drawn since the death of the King on All Hallows Eve. Classes have continued as normal, but voices are more hushed, laughter is more subdued, and rumors spread over cups of tea in the common room late at night. People wonder how the King could have died so suddenly, why no one has been told *how* he died, and what the grieving, merciless Queen will do about it, besides continue her crusade against *meigas*.

Since the All Hallows Eve masquerade, death has hung in the air, and the gloom is palpable in the common room of Berlaise House that evening.

I sit before the hearth with Cerise and Kole, curled up on the sofa. Waffles snoozes lightly in my lap next to my homework. I try to focus on my translations for my advanced ancient Aragoise class, but I've been staring at the same paragraph for ten minutes while I fiddle with the chain of my locket.

Because for the last several minutes Kole's thigh has been lazily brushing against mine, and I can't stop thinking about it. It hasn't seemed to affect *his* concentration. He and Cerise are prattling on with their theories about the King's death, as they and many others often do these days, as though he can't feel the heat of our bodies through our school uniforms.

"Well, I think it was his heart," Cerise says. "Sort of given to fits of rage, wasn't he?"

She stretches her long legs out on the rug, her back leaning against an armchair. Her trousers are tucked into her boots, her school blazer sleeves are rolled up to her elbows, and her tie hangs loose around her neck. Cerise is tall and lithe, her dark hair pulled back in strict cornrows, her eyes sharp and mirthful as she looks at Kole and me, occasionally glancing at where our knees touch and back up to me.

"Could be," Kole answers. My heart flutters strangely at the way the glow of the fire outlines his strong jaw. He removes his glasses and sighs while he cleans them with the tail of his shirt, shifting his leg against mine . . . moving closer.

"Maybe it was the Huntsman," Cerise says with a sly grin.

Kole groans, and I smile. Cerise doesn't *really* believe that the Queen would compel her rumored personal assassin to kill the King, but it's a conspiracy theory that she adores to goad Kole with.

"Not this again," he says, throwing his head against the back of the sofa.

"Everyone knows they didn't get along. And the King's been half loony for ages. Maybe she was tired of seeing an incompetent man in power when she thought she could do a better job."

"Not that she *is* doing a better job," I mutter.

"You're forgetting that the simplest explanation is often the correct one. The King wasn't well. He most likely died of illness," Kole argues.

"A convenient cover-up for murder," Cerise shoots back.

"Saints below, you're impossible." Kole wipes a frustrated hand over his face while Cerise smiles like a menace.

"What's that you're working on?" I interrupt, eyeing the small gold something Kole has in his lap.

He loves to tinker—always has some new contraption he's working on. He and Cerise are in Marquet-Blanc House, the house for students who plan on going into the sciences. Vandenberghe sets students on career tracks early, making them as useful as possible as soon as possible.

Marquet-Blanc has its own common room, but they prefer to spend evenings with me in Berlaise House, the house of the humanities and the arts. Our common room is far cozier—plush chairs and sofas all in Berlaise blue, chess tables, bookshelves that reach to the ceiling covering every wall, and even an upright piano submerged beneath the scrawled pages of half-composed melodies, stacks of books, and dripped candle wax.

Kole holds the small object up for me to see. "It's a key," he says, handing it to me.

It's a strange little thing. I turn it over in my hands, running the pads of my fingers along a row of impossibly tiny gears in the handle.

Kole leans over, pointing, and I can feel his breath on my neck. "It can open any door," he whispers.

"It's wonderful," I say, looking up at him.

He smiles crookedly at me, and I think my heart stops for a full beat. Cerise clears her throat, and Kole blinks, looking away. He plucks the key from my hand.

"Thanks," he mutters.

The common room door opens behind us, and Cerise's head pops up, peering over the back of the sofa. Her mouth forms a cocky grin I know all too well as she sings, "Hi there, Bianca."

A girl with poofy blond hair, who a moment ago was walking purposefully toward us, halts at Cerise's greeting.

"Oh. Hi." An unmistakable blush tints her pale cheeks, and Cerise's grin broadens. I roll my eyes. The merciless flirt.

"Viola, Professor Borges sent me to find you," Bianca says.

"What, now? Why?"

Professor Borges is my academic adviser, but we don't have a meeting scheduled. Besides, it's well past nightfall. My mind goes straight to the altercation with Roze in the Commons, and I resist the urge to glance at Kole. He must've told the dean—it was the right thing to do, after all. I broke school rules. It would have been worse for everyone if he'd said nothing. But if this is about that . . . why is my adviser calling for me and not the dean herself?

Bianca shrugs. "I don't know, but she said it was urgent."

"Vi," Kole says, and I force myself to look him in the eye. "I didn't say anything to Dean Gomes."

"What?"

He shakes his head. "I haven't said anything. I . . . couldn't."

A lump forms in my throat. Maybe it's not about the fight in the Commons. But I can't fathom what else would cause the professor to summon me at this hour.

"I'll go," I say, lifting myself from my seat. "Bianca, will you help Cerise put Waffles back in my room?"

Bianca's eyes widen a little, and she says, "Sure."

From behind her, Cerise holds her hand over her heart and mouths, "You're the best."

I wink on my way out of the room.

CHAPTER THREE

Witch. Witch. Witch. With every step I take, I can hear the hate in Roze's voice as he whispered that damning word in my ear.

Maybe I can bargain with him. It goes against every ethical bone in my body, but I might not have a choice. There are much worse fates than death that the Queen could dole out to a girl with magic in her veins and no family to defend and protect her.

Strictly speaking, I have a family, but I haven't seen them since they left me at the orphanage when I was five years old. They still live somewhere deep in the caverns hewn into the mountainside behind the castle of Aragoa.

When the Mists came, there was little time to plan suitable residences for the nearly seventeen hundred people squashed together within the castle walls. Townsfolk rushed to the castle's safety, protected as it was by the favor of the Saints, and many were still outside when the gates were sealed, left to swallow the poison that devoured them from the inside.

When it was clear that the Mists would not soon dissipate, housing became an issue. The ruling class had sequestered all the commoners in the servants' quarters, which was ridiculous. Hundreds of people, living on top of each other like cockroaches. So the common folk devised their own solution—miners carved their way into the mountainside to create more space.

It wasn't perfect. The caverns were dark and disease-ridden, but the Queen and the nobility mostly left those living there to their own devices.

Still, I was Saints-blessed to get into Vandenberghe, where I could have windows and a real bed to sleep in. So few lowborn children are admitted, and we have to earn our place, while noble students like Roze are handed their spot without having to so much as lift a finger. Most students come from noble families whose money and pride demand attendance at the school, carrying on with hundreds of years' worth of tradition as though society isn't crumbling around us, with the Mists swirling outside our doors and people gnashing at each other's throats. Once, Vandenberghe had been the crown jewel of learning on the continent, where only the most promising students—and, naturally, those whose blood was rich enough to demand it—from every country attended. My professors say it's a shadow of what it once was.

Finally, I enter the library and breathe, taking a moment to stop and crane my neck toward the flying buttresses overhead. Three floors of books—wonderful, glorious books—circling the reading room in the center. The soaring ceiling is the closest thing to open sky I've ever experienced, but I can barely see it when the sun is down. The gas lamps do little to pierce the shadows at this time of night.

I follow a dark hall behind the main desk and find Professor Borges's office.

I knock, and a throaty voice calls from beyond, "Come in."

"Good evening, Professor," I say as I step through the door.

Professor Borges is almost swallowed whole by her massive oak desk and high-back chair. She peers up at me through her round spectacles, her salt-and-pepper hair curtaining wildly around her shoulders.

Her office is large but so cluttered that it feels cramped—stacks of books and papers litter the floor in every corner, and the shelves are cluttered with books, vials, and other strange items: rotting cloves of garlic, a massive horse's skull, and what looks like a dried cat carcass. I've never asked about any of it. It seems safer not to.

"Viola. I wanted to speak with you about"—she pauses, her eyes darting toward the door—"your most recent exam."

I frown as I take a seat before her desk.

"Oh," is all I can think to say. This is about my *exam*, of all things?

Her spindly fingers sort through her papers until she finds mine and hands it to me.

"Your work is meticulous, but your translations are wooden," she says, leaning back and folding her hands in her lap.

I bristle. My translations were perfect. I triple-checked.

"Wooden," I repeat, trying to sound polite.

"Too literal."

I know what "wooden" means.

"I—I'm sorry. I don't understand. Are they incorrect?"

"Not technically," the professor says, "but being correct is not enough. They lack spirit."

Spirit. I bite my tongue to keep from saying what I'm thinking. "Am I not supposed to present the meaning of the text as it is?"

The professor pinches her lips. "All translation involves interpretation, Miss Sinclair. I've given you an opportunity no other student has, allowing you to work on the Hivernian project, and the quality of your work should reflect that privilege."

"Of course," I agree.

I've been spending my spare time assisting the professor with a project for the Crown—the translation of ancient runes that were once the primary written language of Hivernia, the name of the peninsula now occupied by the Kingdoms of Aragoa and Castelle.

Professor Borges has been searching diligently for the lost *Book of Odds*, an ancient text of magic. It's been lost for centuries, relegated to discussions of lore and myth. But recently, interest in it has resurged because of the Mists. All books on magic were destroyed at the end of the Aragoan-Castellian War, leaving the Kingdom helpless against the swirling, poisonous fog, thick as stone, that presses upon the castle. So when Professor Borges found in her research that the *Book of Odds* told of a time when the Mists came before and how they were dispelled, she went straight to the King and Queen. They granted her permission to search for the text, but even if she were to find it, they knew the book was written in

18

Hivernian runes. No one had been able to translate the runes for centuries, until Professor Borges started making breakthroughs in her work. *That* is what the professor invited me to work on with her—to find a way for us to leave this castle, to produce crops, to travel, to live in the sun again. There could be nothing more important.

Professor Borges glances at the door again, and then returns her attention to me, tapping my paper with her long finger. I blink at it—once, twice.

"I'm sorry. I still don't see what's wrong."

She huffs and draws the paper back, straightening her glasses and reading from the paper, "The heart is the dominion of evil."

I nod. It's a line from a very old Aragoise poem. And it's an *accurate* translation.

"You think that's really the best translation?" she asks, looking at me over the rim of her glasses.

Even though I *know* the translation is correct, the look on her face has me second-guessing myself. She narrows her eyes, staring at me with such intensity that it's like I'm meant to understand something significant that's just out of reach.

She exhales through her nose and shakes her head. "Brilliant girl. You have an excellent mind, Viola."

"Thank—"

"But a stupid heart."

I gape. "Ma'am—"

"I have something for you," she says, like she didn't notice I was speaking. She reaches into the drawer of her desk and withdraws a small, black leather-bound book. She lays it on her desk.

On the front of the book is a silver seal—a lion wearing a crown—the familiar symbol of the Kingdom of Aragoa. But the lion is wrapped around a very unfamiliar dragon whose eyes shine like diamonds and who holds a scepter in its gnarled claws. I take the book, looking closer. Around the seal are vine-like patterns, and hidden among the foliage are four symbols woven into the intricate knotted pattern—Hivernian runes. The whole design is oddly . . . violent, unsettling, *off*. My heart twists at the sight of it, like I'm looking into the mouth of a predator.

No, no. It's just a book. Not a living thing.

"You may find it an interesting study," the professor says. "I myself have found it to answer a great many questions."

I look up. "Does this have to do with the *Book of Odds*?"

"Did I say that?"

I don't understand. I'm beginning to wonder if I'm really here to look over my exam, or if something more peculiar is going on. The back of my neck prickles.

"Professor—"

There's a loud bang, and I jump.

"Come in." The professor's tone is clipped, and when I whirl to look at her face, her eyes are narrowed and emotionless.

The door opens, and I turn. There stands a man so large he fills the doorframe—broad and stern with close-cut beard. I take in his maroon-and-gold uniform with the seal of the Crown stitched on his chest—the Captain of the Guard.

"Is this her?" he asks the professor without looking at me.

"It is," she says.

I turn to her, my eyes wide. "What's going on?"

"Come with me, girl," the guard says, grabbing hold of my wrist and yanking me from my seat. Panic seizes me—they must've learned my secret. Either that, or Roze told them what he saw. I try to yank myself free, and his grip tightens painfully.

I look to my professor, my adviser, my mentor, but her expression is cold. "*Please*," I beg.

Professor Borges clenches her jaw and moves toward me. She grabs my other arm, like she's helping the guard, but then she takes the book from my hand and slips it into the pocket of my sweater, out of his sight.

"Submit to the Crown, Miss Sinclair," she whispers. "With the King lie the answers. With the King lies salvation."

I catch her gaze. Her eyes are hard, and I try to read something in them, but whatever message she's trying to convey is lost to me.

"I don't understand," I plead.

But the guard tugs me forcefully by my forearm and drags me from the room.

CHAPTER FOUR

"Where are you taking me?" I demand as the guard pulls me across the glass bridge that connects Vandenberghe to the main castle.

The school was built atop a knoll on the Mist-covered lake, its stony turrets and high walls emerging from the waters. Crossing over the bridge means staring down into the watery depths below. I can see faces there in the water—the corpses of those left behind when the Mists came, choked to death by their vapor.

"Quiet," the guard growls.

I pull against his hold on my wrist again. "You can't just drag me off without telling me *why*."

The guard whirls toward me, slamming my body against the glass wall. My back knocks painfully against the stone casing.

"If it were up to me, *girl*," he hisses, "I would throw your body in the lake right now. But the Queen gave her orders."

Oh Saints . . . *The Queen knows what I've done.*

I glance toward the lake beneath our feet, and for a moment, I imagine my face floating there, gray with death, among the waters, my own wide eyes staring back at me. We burn most of our dead—there is no room for a graveyard in our walls. Traitors, however, are doomed to a watery grave in the lake, thrown into the Mists to choke on them and drown.

"The Queen," I repeat. I say her title the way many do lately—a fearful, choked whisper, like we're all haunted by our sovereign. "What orders?"

"Don't be coy with me, *traitor*."

My blood chills.

"I'm not a traitor," I insist, but it sounds like a lie even to my own ears.

"I know what you are. Your very existence is treachery, little *witch*." The look he gives me is pure disgust.

A witch—Roze must've told them what he saw.

"I'm not," I plead.

"Your words are useless," he says. He grabs my arm once more and drags me farther across the bridge. "Your life is out of my hands."

We pass through the doors into the main castle and step into the grand entrance hall. The chandeliers overhead are as large as my dormitory room. I have never felt smaller as I follow the guard up the carpeted stairs.

The ceilings soar in every hall we pass through, masterpieces on every wall—portraits of kings, works of masters. What I consider extraordinary is ordinary in Prince Roze's childhood home.

Roze.

This is *his* fault. I knew he hated me, but *this*? Telling his mother what I am?

But of course he turned me in. It's in royal blood to hate all *meigas*, and Roze has more reason to hate me than that. Finding out that I was one of them must've been a gift. His cruel smirk flashes in my mind as the captain marches me up the stairs, farther up in the castle . . . not toward the dungeons.

"Where are we going?" I dare to ask.

"*Silence*," he commands.

I decide it's best to obey this time.

Finally, we reach an enormous lancet door, ornate depictions of the moon and stars carved into its wooden surface—the door to the cathedral. I try to take a breath to steady myself, but the guard opens the door and unceremoniously shoves me inside.

"Wait here," he commands, and he slams the door behind me.

I blink, my heart still hammering against my rib cage. I don't understand. Couldn't I just . . . leave? Perhaps the captain is guarding the other side of the door, waiting for someone else to arrive. Quietly, I try to pull the handle of the massive cathedral door. If my life is already at stake, what do I have to lose? But it's locked.

I sigh and turn to the cathedral. It seems empty, though the candelabras are lit with flickering candles, and the barest shimmer of moonlight penetrates the windows that line the walls like sentries—the stained glass faces of saints leering down at me. I step into the space, and the sound of my boots on the stones beneath my feet echoes through the room.

I've been here for religious services before, but never alone, never at night. The silence makes my skin crawl as I pass pew after pew. It's an enormous space, meant to make the parishioner feel small and insignificant, and I feel just that as I approach the altar, strewn with candles, the enormous rose window towering over it.

All around are shadows that seem to move and flicker in the dim light of the candles. I pull my school sweater more tightly around my shoulders. What am I meant to be waiting for?

My fingers toy with the corners of the book inside my sweater pocket. When another minute ticks by and no one appears, I pull the book from my sweater and open it. My first thought when the professor handed it to me was that it could be the *Book of Odds*, the text we've been searching for. If it is, it could be all our salvation—and if I can help Professor Borges lift the Mists, maybe the Queen will overlook my supposed treason.

I lift the yellowed pages carefully. On the very first page, in handwritten ink, there is a single sentence in ancient Aragoise. One I recognize . . .

I frown and close the book again, running my hand over the silver embossment on the front, the thorny vines curling their way around the cover, the lion, the dragon, and those four runes circling them.

I'm not particularly spiritual. I like things that I can see and touch, like a well-constructed sentence or a cup of strong tea. But now, standing before this little black book and the strange symbol in silver relief, I feel the weight of something otherworldly pressing in upon me—whether to warn me or threaten me, I'm not sure. It feels heavy, suffocating.

Something shifts out of the corner of my eye.

I jerk back, dropping the book on the altar.

The great doors to the cathedral creak open behind me.

In panic, I drop to the floor and pull myself under the cloth that covers the altar, barely concealing myself before I hear someone step inside.

The steps are heavy, booted . . . masculine. The guard again? Maybe I should come out of my hiding place—I'm in enough trouble as is. But some instinct tells me to *stay hidden*. My pulse throbs in my throat, and I try to control my breathing. My shadows lick the edges of my fingers. *Not again.*

I am calm.

I am control.

"Girl?" calls the captain's gruff voice. He growls like a beast, and I suck in a breath.

He steps forward, his boots coming closer to the altar where I'm hiding, stops for a moment, then paces quickly down the length of the cathedral.

He's right next to my hiding place. I can see the shadow of his legs by the light of the candles, hear his harsh breathing. And then . . . a chill travels down my spine as I hear him pick up the book. *Stupid.* How could I have left it?

I'm sure he can hear my pounding heart.

Then there's another sound—something from several yards away.

"Is there a reason you're here?" says a familiar voice of twisted silk and spider softness. I'd know it anywhere. *Roze.*

"The Queen requested I come to ensure you've done your duty," says the guard. He has turned now, and I can see the tip of his sword and the soles of his boots beneath the altar cloth. "Where is the girl?"

My heart stops. Roze must have been watching me from the corner the entire time. He *knows* where I am. But he doesn't answer the question. Instead, he says, "What are you holding?"

"This book was on the altar. I thought—"

"Do you make a habit of taking whatever you wish from my family's place of worship?"

"Of course not," the man barks.

Roze comes closer.

"I've already dealt with her," he says.

The guard pauses. "And the body?"

The body. My eyes screw shut. Oh Saints . . .

"I am more than capable of cleaning up my own mess," Roze says.

"And can you explain how you were able to execute the *meiga* and dispose of her body in such a short amount of time, Huntsman?"

The Huntsman?

I suck in a breath, the sound of it too sharp, too audible. I slam my hand against my mouth.

"Are you an expert in *meiga* hunting now, Captain? There is a reason Her Majesty leaves such things to me."

But the guard isn't listening. "Did you hear that?"

No. No no no.

I curl in on myself, making my body small.

I am *calm.*

I am *control.*

"Hear what?" Roze drawls lazily.

"I heard something."

"*I* heard nothing."

The guard takes a step forward.

Roze sighs dramatically. "Your presence is exhausting me."

"My orders were to assist you."

Roze's voice lowers. "I've been doing this a long time, Captain. Your assistance is not required. Leave."

I can feel the guard's attention turn to Roze—the Huntsman. "I'm here on the *Queen's* orders. She's beginning to lose confidence in your ability to perform your duties—always lurking about where you don't belong."

"I'm not lurking about." Roze's voice drips poison. "This is my home."

The guard hesitates for a moment.

"*Leave,*" Roze demands.

The guard finally steps away. "Offer the Queen my regards," he says, halfway to the door.

"I make a point to never offer the Queen anything I'm not required to," Roze says.

"That mouth of yours will be the end of you someday, boy."

My brow furrows. I've *never* heard anyone speak to Roze that way. He's a prince, after all. Then again, I haven't seen his life outside Vandenberghe.

The guard's feet move to the door, and I nearly sigh with relief. And then my foot slips. Just barely, but it's enough to create a sharp squeaking sound. I hold back a gasp. The two men halt.

My heart pounds, and my shadows slip free.

No, no, stop.

I am calm!

I am control!

But it's too late. True terror races through my heart, and they run from my hands, spilling over the floor, snaking under the altar cloth.

No. Oh Saints, no.

I try to reel them back, drawing myself in, but it's not working.

No no no. Tears spill down my face as I desperately try to pull them back into myself, hide them in my skin.

"I *knew* you were a liar," the captain spits. He marches toward the altar. I have nowhere to run or hide—I hear the slick whine of the captain's sword as he draws it from its scabbard.

Roze—the Huntsman—slides in front of the guard, quick as a serpent. I hear a sick *squelch*, a gurgling noise, a heavy *thump*, and the guard's body lands right in front of the altar, right in front of me.

His face is poking under the altar cloth, just inches from my foot. I yelp and jump back.

The guard's eyes are wide, and his mouth opens and closes desperately as blood pools beneath an open slit on his neck—*Roze slit his throat*. He is still alive, blinking at me while he holds his neck, blood so dark it looks like oil leaking through his thick fingers, pulsating with every beat of his heart.

The guard's eyes sharpen into a glare as he sees me, and he reaches out for me with his bloody hand. I squeal and try to kick him away.

And my foot collides with his neck.

I feel the soft give of wet tissue as my toes lodge inside the wound. I try to yank it back, but my foot catches. Even through my boot, I can feel the squishiness and moisture of his open flesh.

Bile rises in my throat, and with it a strange, desperate gasping sound escapes me.

The captain's eyes go wide, and blood spurts from his mouth, sprinkling my skirt and the skin of my arms, my face, my lips. I cry again and try to pull free, try to crawl away, but my boot is pinched securely in the underside of his jaw.

I wrench it, and my foot tears at the man's flesh, impaling him deeper. It doesn't work. *It doesn't work.* The metal pieces on my shoe have caught on something inside his head, and I can feel his pulse in my toes.

I jerk it as hard as I can, and blood bursts from the wound. A pool grows beneath his head, and his eyes widen and deaden.

The thought flashes in my mind—I know I will never be able to cleanse the feel of his jawbone wrapped around my toes from my memories. At last, his head goes limp and his eyes glaze over, staring blankly at me.

I am frozen. I beg my muscles to move, but they don't listen. The fear is too much.

And then I heave, vomiting onto the carpet beside me. My whole body trembles, and in my stupor, I see a gloved hand reach down and deftly lift my foot free from the guard's throat.

Another hand lifts the altar cloth. Roze's sinister, pale face appears.

"Hello, Sinclair."

CHAPTER FIVE

I squeak and try to clamber away, but his hand shoots out, grabbing me by the ankle and pulling me from under the altar. He drags me to my feet, grabbing me by the arms, and I struggle against him.

"Hold still," he growls.

"Get *off*," I shout.

I feel one arm latch around my waist, and he pulls me into him. Roze is stronger than I expect. His arms lock me against his solid frame, my chest pinned to his, hard muscle apparent through his clothing. I try with all my strength to break free, but his arms are like chains, his grip on my wrist like a manacle.

"Stop struggling." His sharp face is pinched in frustration.

"Let me *go*."

"If I let you go, you'll run."

"That's the idea."

"Just *listen*."

He claps a gloved hand over my mouth, and I bite him.

"Fuck." He releases me. I back up several feet into a corner, looking for a way to dodge around him.

He shakes his bitten hand and mutters, "Feral beast." Then he turns his glare on me.

I freeze and take a deep breath. Even as I glower back at him, I'm struck—to my annoyance, not for the first time—by the harsh beauty of his face. He is beautiful, not handsome. "Handsome" is a word reserved for men of valor, and there's no valor in the Prince.

He is pure, lovely dread. Prince of Beautiful Disaster.

"That's better," he croons. "Now behave yourself if you want to live."

"You're the Huntsman," I say. There's no fear in my voice—just pure spite.

He tilts his head. "Some call me that, but I didn't invent the name. That would be my mother's doing. She spreads rumors about her assassin to inspire fear."

"Her assassin," I repeat, my heart pounding against my ribs. "You're a prince. Aren't you too important to play executioner?"

His expression turns bitter. "I don't kill *people*. I kill *meigas*."

I bite the inside of my cheek.

"If you're going to kill me, please hurry. I'd rather that than carry on this conversation with *you*," I say, trying to sound brave when I feel anything but. The knife that killed the guard is nowhere in sight. How many weapons is he hiding beneath his school blazer? He looks completely unrumpled after slicing the captain's throat—not a spot of blood on him. My skirt, however, is splattered with blood, and I can feel it squelch in my shoe.

His eyelids lower ever so slightly. "If I wanted to kill you, I would have done it quickly, cleanly, and as soon as you came in the door."

"Cleanly like the way you killed the guard?"

"He didn't deserve a clean death. Besides, you're the one who made a mess of him. I've never seen someone so brutalized by a foot."

Nausea twists my gut. I'm trying very hard not to look at the body on the floor.

"You were clearly ordered to kill me," I say. "I overheard everything. So why not? You know what I am, and you've hated me for long enough. Don't tell me you've actually grown a conscience."

His chest heaves, and he exhales slowly through his nose. Something flares in his silver eyes, and I find my gaze locked with his, unable to pull away.

"You would deserve it," he spits. His voice is sharp, cold.

The shadows push at my fingertips again, begging to be let loose. *"Why?"*

"You're a *meiga*." He says it so simply. For him, it's enough explanation. I'm a *meiga*. Therefore, I deserve death.

"What did I ever do to you?"

"You can't be serious." The way his eyes glint causes my skin to go cold. "Not since the moment we met have you left me alone. I am royal, a *prince*, and everyone—*everyone*—seems to understand how that works except you. They all fear me. They all respect me. But not you. Never you."

He takes a step closer, until I can feel his breath on my face. "Sinclair, every day of my life, you've been like . . . like an *affliction*, my own personal pestilence."

I laugh mirthlessly. "If I'm pestilence, then *you* are vermin." I cock my head and smile cruelly. "One I can't seem to be rid of."

"You are the source of my every misery. You walk in a room, and it makes me hate the very air I breathe."

"I'd rather choke than breathe your air."

"And that was before I found out about your little secret, you filthy, treacherous *witch*."

I lift my hand to strike him again, just like I did in the Commons earlier, but a gloved hand lashes out like an asp, seizing my wrist. Blood drains from my face as a slow, sinister smile curls on his perfect lips.

"Maybe I should let you," he purrs. "So I can show you what happens to anyone who would dare strike me twice."

His thumb moves slowly over the inside of my wrist, and my skin pebbles.

"Fine with me," I spit in his face. "At least I'll die with the shape of my hand on your cheek."

"I told you I wasn't going to kill you." That thumb is still moving distractingly against my skin.

"And why not?"

He smiles. "Because I want to make a bargain."

31

I snort but keep my mouth shut. As much as I despise the idea of any sort of a deal with Roze, I have no doubt that he *could* kill me, that he's been ordered to, and that this is probably my only way to get out of this alive.

"I'm listening," I say.

He smiles like he's won an argument, and I have to bite my tongue to keep from lashing out.

"I'm an assassin," he says. "A very good one. The *only* one the Queen trusts to deal with *meigas*. She blames my father's death on your kind, and she knows what you are. She's ordered your death."

He finally releases me, stepping away, and the loss of his grip on my wrist feels like plunging into an icy bath. He shrugs off his Vandenberghe blazer, and my eyes widen at the hidden straps he has wrapped everywhere around his body, carrying at least half a dozen blades. He rolls up his left sleeve, revealing pale skin on his toned forearm. Then he holds it up into the candlelight, and there, on his arm, is a tattoo.

It's a rose, like his name. But it isn't beautiful, as a rose should be. It's dark and malevolent, full of sharp lines and jagged angles. There's a curling stem that descends his forearm, and on that stem, jutting out sharply like the teeth of a monster, are seven thorns.

"My mother gave me this this afternoon," the Prince says. His voice is full of loathing, but I don't think it's me he hates this time. "She gives me one each time I'm ordered to execute a *meiga*. A way of keeping me in line." He points to the thorns. "Seven thorns for seven days to kill you. One will disappear each day until it's done."

"And if you don't?"

His eyes are edged with strain and contempt. "If I don't kill you, on the seventh day at sundown, my life will end."

I feel sick. "Why?" I ask. "Why not kill me herself?"

He pulls a handkerchief from his pocket and wipes his gloved hands on it, raising an eyebrow at me. "She's the Queen, darling. She doesn't get her hands dirty if she doesn't have to."

His look is piercing, like he's trying to read me.

"I'm just a girl," I say. "I have shadows that appear at my fingertips when I feel things strongly. That's all. It's nothing special."

He snorts and leans against the railing that separates the apse from the nave, continuing to study me. "If only that were true. You might be simply locked away like an ordinary criminal for what you are instead of killed." He looks me up and down, from my bloody boot to my eyes, and my whole body heats at his perusal.

Something hot surges through my belly, and I look away, wrapping my arms around my middle like I can guard myself against whatever it was. "So you told her what I am. Because of some petty grudge."

He shakes his head. "I didn't tell her."

I forget to be angry for a moment. "What?"

"My mother has her own methods when it comes to weeding out her enemies. I had nothing to do with her learning your identity." He idly inspects the leather of his gloves. "I don't actually *like* this work, you know. It's gruesome."

I pause, swallowing. "So you don't want to kill me?"

He raises his eyebrows. "Are you suggesting that I should?"

"*No*, but you hate me as much as I hate you. If she's had you do this before, why not now? Why are we even having this conversation?"

He sighs dramatically and looks up at the rose window of the cathedral wistfully. "I suppose I'm tired of killing."

I glare at him. "I want the truth."

His eyes cut to mine. "My father is dead. Did you know I was the one who found him?"

I shake my head, unsure of what this has to do with anything.

"After the All Hallows Eve masquerade, I found him alone in a dark hall. There were no wounds on his body. It was like he'd just keeled over. And on his arm"—Roze crosses to the altar and picks up the little black book that is still lying there— "was a tattoo of *these*." He points to the runes around the seal of the lion and dragon.

I stare at the book, my heart beating painfully against my chest.

With the King lie the answers.

33

I close my eyes, remembering the drunken revelry of the All Hallows Eve masquerade, every attendee wearing the face of some fiendish creature, the King's foul, distant mood when he'd danced with the Queen.

"Sinclair?" Roze asks me. "What do you know about this?"

I flinch as I open my eyes.

"Nothing," I say, staring at the mysterious book.

He opens it, staring at the words on the first page. He gently flips through the rest of the yellowed pages.

"It's blank—save for that one line. Why do you have this?"

"Professor Borges gave it to me."

"Why?"

"I have no idea." Not now that it seems to have nothing to do with our search for the *Book of Odds*.

He sighs, sweeping a hand over his hair to smooth it.

"What does this book have to do with anything? What is it?" I ask.

He points to the dragon on the front. "The dragon. That is the symbol of Castelle. The Kingdom of Death. The Kingdom that sent the Mists."

My eyes fixate on the symbol. *The Kingdom of Death.*

"You think Castelle is responsible for killing the King?"

"I don't know, but—" He holds up the book again. "I don't believe for a moment that this was given to you by coincidence just before you were meant to come here for your execution." He rubs his lips with his hand, a thoughtful gesture. His eyes rove over me—cutting, dissecting, inspecting. I feel laid bare every time he looks at me, and I want to hate the feeling. But I don't.

And when he turns away, I find myself wishing he would look at me like that again, like he could swallow me whole in one bite. Finally, he lowers his hand, sliding the book into his pocket. "I don't believe that *meigas* killed my father. I want to find out why he really died. Help me do that, and I can keep you safe from my mother. That's my bargain."

"You actually cared for him?" It surprises me. Roze seems to so clearly care for no one. And everyone knows that the King was a

34

nightmare—drunken and violent and half mad. I can't imagine him being able to endear himself to any of his children.

But when I see the slight flinch in the Prince's expression, I know it's true. He loved him. And he's grieving.

But he doesn't admit that truth. Instead, he offers another. "My mother won't relent from her crusade against *meigas* until we find the true culprit, proving the *meigas* innocent." He inspects the fingers of his gloves, flicking off a speck of dried blood. "I'm done being subjected to my mother's murderous whims."

He's trapped. The thought comes so quickly, so unbidden, that I'm shocked by it. The Prince with everything, who gloats and sneers, who lords over us all, is a prisoner to the Queen.

"You're a *meiga*," he continues. "Some *meigas* can divine things. Find out what others can't."

"Where on earth did you learn that?" Discussion of magic is highly illegal. And books on the subject, of course, were destroyed.

"I have access to books others don't. Maybe I'll show you if you're a good girl."

I glare at him. Despite what Roze might've read, I don't have powers of divination. In fact, I've never been able to divine more than my shadows' uselessness. They've been in my blood and bones since I can remember. Trying to hold them back can feel like trying to douse an inferno with a drop of water, but I've become rather adept at suppressing them over the years. The only time my shadows have proven useful at all has been when I've needed to hide. Oh yes, they're very good at keeping me in darkness.

"Be my oracle," Roze says. "Help me find out why my father died, promise me you'll do everything in your power to find out who or what killed him, and I'll keep you safe from Mother dearest."

I eye him suspiciously. "But won't you die if you don't kill me?"

He grins. "Concerned for me, Sinclair?"

"Hardly."

He cocks his head as he looks at me. "Perhaps there are some things

35

more important than death. Finding out why you have a book with the same symbol as on my father's arm, for example."

I raise my eyebrows. "You're willing to die to find out what happened to him?"

"Not particularly. But while you're helping me find out what happened to my father, I'll look for a way to quell my mother's wrath."

I bite down on my cheek. I could tell him Professor Borges's last words to me before my arrest. Perhaps this is what she was referring to—I need salvation, and Roze needs answers. But how on earth would she have known? I'm on the threshold of something dark and horrible—I can feel it. But behind me is certain death. I don't really have a choice here.

"If I help you—"

He sighs. "Yes? What, beyond not *dying tonight*, are your conditions?"

I lift my chin, projecting all the courage I don't feel. "I'm in charge. We do this my way."

His nose wrinkles. "And what, exactly, does your way entail?"

I shrug. "I study linguistics. If I can't divine the cause of your father's death, we'll try research. We'll follow the trail to figure out what happened to him." I reach out and tap the book in his hand. "Starting with that."

He works his jaw as he watches me, and I wonder if he's imagining wrapping his hands around my throat.

"Fine," he bites out.

"Good," I say curtly. "And how do you plan to keep me safe from the Queen?"

"You are a *meiga*, and I am an assassin of *meigas*," he says. His smile is slick and feline. "Stay close to me, and if you die, it will be by my hands."

Roze has hidden a body before, that much is clear. He left me alone with the corpse for a few minutes and returned to the cathedral with an assortment of tools—some strange material to wrap the body in (for the smell, apparently), mallets, mortar, water. I don't ask how many times he's done this before—how many dead bodies are hidden in the castle. The floor of the cathedral, however, is littered with them, though presumably not ones killed by Roze—graves reserved for nobles. Their bodies rest beneath our feet. But beneath the altar, there is no grave. Yet.

"Why can't we just burn him?" I ask.

"And drag him down to the crematorium? Do you want to have to explain this to anyone out after dark?"

I frown.

He lifts a large mallet overhead and without hesitation swings it toward the floor. The crack of stone echoes in the silent cathedral halls, and I flinch. But Roze barely takes a breath before he's lifting the mallet again and bringing it down hard on the floor. Again. And again. Until rubble flies and dust fills the air. He wrecks the floor, swinging a mallet with unchecked violence, covering himself in dust, and I can't look away. I've never seen him look anything less than perfect, and I get the sense that some beast has been let loose in him as he destroys this small part of his family home.

When he's satisfied with the size of the cavity he's created, he takes a step back, breathing heavily, and wipes the sweat from his brow. Wordlessly, we lift the guard, Roze holding him under the shoulders, and me lifting his legs. Together we drag him into the pit.

I help wedge the body into the crevice, and when his bulk won't fit, Roze lifts his boot and cracks bones with his heel, twisting the limbs to mold into the space like a jigsaw and stamping the body in with his foot.

Roze and I do not speak. I'm afraid that if I do, this will feel less like a bad dream and more like reality. There's nothing to do but keep moving.

Next, we cover the body in the smell-muffling material and replace the old stones with new ones.

"Won't it be obvious what we've done?" I ask, because I can't help thinking this through like it's a homework assignment and not murder. "The priests at least will notice that the stones are new."

"The altar will cover them," Roze says. "Besides, there was always supposed to be a new grave tonight."

My heart stops, and I glance at him, accidentally meeting those silver eyes with mine. This was my grave. I've dug my own grave and buried someone else in it. How existentially horrifying.

The saints watch the entire ordeal from their paned windows, and I can almost feel the stain on my soul for what I've done tonight. But I'll have to deal with my shame later. Tonight is about survival.

When we are finished, we're both filthy, covered in blood, dust, and sweat. I feel sick. My hands tremble.

"Right," Roze says, brushing back his hair. A streak of dark blood mars the snowy locks. He looks at me, his silver eyes assessing. "Now, you're going to help me find out what killed my father. In exchange, I'll keep you alive."

He retrieves his jacket from the railing and folds it neatly over his arm.

"We'll need to stay close together for the next few days so that the Queen doesn't find someone else to kill you."

I swallow and change the subject. "How are we going to explain being around each other? You're a prince and I'm . . ."

"Common."

I glare at him, and he smirks.

"Fine. I'm *common*. But also, practically everyone at school knows we dislike each other."

"There is one possibility." A shadow of a smile breaks over his lips.

I'm tired. My bones ache. I want to wash the blood from my hands and weep into my pillow. "What?"

"You'll be safe if the entire Kingdom believes we're courting."

I blink.

"Courting?" I blanch. "We can't be courting. Don't you think that's a bit—"

"I don't think it's an overreaction to the situation."

"I was going to say far-fetched."

"Why?"

A manic laugh escapes me. He slides his hands into his pockets and watches me.

"You must be joking. I'm . . . Well . . . And you're . . ."

He cocks an eyebrow. "And here I thought you would consider me beneath *you*."

"Why on earth would I think that?"

He snorts. "Viola Sinclair. The star of Vandenberghe. Brilliant. Cunning. And a notorious snob. No one is good enough for her."

My mouth falls open. The hypocrisy of that statement . . . "I am *not* a snob."

He shrugs. "It's what everyone says. You have quite the reputation."

"*Me?*"

"Just this morning you greeted me by mocking my title and calling me an ass."

"You are an ass. That's *your* reputation."

His smile twists. "Well . . . it seems as though we're both far less liked than we'd hoped. Maybe it won't be so difficult to make people believe we're betrothed."

I take a step backward. "You didn't say betrothed."

"That's how it works with royals, I'm afraid. Nothing casual. If we want you protected, you must be indispensable. *Everyone* must believe you're to be part of the family. The Queen wouldn't want a member of her family to turn up with a slit throat—it'll look like she can't even protect those closest to her, much less the nobles who are getting nervous about those restless commoners dwelling in the caverns." He smiles nastily, like the thought of an uprising brings him sick pleasure. "And if you're revealed as a *meiga*, she'll look like she has no control over her wicked, wayward son, latching himself to a treacherous witchling and thus debasing the name of Roquelart."

Why does he make it sound like he would like nothing more than to do just that?

"Don't you need the Queen's permission to get engaged?"

"Not if we pretend like we already have it. But leave that to me."

I'm almost more nervous now than when we were shoving the guard's broken body into the floor. "But . . . suppose our plan succeeds? We find out what killed your father and figure out how to make your mother relent. What then? We get married?"

He makes a face like a toddler threatened with bitter vegetables.

I scoff. "It's not my idea of happily ever after either, but if the alternative is death, then I don't see what choice we have."

"Sinclair, has anyone told you you're in the habit of jumping to the most extreme of conclusions? We needn't get married. Once we've succeeded, I'll pretend to have a change of heart, say I've grown bored with you or something. I've garnered enough of a reputation as a vain and feckless prince, it will be believed."

I fold my arms over my chest. "You've grown bored with me? That's what you want to say?"

He raises a dark eyebrow at me.

I lift my chin to look down my nose at him. "No, I don't think so. I think I'll say I've seen the error of my ways, that after our brief engagement I realized I could never be saddled with someone half as maddening as you."

He smirks. "I drive you mad, Sinclair?"

My face flushes. "Like a bad rash."

He rolls his eyes and says, "No one can simply break an engagement with a royal. You know better than that."

I do, but I'm irritated, and I felt like making a point. "Fine. We say that *you* broke off the engagement after *we* realized the relationship was unsuitable."

"Very diplomatic," he says flatly.

"Indeed," I say coldly. "So then I can go back to a normal life?"

He makes a bored, aristocratic wave. "By all means. Return to your beloved books and rules. I won't stop you."

He leans back on the railing. I look him over—his tall frame, hands slipped arrogantly into his pockets, head tilted back regally as though he isn't covered in the evidence of the murder we have just committed together. The look of a coiled snake in his eyes.

Can I do this? Pretend to be the fiancée of someone who clearly hates me as much as I hate him?

I realize with a feeling like a stone in my gut that I have no choice. I crease my lips together and nod.

His frown twitches. "Good. We start tomorrow."

As we leave the cathedral, the gray ghost boy watches, his face half hidden behind a column. This time, he smiles darkly.

THE SECOND
DEADLY THORN

The Queen had a frightful Looking Glass, and when she stood before it and gazed on her reflection, she said,

> *"Looking Glass, Looking Glass, on the wall,*
> *Who in this land is most dreadful of all?"*

And the Looking Glass answered,

> *"You are more dreadful than all who are here, Lady Queen,*
> *But more dreadful still is the Girl of Shadows, as I glean."*

The Queen was sick with envy. From that time, she schemed to find this Girl of Shadows, and hatred for her filled her heart. That hatred grew like a briar until she had no peace, day or night.

She said to her Huntsman, "This girl is a danger to the Kingdom. I will no longer have her in my sight. Kill her and bring me back her heart as a token."

The Huntsman went to the girl. Though he was a wretched thing, the girl did not fear him, and this perplexed him. Sparrows will not eat a sour berry, and the poisonous Prince would not kill a girl whose power he did not understand, whose darkness called to his own.

So instead, the Hunter-Prince took her heart . . . and kept it.

CHAPTER SIX

I've just committed murder, and I should be haunted by it. Instead, I'm fretting about this stupid bargain with Roze.

In the morning, I pace back and forth at the foot of my bed. Saint Waffles snoozes soundly on my pillow, leathery wings tucked in tight, little piggish snores escaping between his two tusks.

Seven days. The Queen gave Roze seven days to kill me. Now there are six days remaining to learn how the King died while Roze protects me from his mother. Roze believes my shadows give me the ability to divine these things. I'm sure he's wrong, but there are other ways to give Roze what he wants—a culprit for his father's murder.

The little black book that Professor Borges gave me rests beside my bed, and the feeling that it's watching me is like needles on my skin. That book is the only thing we have to go on. It's not the *Book of Odds*, not with all its pages blank. But the dragon and lion on the cover—the symbol of Castelle twisted with the Aragoan lion and the Hivernian runes—those must mean something. Saints, why would the king have Hivernian runes tattooed on his arm? No one could read them. Supposedly.

As though that weren't enough to think about, I also have to pretend to be *courted* by the person I most detest. It wasn't until this morning that the full reality of *that* situation sunk in. It's more than just a fake engagement. For this to seem real, I'm going to have to pretend to . . . to be *in love* with him. Every touch, every glance with Roze feels dangerous, like

I'm walking high on a ledge over a chasm. A small wind could toss me over. And I'd fall.

It's a favorite pastime of Vandenberghe students to complain about the uniform, but I love not having to concern myself with what to wear every day. It's one less thing to think about. It's also a wonderful equalizer between those from the caverns and students whose parents are nobility. I came to Vandenberghe with hardly any clothes, and those I did have from the orphanage were old and tattered. Clothing is nearly priceless in a kingdom that is quickly running out of resources, but the noble class certainly dresses better than those of us from the caverns. Wearing the Vandenberghe uniform spares me the mockery of elitist snobs like Roze.

I smirk. He might be the Prince, but he wears the same old uniform as commoners like me.

I tie the double knot of my navy-and-maroon tie—Berlaise House colors—with a practiced motion so familiar that it causes my heart rate to slow and the worries of the morning to melt. Then I try to tug my wild hair into some semblance of order, a bun barely contained by a ribbon, and slip my feet into my shoes.

I need to get to the library, to start researching those runes. I can't think of any other reason Professor Borges would give me that book unless she knows something, unless it's meant to lead me in the right direction.

What *does* the professor know? How is she involved?

And then the thought that the professor might have betrayed me, might have knowingly sent me to my execution, hits me in the chest, sharp and painful. She's my favorite teacher. Yes, she's strict and holds me to a high standard, but I thought she did so because she cared. The feeling of betrayal is too familiar, too similar to how I felt when my parents left me at the orphanage, and an ugly grief rises with my shadows as they curl around my clenched fists. I squeeze my eyes shut.

Calm.

Control.

I have to stop thinking about it. There's work to do. I take a deep breath and open the door.

Roze is there, waiting. He leans against the wall like he owns it—which, I guess, in a sense, he does. Or at least, his family does. I'm so surprised that I jump back. Saint Waffles is on his feet in an instant, bounding over the edge of the bed, leaping through the doorway. He attacks the Prince with the ferocity of a hellhound, growling and clawing up the Prince's leg.

Roze yelps and jerks back.

"Off!" he commands, trying to shake Waffles loose. But Waffles has the Prince's pants in a snare between his tusks. I want to let him tear the Prince's pants to shreds, because frankly, it would be funny. But since I'm supposed to pretend to like him today, I force myself to pluck Waffles from his leg.

"What is that thing anyway?" growls Roze, eyeing Waffles in my arms. The gargoyle wriggles and roars, still trying to get at the Prince.

"My gargoyle," I say, trying to hush him. "Say hello, Saint Waffles." I rub between his ears—his favorite spot—and he finally relents, softly whining in my arms and glaring at Roze.

"He's disgusting," Roze says with a scowl.

"Well, he's been with me since before I can remember, and I rather like him."

Roze curls his lip at Waffles. "Please tell me he's not going to follow us everywhere."

"Waffles goes wherever I go."

While I lock the door to my room, Waffles growls at Roze . . . and I'm pretty sure I hear Roze growl back.

"So." I look back at Roze with raised eyebrows. This is his stupid plan, after all.

He looks away from Waffles, and a sly smile spreads on his face. "So—" He draws a hand out of his pocket, and in it is a ring.

My heart stutters.

"This is the ring of the Roquelart line," he says. "Not the same one my sister will get as Crown Princess and all, but this crest"—he points to his family's seal on it—"marks you as my intended. You wear this, and no one will question your place."

I swallow, staring at it. It's an ornate, stately thing—the sort that only royals wear. "And how will that stop your mother and her guards?"

"This ring is only given to those who have received the Queen's blessing to join the family. You wear this, everyone in the Kingdom will know your name. And my mother will have a much harder time disappearing you in the night beneath anyone's notice."

"She cares that much about public opinion?" I arch a brow.

"She cares about rebellion. If you haven't noticed, things are rather tense in our little cloistered Kingdom." We both glance out a window at the roiling Mists. "Blaming the *meigas*, sowing fear and hatred . . . you know it's all a distraction from what's really going on."

Neither of us need to say it aloud to know what he's referring to. The Kingdom is dying. Everyone knows it. No one says it. The two decades since the Mists came have felt less like survival and more like a slow death. Plenty have died from disease. Some have gone mad. Soon the Kingdom's stock of medicines will run out. Our emergency stores of grains will grow too thin to support the few small animals that we have kept for eating— chickens and rabbits, mostly. We'll begin to waste away from disease, malnutrition . . . That is, if there isn't a rebellion first, if we don't start tearing out each other's throats like beasts in a cage. We can all feel it— the restlessness and despair tightening around us like a noose. We are walking around in our own mass grave.

"How do you have this?" I ask. "She can't have given it to you."

"Obviously." He smirks. "I stole it."

Of course he did.

He gestures with his hand that holds the ring and lifts his eyebrows.

Oh. Right.

I hold out my hand awkwardly in front of him, and my pulse quickens as he takes my hand in his gloved ones and slowly slips the ring onto my finger.

It looks ridiculous—something that old and ornate and valuable on the hand of a common teenage girl.

"Perfect," he mutters, staring down at the strange sight of my hand in his, his ring on my finger. My heart thunders in my ears.

Then he clears his throat and drops my hand, nearly throwing it back at me.

"Right. From now on, you're not to go anywhere unless I am there. We will dine together at each meal, and I will bring you back to your room in the evenings. Understood?"

My jaw falls open. "What, *constantly*?"

"During the day. I won't be sleeping in your bed with you. Although if you insist . . ." He grins slyly at me, and my stomach twists.

Stop it. He's just trying to get a rise out of you.

"I'd rather share a bed with a corpse," I reply, glaring at him.

His smile broadens, showing every one of his perfect teeth. "Such a morbid sense of humor, Sinclair. How delightfully unexpected."

"You're a troll."

"Come on now, you find me charming."

I cross my arms over my chest. "What if I don't *want* to be with you day and night?"

"I'm afraid this is the price of staying alive, *meiga*."

"I don't need you haunting me every moment of the day. I'm entitled to some privacy."

He waves me off, like my wishes are a mere annoyance. "You can forget about *that* notion right now, Sinclair. You're about to lead a very different sort of life."

"We said *I* was in charge."

"Of our investigation. *I*, however, am in charge of your safety."

Then he steps close, towering over me. His cool breath whispers against my cheek, and I catch the scent of him—spice and winter and something that makes me shiver and want to pull away . . . or pull closer. I'm not sure.

"You *will* stay close to me, little witch, because it's what's expected of

49

you as my fiancée. And because *you* are the key to finding out how my father died. I won't allow anything to happen to you until you do."

Strange how it feels like both a threat and a comfort.

———

Roze is true to his word. He sticks to me like a leech.

He wants to go to breakfast, but I insist that we go to Professor Borges's office first. My need to know *why* is eating me alive—why she acted so cryptically, why she gave me the book, why she sent me into the mouth of the lion now prowling beside me.

But when we knock on the professor's door, there's no answer.

I stand outside for several minutes waiting, chewing on my lip. Eventually, Roze sighs and stands up straight from where he's been leaning against a wall. "Time to go, Sinclair."

"But—"

"You can check later. It's still early."

I nod. "Perhaps . . . she's at breakfast."

"Where all reasonable people are at this hour, and where *I'd* like to be."

Saints, he's cranky on an empty stomach.

Minutes later, we enter the dining hall, and a sick, ominous feeling forms in my gut when I don't see Professor Borges seated with the other staff.

"Where could she be?" I whisper to Roze as we take our seats.

He shrugs and says, "She's sort of an odd old duck, isn't she? I wouldn't be surprised if she spends her off hours convening with undead spirits or something."

His tone might be sarcastic, but there's a twinge of apprehension in his eyes, and I know he's worried too.

"Hel-lo," sings a male voice, and a handsome boy I've seen with Roze before rounds our table and takes the seat next to mine. "Who's this?"

Roze's expression goes flat. "Ed, you know Viola."

Ed props his head on one arm as he looks at me, cocky grin on his

50

face. "Of course I know *of* her, but knowing *of* is not *knowing*, and I'd very much like to make her acquaintance." He flashes a broad grin, his cheeks dimpling as he holds out his hand. I can hardly hold back a grin of my own as I place my hand in his. "Edward Paschal, but you, gorgeous, can call me Ed." He actually kisses my hand and winks at me. I snort and Roze glowers at his friend.

"Get your paws off my fiancée, Paschal, or I'll have you drawn and quartered."

Ed rolls his eyes and leans toward me conspiratorially. "He always gets medieval before his second cup of tea."

I almost laugh, but then shock flashes on Ed's face. He whips his head toward Roze. "*Fiancée?*"

"She's our boy's new betrothed." Fletcher Llopart, a tall boy with dark skin and serious eyes behind rectangular spectacles, settles next to us. I know him from an economics seminar last semester. He, at least, gives me a decent amount of personal space. He takes a bite of a slice of toast. "His *bride.*"

"How do you know?" Ed asks.

"Half the school is already discussing it."

I swallow thickly. "They are?"

"Rumors spread quickly in Vandenberghe," Roze drawls, looking pointedly at me, and I catch his meaning. He sowed these rumors—the faster the news broke that Roze and I were betrothed, the sooner I was protected.

"Well, I'm in shock," Ed says. "Roze has allowed a *woman* within spitting distance of him?"

"Perhaps it was that punch she threw at him yesterday," Fletcher remarks.

Ed cackles. "Quite the masochist, aren't you, Rozy?"

"Rozy?" I say, raising an eyebrow at Roze, unable to hide my smile. He glares daggers at me.

Ed grins. "Good luck with this one, Sinclair. Or should I say 'Princess'?"

"Princess?" I choke on the word.

Fletcher rolls his eyes. "She's not a princess yet."

"Not until our wedding," Roze says.

The words send a shock through me. When I look at him, his eyes are on his breakfast, picking delicately at his food. He just lied so fluidly, made it sound so . . . real.

"You'll learn to ignore these two," Roze says. "I'm afraid they're impossible to get rid of. I've tried several rat poisons, but it seems to have only turned them more feral."

"I take offense to that," Fletcher mutters. "Don't lump me in with this idiot."

Ed salutes him, and as he does, I catch sight of a mark on his wrist—a moth.

"What's that?" I ask, pointing to it. "Do you have the same tattoo as Roze?"

"Um, yeah," Ed says a little awkwardly, pulling his sleeve back over the moth.

I laugh. "Why? Are you all in some sort of little club? How sweet."

Ed looks questioningly at Roze, who shakes his head.

"Excellent pottage today, don't you think?" Fletcher says. "Fewer lumps than usual."

It is not excellent pottage.

"Hold on," I say, now slightly more serious. "Are you? Is it some sort of . . . society or something?"

Ed nearly chokes on his tea. "Damn the Saints, darling, keep your voice down."

Fletcher levels me with a very serious look. "Don't speak of this if you know what's good for you, Viola."

I raise my eyebrows at him. "Are you threatening me?"

"He knows better than that," Roze cuts in, giving Fletcher a cutting look. "He only means that a particular . . . group, which may or may not exist, is hardly something that should be discussed over breakfast." There's a tone of command in his voice, and I bite my lip, turning back to my food.

"What about you, Princess?" Ed cuts through my thoughts while refilling my cup of tea. It's not *real* tea. That I can only get from Professor Borges, who's hoarded it since before the Mists came. The stuff they serve with breakfast is made from mushrooms and boiled water. It's bitter, earthy, and doesn't compare to the professor's stash, but it isn't bad once you're used to it. "Tell us about yourself. You're Roze's girl, and somehow we hardly know you. How long has he been keeping you a secret from us?"

Roze's *girl*. Somehow that sounds more serious than "princess," and my stomach does that funny little twist again.

"You don't have to answer that," Roze says, standing from his seat and buttoning his jacket. He rounds the table and holds out his hand for me to take. "I'll walk you to class."

I place my hand in his gloved one and rise to my feet.

"Oh, come on, Rozy, don't be possessive—"

"It's far too early to hear this much of your voice, Ed. It's grating."

Ed smirks and winks at me as we walk away. "*Fiat tenebrae*, Rozy, old boy."

Roze castigates him with a look, and as we leave the dining hall, he whispers in my ear, "Forget everything you just heard, Sinclair."

And because he tells me to forget, I make a point to remember everything.

CHAPTER SEVEN

We're surrounded by other students streaming into the lecture hall for Early Modern History when Roze stops and looks down at me, frost in his eyes. "I'll be back by the time your class lets out. Do *not* go anywhere without me."

"Yes, Your Highness," I say with a bite in my voice and a mocking smile.

He glances around at the other students, most of whom are blatantly staring at us together. At our joined hands. At *my* hand with its obnoxiously large engagement ring.

Roze turns his gaze on me, a hard, fiery look in his eyes. My breath catches. I'm not sure how I know, but the air around us has changed, and I'm certain . . . he's going to kiss me.

It's for the benefit of the crowd. It shouldn't *matter*. Because he's awful, and a beautiful face doesn't change that. And yet, my heart is thumping wildly against my ribs, and my eyes fall of their own accord to the perfect bow of his lips—lips I'm so used to seeing curled into a sneer. But they're not sneering now. They're relaxed and open and—

I don't remember deciding to wet my lower lip with my tongue, but when I do his eyes unmistakably catch the movement. The knot of his tie bobs with his swallow. Something swoops in my chest, and suddenly, I *want* him to kiss me, even if it's a horrible idea, even if I'll regret it later. In this moment, all I know is an undeniable need to feel his lips on mine, to know whether they're soft or needy, careful or as cruelly demanding as he is.

But then Roze quickly leans down, grabs my hand, and kisses it. His lips never even touch my skin. Instead, he kisses the enormous Roquelart ring on my finger. His own family's crest.

He can't even stand for his lips to touch my skin. He finds me *that* repulsive? Sure, kiss the Crown jewels. Stay far away from commoner skin.

I tear my hand away from his a little too harshly and plaster on a saccharine smile. "I'll see you soon, Prince," I say sweetly.

He doesn't even reply—just offers a swift nod, turns on his heel, and strolls off. Saint Waffles yips at him as he leaves, as though he were the one to scare him off.

"What the hell?" says a voice behind me.

Cerise. I'd been so focused on watching Roze leave, I hadn't noticed her approach. Saints, I haven't thought through what to say to her about the engagement. I'm burning to tell her everything—the whole nasty ordeal.

But I can't.

Because I'm a murderer. I covered it up. And the Queen, of all people, wants me dead. There is only one person who I can trust with that information, who is already as much at risk as I am—Roze. For Cerise's sake, there's no way I'm going to drag her into this.

I turn toward her, and her expression turns guarded as she glances between my face and the Roquelart ring. "Viola, what happened? You went to see your adviser, and now everyone's talking— Tell me you're not *actually* engaged to Roze Roquelart."

Word travels fast. How many people saw us together at breakfast?

I chew on the inside of my cheek. I have to come up with a lie, and quickly. "It's true," I say carefully.

Her eyes go wide. "But you hate that little weasel."

"I wanted to tell you," I say, looking down as I fiddle with the hem of my sweater. "But . . . you know, with him being a prince and all, we didn't want the pressure, so we kept it a secret."

She blinks. "For how long?"

I hesitate. It must be long enough that an engagement would be reasonable. I shrug. "A few months."

"A few months?" she nearly screeches. People are starting to stare.

I sigh and grab her by the elbow, leading her out of the crowd waiting outside the lecture hall and finding us a semiprivate spot beside a suit of armor. "Yes, a few months," I say. "I would've said something, but I had to keep it quiet."

Her face doesn't relax. Instead, she knots her brows. "How . . . how did this even happen?"

"That's . . . hard to say. It just sort of did."

Her glare clearly tells me I'll have to do better than that.

I shuffle my feet, wrapping my arms around myself as I try my best to lie like my life depends on it to my best friend. "A few months ago, at the start of term, I was . . . in the library one day, and he was there. Just up to his usual antics with his friends, I suppose. Anyway, I told him off, and we started arguing. After a while his friends got bored and left, but Roze and I were still at each other's throats. And then somehow arguing turned into . . ."

An image unfolds completely unbidden in my imagination—a dark corner of the library, my back against a wall of books, Roze's face buried in my neck. My head is flung back, and his hands are running up my sides.

I shake my head, banishing the image.

"Why didn't you tell me?" she asks. "You know you can trust me."

Saints, she sounds so sincere. My heart squeezes painfully. It hadn't occurred to me until now that the hardest part of this nightmare isn't going to be staying alive or spending time with Roze. It's going to be lying to my friends.

"I know—"

"What about Kole?"

I take a deep breath. I told Cerise weeks ago about my growing feelings for Kole. I hadn't wanted to deal with that reality yet—what he'll think now that I'm engaged to the Prince.

"A . . . decoy," I lie. "I told you I liked Kole so you wouldn't pick up on things between Roze and me."

She looks so *hurt*, and my heart feels like a rubber band is squeezing it.

"I'm so sorry, Cerise," I say, putting a hand on her shoulder. "I trust you. I do."

But she's not looking at me. "You sure lie a lot for someone who does."

"I'm sorry," I say again. What else is there to say?

Behind her, the doors to the hall have opened and the bells signaling the beginning of the lecture period have started to chime.

"I don't want to be late for class," she says, not meeting my eyes. Her face looks gray. "See you."

She enters the lecture hall without waiting, going to a seat near the back, far away from where she usually sits beside me.

I leave Waffles outside, where he takes up his usual sentry position by the door, and find my way to my seat, fighting the weight of my heart in my stomach. The lecture hall smells of thick dust and polished oak—pure academia. It's a smell I've come to associate with home, joy, friendship . . . But today, it makes my chest ache. The whole world can burn around me as long as Cerise and I are okay. But if she's mad? If I hurt her?

Saints, all I want to do is crawl back in bed and pretend this day never happened.

Kole is already in the seat beside mine, bent over his notes on the small foldout desk. All three of us coordinated our schedules to have this class together this semester to fulfill our history requirement. Our professor, Sir Patrick Porcher, is notoriously difficult, and we knew we wouldn't survive without each other.

As I go to my seat, heads turn my way, and whispers scatter across the room. I drop my eyes to the ground. I wish this stupid ring wasn't so conspicuous. It feels like a beacon on my hand.

I slip into my seat beside Kole and mutter a rushed greeting, hoping to avoid eye contact. After Cerise's interrogation, I'm not keen to hear what Kole thinks of my engagement.

"Morning," he mutters.

I look up, meeting his eyes, and my heart warms the way it always does with him. His hair is slightly unkempt today, like he's just woken up, and his expression is tired but pleasant. The only word that could describe him like this is cozy. He's the human version of a wool sweater and a hot cup of tea. Adorable.

"Congratulations, by the way," he mumbles, and my heart sinks.

"Oh . . . uh, thank you."

He's silent for a few moments, apparently reading his notes. But that can't be it, can it? That can't be all he has to say. I just got *engaged*.

"You approve?" I ask.

He blinks and lifts his eyebrows. "Sure. If he makes you happy."

I stare, completely dumbfounded for several seconds before I remember that I'm supposed to be pleased. I nod and try to smile, but my stomach turns sour.

I didn't realize until just now that I'd hoped to see a glimmer of . . . of *something* from Kole. Shock, protectiveness, maybe even a little jealousy. But he seems perfectly content to accept that I'm now engaged to a man I claimed to hate only yesterday. It's like he doesn't know me.

But I'm reminded that no one *really* does. Not with my secrets.

I busy myself with retrieving my notes from my bag, but my heart is aching in my chest, and shadows push at my fingertips.

I quickly hide them under the table and take a steadying breath.

Calm.

Control.

I *can't* lose it now. There's too much on the line. I'm taking deep breaths, begging my body to steady itself. Kole doesn't even notice—he's so fixated on his notes. I'm normally the one who can barely peel myself away from my homework, and yet here *he* is, so distracted by school that he isn't even aware that I'm imploding in the middle of the lecture hall.

Calm.

Control.

And then there's Cerise. Who *would* have noticed, *should* have noticed that something was wrong, but she's at the back of the room, quick to abandon me as soon as she thought I'd slipped up. But I *hadn't*. I hadn't lied to her about some months-long dalliance with the Prince of Aragoa or pretended to be infatuated with Kole to cover it up. I *hadn't* lied until today, and only because I had to. I didn't have a *choice*. Did she give me the benefit of the doubt? Did she stick with me, promise to talk it through? No, she got hurt and shut me out. Was our friendship that fragile? Was I that easy to leave?

And now . . . I'm alone.

I am utterly alone.

Calm!

Control!

Darkness snakes around my fingers as my vision blurs with unexpected tears. Damn Cerise. Damn Kole. Damn Roze. Especially Roze. Damn my horrible, treacherous shadows!

I try to hide my hands under my thighs, but the darkness creeps up my wrists now, and with it, my walls begin to fall. I'm so tired. So tired of trying not to feel, of holding everything down, everything back. I've been pretending that I'm fine, that I'm *normal*, every day of my life, but I'm tired of pretending. What if I didn't care anymore? What if I let them come? Let them all see what I am, consequences be damned? Saints, it would be a brutal, disastrous relief . . .

"Notes out, lips *silent*," booms a voice from the back of the room, and with a jump, my shadows snap back. I quickly wipe the corners of my eyes dry and finish rustling through my bag for my notes.

That was too close. I can't let myself get worked up like that again, no matter what's going on. Too much is at stake.

Sir Patrick marches his way past row after row of seats, his broad frame filling the aisle. "One of you had the gall to suggest to me before class this morning that you should be granted an extension on your essay on the Holy Virtusian Empire, because of the effect that the loss of our late King, Saints rest his weary soul, has had on morale this semester. You can thank that inspired individual for the extra three sources I'm requiring for your bibliography."

The class collectively groans, and Sir Patrick turns swiftly behind the lectern, silencing all of us with a glare from beady, ratlike eyes. Sir

Patrick is a portly man with shoulders as wide as the aisle between desks and a ruddy face. His size only makes him more formidable; his presence commands the room.

"I realize that this semester has been far from ordinary with the death of the King and the whole Kingdom in mourning. However, now is *not* the time for complacency. As all of you are aware, I was a general in His Majesty's armies during the war. Let me tell you something about King Alexandre during his glory days. He was relentless. Let that be a lesson to all of you that laggards will not be tolerated. Now"—he turns tightly toward the blackboard behind him and lifts a piece of chalk— "second-century political uprisings. Who among you can tell me precisely when the Holy Virtusian Empire dissolved?"

My hand shoots up—the answer is such a good one. Yes, I have a habit of answering too many questions, but maybe if I answer just this one, I'll let someone else answer others. Sir Patrick scans the room for a moment, and I glance behind me to see no other hands raised. I know at least some of them *know* the answer. I don't understand why they don't find this fascinating.

Sir Patrick exhales and says, "Miss Sinclair?"

"It's a trick question," I say as though I'd been holding my breath. "The HVE didn't end overnight, and it's impossible to put a date on its dissolution, since parts of it technically still remain in the form of smaller kingdoms in the southern part of the continent."

Sir Patrick's mustache bristles. "All true. Although I would've also accepted 'Approximately one thousand years ago, sir' as an answer."

Several students snicker around me, but I refuse to be embarrassed. Am I supposed to be ashamed of knowing more than what he wanted?

He continues, "The HVE weakened and fell over the course of more than two hundred years, and the continent thus fractured into warring kingdoms, ushering in the reign of darkness and chaos. Here, on the Hivernian Peninsula, conquering bands destroyed the ancient Hivernian culture and formed smaller kingdoms between four and five hundred years ago. Those kingdoms then fought for dominance of the peninsula. And what happened when they fought, Vandenberghe students?"

He eyes the class sharply, but every head is down, madly scribbling notes. Sir Patrick is notorious for including the smallest details from his lectures on our exams.

When no one raises their hand, he sighs. "Miss Sinclair, would you like to answer the question?"

I try to hold back my grin. "Aragoa and Castelle conquered the other kingdoms. They became the two dominant forces on the peninsula."

"And?"

I swallow, losing a little of my enthusiasm as we near the subject that everyone in the Kingdom readily avoids. "And we've been at war ever since."

He meets my gaze, his eyes cold, haunted even. "Indeed we have."

Sir Patrick turns his eyes away and continues with his lecture. I turn my attention to my notes, but then a chill skitters over my skin, raising the flesh on the back of my neck. Head down, I glance out of the corner of my eye instinctively toward the latticed windows. And there is the face that, no matter how often I see it, still chills my blood.

The little ghost boy is outside the windows in the Mists. Panic jolts through me. Nothing that even appears alive belongs out there, and it almost makes me want to rescue him, break that glass and pull him through to safety.

He presses his small hands to the window, his large eyes staring woefully into mine. Sir Patrick's voice fades away as I watch him. The Mists wrap their way around him, like the limbs of a carnivorous plant, folding its arms almost lovingly around the boy. He screams silently, tears welling around his eyes, fingers clawing at the window. I can't look away. In a moment he's swallowed by the Mists, and I squeeze my eyes shut.

When I open them, the Mists writhe over the glass like nothing has happened, like they didn't swallow a spirit a moment ago. Then again, maybe the boy was performing that whole scene just to torture me. He loves to frighten me—something I've learned in the weeks since he decided to haunt me.

I watch the Mists undulate quietly. Our ever-present threat . . . because of the Kingdom of Castelle. My memory flashes back to the symbol of the lion and dragon wrapped around each other on the cover of the book the professor gave me. It's the only starting place I have for finding a culprit for the King's death, but Castelle, the war . . . They're hardly ever discussed, like we're all afraid to look too closely at the threat of death closing in all around us.

"Professor." My voice cuts through the classroom, and I hardly remember making the decision to speak.

The chalk squeaks on the chalkboard, Sir Patrick's lecture coming to a sudden halt. He turns toward me, nostrils flared, his movements slow, like a cat approaching a mouse. No one interrupts Sir Patrick's lectures.

He scans the room and then sets his eyes on me. "Miss Sinclair."

"I—I know we're covering the second century, but I wondered if you might answer a question I have about . . . about the recent war." A hush falls over the classroom. Those young enough to not remember the war know better than to bring it up, and those old enough to remember never speak of it. "Only because I know you were so crucial in the fight against Castelle, weren't you?" I say quickly. "As a general in His Majesty's army, you had firsthand knowledge of what happened."

He narrows his eyes at me, and I'm certain he's going to tell me off for being dreadfully off topic. I'm just praying his pride will lure him into telling us more.

"Go on," he says cautiously.

I clear my throat. Everyone is staring at me as though I've just started dancing a jig and whistling the national anthem. "During the war, *meigas* sided with Castelle, right? They sent the Mists." The atmosphere in the room chills at the mention of *meigas*—I've just taken an enormous risk in bringing up magic at all. "But the Mists weren't able to penetrate the castle walls. We're protected."

Sir Patrick raises an eyebrow. "What is your question, Miss Sinclair?"

I muster every last ounce of courage I have. "I was just wondering if—if magic created the Mists, is it magic that also protects us from them as well?"

The room goes silent as the grave. What I've just suggested is verging on heresy. Magic is wicked—a truth that is drilled into us with our first nursery rhymes.

One witch, two witches, hanging in the gallows . . .

Sir Patrick surveys the room like he's scanning for threats and slowly clasps his arms behind his back. "This is hardly an appropriate subject for this class. However, I recognize that you all are too young to remember the war and may not understand why we don't discuss such things in polite company. Perhaps this will help you understand."

I can feel every single body in the room lean forward. Beside me, Kole sets his pen down and inches closer.

"The Mists are a phenomenon produced by the *meigas* who fought with Castelle in the Aragoan-Castellian War," he says, speaking slowly, facing us now instead of making notes on the blackboard. "The war started as a dispute over land and power, and over centuries turned into a philosophical conflict. As such, the two sides were utterly irreconcilable. It's true that many *meigas* did side with Castelle. And . . . a few *did* side with Aragoa. They created the wards around the castle that protect us from the Mists. They allow smoke from our chimneys and fresh air from the outside to pass through, but they hold the Mists back. Those wards, not these stone walls, are our blockade against the death that Castelle wishes upon us." He gestures to the shadowy Mists twisting outside the windows, and all our heads turn that direction. "The *meigas* of Castelle have a darker, more sinister magic, the sort that can only be produced from truly corrupted souls. Make no mistake, were they to have their way, every last citizen of this Kingdom would choke and burn on their magic—our whole existence snuffed out like a lamp."

A chill passes over the room, and though I know it's not logical, I feel exposed, like every person in the room knows my secret, can see me for what I am—the monster lurking in their midst. It takes all my strength to pull back on the shadows pressing through the layers of skin on my palms.

But then reason—beautiful, glorious reason—cracks through my fear like a beacon in the night. Sir Patrick says the *meigas* of Castelle are to blame for the Mists. But if some sided with us, if some created the wards . . . perhaps not all *meigas* are dangerous. And perhaps there are some who know it.

Sir Patrick notably stiffens, standing taller. "Aragoa's mistrust of *meigas* exists for good reason. The Mists you see outside are indeed deadly, and they're just a small demonstration of the sort of thing I saw those *meigas* produce during the war." His eyes darken. "All power corrupts. Supernatural power, the sort that makes gods out of men . . . Well, you can see the level of its corruption in the lake surrounding us. The Mists wiped out nearly our entire Kingdom in a matter of—"

I raise my hand, and Sir Patrick's eyes flash at the interruption. "Sir, what about the *meigas* on our side? Was their magic more . . ." I search for an appropriate word. "Good?"

His lips pinch, and I know I've asked something important . . . and that Sir Patrick doesn't want to answer it. I hold my breath as I wait for an answer, fearing that if I breathe wrong, the spell will break, and he won't give one.

"Let me be perfectly clear," he says slowly. "There is no such thing as good magic." He punctuates every word like it's a death sentence, and for a moment, I'm sure my heart stops. "The *meigas* of Aragoa were once believed to have a nobler magic—a light side to meet the dark. But the great lesson of the Aragoan-Castellian War was that there is no light side of magic. King León of Castelle—the Death King, as he is often called—made a deal with his *meigas*, offering them more power and influence than they'd ever been granted before. And there is nothing that a *meiga* craves more than power. In exchange, they helped create the cursed Mists, a weapon meant to eliminate the entire capital city in one fell swoop. And that it did, rolling through our streets and choking to death all who could not make it into the castle in time.

"Ah, but the *meigas* who sided with us, those you suggest, Miss Sinclair, might've been good . . ." His eyes narrow on me. "They were discovered to have been colluding with their *meiga* brethren in Castelle. They had a plan to end the Roquelart line from the inside. Were it not for the Queen's discernment and the King's mercilessness, the entire Roquelart line might've been wiped out in a night."

I raise my hand again.

Sir Patrick lets out a breath that's half growl, half sigh. "Sinclair?"

My voice is reedy when I speak. "What happened to them—the *meigas* who were on our side?"

His lips thin. The air is sucked from the room. And it's like he's speaking right to my own soul as he says, "They were tried, convicted, and finally executed for high treason. Such is the fate of all who dare oppose the Roquelart Crown."

CHAPTER EIGHT

I leave class with my arms wrapped tightly around myself, and I don't even look in Waffles's direction as he trots up to me, rubbing against my shin.

Executed for high treason. The words echo in my head with every step. No wonder the Queen wants me dead.

"Are you all right, Viola?" Kole asks, a gentle hand on my shoulder. I nearly jump out of my skin, and he pulls his hand back quickly.

"Hey," he says softly, concern on his face as he cautiously puts his hand back on my shoulder. "What's wrong? You were asking those questions in class and now you're eons away."

I take a deep breath and come back to myself. The rest of the class streams around us like a river breaking around a rock. Waffles sits between my legs protectively, like he can feel my anxiety.

I shake my head. "I'm sorry."

"You don't have to apologize for anything. Just tell me what's going on."

I look up at him, the familiar snap of my heart reminding me how good it feels to be this close to him. His thumb is rubbing little circles on my shoulder, and everything in me wants to melt into him.

But then my treacherous brain recalls those words he said to me not an hour ago. *Congratulations. If he makes you happy.* Friendly words. Indifferent words.

I force myself to take a step back and smile. "I'm fine, Kole. I promise. I just didn't sleep well last night."

Kole frowns but accepts this answer with a small nod.

I don't give him time to inquire further. "Prefect meeting later, remember? I'll see you then." I turn away.

"Viola, wait—"

I stop short, seeing Roze leaning against the wall down the hallway. His stance is relaxed, but his eyes are those of a predator, pinned on me.

"I'll see you later," I mumble to Kole, and hurry over to Roze.

He merely raises an eyebrow before extending a hand to me. He *really* needs to practice the whole affectionate fiancé thing before people get suspicious.

"What's wrong with your face?" he says as we walk hand in hand down the hall.

I clench my jaw and hold back an eye roll. "My face is *fine*."

"No, it isn't," he drawls. "You look like you've seen a ghost."

I have, but that's neither here nor there. Obviously, I'm not going to tell him about my conversation with Kole or my fight with Cerise. I need to fill him in on what Sir Patrick said, but later.

"I want to go to the library," I say.

He snorts. "Shocking."

I send him a glare. "I want to research some local history. I think it could be tied to your father's death."·

He sighs and says, "Very well," as though he's doing *me* a favor, not the other way around.

———

After an hour poring over text after text on the war with Castelle, I'm nearly pulling my hair out at the roots, biting on the end of my fountain pen as I search for *anything* on the role *meigas* played in the fight. I discover a mountain of graphic details on the final days of the war, but there's no mention of magic at all.

I'm reminded of what Sir Patrick said this morning—magic isn't discussed. Ridiculous. How is fear of speaking of a thing supposed to protect us from it? How is ignorance supposed to produce answers?

I shouldn't be doing this. We only have a few days, and it feels self-indulgent to cling to this hope that maybe, just maybe, I might not be the wicked thing they would all think I was if they knew about my shadows. Yes, Sir Patrick thinks that all magic is rotten, but what I heard in his retelling of the events of the war was that those *meigas* made a *choice*. Maybe I have a choice too.

Besides, this research does have something to do with Roze's father's death.

On the King's arm was the tattoo his own son didn't recognize—the same runes that encircle the crest on the book: lion and dragon, Aragoa and Castelle, twisted together, as though embroiled in a fight. If the King holds the answers, maybe the war is a clue.

I glance up at Roze.

He sits opposite me while I read, his feet propped on the table obnoxiously, holding a book in his hand. I glance at the cover—a book of poetry, of all things.

"Are you going to help?" I ask.

He doesn't look up. "I thought this was your area of expertise," he says.

"What, reading?"

"Research."

I slam the book shut, the sound of it echoing through the hallowed halls. Several stray students look up, and the librarian shushes me with a sour glare. "We're here trying to solve *your father's* death, so if you don't mind, please put in just the smallest amount of effort."

He finally looks at me over the top of his book. "Darling," he purrs with a lazy smile. I narrow my eyes at the false term of endearment—meant to rile me, clearly. "How do you know I'm not?"

"How could a book of poetry possibly be useful?"

"And the books you're reading? Have you found them to be useful?"

I grind my teeth as I glare at him.

He glances over my stacks of books. "The Queen likely removed all information on magic from public records."

I groan and massage my temples.

"I need a cup of tea. Let's take a break for lunch." I stand and move to return the books to the shelf. Roze shrugs and follows me.

I find Waffles cornering the beloved library cat atop a bookshelf. The poor thing assumed that she could escape him by climbing up high—those little wings of his might not be good for much, but they can certainly help him scale a wall.

"Waffles," I whisper-call. "Down. It's time to go."

He looks at me and back at the cat, its hair raised and mouth hissing. He volleys one more combative growl in its direction before fluttering down to meet us, knocking Roze's hair askew with the tip of his wing on the way down.

Roze curses and mutters, "Foul creature," smoothing his hair back into place, and I pretend to cough to hide my laughter.

As we cross under the peaked archway of the library, I notice Roze still has the book of poetry in his gloved hand. I open my mouth to ask about it—

"Oh, I meant to mention," he says, his voice bored and aristocratic. "We're expected at dinner."

"Dinner? Where?"

"With my family, of course."

I come to a dead stop in the middle of the hall. He turns around and raises an eyebrow at me.

"You must be joking," I say.

He gives me a bemused look. "What did you think being my fiancée would entail?"

Not that, I want to scream. "Your mother sent an assassin after me!"

"And I've assured you that said assassin has no intention of harming you," he says with a smirk that's all too charming. "If we want to convince my mother that this courtship is real, we have to show her."

I feel the blood drain from my face. "You mean act . . . in *love* . . . in front of your family?"

"Obviously."

My heart does a funny flip.

"I can't do this," I say, and I feel my shadows nipping at my fingertips.

He gives me a strange look, like he's struggling with something. "Viola Sinclair, the rising star of Berlaise House? Surely, she's not afraid of a bunch of stuck-up royals."

"But—"

I don't want to say what I'm thinking, because it would only be fodder for Roze to mock me. *They'll see right through me—not only to the* meiga *that I am, but to the unwanted child, afraid of her own shadows.*

I'm caught up in my own world when I feel a hand on my shoulder. I automatically flinch at the touch, and Roze pulls his hand back like he's been stung.

"Sorry," he mutters. I think it's the first time I've ever heard him apologize for anything.

Was . . . he trying to comfort me?

I blink, and his aloof expression has reappeared. "You don't need to concern yourself with making my family like you. They make a point of disliking everyone—especially commoners. You never really stood a chance."

"How very reassuring," I growl.

He shrugs. "Take what you can get, Sinclair. We only need to convince them that you like *me*, not them."

I snort. *Easier said than done.*

He gives me his best exasperated expression. "This is the surest way to guarantee your survival. We'll convince my mother that we've been grotesquely in love for months and that I've declared my intention to marry you in a desperate hope that she will remove the thorn tattoo from my arm."

I glance down at his forearm, where the rose and its wicked thorns are covered by his sleeve. "And will it? Convince her to remove it?"

His face goes cold, something dark and haunted passing over his eyes. "Not for my sake. She'd slit your throat herself if she thought it would hurt me. But if my sisters, the Court, and the whole Kingdom expect a royal wedding, she won't risk your sudden disappearance. The death of someone close to the family . . ." He shrugs. "It would make her look weak. Like she couldn't protect those closest to her."

I take a deep breath. "All right. So I'll just pretend"—I look up, meeting those quicksilver eyes, spearing me each time I meet them like a knife through the chest, and yet, I'm always caught off guard by them— "pretend to . . ."

"Be in love with me," Roze finishes, inclining his head. "Don't act like it's some great millstone around that pretty neck, Sinclair. I won't bite."

I choke on my air, but he hardly notices. He turns on his heel and says, "Let's go to lunch. Hurry up. I'm starved."

———

It's late for lunch, but there are still a few students in the dining hall. Heads turn our direction as we enter and pairs of eyes throughout the hall glance down at the Roquelart ring on my hand as I pass them. By now, the rumors must've spread—I'm known throughout Vandenberghe Academy as the Prince's betrothed. I can only imagine what they're thinking of me, the common girl who snagged a prince.

Despite the fact that students at Vandenberghe come from both the caverns and the main castle, where the noble families all live in relative comfort compared to the squalor of the lower class, the two groups don't mingle much. The school has tried, hoping the camaraderie that house loyalties inspire will breach those lines, but honestly, the effort is laughable. The nobles dine on meat and wine while those in the caverns fill their babies' bellies with warm broth to keep them from starving. It's disgusting, and forcing us to wear matching ties won't make us the same.

A table full of sophomores from the caverns goes silent. As we pass, I hear one of them hiss, "Roque slut."

My breath catches, but I have to keep my expression blank as I pass. A traitor—that's how they see me now. I'm a traitor to their families living in squalor if I marry into the family at the root of their oppression.

I brace myself, expecting Roze to do something drastic and cruel, to threaten the one who said it at least. But instead, he slows his step till he's right beside me and slings an arm around my shoulders. He looks down his nose at those at the table as we pass, pulling me in close. The warmth of his body beside mine slows my racing heart, and suddenly I don't feel quite as alone as I did a moment ago.

He pulls me close, buries his face in my hair like he's giving me a kiss on the head, but instead he whispers, "Don't listen to them, Sinclair. Head up. Eyes forward."

I wonder if he's had to tell himself the same thing before.

As we move toward a table on the far side of the room, I try to ignore how his arm feels on my shoulder, casual and cocky, like he couldn't be more pleased to shove his new fiancée in the face of everyone he sees. I also ignore how it feels to be nestled into his side, his shoulder fitting just over mine, his gloved hand hanging just above my breast.

The scene that flashed in my imagination earlier returns—some dark corner of the library, lips and hands everywhere. Except this time his hands aren't on my sides, but under my shirt. The cool leather of those gloves is sliding over my hot skin, teasing me until I'm breathless and begging.

I take a deep breath to shove the image out of my mind.

Cerise is always trying to get me to loosen up about sex. If I'm honest with myself, I wish I could, but when I think about having that first time with someone who I don't deeply care about, I know I can't do it. I don't judge Cerise—she's seemed happy with every dalliance she's had. But I don't think I'm capable of that sort of casualness. It's just not me.

That's to say nothing of my shadows. I have no idea what they'd do in *that* situation.

But Roze already knows about your shadows, a treacherous voice whispers in my mind. *You know he won't betray you.*

No. I *cannot* let myself think that way. Roze is awful and dangerous and—

I hear my name whispered on someone's lips.

"*Viola Sinclair, of all people?*" a girl nearby whispers to her friend.

I catch her eye for a moment and then whip my head away, urging the redness I feel on my cheeks to cool. I wish I could turn and run from the room. Forget lunch. I'd rather starve than be fodder for gossip.

"Could you try to look less like you're repulsed by me?" Roze mutters in my ear as we finally sit down.

"Sorry," I mutter, trying to force my face into something more agreeable. A group of girls laugh at a table nearby.

I smile to myself to pretend not to notice.

"Not like that," he says, a bite in his voice. "You're smiling like a lunatic."

"Well, this might come as a shock to you, *Your Highness*, but I've never been engaged to a prince before. I don't know how to do this."

He sighs and his voice softens. "Just relax." His fingers slip down my spine, searing my skin despite the leather gloves and my sweater between us. His hand curls around my waist and pulls me close, so that our thighs are touching.

Oh Saints.

I can't *think*. I can't *breathe*.

I can feel the pressure of his hand on my waist so distinctly—the length of his fingers, the elegant bones inside them.

"Perhaps if you would stop touching me so much, I could act more naturally."

He scowls at me. "The touching is what makes it natural, Sinclair. Have you ever seen two people in love, or was that not in any of your books?"

I bite back a retort. My face warms again, partly because this is a painful reminder of just how loveless my life has been. I didn't grow up watching my parents show affection. But, I suppose, neither did the Prince. Yet somehow, he's developed social graces, and I haven't.

"Let's just get through this," I mutter, consciously scooting closer to him. He stiffens, like I've surprised him, and I can't help but smirk as I reach into my bag. I draw out the book that Professor Borges gave me and examine it on my lap, running my fingers over the Hivernian runes—symbols that are familiar but still a mystery to me. And here they are, wreathing the symbol of Castelle. I've been reaching for the book at odd moments, fingers skimming it in my bag while we walk the halls, like I almost can't help but touch it. Roze desperately wants a culprit for his father's death. I would rather leave those secrets for only the walls of the castle to know, but I do want to know why my professor gave me this book.

I glance toward the door and see Cerise stroll in with her hands buried in her pockets. She doesn't spare me a glance, heading instead for her friends in Marquet-Blanc House. Before she sits with them, she looks up and meets my gaze. And then her eyes swing to Roze. She hesitates for just a moment before changing direction and heading to our table.

"Oh Saints," I breathe.

"What?" Roze asks.

I turn to him quickly. "Cerise is my best friend. She thought I hated you and now thinks I've been lying to her for months. She's furious, but she means the world to me, so *don't* make this any worse. I'm begging you—"

He raises a brow. "Begging me, are you?"

"*Roze*—"

"Hello," Cerise says frostily, but she's not looking at me. She's looking at Roze.

"Hi," I say. My voice is too high, too bright.

"Hello," Roze says, his tone cold.

She locks her jaw. It's a split second before she makes her decision. Then she's dropping her book bag by our table and pulling up a seat. Her body language is anything but warm, anything but casual, as she takes a roll out of the basket in the center of the table and stabs it aggressively with a knife, slicing it open like it's either Roze's neck or mine.

"You know," she says as she dips her knife into the beet jam and slathers it like blood across the roll's insides, "I've had some time to mull this"— she gestures with her knife between Roze and me—"over, and I've decided it makes sense. I think you'll be good together." Her words are biting, practically dripping in sarcasm. "Both stubborn and opinionated. Excellent at lying, keeping secrets. There's a lot in common there."

I can't stand this. "Cerise, I'm so, *so* sorry. I wanted to tell you. I really did." *I didn't lie to you. Not once.*

"I'm afraid this is my fault. Cerise, is it?" Roze interrupts. His hand moves to my back, and a smile plays on his lips. "Viola wanted to tell you about our relationship, but I insisted we keep it a secret. It was mortifyingly selfish of me, and I apologize."

He smiles, and I swear my heart fails for a moment. For a face that is almost always wearing a scowl, his smile is breathtaking. Earth-shattering, really. He could destroy kingdoms with that smile—never mind lovers.

Charming. That's the only word for this version of Roze. Completely, devastatingly charming.

Cerise narrows her eyes, not one to be reeled in by a handsome smile. She looks at me as if asking for my response. I grin sheepishly at her and shrug.

"I see," she says.

Roze's hand presses more firmly into my back. "Darling, may I get you a cup of tea?"

Darling. There's that word again.

I turn and smile at him. "That would be glorious. Thank you."

He takes a moment to let his eyes pass over my face. His jaw clenches. And then he stands, strolling elegantly toward the tea station. I watch him walk away for a moment and then turn to Cerise.

"Cerise . . ." I want to have a speech prepared, some sort of properly outlined treatise on why I deserve her forgiveness and friendship. But I have nothing. So instead, I just stare at her, silently begging for mercy.

She frowns, takes a bite from her roll, and shrugs. "I wasn't entirely joking when I said it makes sense," she says carefully. "You've been picking fights with Roze for years."

I raise my brows. "And . . . how does that make this make sense?"

"All that rage—it's a type of passion. It has to go somewhere. Sooner or later, you were either going to kiss him or kill him." I gape at her, not sure how to respond to *that*. "You still didn't have to lie to me about Kole, though."

I bite my lip. This is the worst of the lies—how do I explain why I broke down to her that night weeks ago and confessed how I felt about Kole? She's always been open with me about anyone she's been interested in, and I've guarded that trust like a sacred thing.

Now she thinks I've spat on her trust.

"I was nervous," I lie, hating every word. "I invented all that to throw you off the scent. I was so worried you'd see through me, and if you found out . . . I just couldn't let anyone know. Not yet."

"Why? Afraid we'd all think you were getting cozy with the royals?" Her eyes darken. "Do you know what they're calling you in the halls, Viola?"

"I've heard what they're calling me," I say, emotion clogging my throat. "I never thought you'd think that about me, though." Shadows press against my fingernails. How many times today have they begged to be set free? This must be a new record.

Her next words are vicious, each laced with poison and the bitterness of a thousand injustices. "The nobles have spent the last eighteen years getting fat and happy while the rest of us waste away in the caverns. And that—that *family*—*his* family is the worst of them all. They're pigs—you know that."

"I know what they are," I whisper. "I'm still the same person I've always been, Cerise."

"The person I know, my *best friend*, wouldn't be marrying into a family like that. Not when she knows I lost my own"—her voice chokes now, and to my horror, angry tears start to slip over Cerise's cheeks, and she looks away—"I lost my own dad because of the stupid medicine rations the Roquelarts instituted to keep *themselves* and those like them comfortable while the rest of us suffer."

The blood drains from my face. "I—"

"No," she says. "There is nothing you can say to make this better. If you become a Roquelart, you and I *cannot* be friends." She sniffs and stands. With a final glare, she says to me, "And if there's ever a crown on that brilliant head of yours, don't expect me to bow to it." And then she's gone.

My stomach bottoms out. I feel hollow, unmoored.

I'm lost in bleak thought for just a moment. Then Kole appears, dropping his bag like a sack of rocks at the table, and he falls into the seat beside me—Roze's seat.

"Afternoon," he says. "Vi, I wondered if you still had your Rhetoric notes from last semester— Saints, what's wrong?"

I blink and look away. This is the second time today that Kole has caught me on the brink of a breakdown. "I'm fine. Sorry," I say, blinking away the sting in my eyes. With a deep breath, I feel the shadows in my veins receding, calming, the thrashing seas inside me finally settling.

But Kole's brow is still knit with concern. He reaches out and grabs my hand where it sits in my lap. "This isn't like you," he says. "Listen, if Roze isn't treating you right . . ."

My heart clenches. "No, it's really—"

"What's that?" Kole points to the book that rests on my lap beneath our joined hands.

"Oh. It's . . . just a book that Professor Borges gave me," I say, deciding to offer at least some of the truth.

"Viola," Kole says, his face grave as he looks up at me, "is that the dragon of Castelle? You know anything with that symbol is illegal. What's Professor Borges thinking, giving something like that to a student?"

"It's purely academic," I reassure him, covering the seal protectively. "She thinks this could have something to do with the *Book of Odds*. Look, Hivernian runes." I show him the cover of the book.

He frowns. "Well, I'll admit that's peculiar. The dragon of Castelle with the lion of Aragoa? And what would these runes be doing on a book with the Castellian dragon? Runes hadn't been used in centuries by the time Castelle existed."

"There's some unknown link between the two," I say, the familiar thrill of discovery quickening my pulse. And maybe because our hands are still clasped in my lap. "This book is proof of it—I just need to find it."

Kole nods. "You know, the war is fascinating, but people who fought in it never want to talk about it. My father was an engineer in the garrison here, and he's told me a few stories, but very little."

"Oh? What stories?"

"Well," he says, sweeping a hand through his hair. "For example, he told me that before the Mists came, they thought the war was almost over. They were so hopeful that he wrote to my mom that he was coming home. There was an armistice, and it looked like there might be a treaty signed, but it didn't last."

"Why not?"

A clearing of a throat.

Kole drops my hand like it's burned him, and we both turn in our seats. Roze is holding a cup of tea, staring down at Kole, and the way he's looking at him . . . Objectively, there is no expression there. Every muscle in his face is utterly relaxed. But there is something lethal behind his eyes that makes me infinitely glad I am not on the receiving end of that look.

Roze's un-expression falters. He smiles congenially. "So sorry," he says, his tone absolutely dripping with condescension, "but it seems you're sitting in my seat."

"Roze," I say. "Don't—"

Kole looks taken aback. "It's just a seat."

"It's *my* seat," Roze fumes. "Get up, Belcamp." His voice is louder than necessary, and several students eating nearby turn to watch.

Kole doesn't hesitate now.

He shoulders his bag and stands, sparing me one final glance. "I'll see you later, Viola." He hurries from the dining hall, apparently preferring to forgo eating entirely rather than endure whatever Roze might do to him next.

I groan and let my head fall to my hands.

Roze acts none the wiser, taking Kole's seat in what can only be described as a merry manner—at least, merry by Roze's standards. He sets the cup of tea before me and pulls an apple from his bag. I fully expect him to bite into the fruit in front of me, flaunting his status with it as always.

But then, to my utter shock, he holds the apple out to me. I stare at the bloodred fruit in his gloved hand. I have never in my life tasted an apple, and surely he knows this, surely he knows the significance of what he's offering.

And then I realize—of course he does. This is his answer to what just happened with Kole, when Roze walked up on his fiancée holding hands with another in public. This is a statement to everyone in the room . . . and possibly a reminder to me as well. The moment feels weightier than when he gave me his ring.

I look up into his eyes, and he raises an eyebrow at me. I take the fruit from his hand, feeling the firm texture beneath my fingertips, lift it to my lips, and bite.

Oh Saints.

My eyes flutter shut, and I barely stifle a groan. When I open my eyes, Roze is staring at me, frozen.

"What?"

He closes his lips and lifts a hand. Now it's my turn to freeze as his gloved thumb wipes a fleck of apple flesh from the corner of my mouth . . . and then he lifts it to his own lips and sucks the spare fruit from his thumb.

"Waste not," he mutters.

I think my whole face is on fire.

He takes that infernal apple from my hand and bites right over my own bite mark, juice coating his lips.

I will burn to death before this is over.

CHAPTER NINE

There's work to be done. I want to continue our research in the library, but Roze has other ideas.

"Where are you taking me?"

"We spent the whole morning in the library, Sinclair. It's time to try things my way."

"We *agreed* that I was in charge."

"And how far has that gotten us?" he muses, dragging me along a corridor of the main castle, Waffles, of course, in our wake. Our fingers are linked, and the feel of his hand in mine doesn't match how obviously exasperated he is.

"You still agreed to let me take the lead," I grumble.

He sighs theatrically. "Fear not. I'll get you back to your books soon enough. But humor me first. There'll be a surprise for you if you're a good girl."

A strange flare of heat pulses through me at his words. But they also spark a memory from the day before. "You said you had access to books others don't."

He looks at me over his shoulder, his smile fiendish. "And now you've ruined my surprise."

I can't help the grin that spreads over my face. Does Roze have a secret stash of books somewhere? One that hasn't been censored, all references to magic and Castelle removed?

We climb staircase after staircase, venturing up into the parts of the castle I'm unfamiliar with. These areas are less crowded than the rest of the castle. Noble families live in rooms that were once galleries, dining rooms, and drawing rooms. Their conditions are still cramped, but they're far superior to what I grew up with, what those who live in the caverns endure.

But soon, the halls are sparser, and it's been several minutes since I've seen a soul.

"Where are we?" I ask.

"Quiet, you," he mutters. He's distant and tense, and he won't look me in the eye. Nevertheless, he hasn't let go of my hand since we left Vandenberghe.

"Where is everyone? I didn't know there was a part of the castle that was this empty." Even where the nobles live, they are squeezed together like mealworms.

He exhales a long-suffering sigh. "It's a simple request, Sinclair. *Silence.* We don't want to run into my mother or sisters before dinner if we can help it."

I stumble over my feet, but Roze jerks me forward.

"What do you mean? Are we . . . in the royal residences?"

"Of course, where did you think?"

My stomach sinks. I look around the dimly lit halls with new eyes. This place isn't open to the public, and everything about it—the dark, ornate architecture, the masterpieces on the walls, the chandeliers that hang over my head like guillotines—tells me that I don't belong.

Roze stops before a door at the end of a hall. "My mother should be at tea," he says as he turns the handle. "She won't be anywhere near her bedroom."

"Her bedroom?"

Roze jerks me into the room, and I stagger inside.

Despite knowing that I *shouldn't* be curious about the Queen's private chambers, I can't help but look around. A four-poster bed takes over one wall, the dark, velvet bedding spilling onto the floor around unlit candelabras and a vast arrangement of . . . *roses.* How does the Queen have flowers, of all things—something so frivolous that no one has bothered to attempt to grow them with our limited light and soil in two decades?

On the opposite wall is a magnificent hearth of dark marble, over which hangs a painting of the Queen and late King, and it's . . . surprising. A young Queen sits on a stone bench in a rose garden—the sort that would've surrounded the castle before the Mists came. Her hand rests lightly in the King's palm while she stares adoringly up at him. King Alexandre stands proudly, smiling down at his wife. I tilt my head, studying the King. This is a private family portrait, one clearly meant to portray domestic bliss between the royal couple. But I see the stiffness of the King's shoulders, the lines of his face, the tightness of his eyes—though he is smiling at his wife, he seems . . . tired. Removed. The coldness of him is unnerving, and that's when I realize where I've seen that look before. The deadness of his eyes. The mask. Roze often wears that same expression. I shiver and look away.

In the corner of the room, Roze is inspecting a tall, stately mirror with a florid gold frame. It somehow seems oddly separate from everything else in the room. Like a spider that's fallen into porridge.

"What is that?" I ask Roze, unable to look away from the mirror.

"This," he says, "is how you're going to help me. A magic mirror."

I take a step toward it without completely understanding what I'm doing. And then I see why it seems so out of place.

There, in the glass . . . There's no reflection. The glass is black as a pit, dark as the corpse-filled lake.

"How?" I ask. I'm not sure why I'm whispering.

"Look."

He pulls me directly in front of the mirror. I'm standing before it. There should be a reflection, and yet, it is black.

"Ask it a question."

"Like what?"

"Like what happened to my father, of course."

I swallow, a rock forming in my stomach. "It's not going to work," I say.

82

"Humor me, and try anyway," he says darkly. There's a note of warning in his voice that reminds me why he's called the Huntsman.

I don't want to do this. If the mirror is magic, there are things it could show . . . things about myself I'd rather Roze not see.

"I'm waiting, Sinclair," Roze says.

I steel myself, knowing I have no choice. "Magic Mirror," I say, "what happened to the King?"

Its surface remains dark as night, and I sigh. And then something like mist swirls on its surface. When it clears, I see an image—my own face, perfectly reflected, just as it is now. Roze stands beside the Mirror, that grimace still on his face while he waits.

"What am I supposed to be seeing?"

"What *do* you see?"

"My reflection."

His frown deepens. "What do you mean?"

"I see myself. Like a normal mirror."

"And it's not . . . not *doing* anything?"

"The reflection?"

"Of course."

I look back into my own tawny eyes.

"No. It's just ordinary."

Roze sighs and rubs his eyes.

"You're a *meiga*. You're *supposed* to be able to see things in the mirror." His tone is full of blame and frustration.

I rip my gaze away from my reflection to glare at him. "Well, I'm sorry, Your Highness, but despite whatever wild rumors you've heard, that's not a skill I possess."

He gives me a chiding look. "That's impossible."

"And you're an expert on *meigas* now? Tell me, how does this work, because I've been living with magic my whole life, and I've never been able to figure it out. Why does your mother even have this? Shouldn't it have been destroyed?"

"The most valuable items were kept in the family."

I scoff. "Of *course* they were."

He furrows his brow, tilting his head thoughtfully. "What *can* your magic do?"

Maybe it's the subtle note of accusation in his tone. Maybe I'm just not used to discussing my magic. Whatever the reason, I feel my face pale. "It's not much. Just shadows."

He lifts an eyebrow. "Just shadows?"

I nod. "Sometimes they help me hide."

He studies me. "You're used to hiding, aren't you?"

I feel laid bare under his gaze, and I look away. "Can you blame me?" My whole life has been spent living in fear of what I am.

He takes a step closer to me—close enough that I can feel the warmth of him. "Sinclair," he says, and for some reason that pulls my gaze to his. Silver irises, intense and unyielding. Like ice so cold it burns. "You were never meant to be hidden away in the shadows."

His words choke the breath out of me. "And how do you know?"

"It's who you are. World's worst show-off. Defender of the victims of harmless pranks. Incorrigible know-it-all. Imagine what you could do if you didn't have to be afraid of your magic. You'd be unbearable. Unstoppable."

My lips tilt. "I think you might be trying to compliment me."

"Don't read too much into it," he says with a glower.

"It wasn't a harmless prank, though." I can't help but point that out. "I think you might've traumatized that poor freshman."

Something ruthless flashes in his eyes. "That *poor freshman* was handing over the names of suspected *meigas* to my mother's guards."

I gape. "What?"

Roze lours. "He was greedy for the rewards and was giving them names on the slightest suspicion. I doubt if any of the names he provided were legitimate. Johnson was a slimy little rat, too immature and idiotic to realize how many lives he was ruining. Anyway, that's why I was sorting him out."

Of all the surprises the Prince has handed me in the last day, this might be the most shocking. "And why would you care?"

His lips go taut, and he looks away. I've never seen the expression that graces his face now—if I didn't know better, I'd call it vulnerability.

He turns back to the mirror. "Try again."

I don't want to let it go—could Roze Roquelart, prince of bullies, actually have defended *meigas*? Why? I want to press the issue, but I know from the cold look in his eye that he won't answer my questions now.

"What's the point? It won't help."

He groans, tossing his head back, and I get a full view of that moth painting his neck and the smooth curve of his Adam's apple as he swallows. "Must you question everything?"

"Yes."

He looks at me and seems to consider for a moment. "Do it because I'm asking you to. *Please*."

I've never heard him politely ask for anything. I suppose good behavior should be rewarded. "Fine," I say with a sigh, and focus on the mirror again. "Magic Mirror, what happened to the King?" I brace myself, but nothing but my own face stares back at me.

"Well, there you have it," I say. "I've never in my life been able to divine information out of thin air. If I were you, I would stop putting all your faith in supernatural nonsense and get back to the *research*."

"Says the witch."

I glare at him. "*Don't* call me that. It's crass. And you know I'm right. We need to be focusing on the book and on Castelle. Those are the only clues we have about your father. *That's* how we'll find out what led to his death."

He meets my gaze for a moment, assessing. "Fine." He turns to the door. "Let's go before a servant catches us in here."

———————

Roze stops abruptly before a tall pair of doors, and I crash into him. He lets out an *oof* and steadies me with his hand. "Head out of the clouds, Sinclair; you nearly bludgeoned me with your hair."

I glare at him.

A smile blooms on his lips. "Wipe the scowl off your face, darling. I'm making good on my promise."

"What promise?"

"My surprise."

His hand leaves my shoulder, and he backs into the doors, smiling wickedly the whole time as he opens them. I step into the room, and for a moment, I can only stand there, my heartbeat audible in my ears.

And then . . . I'm wonderstruck.

When Roze said he had access to books that others didn't, I imagined that he meant a small collection in a family study, but the room I'm standing in could hold a dozen of the stone-hewn hovels I grew up in, and every inch of it is filled, wall to glorious wall, with books.

It's markedly different from the gloomy and ostentatious Vandenberghe library, with its Gothic architecture and dizzying ceilings. The Roquelart private library feels like the morning of the Winter Solstice—crimson carpets, flickering candles, and gilded molding along the bookshelves. Several jewel-toned velvet chairs are arranged around the room with paintings set on display easels around them. Tables full of trinkets—porcelain, silver, and rubies. Expensive things. Ancient things. Items so precious the royals hoard them all to themselves like regal dragons. Actual wood waits in the fireplace, waiting to be lit, should anyone request it. The excess of it all is mind-boggling.

And then there are the books. Glorious books.

I rush to the shelves and run my hand over the volumes, scanning the titles as Roze stands by the door, watching me. He wasn't joking—these titles would *never* be allowed in Vandenberghe or anywhere else in the Kingdom. Any other time, I would bristle at the hypocrisy, but right now, I'm far too curious. I pull a volume off a shelf at random and flip it open, only to be assaulted with gruesome illustrations of torture techniques.

"Ugh!" I exclaim, and Roze chuckles.

"Welcome to the hall of banished books," he says.

"Is that really what this is called?"

"It's what I call it," he says, eyes glinting with mirth. He saunters toward me, hands in his pockets. "This morning, we exhausted our options with the school library. I thought this might provide us with more adequate research materials."

I eye the door suspiciously. "And no one will find us here?"

He inclines his head. "How much do you think my nitwit sisters read?"

———

We spend the rest of the afternoon in the Roquelart library, skipping classes. Roze keeps stacking books next to where I'm spread out on the floor, volumes surrounding me like a moat. I've been scribbling notes for hours, Waffles dozing at my side. At some point Roze brought tea, but mine has gone cold, abandoned amid the towers of texts.

I can hardly believe the information I've found. There are dozens of books on magic, on Castelle, on the war. I linger far too long on several instructional texts for *meigas*, marveling that there was actually a time when we *studied* magic instead of hiding it. But I struggle to understand them. It's as though I'm missing some context, some elementary education in the fundamentals of magic that all these texts take as a given. They refer to the "wholeness" of magic being its strength and encourage *meigas* to harness that wholeness, but they never explain what that means. And though I'm looking for some instruction on controlling my magic, gaining strength and power seem to be all these *meigas* are interested in.

But I need to focus on the book Professor Borges gave me and its runes. Unsurprisingly, I can't find anything on them, even here in the Roquelarts' secret library. Professor Borges has spent ages trying to decode the Hivernian runes. If there were a book easily translating ancient Aragoise to runes here, the Queen would have provided it.

There is a shocking amount of material, however, on the war. Kole was right—there was an armistice, a brief one, in the last years of the war. In fact, a peace treaty seemed to be all but signed, but Castelle betrayed Aragoa, using its *meigas* to send the Mists. One text vividly describes the day the Mists came, and I can hardly bear to read it—the way they first appeared on the horizon like a bad storm and then began to roll into the valley of the capital city, first burning the forest, and then the farmland, before falling on the heart of the city itself. There were only minutes— less than an hour, it says—for anyone who could to get inside the castle to rush to safety while Aragoa's own *meigas* set up wards to protect those inside.

But there's no mention of the *meigas'* betrayal. I suppose the Queen doesn't want that information even in her own library—a reminder of rebellion.

"Sinclair?"

Roze's voice heaves me out of the depths of my thoughts. I've lost track of the hour, but the sunlight barely piercing the windows through the Mists has dimmed to a kohl gray.

I look up at Roze, and he's strewn himself lopsided in an armchair so large it looks made for a giant, a weighty volume open on his lap. My heart does a funny flip at the way the dying light illuminates half his face, the way his eyes are glazed and half open from hours of research.

"I know you would stay in here until you rust, but I'm afraid if we don't leave now, we'll be late to dinner."

CHAPTER TEN

Dinner with the royal family. Never did I think this school year would bring me here. Roze and I cross the glass bridge together, the Mists and the faces in the murky water below us lit only by the light of gas lamps. The sun behind the Mists has set, the world around us gone dark.

I've done my best to look the part of a royal's fiancée, leaving Waffles in my room and trading my school clothes for a deep red dress—the only one I own. Roze, on the other hand, wears a suit so elegant that I'm sure it could've purchased a hundred of these dresses. The shirt and tie are the same color as my dress—something we discussed, even if my clothes look pathetically shabby next to his. The collar and tie are embroidered with black and silver thread in intricate damask patterns. He even wears a small silver tie clip etched with a rose and skull, along with matching cuff links. And, of course, black gloves. I eye those as we cross the glass bridge. I intend to ask him about them at some point. Perhaps he has a phobia of germs . . . or of touching commoner skin.

But I'll admit, he's even more breathtaking than usual. His white-blond hair is combed back elegantly from his face, accentuating his sharp features, just a lock of it falling lazily over his forehead. He makes me think of wine and smoke and silk, and for a moment, I imagine the feel of those leather gloves gliding across the bare skin of my stomach.

Saints below, what is *wrong* with me? I can't, I *won't*, begin to think that direction, no matter how good he looks in a suit.

Once we enter the main castle, Roze's posture tenses. The gas lamps flicker around us, the shadows moving like serpents on the walls. We pass through halls carpeted in thick scarlet weave, walls masked in ornate brocade patterns, ceilings adorned with chandeliers muddied with dust. The castle has fallen into disrepair—rooms that were meant to be largely decorative are strained with overuse, and a shortage of labor means that many things go uncleaned and unrepaired.

We are standing in ruins. We're a heart still beating inside a corpse that's already gone brittle and dry. How long can it hold us?

Roze has taken to leading me around by the elbow, his grip on me like a vise.

"If this is your idea of affection," I say when his grip turns so strong it's painful, "then I pity your future wife."

"My future wife will loathe me as much as you do," he says darkly. I roll my eyes, and he pulls me closer. "*You* need to keep your wits about you, Sinclair. We're about to face my mother."

I know he's right, but I say anyway, "Shouldn't she make nice with her son's fiancée?"

His face comes closer, his eyes glaring into mine. "You're a *meiga*, Sinclair, which means she hates you even if we're courting. And even if you didn't have magic, you're not exactly who my mother would have chosen for me."

"So sorry to disappoint you," I grumble.

"I'm a prince. My parents would have made a match for me from among the nobility, not some common girl from an orphanage."

I bite my tongue hard enough to sting. "Aren't all your noble families inbred enough?"

He narrows his eyes. "It's the world I live in—the one you're stepping into. Try to at least pretend like you can appreciate that."

"Elitist prick," I mutter. That fragile truce we'd established is gone. Now he's back to his normal self again. Mean, classist, and vile. Is he that nervous about dinner with his family? Shouldn't I be the one who's nervous?

I straighten my back and approach the door, waiting for him to knock. He lifts a hand, glances at me, and then lowers it.

"Hold on," he says. He takes a step back, surveying my appearance. "I need to make sure you look the part."

I glare at him, telling him with a look exactly how I feel about *that*.

"Angry at me again, Sinclair? I'm trying to help you."

"Oh, is that what you're doing?" I ask as he circles me. "Here I thought you were making sure I don't embarrass you."

But he doesn't reply. Instead, I feel his hands in my hair, and I have to hold back a small gasp. Why do his fingers feel like burning ice through those gloves? I feel a tug, and then my hair falls free from its ribbon. He continues to circle me until he's facing me again, and he arranges my hair on my shoulders. "Down is better," he murmurs.

I gape at him, and he stands back, eyes glazing over slightly, and the moth tattoo on his neck moves as he swallows. Some line has been crossed, but I can't quite put my finger on what it is. He clears his throat and faces the door once more.

"Right," he says. "Onward."

He pushes through the doors without knocking.

Roze's sisters stand in a ring around the room, grouped together in clumps of conversation. As we enter, their eyes swing toward us—toward *me*—and gooseflesh rises on my arms.

There is something deeply unsettling about the six princesses of Aragoa—Wisteria, Azalea, Oleandra, Narcissa, Hemlock, and Belladonna. They are all close in age, and they look far too alike, moving as one, like they share some sort of hive mind.

Each has dark, silken hair, plaited and arranged elegantly on their heads, showing off their long necks. They all wear the same sour expression as they survey us. Their arms are covered in silk gloves that pass the elbow, and I instantly feel out of place. I have no silk gloves, but it's clearly proper dinner attire. Why didn't Roze say something?

They watch me, and I feel like I'm expected to speak. But I have nothing to say.

"Oh dear, who let the dog in?" says the princess at the back. She grins broadly, perfect lips and tall forehead noticeably the same as Roze's. There's something about the way she holds herself, the way the bodies of the other girls are unconsciously angled toward hers, the way she wears her tiara like she was born with it already attached to her head, that tells me this is the eldest of Roze's sisters—the Crown Princess Belladonna.

The others cackle in delight. "Hello, brother," she finishes.

"Bella," Roze says.

He places his hand protectively on the small of my back—no, not protectively. It's obviously a performance for their sakes. But then his thumb skims the skin just above the hem of my dress where it meets my bare back—something the princesses, of course, can't see—and my breath catches. A shiver runs down my spine.

I should pull away. I should *want* to pull away. But I don't.

"And what have you brought with you?" Belladonna asks.

Before Roze can answer, a double door across the room opens.

Queen Maria—stately and formidable and just as breathtaking as her son—crosses the threshold. The Queen is still in mourning for the King, a fact made obvious by more than just the black dress she wears and the matching veil that hangs from her head like tree moss. Her skin is grayish, ghostly, almost translucent, like she has no blood left in her face. Her hair is arranged elaborately on top of her head, pulled back from her brow so tightly that I can see the bones of her skull. She's beautiful, but corpse-like—the dark attire is a stark contrast against her pale skin, and her cheekbones and collarbone jut out sharply. The weeks since the King's death haven't been kind to her—she looks ready to take her place beside him.

The princesses immediately drop into curtsies, and Roze bows deeply. I stumble into some semblance of a curtsy, and when I raise my head, I find the Queen's eyes fixed on me. Her expression betrays nothing.

This is the woman who wants me dead.

"Mother," Roze says, his voice anything but warm, anything but affectionate. "This is Viola Sinclair, my intended."

The Queen's face contorts into a false smile. "Of course." Her smile broadens, and I wonder who it's for. No one in the room believes she's pleased. But she doesn't mention that she's just as surprised by our engagement as everyone else—she has to pretend that Roze asked for her permission or risk appearing like she doesn't have control of her own son.

I can't help wondering what the princesses think of their mother allowing Roze to marry someone like me, if they've had conversations about it yet. What excuse could the Queen have come up with?

"Well," Queen Maria says. "Let's get to know the young lady, shall we?"

She gestures for the family to sit. A team of butlers lining the walls step forward to pull the chairs from the long dining table. I feel awkward being treated with such deference, so I look up into the face of a butler to say "thank you" . . . and I jump, nearly toppling the chair behind me.

The butler has no face.

I feel Roze's hand grip my elbow. I twist around toward him and his family. The butlers have all stepped away—each one of them is missing eyes, noses, mouths. Their faces are lumpy, squashed, and clay-like, as though their heads were scrubbed clean of features.

"Goodness. Are you all right, Miss Sinclair?" the Queen asks.

I turn toward her. She's taken her seat at the table ahead of the rest of us. Her expression is genial. Roze's sisters wear smiles that clearly hide their laughter. Can they not see the faceless butlers?

I turn to Roze. His brows are knotted, and his lips are pinched. I think he might be angry with me. "What are you doing?" he hisses.

"I—" I look around at the butlers, but . . . they're normal. What . . . just happened? My head feels suddenly floaty.

I look to the Queen. She smiles pleasantly.

"Apologies, Your Majesty," I say, recovering. "I think my shoes pinched."

"I suppose that's what happens when you find your footwear in the garbage," muses Belladonna.

The sisters chuckle lightly behind silk-gloved hands. I frown, feeling even more awkward as I move to take my seat.

But my thoughts come to a screeching halt as Roze drawls, "I'm afraid

Viola has little time to concern herself with footwear, busy as she is actually using her brain."

Was that a compliment, or am I dreaming? I suppose he is playing the part of my loving fiancé.

Six sets of vicious eyes pin Roze, and Princess Wisteria says, "Excuse me?"

"We can't all have your shared endurance for conversation topics as fascinating as ribbons and fabrics, Wisteria," he says.

I fight to hide my smile as Roze takes his seat next to mine and Wisteria shoots a glare at me.

"So defensive of her." Princess Belladonna preens from her seat next to the Queen as the butlers approach with the first course. "I have to say I wasn't sure I truly believed you were engaged. And especially to a common girl. You've always had such a distaste for them."

I bristle. Belladonna's eyes are cutting, as sharply intelligent as Roze's. This is a test, and we have to pass it.

Roze's cold gaze meets his sister's. "Viola is different."

I clench my teeth at the implication. *Different.* Because he wouldn't be caught dead with the rest of the rabble. Saints, I want to hit him again.

Instead, I look down and focus on my soup. And . . . something moves in it.

I jerk back in my chair.

A black speck grows in the liquid, bubbling to the top, and a *beetle* struggles on the surface, wriggling its legs as it bobs in the greenish fluid. My stomach roils.

"What's wrong with her now?" scoffs another sister—Azalea, I think.

"I don't—there's—" I stutter, but Roze and his family are all looking at me with the same mixture of judgment and bewilderment.

"Eat your soup, Miss Sinclair. Or the cook will be insulted," the Queen says, and more quietly, "I know I certainly am."

The sisters cackle again. Do none of them see it? Does Roze? Is this all some elaborate joke to mock me?

I am failing at this.

I feel a hand on my knee and look up at Roze. He's frowning at me—an expression that is almost kind.

Fine. If they all want to play this game, then I'll play as well. And I'll beat them at it.

"I'm fine," I say. "Just a chill."

Carefully, I pick up my spoon and lower it into the bowl of soup as far from the beetle as possible. He scurries toward my spoon, tiny, feathered legs swimming through the steaming liquid, but I lift the spoon quickly from the bowl and sip before I lose my courage.

I force myself not to gag and smile pleasantly at the royal family. Roze is still watching me strangely.

A moment longer, and they're all bored enough to turn back to their own conversations.

Princess Oleandra pipes up, "Mother, when are we going to have the winter fete? I have a new gown that I'm dying to debut—"

I look down at my soup. A *second* beetle is bobbing along with the first. They crawl over each other frantically, searching for purchase, latching together, antennas wriggling. I breathe, keeping my face blank.

"Oh, mustn't we have a ball for Roze, to celebrate his betrothal?" Princess Hemlock says, smiling as wickedly as Roze himself often does.

"That really isn't—" Roze says.

"Come on, Roze. Surely you want to dance with your fiancée before the Court. We all want to witness your . . . happiness."

The way she says it sounds like an accusation, and I know this is the moment I'm supposed to play my role convincingly. Swallowing the bile in my throat and ignoring the horror taking place in my soup, I turn to Roze and do my best to look at him adoringly. "I would love to dance with you," I say.

His face turns statuesque, that beautifully carved marble that I can't help being captivated by. And then he reaches into my lap, lifts one of my hands to his lips, and kisses it, never breaking eye contact. His lips barely brush my skin, like he's purposefully trying not to touch me, and I should be insulted by it. Instead, there's something about the barest touch that sends lightning through my body. My pulse quickens, and I'm held captive by the wickedness in those silver eyes.

He's awful. I shouldn't enjoy this.

Maybe with worse enemies surrounding me, I'm forgetting to see him as one.

"Yes, I agree," the Queen declares, interrupting the perilous path of my thoughts. The tone of her voice lets everyone know that it's the final word on the subject. "Tomorrow night, I think. It will help turn the Kingdom's thoughts toward happier things after the death of your father. Tomorrow we will host a fete in honor of your betrothal." Her eyes watch me as she lifts the spoon to her lips. "I'm sure it will be quite the event."

My stomach sinks. I know what this is—a punishment for this attempt to evade her. She thinks that if she can detach Roze from me quickly, killing me will be easier. We'll have to work even harder to convince everyone that this engagement is real.

I turn back to my soup.

Oh Saints.

There are dozens of beetles writhing in the thick liquid, some scampering toward the edges, some floating on their backs, clearly dead. They latch together and swim about, getting tangled and dunked.

I clench my teeth together and grip the sides of my chair, trying to keep still, trying to look *normal*.

Roze takes another bite of his soup, glancing at me, raising his eyebrow in question. I lean close to him. "Can you see this?" I whisper, my voice as close to silent as possible.

"See what?"

"My soup—"

I turn back to it. The beetles are gone.

A tingling sensation fills my head. I think I'm floating—I feel ungrounded, adrift.

"Sinclair?" he whispers. His hand is back on my knee, squeezing. Somehow that grounds me.

"How is it possible that *Roze* will be married before I will?" Oleandra whines. "He hasn't even mentioned her before yesterday."

"That's a good point. How do we know she's not just seducing him for his title and fortune?" Azalea chimes in, narrowing her eyes at me.

I almost expect the Queen to chastise her for her rudeness, but Queen Maria pretends not to hear the conversation as Belladonna responds.

"Perhaps it's true love."

The Crown Princess is defending me? But when I see the mischief in her eyes, I know I'm mistaken.

"Is it, Roze?" Belladonna croons with a serrated grin. "Do you *love* her with all your rotten heart?"

Roze looks at his sister with nothing but coldness. "Of course I do."

Belladonna hums and the sisters grin, sensing a game at play. "And what about her? Does the cavern girl love you? Or does she, like Azalea has wisely warned, love the idea of marrying a prince?" She sneers in my direction. "Cavern scum are always trying to wring from us more than their lot."

"I love him," I snap. The sentence comes out angry, like I can lance her through the chest with it.

Belladonna hums again. "You could prove it."

The sisters' smiles broaden.

I glare at Belladonna. "You can't prove love."

"Oh, I don't know about that." She spins her fork thoughtfully. "I think if we were to, say, witness a kiss, we could very well tell whether your relationship was sincere."

Roze's face drains of color next to me. "Bella, stop it."

I glance at him. Does he consider it that much of a burden to kiss me? I'm not eager to do it either, especially with his whole family watching, but I'm sure we could make it convincing if we needed to.

"What's the matter, brother?" Belladonna mocks. "Surely you've kissed your own fiancée enough that it should be no burden to do so now."

Roze purses his lips. "I don't like open displays of affection."

Belladonna cocks her head. "It's just one kiss."

"I—"

"Roze," says the Queen. I hadn't even noticed she was paying attention, but now her dark eyes are set squarely on us, her hands splayed regally on the table before her. "Kiss your beloved."

Roze's face turns to stone, his eyes wide as he meets his mother's gaze. He looks utterly terrified, and now I'm completely confused. But the command in the Queen's voice leaves no alternative option.

Roze turns to me, his face serious and things I can't discern swirling in his eyes. I'm completely uncomfortable, all too aware of the sights of every one of the sisters as well as the Queen on me, analyzing for sincerity. But then Roze's gloved hand cups my cheek.

"Viola," he whispers, "eyes on me."

I look at him. My breath shudders as I watch him study my face like he's searching for something, scanning down from my eyes and finally landing on my lips. He brings his face closer, and when I feel the coolness of his breath across my lips, my eyelids flutter shut of their own accord.

His other hand cups my other cheek, taking total control of my head, and I can feel the ghost of his lips over mine, the crackle of energy where his nose is almost brushing my cheek. But he isn't kissing me. Not yet. I don't understand why he's waiting, but despite the others watching, it has my toes curling in my shoes. I want his mouth on mine. In fact, I *need* it. I almost cross the distance between us on my own, when I hear him whisper, "Hold on. Please, just . . . hold on."

Hold on? What does that mean?

My eyes open a sliver to see Roze's face, close to mine with a look that can only be described as desperate, tortured, and . . . longing? But then I catch something behind him.

In the corner, the little gray ghost boy stands half submerged in shadows. His face smiles cruelly as he holds a small mirror, its surface cracked into a shattered mosaic. But in the glass, there's an image. A face.

I squint, and I can just make out the blur of familiar cheeks and freckles across a nose, eyes openly frozen in death, face drained of blood, icy lake water sloshing around curly hair. My own face. Dead in the water of the lake.

I think I'm going to be sick.

"Excuse me." I wrench myself from Roze's grip and stumble from my seat, even though I know I shouldn't, even though it breaks every rule about dining with the Queen. I can't sit in that room for another moment. I hear Roze stand behind me and hurriedly say something to excuse our absence as he follows me from the room.

Once we're in the hall, I heave into an empty urn situated on a pedestal and pray it's not very old or expensive.

"Sinclair?"

I pull back, and he stops at the sight of my face. I keep seeing all these things—visions, omens, hauntings, whatever they are. I can't trust my own eyes, my own mind. And the sight of my own dead eyes staring back at me . . . It seemed like more than just a ghostly trick. It seemed real.

"Tell me something true," I say, desperate to ground myself.

His face slackens, a whisper of understanding passing over it. He takes a step forward.

"You are at dinner with my family. I'm courting you so that my mother won't kill you. You're going to help me find out what killed my father so we can get rid of the thorn tattoo and neither of us has to die."

That lines up, but it's a small relief.

I heave again, vomiting into the urn. Roze comes up behind me, pulling my hair gently away from my face.

"You killed a man with your toes last night, but now you can't tolerate dinner with my family?"

I wipe my mouth with my wrist. "There were beetles in my soup. Big, ugly black ones. You didn't see them?"

"No," he says.

"And the butlers. Did they . . . have faces?"

"Of course they did."

I shake my head. "I think I'm losing my mind." I don't know what to think. I only know what I saw.

99

He sighs deeply. "You're not losing your mind."

He rubs my back as he holds my hair, the movement so kind and so foreign that it makes me lightheaded again.

"I don't understand," I mutter.

Slowly, I right myself. I feel wobbly on my feet, and the world is tilting strangely.

"I'll tell you the truth if you promise not to hit me again," he says.

I snort crudely. "Fat chance." I stumble a little, and Roze tightens his grip on me.

"Easy," he says. "Is this what you're like drunk? Saints, I'd love to see that."

"I can hold my liquor," I say defensively, though I've only had alcohol twice in my life—once when Cerise stole a bottle of port from the school cellars for my birthday, and then during the All Hallows Eve masquerade.

"I'll tell you the truth, but you're not going to understand at first. So I'm requiring you to hold your questions until I'm done explaining. Understood?"

I make an ambiguous grumble, and he seems to take it as permission to continue.

"There is a reason my mother is so hell-bent on finding all *meigas* and destroying them. It's not because she considers you all traitors. My mother is a *meiga*."

I look up at him. "*What?*"

He closes his eyes and pinches the bridge of his nose. "I told you to not ask questions—"

"Your mother is a *meiga*?" I'm nearly screeching, and he shushes me. In a whisper I demand, "When exactly were you planning on telling me this?"

"Soon enough," he bites back.

"You didn't think it was pertinent information? We have *six days*, Roze."

"I *know*," he growls. Suddenly he grabs his left wrist, rips open his sleeve buttons, and shoves his sleeve up to the elbow. "It's my life on the line as well, remember?"

He brandishes the tattoo in my face, and it's shocking to see not only the sinister tattoo, but to see his *skin* when he keeps himself constantly mummified beneath layers of clothing. I fall silent.

He lowers his arm and meets my eyes with a glare. "Just let me explain, will you?" He pulls his sleeve back down. "My family has many secrets, and *that* is one of our most precious. Do you have any idea what the nobles would do if they found out what my mother is? There'd be an insurrection, Sinclair. She already has those snakes constantly trying to wheedle their way to the Crown. Did you know she's had five marriage proposals since my father's death? *Five.* And half the nobility want to assassinate my entire family and take the throne for themselves. You think conditions are poor for your precious commoners in the caverns now? You have no idea how bad it would get if the monarchy fell."

Despite the weakness of my body, my mind is buzzing. If the nobles are as two-faced as Roze says, perhaps one of *them* had motive for killing the King.

"That still doesn't explain why she hates *meigas*," I say.

"I'm getting to it. *Patience*, Sinclair." He sighs. "My mother believes that magic belongs only in the hands of royalty. She considers all magic outside of royal veins a heresy, and blaming *meigas* for some of the Kingdom's ailments helps her save face before the Court. It distracts them from worse problems—food shortages, disease, that sort of thing."

A wave of pure rage washes over me. "Unbelievable. So she's hunting me down because she thinks that executing me will make her popular with the nobles?"

"It's not just that she thinks it will. It has."

"What does that mean?"

He cringes and glances at my face. "I'm afraid you're going to like this part even less. You remember how there were *meigas* who sided with Aragoa during the war?"

My mind flies back to Sir Patrick's lecture from this morning. "Yes."

"When the Mists came, the *meigas* on our side put the wards in place on the castle walls to protect us. Most believe that Mother had them all killed because they betrayed the Crown, that they were plotting with Castelle to overthrow the King, but . . . that was less than true."

I narrow my eyes. "Less than true?"

He nods. "Another of our family secrets. She didn't trust that many *meigas* in an enclosed space together. She thought it would be too easy for them to turn against the Crown, so she executed them."

I gape at him. I can hardly believe what I'm hearing. I knew the Queen was a tyrant . . . I knew she wanted me dead, even. But I still didn't *truly* believe that she was evil. Some part of me actually believed what I'd been taught my entire life—that magic was corrupt, immoral, wrong. I've believed for so long that *I* was wrong, that on some level I deserved their hatred.

But if what Roze is telling me is true . . .

There were good *meigas*. And the Queen killed them because she wanted to be the only one with power.

"One of the *meigas* escaped," he continues. "And cursed her so that she cannot personally harm another *meiga* again."

"That's why she sends you," I realize. "It's not just because she'd rather not do the dirty work herself."

Roze nods, his gaze distant. "It's why she wouldn't merely reach across the table and choke the life out of you herself tonight."

"I knew public opinion wouldn't really be enough to hold her off."

"I'd hoped it would help," he says with a shrug, "as I hoped convincing her we were in love would help."

I click my tongue. "I can't imagine her caring about such a silly thing."

He lifts his eyes, meeting mine. "Silly? That's what you think of love, Sinclair?" After a beat, he looks away. "Even my mother can be a romantic, you know. You'd be surprised."

I am surprised. The cold, cruel woman in that dining room doesn't seem like the sort to be swayed by love.

Another thought occurs to me. "Are . . . are you a *meiga*, Roze?"

He shakes his head. "No."

My heart falls, and I'm more disappointed than I should be, the hope that maybe I'd finally found someone who could understand evaporating.

He continues, "So, my mother is a *meiga*. That's why you saw what you saw tonight. I don't understand much about how her magic works, but I know that she has the ability to create. Because of the curse, she can't harm you. She's trying to scare you instead by creating illusions."

"Illusions." It wasn't real. None of it. "So she made me see those things to . . ."

"Embarrass you. Terrify you. Make you come unhinged. She's used to getting what she wants. I don't doubt she's furious that I'm trying to defy her orders."

That doesn't explain the ghost boy. He scared me out of that kiss with Roze, but the Queen was the one who demanded that we kiss.

I look up at his face, but he's looking pointedly away from me. "Have you ever done this before? Defied her orders?" I ask.

He pauses, flicking his tongue against his lower lip, and my gaze is stuck to it for longer than is advisable. "I tried to . . . when I was younger. I don't attempt it anymore," he says. "It doesn't go well for those who do."

I blink and look away. "Do you think it's possible that the Queen killed your father?"

"I was with the Queen when the King passed."

"Oh." I want to say that she still could've done it, that it could've happened at another moment, especially with power like hers, but I know I shouldn't. Not now.

He shifts on his feet, then takes a step toward me. "Listen, I know this will be difficult, but we have to go back inside. We *must* convince my family that this engagement is real."

"You seemed bereft at the idea of kissing me. I think you should take your own advice."

He bites the inside of his cheek. "Trust me, Sinclair, you don't want that."

I cross my arms over my chest. He has such a problem with kissing me but won't say the real reason—that he thinks himself above me. Well, I'm going to make him admit it. "And why wouldn't I?"

The corner of his lip curls. "Because a kiss from me would be devastating. It would ruin you."

Arrogant bastard.

Before I can argue, he leans close, tilting his head and lowering his voice to speak in my ear even though the hall is empty. "After dinner, the family always does drinks and games in the parlor. There, I can talk to my mother. Perhaps we can make a bargain with her."

"You're certainly one for bargains, aren't you?"

"She may be willing to remove the order to kill you—and remove this tattoo on my arm—if we can convince her that we can find the King's true killer. It's what she wants more than anything, even eliminating other *meigas*."

I exhale a shaky breath. "So I just need to . . . get through dinner."

He nods. "And remember that none of it is real. Don't let her rattle you."

I scoff. "You didn't have beetles copulating in your soup." Or the image of his own corpse tormenting him.

His expression is so disgusted I almost laugh. He offers me his arm, and I loop my hand in his elbow as we pass back through the doors.

———

I make it through dinner by keeping my head down and saying very little. Luckily, Wisteria keeps her mother's attention occupied with chatter about the fete that the Queen is now throwing tomorrow night in honor of our engagement. As though it wasn't going to be difficult enough to perform in front of his family—now I'll have to do it in front of the Court as well.

When dessert is finished, we follow the Queen through the far doors of the dining room, Roze and I trailing behind the princesses.

"Well done, Sinclair." Roze's hand brushes the small of my back. "The after-dinner drinks are a much more casual affair. You're going to need to loosen up."

"Loosen up?"

He smirks. "I know—a difficult task with that stick up your—"

I elbow him in the stomach, and he doubles over in pain. Princess Narcissa eyes us over her shoulder as she follows her sisters, and I smile sweetly at her while Roze coughs to cover his pain.

"Saints, Sinclair," he whispers. "Pretend to actually like me if you want to convince them."

The parlor is dimly lit, a fire already warming the sitting area. Several of the sisters have a deck of cards out and are taking their seats at the game table.

"Do you want to play?" I ask Roze, desperately hoping he doesn't.

"Saints, no," he says, taking two glasses of wine from a butler's tray and handing one to me. "I prefer to brood and get drunk, if you don't mind." He tosses back a gulp of his wine.

"Sounds glorious," I mutter, sipping from my own cup.

He pulls me by the waist with his free hand toward the sofa next to the hearth, falling into the cushions and pulling me down with him. He's more sprawled than sitting, which leaves me half-lying against him, his arm securely around my waist as he takes another deep drink from his glass. I'm surrounded by him—the warmth of his body touching me from shoulder to knee, the scent of him, apples and winter spices, overpowering me. My cheeks flush, and I take a deeper drink of my wine. For the next few minutes, I study the Roquelart family to distract myself from the all-encompassing presence of Roze.

Four of the sisters are playing cards, which, based on their prim posture and upturned noses, seems to be more about out-peacocking each other than actually winning the game. Wisteria is attempting to play the piano and doing a terrible job of it. Each time she hits a wrong note, a muscle in Roze's jaw twitches, like it's physically painful for him to listen.

And Belladonna . . . she stands talking in a far corner with the Queen. The Crown Princess's expression is bored, but there's a hardness in her eyes that makes me wonder how much of that is an act. The Queen's face is sharp as a viper's as she speaks to her daughter, and Belladonna isn't uttering a word.

"What's your mother saying to your sister?" I whisper to Roze.

"Who cares," he mutters, clearly more interested in the wine. He must be well on his way to getting drunk—his arm has worked its way up from my waist and he now has a curl of my hair wrapped around one of his gloved fingers. He toys with it, studying it like it fascinates him. He's taking quite a few liberties with this ruse—no doubt to rile me.

I do my best to ignore him and instead watch the interaction between Belladonna and the Queen. Queen Maria looks furious, nearly spitting her whispered words in Belladonna's face. When I see Belladonna's gaze start to wander from her mother's, the Queen grabs her by the jaw, and my breath stops. The Queen's nails dig into her daughter's cheeks like talons as she hisses something to her, eyes aflame. Belladonna has the look of an abused animal—frightened and furious. A moment later, the Queen releases her jaw roughly—a dismissal. Belladonna slowly lifts her head . . . and sees me watching.

Pure rage washes over her face. She quickly curtsies to her mother before crossing the room to us.

"Oh no," I whisper.

"Hmm?" Roze mumbles, eyes half open as he fiddles with my hair.

Belladonna approaches, stopping just before our spot on the sofa. "Viola Sinclair," she says, her voice dripping with poisoned sugar. "Find something interesting to gawk at?" Then she leans down close, all sweetness gone. Roze stiffens, his sleepiness evaporating. Belladonna snarls, "You have some nerve sitting here, like you're one of us, like your veins aren't full of filthy, common blood."

Something snaps in me. Against my better judgment, I say, "At least my filthy common blood doesn't cower before the Queen."

Pure violence crosses Belladonna's face. And then she pours her wine onto my lap.

Roze jumps to his feet. I gasp and try to keep the wine from falling on what I'm sure are the most expensive pieces of furniture in the entire Kingdom.

Roze, however, is in his sister's face, and . . . he has a knife out. Oh Saints.

"Guards!" squeals one of the princesses at the card table.

A moment later, two guards storm into the room, hands on their swords. Roze doesn't look at either of them. His knife is against his sister's throat. His other hand holds the back of her head.

"You're forgetting yourself, Bella," he whispers to her. "And you're forgetting me. What I am."

Her face has paled, but she glares at Roze. "I could never forget what you are, *brother*." She says "brother" like it's an accusation, and I don't quite understand.

"Unhand the Princess," one of the guards commands, drawing his sword.

Roze eyes the guard and then reluctantly obeys, releasing his sister and taking a long step back. He paints his face with that charming smile of his. "Sibling squabbles. All in good fun."

The guards look warily from Roze to the Queen, who sighs and says, "You're dismissed." They bow and are gone in an instant. "And Belladonna, go to bed," the Queen continues wearily.

Belladonna glowers openly at Roze, her chest heaving, her hair disheveled from where Roze grabbed it. She points a long, painted finger in Roze's face. "You and your little w—"

"*Belladonna!*" the Queen snaps, and the Princess flinches. The Queen's face is livid, and I feel goose bumps rise over my arms, like I can feel the malevolent power lurking under her pallid skin. "*Leave.*"

Roze smiles wickedly at the Crown Princess. "Go on, sister. Off to bed."

Belladonna's face is pure malice, her eyes so alive they almost look like they spark with light. She manages a half-hearted glare at him before fleeing the room, head bowed but spine erect.

Had Belladonna been about to call me a witch? Had the Queen told her daughter the truth about me? It doesn't seem likely, given the sourness of their relationship, but this family keeps surprising me.

Roze stows his knife beneath his sleeve and returns to his seat beside me. "Is your dress all right?"

I look down at the damp fabric in my lap and shrug. "It doesn't matter." A lie. This is the only dress I own, but I'm not going to tell Roze that.

He frowns. "Tomorrow I'm going to have some new clothes purchased for you."

I pull back to look him in the face. "That's completely unnecessary."

"On the contrary, your clothes are awful. If you're going to be my fiancée, then you need to look the part."

My mouth pops open, about to tell him off for being rude, but he's already moved on. "It's nearly midnight, Sinclair. We should speak to my mother."

Roze gets to his feet and offers me his hand. I toss back the last of my wine for courage, set the glass on the nearby table, and take his outstretched hand.

Queen Maria has taken her place in a chair near the game table, looking every inch a queen on her throne as she watches her daughters with a stony expression. With her black skirts splayed out before her, the woman is like winter itself, so dark and cold, full of treacherous beauty.

"Mother," Roze says when we approach, "Viola and I would like a word."

The Queen surveys us slowly, her eyes piercing, and my stomach sours with nerves. My shadows itch at the edges of my fingertips, as though in response to the magic in the Queen.

"Very well," she says.

Roze glances at his sisters, who are preoccupied with cards and the piano—they pay us no mind.

"Mother, we're here to make a bargain," Roze says.

She laughs—a high, clear sound, like clinking crystal—and I flinch. "You defy my orders, undermine my authority, and force my hand with this farcical engagement, and now you have the nerve to pursue a bargain? With *me*?"

"It's true," I say, forcing sincerity into my voice. "It's not a farce."

The Queen raises an eyebrow and turns to her son.

"I love her, Mother," Roze says. He sounds so utterly convincing as he places a hand on the small of my back.

The Queen's smile is catlike. "And yet, the rose remains on your arm, Prince." She turns her icy gaze on me. "Magic is treason. There is no worse wickedness. And once the Kingdom learns of your true nature, I doubt there will be a soul who will defend you, Miss Sinclair."

I open my mouth, about to bite back that she's a liar and a hypocrite, that I know what she is, that she can't use my death and the death of every other *meiga* for her own ends. But then Roze's hand tightens on the back of my dress, and I understand his meaning—*Hold your tongue. Don't show her what you know.*

I snap my mouth shut, still glaring at the Queen, who continues to watch me with those too-perceptive eyes.

Roze interjects, "I know how Father's death has plagued you. And we both know that Viola isn't the one you're after. Let us find the real culprit and deliver them to you. The Court will be mollified; justice will be satisfied. And when we do, you'll remove the tattoo and let Viola live."

The Queen's jaw tightens. The air around her darkens. I doubt Queen Maria is used to anyone denying her anything, holding any sort of power over her—she'd rather have me dead *and* find out how the King died. She inhales deeply, and I feel death fill the air, surrounding the Queen. The hairs on my arms rise, and for less than a blink, I'm sure Queen Maria's eyes flash bright red.

And then her appearance is ordinary once more, the air cold with winter chill.

"You *will* find his murderer. If you do so within the time frame of the thorn tattoo . . . I will consider lifting it."

I take a deep breath, finding my voice. "You're so certain that he was murdered? Wasn't he in poor health?"

Her eyes flash. "I knew my husband. His mind was addled, but his body was strong. It did not fail him."

"Then we'll find his murderer," Roze says, his mother's rage reflected on his face.

"But," the Queen continues, "*if* you find the culprit, when the last thorn disappears, this engagement must hold. Miss Sinclair will marry into this family."

My legs nearly give out. "Why?"

Roze's fingers press into my back—a warning. I glance at him. His eyes are set on his mother, his jaw clenched, surety in his gaze.

The Queen's eyes narrow on me. "I will not be made a fool before the Court because of your scheming. A broken engagement, a fickle young prince . . . the smallest sign of weakness and those vipers will smell blood." She looks at Roze. "We've lost your father, our lion. But this family will remain strong. I'll make sure of it." She turns back to me. Every time I meet her eyes, I remember what it felt like to plunge into the pools of the caverns as a small child—the freshly melted snow shocking my body so brutally I could scarcely breathe. "I protect my family at all costs, Miss Sinclair. You'll do well to remember that."

THE THIRD
DEADLY THORN

Though a bargain was struck, there was no peace for the Prince and the Girl of Shadows, for nothing could protect them from the wicked plot of the Queen. All alone and afraid, the Shadow Girl disguised herself as an ordinary maiden—pleasant and light of heart, burying her darkness so deeply within herself that she hoped even she would forget it was there.

But some things will not stay in the dark, even when locked away, gagged and chained, threatened and beaten into silence. Some things are stronger than fear.

And no matter how afraid the Shadow Girl was, she could not escape herself.

CHAPTER ELEVEN

It's the third day. Another thorn will disappear at sundown, and we're running out of time. I must have slept, but it doesn't feel like it. After hours of tossing and turning in bed, my limbs tangled in sheets as much as my mind is tangled in questions, I finally accept defeat and dress for the day.

Over my uniform, I pull on my sweater with the Vandenberghe patch sewn over the breast and then go on the hunt for my shoes under the bed. Instead, my hand finds the worn wool of my slippers, and I groan.

"What's this?" I say, waving the slobbery, shredded slipper in Waffles's face where he's sprawled upside down in my vacated spot on the bed. He has the nerve to look back at me with big, sad eyes, and I glare at him. "I should change your name to Demon Waffles."

He nuzzles my hand, and I relent, scratching his ears. "You little hell beast."

I slip on my thankfully unmutilated school shoes, vaguely wondering if I can talk Roze into including new slippers in his offer of clothing worthy of his fiancée. If I have to tolerate spending this much time with him, I might as well enjoy the perks.

Although I have to admit, he was . . . less deplorable last night. Positively tolerable, in fact. Only vaguely irritating. I remember how he held my hair while I vomited my dinner into an urn. It was almost gentlemanly. If I was feeling generous, I would call it kind.

I shake my head on my way to the common room. I have enough on my mind without analyzing Roze's change in behavior.

I thought the common room would be empty at this early hour, but it isn't. Kole is hunched over a table, various metal springs, nuts, and bolts spread over it on a leather cloth. I'm surprised to see him. For once, I wasn't looking for him. He's always been an early bird, and we often meet in my much cozier common room to do homework together in the quiet morning hours.

"Morning," he says brightly. He kicks a chair out with his foot. "Come sit."

I fall into a seat and Waffles jumps up and settles onto my lap. The common room is awash in pink haze—the morning sun straining to pierce the Mists. I find the Mists almost lovely at this time of day. The whole scene is eerily ordinary, as though the last few days of my life haven't felt like a slow march to the gallows.

"So," Kole says, using a tool to wind one piece of metal around another. "Any progress on the project for Professor Borges?"

"Oh," I say, almost forgetting that I'd shared the book with him the day before. Lunch yesterday seems like forever ago. "Um, not really. Although I did find out that your dad was right about the armistice. The war almost ended peacefully."

Kole's shoulders sink a little. "Yeah. It's a shame."

He bows his head toward his work again, and I notice how the morning sun lights up the amber in his hair. I pull one of my books from Roze's family library out of my bag and open it on my lap.

"What else does your father remember about it?" I ask casually.

Kole shrugs, his eyes narrowed on the little tools in his hands. "He said there was strong support for a treaty even when he was at Vandenberghe. He was in some sort of student organization that fought for peace."

"Really?"

"Yeah. Can't remember which one. But he said even the King was in it with him when he was a student. You know, before he was King and all that."

My head pops up from my book. A young Prince Alexandre

Roquelart was in a student organization that fought for peace? But Roze's grandfather was waging the war with Castelle. If Alexandre was fighting for peace, wouldn't he have had to keep that information secret?

I glance up at the wall of books below the windows. On the topmost shelf there are dozens of leather-bound yearbooks, recording the members of each class of Berlaise House going back ages. Every house has its own set. I know that Alexandre Roquelart was a member of Berlaise—houses tend to get competitive about their famous past members, especially royals. I'm suddenly very curious to lay eyes on teenage Alexandre. Alexandre the Prince, Alexandre the secret peace fighter.

I cross to the shelf and climb the stepladder in front of it, and . . . I'm still too short to reach.

"What are you looking for?" Kole asks, following.

"I'm just curious about something," I mutter, stretching. I'm too far up to grip the ladder with my hand now, so I lean my elbow against the bookshelf to steady myself while I search, running my fingers along the golden dates on the books. I find the one containing the records from the years around the end of the war and reach high, trying to slide the volume loose with the tips of my fingers.

The weight of the book tips forward, and it starts to fall toward me. My foot slips—

"Vi!"

I tumble from the ladder. The book collides painfully with my shoulder as two arms wrap around my middle.

There's a loud *oof* as Kole collides with the floor, and I collide with him, landing right on top of him.

"Saints, I'm so sorry," I say, turning and lifting myself on all fours.

"'S'all right," Kole says, wincing as he lifts himself onto his elbows. His glasses have fallen from his face on the way down, and his unfocused eyes meet mine.

This is the closest our faces have ever been to one another, and suddenly I'm frozen. The sun and the fire warm the green in his eyes to a mossy color. I wonder—are they the same shade as grass was before the Mists came? Are they greener?

My gaze falls to his lips, and for a moment, almost out of habit, I wonder what it would be like to kiss him.

Kole blinks and clears his throat, pushing himself into a sitting position. I hand him his glasses, and he adjusts them on his face.

I smile. "Thanks for breaking my fall."

"I would say anytime, but I think you might've bruised a rib."

I huff a laugh, and my eyes fall to the book. I pull it into my lap and quickly turn to the class pictures toward the years at the end of the war.

"When was your father at Vandenberghe?"

Kole tells me his class year. I turn the page, and my eyes immediately snag on an old photograph that I know is what I'm looking for.

Four lines of Berlaise students, nearly triple the number we have now. Their expressions are serious, but I can tell that their clothes are newer, and they have the shape and brightness of health in their bodies. And then there are the sharp shadows behind them—the sort that can only be created by actual unfiltered sunlight. The photograph was taken outside, where there must have been fresh air and grass beneath their feet. It's enough to make my heart squeeze.

But my eyes are almost instantly drawn to one particular boy in the front row. I don't need to read the list of names below the photograph to know this is Prince Alexandre. His face is familiar to everyone in the Kingdom, distinguishable even at this young age. Another handsome boy stands beside him, their stances suggesting they're in close confidence. Their heads are held high, their expressions confident, even cocky. And beside them is a line of writing in scrawled, faded ink.

Bone. Blood. Breath. Bite. Fiat tenebrae. —L

I stop breathing. I rush to my feet, heaving the heavy book with me.

"Viola?" Kole asks, standing.

"I've—I've got to go," I say, not bothering to come up with a better excuse. "I'll see you later," I call over my shoulder as I race down the hall, leaving Kole standing by the bookcase with a confounded expression on his face.

———

Roze isn't answering his door. I pound on it louder, not caring if it's too early for his spoiled—

"Sinclair?"

I spin around, and Roze is standing inches behind me. I nearly jump out of my skin. He's dressed and looks like he's been up for hours, that ice-white hair perfectly coiffed as always so that a single lock falls over his forehead, one dark eyebrow raised at me. Seeing him face-to-face forces me to confront what I've been ignoring since last night—that even if we survive this, I'll have to marry him. The thought shortens my breath, and the Roquelart ring weighs heavily on my finger.

"Don't *do* that."

"Do what?"

"Sneak up on a girl."

"You're standing in front of my room."

I huff and look past him down the hall. "Where were you, anyway? I didn't see you in the common room."

He shrugs. "I was out."

I lift a brow. "Out?"

"Yes."

I pause.

"Are you going to provide me with further details, or—"

"It's *private*, Sinclair, fucking Saints."

I purse my lips and look away. Something occurs to me that hadn't before—that Roze might have a lover. Maybe he slips off at night to see them. The thought turns my stomach sour, and I quickly distract myself.

"Have you seen this?" I ask, pushing the book into Roze's chest.

"A dusty old yearbook? I can't say I have."

"Not that," I say impatiently. "*This*." I open it to the page with Prince

117

Alexandre and point to the note scrawled on the edge of the photograph. "Next to your father."

Roze takes the book from me and turns it to look at it properly. His gaze is on the photo, but mine is set squarely on him. I watch the blood drain from his face.

I can't contain my smile. "*Fiat tenebrae*. It's what Ed said to you in the dining hall yesterday morning. Roze, this secret organization that you and your friends are in . . . was your father also a member?"

He sighs. "Shit."

Victory.

"I'm right, aren't I?"

He groans and massages his brow. "It's too early for an inquisition, Sinclair."

"Kole said his father was a part of a student organization fighting for peace." I know my next conclusion is a leap, but I have a hunch. "Was that your club? Was your father fighting for peace before he was King?"

"Stop calling it a club."

"Aha! So it does exist."

"Could you try to be marginally less chipper about this?"

"Not a chance."

"Sinclair—"

"Don't you see? This is the connection. Your father did something shady, something I'm sure would have been kept secret—" I've discovered a feasible explanation for the King's death, one I cling to.

"*Sinclair.*"

"I don't know what that has to do with this book that Professor Borges gave me yet, but whatever he was involved in might have given the older nobles reason to have a vendetta against him, especially if he was working against his own fa—"

His leather-clad hand claps over my mouth, just the way it did in the cathedral two nights ago. He drops the book and backs me into the wall until he has me pinned with his hip, one hand holding my mouth and the other gripping my arm. I can feel every hard line of his body, the heat of him seeping through his clothing. He brings his face close to mine, our lips separated just by the gloved hand between us. His eyes bore into me like knives.

"You might find this amusing, some fun little mystery to solve," he breathes. "But I promise you, there is nothing pleasant about the risks our organization takes. If the nobility, or the royal guard, or worse, my mother, were to catch wind of our existence, you have no idea how hard the sky would fall. So while I know that I'm asking the impossible of you, I'm going to have to insist that you *hold—your—tongue*."

I don't breathe. I don't blink. I stare widely up at his silver eyes, both captive and captivated. Every time I become too familiar with Roze, every time I start treating him like just another Vandenberghe boy, he reminds me that he is something completely *other*—the Huntsman. Assassin and Prince.

Slowly, he releases his grip on me and backs away, giving me back my space. His expression is cold and controlled—I imagine he thinks he's won some sort of battle. But I'm just getting started.

I glare at him. "Let me be clear about something," I whisper. "If you want me to hold my tongue, then stop dodging my questions. You asked for *my* help."

"Which was not a license to put your nose in every aspect of my personal life."

"If I think it's relevant to what happened to your father, I'm going to investigate it."

"This isn't."

"I disagree. And you need my help or you certainly wouldn't have asked for it. You don't strike me as someone who asks for help easily, Roze Roquelart. So I'll repeat myself—*stop* hiding things, and for the love of the Saints, *stop* threatening me." I take a deep breath, calming my thundering pulse. "If you think you can do that, then you can trust me to keep whatever secrets you and your friends have."

He looks me over, thinking. I can almost feel him about to relent, but then—

"No," he drawls. "Sorry, darling. This is off-limits." He turns on his heel and struts down the hall.

"Wait—where are you going?" I call after him.

"After this discussion, I find myself in desperate need of a cup of tea. You're giving me a headache."

"*Me?*"

I allow him five minutes in the dining hall. Five minutes of silence so he can drink his precious tea. I think I'm being rather generous considering what a complete ass he's been.

And then I'm pursuing the yearbook lead again. "You need to tell me about this—"

"*Don't* call it a club."

"This *organization* of yours. Don't you see? It's the missing piece. Your father's death, the war, the armistice—it has to be the reason he was killed."

"No."

"You don't think this is why someone would want him dead?"

"He was the sovereign, Sinclair. Half the Kingdom wanted him dead."

I throw my hands up in the air. "Well, if you won't be helpful, I'm out of ideas."

"We should go back to the mirror."

"Absolutely not."

Trying to coax helpful answers from him is like negotiating with a toddler. Actually, he reminds me of Waffles when he's like this. Those two would get along wonderfully if they would stop growling at each other.

"What was your relationship like with your father?"

He hesitates a moment, swirling his tea in his cup. I think he's going to snub me again, but then I watch his guard lower just a smidge. "It's an odd thing, being the son of a king. When your parent is the sovereign, you're nothing like a normal family."

Something familiar twinges in my heart. I understand what it's like to long for the embrace of a loving parent, what it's like to give up on that hope.

"But regardless, my father and I—" I watch him struggle with the words while brushing imaginary dust off the leg of his pants. "We had a bond. We were separate from whatever my mother and sisters were."

I think of those six nearly identical faces. Six sets of piercing eyes. Six cruel smiles. In a family like that, I can imagine Roze and his father clinging to each other for sanity.

"My mother has a habit of treating me like her own personal henchman. But my father . . . he actually talked to me like a son."

"What did you talk about?"

Roze shrugs, a distant look in his eyes. "Art. Music. Great works of literature. He loved the opera—patronized the opera house before the Mists. I suppose that's why I decided to study music. That and because Mother thought it was a ridiculous pursuit for a prince." He smiles mischievously.

"Roze," I say, not sure how I'm going to finish the sentence. There is no proper way to phrase what I want to ask. "Your parents—"

He cuts me off with a warning glare.

I know I'm not the first person to wonder about his parents' relationship. There had always been a tangible coldness between the King and his Queen Consort. And yet . . . *seven* children, all born within a few short years of each other. And there was that seemingly happy portrait in the Queen's room. Whether it's impolite to ask or not, I need insight into his father, what might have been on his mind the night of his death.

I clear my throat. "Your father . . . did he love your mother?"

There's a growl in Roze's voice as he says, "Careful, Sinclair."

"I *need* to know more about them."

"The relationship between your King and Queen is none of your business."

"We've exhausted our leads. We know your father was a part of *something*, but you won't tell me what. We know that your mother killed the *meigas*. Are you sure it wasn't her who killed him?"

He bristles. "I told you—I was with her."

"But how do you know *exactly* when he died? It could have been any time between when he left the party to when he was found, right? Were you with your mother that entire time?"

"You're reaching, Sinclair. I told you it wasn't my mother."

"I don't understand why you're dismissing the possibility. You don't seem to have any real love for her, and we know what she's capable of. Plus, now that we have this new information about your father, there's possible motivation—"

"I know because my mother loved my father. To an insane, illogical degree."

I blink. "That just doesn't seem possible—"

"What would you know about it? About love or family or any of it? Your parents abandoned you."

Ice slides down my throat. How did he find out about that? "Have . . . have you been researching me?"

His expression is arrogant and cold. "And why not? You're my fiancée." He cocks his head. "Why did they toss you out, I wonder?"

"Don't—" I say. I try to make my voice sound commanding. Instead, I just sound as angry as I feel.

"Is it because you're a *meiga*? Did they find out? Or did you get on their nerves as well with all your incessant questions?"

I glare at him, hatred stinging my throat. He's deflecting, I know, drawing my attention away from my questions, trying to get a rise out of me. But it's working.

"Martin and Elise Sinclair are doing well, in case you were wondering," he says, swirling his tea. "I know you haven't been to see them in years. They seem happy without either of their children. What happened to their son, by the way? You must have been, what, four when he died?"

I want to hit him again. I want to burn him alive. But my throat is raw, and I don't want him to see me cry.

I shove away from the table and snarl at him, "I don't need to ask why your family hates you. You're as lovable as a plague."

I storm away, hearing him chuckle behind me. "Darling, I *am* a plague."

I don't know where I'm going as I storm from the dining hall, feeling my shadows leak from the tips of my fingers. I curl my hands inside my sweater to hide them as I bow my head. I'm nearly through the doors when I collide with something solid.

"Viola," Kole says, grabbing hold of my shoulders to steady me. I'm taking deep breaths, keeping my eyes on the floor, but I'm frozen. I want to hold on to him, someone familiar enough and, for goodness' sake, *normal* enough, to ground me.

"Are you okay?" he asks. "Viola . . . are you crying?"

I bite my lip. "I'm fine."

I try to move past him, but he stops me, holding my arm. "What happened?"

He looks around, turning in the direction I came from, where Roze is likely still sitting at the table drinking his tea like the arrogant ass he is.

"Oh," Kole says. His body tenses, and then he backs away from me. "Tell me what he did."

"Kole—"

"Did he hurt you?"

I almost say no. But he *did* hurt me.

It's petty. It's wrong. But I pause long enough to let Kole draw his own conclusions.

His lips form a hard frown. "I'm going to take care of this."

"What? No, Kole, don't—"

He crosses the room, not paying attention to my protests. My stomach clenches as I follow him.

"What did you do to her?" Kole demands, standing over Roze where he lounges at the table. His legs are still crossed lazily, and he doesn't even look up at Kole.

"Your Royal Highness," Roze corrects.

"Excuse me?"

"What did you do to her, *Your Royal Highness*?"

I have never seen such a look as what passes over Kole's face. He looks like he might impale Roze.

"I don't care who you are. You can't go around torturing everyone in this school. Stay away from her," Kole says.

Roze looks up at him, studies him coldly, and then, deadly and slow, he stands to his feet. "Let's you and I clear a few things up, Belcamp. You do not tell me what to do for several reasons. Firstly, because I *am* your Prince, whether you like it or not—"

Kole opens his mouth, but Roze raises his hand, wagging a gloved finger at him. "Ah, ah. Remember who you're speaking to."

Kole clenches his fists at his sides but stays silent.

"Second, because I am looking out for Viola's best interests, and she is *my* fiancée, not yours."

Why was that distinction necessary? Kole's face reddens as the wrath between them sizzles.

"And third, because if you do, I'll destroy you." He says it plainly, mercilessly, less like a threat and more like a fact.

I put my hand on Kole's arm. "Just go. Please."

But Kole doesn't move. He glares at the Prince, pure spite on his face. "You're pathetic. Without your money and your title, what are you?"

Roze smiles, a sight so disturbing that a shiver ricochets down my spine. "Something much worse."

I put myself between them, facing Kole—my back to Roze's chest. "*Go*, Kole," I demand.

He looks perplexed and stricken.

"*Please*," I beg.

He obeys, turning on his heel and stalking away with fists still clenched, leaving me standing with Roze. I've never been more furious with Roze, even as the scent of him fills my lungs—winter, spice, and poisoned apples. I am lightheaded and dizzy and can hardly ignore the feel of him, the warmth of his chest through his button-down shirt.

I shove him away. "*Stop* threatening people."

He looks unperturbed. "I'll threaten people when I need to."

"Kole did *nothing* to you."

"Didn't he? From the looks of it, he was trying to get between me and my fiancée."

"I'm not *your* anything." My voice is louder than I intend, but I can't fathom the sheer audacity of this arrogant, arrogant man. "I don't belong to you. I belong to myself. And you were being an ass."

He adjusts his gloves with precise movements, not looking me in the eye.

"You need to apologize to him."

"The only words Belcamp deserves from me are to tell him to kindly fuck off."

My throat burns with anger. I hold back my shadows. "Kole is my *friend*, and you're ruining that."

"He's manipulating you," Roze spits.

My mouth falls open. "*Manipulating* me?"

A frustrated growl escapes Roze's throat, and he smooths back his hair, looking away. "Sinclair, listen . . ." He frowns, shifting his weight, clearly agitated about something. "You need to watch out for Belcamp."

I laugh. "This, coming from you? Kole is the most harmless person I know."

"He's an opportunist. He's ambitious, and he doesn't care who he tramples on along his road to success."

"What are you talking about?"

Roze steps closer, looking deep into my eyes now. "He spends time with you because you're smart and accomplished. It makes him look good. But he's not as clever as you are—I doubt he would pass half his classes without your help."

I blink. "You're saying he's my friend because we study together?"

He gives me a meaningful look. "Men like him discard people as soon as they fail to prove themselves useful. He *knows* you like him, Sinclair. He's using it to his advantage."

I gape at him. "That's absurd."

He sighs. "When we started at Vandenberghe, he stuck to me like a tick. He was desperate to become my friend. But I can smell a social climber a mile away. Eventually he gave up on winning me over and moved on. To you. He smells success on you. Be angry at me all you like, but you need to cut Belcamp loose."

My hands clench into white-knuckled fists, like I'm holding my shadows by the reins. He's wrong. *He's wrong.* I know Kole. He's a good person. He would never—he defended me against Roze, didn't he?

He did . . . as soon as Roze took me away from him. A sick, dark feeling fills me.

"I don't want to talk about this now," I say. "Let's just get through this."

———

Roze thinks we should take a look at where the King was found, but I don't want to—I want to find Professor Borges. I didn't see her around the school at all yesterday, and it's starting to trouble me. But after a not-so-brief squabble about it, Roze refuses to do anything other than return to the site of the King's demise. I'm tired of fighting him, so to the murder scene we go.

Roze leads me to the halls that surround one of the castle's extravagant ballrooms, where the All Hallows' Eve masquerade was held, and I'm filled with memories from that night. Cerise, drunk out of her mind. Me, thinking only of returning to my dorm, where I could curl up with Saint Waffles and a book that I wanted to finish. The music and the madness.

These halls were a world of beauty and grotesquerie, everything dark and dimly lit, all the faces of the revelers hidden behind the gruesome, smiling masks of animals and fiends, outlined in gold and jewels.

But Roze leads me to a far-off hall, where the party would certainly not have ventured. "This is where I found him," he says darkly. "Slumped on the floor. His skin was already cold as ice. Not a mark on him, except those runes."

I look around. By all accounts, it's an ordinary hallway. There are dozens of others like it in this part of the castle. The carpet is worn and the polish on the molding has gone dull from lack of upkeep. Artwork lines the walls—portraits of kings, nobles, and battles. The only thing at all peculiar about this corridor is that it's a little darker than some of the others. There are no windows, and no one has bothered to light the gas lamps.

"Don't any nobles live on this hall?" I ask. "Why is it empty?"

"These were my father's personal rooms. He insisted that they be kept dark, and he never allowed anyone to come down this way, not even servants."

I grimace and walk a few paces into the darkness, scanning the space. "I don't see anyth—"

My breath catches. My heart stops.

There on the carpet, barely perceptible among the shadows, is a dark, wet spot.

"Sinclair?" Roze asks, watching me.

I take a step backward, and my knees wobble.

"*Sinclair?*" Roze insists.

The puddle is dark and wine colored. I back up another step, and then the smell hits me—the unmistakable, metallic scent of blood. The air around the stain shimmers—silver and blue coalesce to form a shadowy shape. The gray ghost boy sits in the middle of the stain, his face and his hands covered in blood leaching from his pores, oozing from every crevice, running in thick streams down his small arms and legs, matting in his clothing.

And then, the boy speaks. His voice is small, weak, and garbled from straining to speak through the blood that pours over his lips and nose.

Tongues of shadow burst from my fingers, licking around my hands.

Calm.

Control.

The ghost boy opens his mouth and hisses, "Bloody Annie. Bloody Annie. Bloody Annie."

I choke on the air in my throat. The ghost has never spoken before.

The boy stands, gliding closer as the blood streams down his clothes, his innocent face.

My shadows wrap around my arms like armor.

No, no, no.

I am calm. I am in control.

Distantly, I hear Roze's voice, but something is keeping him back. I screw my eyes shut. A hand like winter ice touches my chest, piercing my skin, slithering past my rib cage, seizing my heart.

And the last echoes I hear are the name, this time in my own voice, in my own head.

Bloody Annie.

Bloody Annie.

Bloody Annie.

CHAPTER TWELVE

Leather on my cheek, breath on my skin, and I open my eyes. Roze looks down at me, his hands holding my face, his expression almost panicked. He pulls back immediately, like I might bite, and sweeps his hand over his hair. "Fuck the Saints, Sinclair." He takes a deep breath, watching me with wary eyes. "You weren't breathing."

I lift myself gingerly into a sitting position.

"What happened? Did you have a vision?"

I close my eyes, the image of the boy's bloody face flashing in my mind, the feeling of his cold hand around my heart . . .

I can't tell him.

He would hate me if he knew the truth.

"No."

"It's all right," he says, smoothing his hair back again. But I can tell it isn't. We're not making any progress, and it's bothering him as much as it is me.

While he stares at the floor, I watch him, studying that tattoo on his neck—the one that matches the tattoo Ed has on his wrist. This organization he and his friends are a part of . . . whatever they do that's so dangerous, whatever his father did as a student as well . . . There has to be something there. I can imagine a dozen reasons certain nobles might want a ruler like Alexandre dead if he didn't support the war. Maybe they even blame him for the Mists.

I'm on the verge of discovery. I can feel it—I just need to learn more about this, even if Roze wants me to stay away. If he won't be cooperative . . . Well, I'll find a way around that.

"I think I need to lie down," I say, making my voice sound weak.

Roze looks back at me, examining my face. "Right. Of course." Though I can tell he's disappointed. He wants to keep trying to solve his father's murder. We're both feeling the constraints of time, which will be further cut short this evening with the fete.

"Let me take you back to your room," he says, getting to his feet and offering me a hand.

If Roze won't talk, I'll go to someone who will, and I know just where to find him.

Bosc House is far more ostentatious than Berlaise. Its common room is decked in green-and-black banners celebrating the accolades of its former members. High-back chairs are arranged around long tables as though its students are expected to always study with straight backs and perfect posture.

I find Ed flouting these expectations with one leg propped on a table and the other crooked over the arm of his chair. His nose is deep in a book titled *Economy and Society: The Necessity of the Noble Class.* I wrinkle my nose at the book, resisting the urge to gag.

"Hello," I say, falling into a seat beside him.

He jumps. "*Saints.*" He takes a moment to register me and pulls his expression into a charming grin. "Princess, what a surprise. Where's His Surliness?"

I wave dismissively. "Prince duties. But I had some free time, and I thought I'd come find you."

"Oh?" he says. "Roze leaves you alone for a few minutes, and you're already pining for my company? I have to warn you, I don't recommend betraying someone like Roze. Not that I can blame you."

I roll my eyes. "Merciless flirt."

"Always," he says with a grin. "But really, what brings you here?" He sets his book aside.

"Well . . ." I'm winging this conversation. I think the best way to get information from Ed, who seems far more loose-lipped than Roze, will be to act as though I already have it. "Roze told me a bit about your . . . organization, and I'm fascinated. I'd really love to hear more."

He chuckles casually, but I can see a note of apprehension in his eyes. "What would you like to know?"

"Well, for example, if I wanted to join, how would I do that?"

He keeps the smile on his face, but his eyes flicker away from mine before answering. "We've never had a female member, I'm afraid."

My own pleasant expression turns sour. "How very enlightened of you."

"Don't think I'm sexist, love. It's not me who wants the females out— it's tradition. If you ask me, it's high time it changed."

"Wonderful to hear," I reply flatly. "So what would I need to do?"

Ed looks taken aback. "Well—I— You'd have to be sure you want to dedicate yourself to it. It's a lifelong commitment, and not one to be taken lightly." He eyes me carefully. "How much has Roze told you?"

"Enough."

He makes a noncommittal grunt in his throat.

Maybe this is going to be harder than I thought. "Listen, Roze and I are working on something really important, and I think you and your *friends*, whoever you are, could help."

"Help how?"

I offer him a version of the information I have, sanitized of magic, the thorn tattoo, and the Queen's call for my head on a proverbial platter. We need to know about the King's death, and the King's death is linked to this secret society that Roze and Ed are a part of.

"You and Roze are investigating the King's death? Damn, you're as devious as he is." Ed taps his fingers on the table thoughtfully. "We don't talk about this, Princess."

"I understand."

He shakes his head. "No, you don't. What we do—" He sighs and leans in close. "If a word of this were to get out . . . You have to *swear* to me on your life that you will take this secret to the grave."

Ice fills my veins, but I nod. It's entirely disconcerting to see someone normally as cheerful and foolish as Ed be this sober about something.

His jaw tightens. "We're called the Grimmstone Society. We collect and guard knowledge—histories, lore, old science, artifacts—the sort of stuff certain people don't want lying around. And that guardianship is more essential, and frankly, more dangerous, than you can imagine."

My heart flutters as my mind flies immediately to the *Book of Odds*. I'm practically salivating at the prospect. This is exactly the sort of information that someone would kill for, and if King Alexandre was at the center of it, that's certainly a motive for killing him.

"What sort of knowledge?"

"That's as specific as I'm going to get with someone on the outside, as much as I like you, Princess."

I bite my lip. "Are there books in ancient Aragoise?"

Ed stares at me, saying nothing. But the silence is enough confirmation for me—of course there are books in ancient Aragoise. "Are there books with Hivernian runes?" I whisper.

The slightest twitch of his lip makes my breath hitch.

"You know how good I am with translation. I can help."

"No one except members get access."

"So let me join!"

Ed works his jaw for a moment, considering. "Roze would never approve."

As if I need Roze's approval for everything. "Let me deal with Roze."

"You *don't* want to cross him. Besides the fact that he's head of the Grimmstones, he's dead scary."

"I'm not afraid of him," I say, realizing that it's at least partly true. Sometime in the past few days, my fear of Roze has dissipated. "Think of all that I might be able to do if I just knew what information the Grimmstones had, what secrets you yourselves don't even know you possess, just because you don't have a good translator." I smile at him. Ed is loyal to Roze, but I'm guessing there's something stronger than his loyalty to (and slight fear of) him—his desire to help him. "I'm not crossing him. He wants to find out who or what killed his father, and access to the Grimmstones' knowledge is what I need to help him do that."

Ed frowns. "He's terrified of something happening to you. I was serious when I said joining the Grimmstone Society is a lifelong commitment. It's also a lifelong target on your back. After the war, the Crown had all information on certain subjects—Castelle, magic—removed from public access. The Grimmstones saved as much of it as they could, hid it away where only we could find it. If anyone were to learn who we are and what we've done, every last one of us would hang. The Grimmstones guard that knowledge with our lives. I'm risking all our lives by even telling you that much." He rotates his shoulders and looks away from me. "After school, it only becomes more dangerous to be one of us. Vandenberghe Grimmstones are the guardians of that sacred knowledge. But alumni are the hunters of it. They find secrets, and they hide them so that they never fall into the wrong hands."

My breath shallows. "What sort of secrets?"

"*Any* sort," he says, turning back to me, his eyes stony. "Political, historical, scientific—you name it. We guard knowledge until the time is right for the world to know it. Sometimes it never is."

I stare down at my hands in my lap. Is this why Roze was so secretive? It didn't make sense to me before, to avoid danger when death already looms over my head. But this is different. If I live through the next four days, would I want to live the rest of my life hunted, the way I am now?

My heart pounds against my ribs as I look up into Ed's eyes. They're so dark, so grim, that I know I'm already in this too deep. This life of danger, of secrets—these boys will live with an axe upon their necks the rest of their lives.

But that knowledge, that mission . . . even with the threat of death, it's like a beacon calling to me. And after two days of study and investigation, I know this is the only way forward, the only way to find out what Alexandre was a part of, what he knew.

"Please, Ed," I say. "I understand the risks. I want to do this. Let me help you. Let me help Roze."

Ed sighs and looks down at his shoes. "Damn it." His eyes swing up to mine. "Promise me you'll keep Roze from killing me for involving you in this."

I smile, feeling devious indeed.

One doesn't grow up in the caverns without picking up a few handy tricks—pickpocketing, how to evade the royal guard, and most usefully today, lockpicking.

Ed will help me pledge myself to the Grimmstone Society at their meeting tonight, disguised so that Roze won't realize it's me until it's too late. In the meantime, there are still hours before the fete, so I've decided to search for the professor again. I wouldn't normally consider breaking into Professor Borges's office, but she's still not responding to knocks on her door, and time is slipping through my fingers.

The lock gives way after some persuading from a hairpin, and I inch the door open. The room is dark. Misty gray windows near the ceiling provide barely enough light to see by. There's been no sign of the professor, but perhaps there's some indication of where she's gone in her office. I'm far past caring about the invasion of privacy as I slink into the room. I need to find out where she's gone *now*.

A strange collection of skulls watch overhead as I approach the professor's desk. She's always kept it in a constant state of chaos—stacks of papers, books, and copies of ancient manuscripts strewn about. Many of them contain Hivernian runes, ones that she and I have struggled to decipher together. I shuffle through them but don't see any of the runes embossed on the cover of the book she gave me.

I open her drawers one by one, not even sure what I'm looking for, pulled along by a hunch more than anything. I move a scroll of parchment aside, and my hand freezes. Beneath my fingertips is a long, metal object like a stake. It's an odd thing to keep in a drawer, but no more peculiar than anything else in her office. What has my breath freezing in my lungs is not the object, but a small shape carved into it—a spiraled dragon closely resembling the one on the cover of the book.

"Funny, I remember leaving you in your room."

I jump and slam the drawer shut. Roze is standing casually in the doorframe, so silent I didn't even hear him approach. How does he do that?

"I'm—I'm feeling better," I stutter.

He glares darkly. "Didn't I warn you not to go wandering off alone? Or did you just forget that the Queen wants you dead?"

I clench my jaw. "We made a deal with her. And I didn't know where you were. I didn't want to waste time when I could be investigating." I eye him suspiciously. "How did you know I'd be here? Have you been following me?"

He snorts. "No. Should I be?"

I ignore that. "Then how did you find me?"

"I didn't. I'm here for the same reason I assume you are. I was looking for Professor Borges to question her about the book."

I'm annoyed by how much sense that makes. "Well, she isn't here."

"Obviously." We stare each other down for a long moment before he sighs and turns back toward the hall. "Come on, Sinclair. I'll chaperone you back to Berlaise, since you clearly can't be trusted. It's time to get ready for the party."

CHAPTER THIRTEEN

Roze did, in fact, buy me new clothes. When we come back to my room, a dress for tonight's fete is hanging in front of my wardrobe.

I ask him how he knows my measurements, and he just snorts and lets his eyes fall down the length of my body and back up again. I glare at him and try to calm the rush of heat that climbs up my body.

Roze leaves to let me get ready, and I study the dress he chose for me. I have to admit . . . I don't hate it. It looks like death itself—lovely and dark, like falling asleep and never waking up. I slide it on and study myself in the mirror.

Black gauzy fabric is interwoven with gems in moody hues—garnet, amethyst, and lapis—forming an intricate pattern that reminds me of the brocade on Roze's tie from yesterday. The dress wraps tightly around my torso, falling loose at the flare of my hips. I feel like a dark jewel, a glittering nightmare. It suits me.

Roze and I agreed to meet in the entrance hall of Vandenberghe. I arrive at the apex of the grand staircase that sweeps downward toward the entrance doors of the school.

The great chandelier casts gloomy light over the damask wallpaper and velvet carpets, barely illuminating the gilded scrollwork on the railings and walls. I make my way carefully down the treacherous steps in my heels, the chandelier blocking my view of the floor until I round the turn.

And there he is.

If I am a nightmare, Roze is the night itself. He wears a suit black as ravens' wings. The jacket is textured with velvet roses, and his tie, squared against the tattoo on his throat, is detailed in shimmering green thread. His snowy hair is combed back in a way that looks both genteel and criminal. He is blazingly gorgeous, wearing that same austere, bored expression that has my blood instantly burning to wrap my shadows around his throat.

He glances up, and our eyes meet.

I would be lying if I said I don't enjoy the way his lips instantly part. He closes them quickly, his mouth set back in its grim expression, and I descend the stairs with my head held high.

He's keeping his face blank, but his eyes are glued to me. They pass down my body from my head to my toes, like they're tracing every inch of me, cataloging, measuring, memorizing. Those eyes travel back up again, and when they meet mine, my breath stops cold. I swear his eyes could lance a girl straight through the chest, like a moth pinned to the wall for his study.

This would all be romantic if we weren't pretending, if we didn't hate each other, if the order to kill me didn't still mark his forearm.

"You look . . ." He gives me another long perusal. I watch the moth on his throat move as though alive as he swallows and sucks in his cheeks. "Tolerable."

"*Tolerable?*" I say, barely keeping my indignation in check.

"Did you expect me to get on bended knee? Compose an ode to your beauty?"

I glare. "A simple 'you look nice' would have been sufficient."

He snorts but then extends a gloved hand to me. He's exchanged his leather ones for ebony silk this evening, and as I take his hand, I try to ignore the warmth that cuts through the thinner fabric.

His skin is warm.

I brush away the thought. Or try to. But that thin slip of fabric is the closest I've ever been to touching the Prince with my bare hands.

Besides, of course, when I punched him in the nose.

He helps me down the last step and then extends his arm. I place my hand on his forearm like I think a princess would. But as we leave the school's entrance hall and cross the glass bridge over the corpse-filled waters, I don't feel like a princess. I feel like I'm being marched to the gallows.

The Kingdom of Aragoa is small compared to what it once was. But the wealth we've held on to, the accumulation of centuries of dominating the western plains of the Hivernian Peninsula, is obvious as I walk under a ceiling painted with scenes so exquisite that I want to weep. The walls of the ballroom are molded in gold and violet, and the black terrazzo floor is snaked with sparkling filigree. I know Roze will mock me if I gush about the history that is contained in this room. He probably grew up throwing tantrums on this very floor, persecuting some poor governess to within an inch of her life.

I nearly smile at the thought.

The crowd parts before us as we enter, my hand on Roze's outstretched arm. I have to resist every urge to point my gaze at the floor.

Finally, we reach the dais where his mother is perched on her throne, her spine ramrod straight as she looks down her nose at us. Her black mourning dress and cape, lined with dark fur, fan out around her feet. The crown on her head is as sharp as her expression, and I force myself not to swallow as I approach the woman who wants me dead.

On either side of the Queen, the six princesses stand in a line like pawns. Each of them has the same cruel, feline smile painted on their ruby lips.

Roze bows low, and I sink into my best curtsy.

Don't fall. Don't show your fear. Look demure and unthreatening.

This is the test, the most difficult part of the evening. After this, it will just be dancing . . . with Roze . . . while everyone watches.

A hint of a smile spreads on the Queen's lips as I right myself.

Something about the look on her face makes me think that she's mocking me.

"Prince," the Queen greets her son.

"Mother," he says, his voice void of emotion. "May I introduce Miss Viola Sinclair."

I have already met her, of course, but this is for the Court's benefit.

I offer another little curtsy, only because it feels right. "Majesty," I say.

"This fete is in your honor, Miss Sinclair," the Queen says. "I hope it meets your expectations. I know your tastes are . . . aspirational."

The sisters' smiles broaden.

I smile back, as though I didn't understand the insult.

"It's lovely, Your Majesty," I say. "I'm grateful for your warm reception."

She frowns. "Enjoy the ball with your betrothed, Prince Roze. I hope to see you both dancing." She waves us off, and the music starts up again.

I take a deep breath as we step away from the Queen.

"Calm down," Roze murmurs in my ear. "You did fine."

"That's easy for you to say. Your life isn't hanging on the whims of a bloodthirsty royal."

"Isn't it?" he muses, snatching two glasses of champagne from a passing tray and downing his in one gulp. He somehow manages to make even overindulgence look sophisticated.

He lowers the glass and smiles. "Let's not fight, darling. It's a party."

I force myself to look away from that expression on his face, the one that makes him look like a boy, foolish and flirtatious, and not like the snake I know him to be.

I glance at that great moth on his neck out of the corner of my eye, the eyes of its wings level with my own as it twists with his turned neck. What would it be like to run my lips over that moth?

I set down the glass of champagne, deciding I've already had enough.

"You should know the important members of the Court," Roze says over the noise of the party. "There's Fletcher's father. Lord Llopart." He nods toward a gangly, potbellied Black man whose cheeks are already reddened from drink. He laughs with a group of other middle-aged men, his eyes watering. "And there's Ed's grandmother, the Dowager Countess Paschal. She's vicious—watch out for her." The dowager's wrinkled neck cranes over the crowd, a severe frown painted on her face. Roze then points to a man sporting a decorated uniform and an equally impressive mustache. "That's Lord Basa. He was a general in the war. But rumor has it"— Roze leans in close, so that his lips nearly brush the shell of my ear—"he's killed three of his wives, one after the other, for failing to give him an heir."

"That's horrible," I breathe, but what's really horrible is the effect Roze's closeness has on my heart. It feels like the edge of an axe at my neck. But I can't step away. We're supposed to be in love.

"And her—" Roze whispers, pointing to a woman in a black mourning gown, a dolorous expression on her young face. I silently beg him to back away. Apparently, he doesn't get the message, because a gloved hand grazes down my arm, causing my whole body to tingle, as he continues to whisper, "Lady Toussaint. She's rumored to have killed herself after the death of her brother, who, if you believe the gossip, was her secret lover."

I turn to him, shocked. "Her brother was her lover?"

"Nefarious, isn't it?" he says with a wicked smile.

"It's obviously untrue, is what it is. She can't have killed herself. She's here, isn't she?" I ask, my mind very much on that hand on my bare arm.

"That ribbon on her neck," Roze says, pointing to the black silk, tied in the back beneath the woman's elaborate hairstyle. "It's said to hold her head in place where it was severed. She never takes it off."

"That's ridiculous," I mutter.

Roze chuckles. Something molten races to my core at the sound of it in my ear, and I jerk away, using the excuse of grabbing another glass of champagne to hide my reaction, deciding that I actually *haven't* had enough. I take a long gulp, and when I look back at him, his brow is arched and he's frowning.

"Are you all right?" he asks.

"Is that actual concern I hear?"

He smiles like a devil. "Never."

He extends a gloved hand to me. I must look foolish as I glance between it and his face several times before he gives me a long-suffering look. "Dance with me."

"Why?"

He purses his lips and says under his breath, "Because we are *expected to.*"

Oh. Right. I set the glass of champagne down next to his on a nearby table and place my hand lightly in his.

I've only had minimal training in courtly dances—there are few that commoners are invited to these days, but Vandenberghe students are required to take dance lessons in the first year. I've learned enough to not embarrass myself.

I try to remember my steps to distract myself from Roze's closeness as he places a hand on my hip. The string quartet strikes up a new tune, and I look anywhere but at his face.

I can see the crowds in my periphery, and many of them have turned to watch us—the rogue Prince and his mysterious commoner bride. I feel unsteady on my feet. The ballroom is too hot and crowded, and I'm terrified I'm going to trip over my own feet.

"Relax," Roze whispers. "Focus on me. Think about the steps, not them."

So I focus on the waltz and the music.

And after a while, I forget about the eyes of the crowds and the Queen. Roze, unsurprisingly, is an incredible dancer, moving with grace and precision, and I'm able to put aside my worries with him leading me, the weeping of the violin strings wrapping around me, the chandeliers dazzling overhead.

He spins me, and, Saints help me, I smile.

Perhaps I've had more champagne than I realize. Perhaps fear at some point just makes one reckless and silly. I unconsciously move closer to Roze, my chest pressed flush against his. And then even he cracks.

I smile up at him before I know what I'm doing, and something sparks to life in his eyes—something like shock as he looks down at me. I laugh at him, not to mock him, but because I feel for the first time like I'm seeing a real boy behind the mask—there truly is flesh and blood beneath those black gloves that grip my waist and my hand.

The edge of his lip quirks, as though he's tempted—so tempted—to smile, but he doesn't. Instead, as a compromise, he pulls me close against him and holds his head over mine, just shy of resting our foreheads together.

I'm beginning to become familiar with the dizzy feeling that overcomes me whenever he's near. He whispers in my ear, "You're quite the actress, Sinclair. You have them eating out of the palm of your hand."

I glance around at the lords and ladies. He's right—their disapproving looks have turned to wonder and interest. Some are even smiling.

We dance till we are both breathless and exhausted and then take a break so that Roze can greet members of his mother's Court. He guides me around the room, introducing me to various nobles—there's no way I can keep them all straight, not when I'm dizzy with champagne and the exhilaration of dancing.

"Every gentleman in this room reeks of jealousy," he says to me as I sip champagne. "You've done far better than I expected."

I lower my glass and glare at him, a little hurt, if I'm honest. It's just like him to wreck the way things were going by insulting me.

Prince Roze Roquelart—the ruination of perfectly pleasant evenings.

I don't know why I'm surprised.

He lowers his eyelids, his hands folded neatly behind his back. "Don't look sour. Was I supposed to expect a common girl from the caverns to be able to charm courtiers? Half of them have daughters they'd rather me marry."

"Well, by all means, I'd hate to keep you from someone willing to bat her eyelashes and thank you for your unpleasantness." In a shrill voice, I mock, *"Yes, Your Highness, I am a nauseating bimbo. Thank you so much for saying so. I'm just lucky to be in your superior pointy-faced presence."*

"Pointy-faced?" Roze's eyes narrow and his lip twitches. "I see there's someone else who's jealous tonight."

I snort, a sound I realize too late is unladylike for the present company. "Don't flatter yourself."

I take another swig of my champagne, swirling the bubbles over my tongue. A gloved hand snatches the flute from me. "Keep your wits about you, darling," Roze says, looking over my head. "Can I trust you to not get yourself into trouble while I have a word with my mother?"

I whirl toward him. "What? You're leaving me?"

He looks down at me, spider-silk skin creasing at the corners of his eyes. "Don't worry, Sinclair. You have them more than handled." He glances around the room. "Dance with Lord Basa. He's been eyeing you all evening."

I ignore the fact that he's keeping track of who's watching me.

"You told me he kills his wives."

Roze shrugs. "So don't marry him." With a fiendish grin, he turns toward the throne. I watch the crowd part before him as he strides toward his mother. What would it be like to walk through the world expecting obstacles to jump out of your way? I watch him bow deeply to the Queen, and after a few moments of conversation, she disappears with him to a room somewhere behind the throne.

In the Queen's absence, the mood of the party picks up. The musicians start up a new song, and the revels turn boisterous and loud.

I'm out of my depth here. Just like Roze said—I'm a girl from the caverns in a room full of nobles, a rabbit among wolves. But I'm also in a room *full* of people far more familiar with the King than I am, people who might've had reason to see him dead.

I snatch another glass of champagne off a passing tray and rove about the room, nodding and smiling blandly at various courtiers, hoping to pick up on any useful conversation. Most of them, disappointingly, discuss nothing of importance. They critique the party, complain about the size of their quarters, discuss the eligibility of certain young nobles . . . I become more and more frustrated as time passes—at their utter selfishness, their vanity, and my inability to learn anything useful from them. I almost give up. Leaning against a column, just behind a collection of older gentlemen, I overhear them in deep discussion, their arms folded in a gentlemanly way behind their backs, above stiff tailcoats. One of them is Fletcher's father, Lord Llopart, who, if it's possible, appears even more drunk than before. I try to look as though I'm taking a break after a long night of dancing, resting my legs and fanning myself.

"—concern to us all, economically, socially," one of them says.

"But the idea is absurd, isn't it? We're not talking about trained spies, are we? These are not intelligent folk living in the caverns. They can't even feed themselves, and yet you're suggesting one of them killed His Majesty without leaving a mark?"

My breath hitches. This is what I was hoping to hear.

"Don't underestimate the sewer rats, Bartolome. They outnumber us three to one."

"Not if the Queen keeps restricting their rations, they won't."

The whole group chuckles, and my blood boils. Are they suggesting . . . that the rationing of food, of medicine, isn't a mere preference for keeping the nobility alive and healthy but an actual attempt to thin out the population in the caverns?

The bastards.

"Quite a different world from Vandenberghe, isn't it?" slithers a voice in my ear, and I nearly drop my glass.

CHAPTER FOURTEEN

Belladonna Roquelart glowers down at me. Her cold expression is strikingly similar to Roze's, and yet its effect on me is completely different. I take an inadvertent step back before I remember to curtsy.

She smiles, catching the gaffe.

"Your Highness," I choke out, trying to recover. "You surprised me. I thought you'd be dancing."

She scoffs and looks out over the crowd. "There's hardly a partner here to interest *me*."

Saints, her arrogant aloofness is an absolute twin to Roze's.

"No?" I ask. *What does interest her?* I wonder. *Power? Privilege? Making babies cry?* "Because they bore you?"

"Because they're all men. I prefer the company of a fair lady over any of these dolts," she says, gesturing to the group of gentlemen I'd been eavesdropping on. I raise my eyebrows. She looks back at me and tuts while she fans herself. "Oh, don't get excited, Sinclair. I'd hate for you to think I was confiding in you. It's common knowledge. Not that it matters— there's that pesky duty to produce heirs and all. I'll be wed to one of these mustaches whether I like it or not."

She sighs dramatically, and it reminds me so much of Roze. "But enough about me, I want to learn more about you." Her pleasant smile is deeply unsettling. She's acting as though last night didn't even happen, like she didn't pour wine on my dress and go head-to-head with her brother. Roze might be a snake, but his sister is a wolf in princess's clothing.

"I wondered if you could satisfy my curiosity," she says, folding her fan and elegantly crossing her hands over her waist while mine tap my drink nervously. "How is it that you've managed to capture the attention of my brother so quickly? You see, he hasn't told us the story. And Roze has never shown serious interest in any young lady before now."

"We met our first year at Vandenberghe," I say. My voice sounds a little too breathy.

"And you've known each other all that time, but he hasn't admitted attraction until now? How strange."

"We . . . wanted to keep it a secret for a while."

"Ah, so it's been going on for longer than you let on. I thought so."

I raise my eyes to look at her face. "What do you mean?"

Her false smile widens. "The Prince seems unable to keep his hands off you. You must understand what a rarity that is. He hates touching people, you see."

He hates touching people. Is that why he wears the gloves?

She narrows her predator's gaze. "I've had an eye on *you* for a while, but I'll admit that even I was surprised when he dragged you to dinner yesterday."

I wet my lips. "You've . . . had an eye on me?"

"Don't look so terrified. Of course I did. Roze thinks that we don't pay attention to what he does, that if he performs his duties adequately, we'll leave him be. That might be true for my sisters, but he's my closest sibling in age. I understand him too well." She finally turns her head my direction and takes a single step toward me—just a step, but it feels like she has her hand wrapped around my throat. "I know Roze has his secrets. When he started complaining about the busybody girl in Berlaise House at every family dinner, droning on about how irritating he found you till I thought I'd rather slit my own throat than listen to him whine, I suspected you were one of those secrets."

Roze has been talking about me? For how long? I want to contradict her—tell her that it means nothing, that Roze and I loathed each other.

But before I can open my mouth—

"Your Highness," a spirited voice says over my shoulder.

I turn to see Ed stepping up to join our conversation. His grin is broad and cocky, his chestnut hair combed back neatly. He looks remarkably handsome in his coattails, like a prince from a fairy tale.

Ed bows deeply toward Belladonna. "You look lovely this evening, Princess."

Her expression immediately sours. "Paschal," she says. "I didn't realize Roze invited his band of merry men."

He nods good-naturedly. "I'm afraid you have my family name to thank for the invitation, not His Highness."

"Oh yes, I'd forgotten your grandmother is a countess," Belladonna says dryly. "I suppose we're extending invitations to every earl's second cousin twice removed these days. It's a wonder half the Kingdom isn't here."

Ed doesn't react to her barbs; instead he broadens that charming smile and sighs. "Unfortunately, I'm still two funerals away from an earldom. But one day I'll relish governing Salverre under your benevolent rule, Highness."

"Perhaps the Mists will finally recede, and I can send you there, far away from here," Belladonna drawls.

"Oh, but then how would I sully your parties with my congenial company?" Ed says with a wink.

"Your family governs Salverre?" I ask Ed. He hadn't mentioned his family's ancestral lands before. It's not a large territory—a little province west of the Pirineus Ridge—but before the Mists fell, it was a crucial fishing and trade port.

"Oh, you'd love it, Sinclair," Ed says brightly. "Father says the waters sparkle like sapphires." He elbows me in the side. "If it weren't for these dreadful Mists, I'd say you and Rozy boy should honeymoon there."

I gulp and take another sip of champagne.

Belladonna gives Ed a flat, disapproving look. "Yes. Well, as fascinating as this conversation is, I must return to my sisters. It was very . . . educational speaking with you, Viola."

I curtsy, and as she glides away, I let out a long breath. "Hello," I say, turning to Ed with a smile.

"Hello, lovely," he says with a cheeky grin. "I saw you under siege and thought I'd come to your rescue. Rather chivalrous of me, don't you think?"

I roll my eyes but smile.

He grins back. "I've been sent to chaperone you while our boy takes care of some business."

My face falls. "What business? Is he still meeting with the Queen?"

"Don't worry your pretty head over it. Dance with me." He takes my hand and starts to pull me toward the dance floor.

I huff as I'm pulled into his embrace. Ed is sweet—charming as a trained poodle—but I don't like men thinking they can distract me with compliments. "What is Roze doing, Ed?"

"Princely things, I imagine," he says as the music starts up. This dance is a faster-paced, lively one, and as Ed spins me around the room, my head starts to spin with it. I shouldn't have had that last glass of champagne.

"I mean it, Edward. You can't keep me in the dark about what he's doing. Is it about the—" I give him a look, indicating I'm talking about the Grimmstones.

"Edward? You sound like my mother."

I sigh, and we go back to dancing in silence. I let myself get swept along with the music, watching the colorful gowns of the women twirl about the dance floor and—

Saints, no. No, I'm imagining things.

There is a face in the crowd, one I recognize. But it *definitely* shouldn't be here.

It should be buried beneath the cathedral floor.

My heart thunders against my ribs as I watch the unmistakable face of the Captain of the Guard peer out over the crowd. His head turns slowly, scanning every face . . . until his eyes lock on mine.

I choke.

Dead. Dead. He's supposed to be dead. We buried him beneath the altar.

But he's standing there, in the middle of the room, as clear as crystal.

"Viola?" Ed asks, his hand on my arm.

I barely hear him.

Run. What are you doing standing here?

But I'm glued to the spot.

"Viola, what's wrong? You look like you've seen a ghost."

A lethal sneer spreads on the guard's face.

My skin turns to ice. My shadows beg to be set free, to spread around me, shield me from him.

Calm.

Control.

Oh Saints below.

My boot was lodged in his neck. I watched Roze slit his throat. But that throat is now covered with the collar of his uniform. Standing. Alive. It must be a trick—one of the Queen's illusions.

As though sensing my intention, the guard moves, pacing toward me, weaving through the crowd. Several people step back to let him pass. Definitely *not* an illusion.

Roze. I have to find Roze.

"Sorry, Ed," I say, rushing away from him. "Bathroom."

"*Wait!*"

I push away through the crowd, searching frantically for the exit, keeping my head down. A face of yellowing teeth and unkempt eyebrows steps into my path.

I jump back.

"Miss Sinclair, is it? Delighted," says the elderly gentleman, smiling at me crookedly. Out of the corner of my eye, I catch the face of the guard moving closer. The way he touches the other guests looks so real. Some even nod in his direction.

149

Not a ghost. Not a trick.

"I am Margrave Fraisse. I hope you—"

"Nice to meet you," I interrupt the old man, and hurry off. I can hear a huff of offense behind me, but I don't care. I all but sprint through the open archway.

Something tugs my waist. A hand fists in my skirt as I'm yanked to the side.

I scream.

CHAPTER FIFTEEN

"*Quiet, Sinclair*," Roze's lips whisper in my ear.

He pulls me into the shadows of an alcove, and though my heart rate is still thundering, I'm flooded with relief. Here I'm safe. In the darkness. With the Huntsman, ironically. Being close with Roze is like being friends with a snake. At least he's willing to bite other people on my behalf.

I clutch his forearm, breathing erratically.

"Sinclair? What's the matter?" Roze asks, turning me and examining my face.

"The guard," I choke out. "He's—Roze, he's here."

He frowns. "What guard?"

"The one we *killed*. *That* guard."

"That's impossible."

I grab his sleeve desperately. "We don't have time for you to question me about this. I'm telling you—he *saw* me. He's *coming*."

He puts his hands on my shoulders. "Okay, okay. Do exactly as I say. Follow me, and *don't* ask questions."

"But—"

He gives me a look. "*No questions*, Sinclair. For once in your life."

I don't even want to argue with him, terrified as I am. I will do whatever he says to get away from the undead man in the ballroom.

He takes my hand and drags me away. At nearly a run, we sweep down the corridor, eerily quiet and dark after the noise and ruckus of the dance.

Our footsteps are muffled by the thick carpet beneath our feet, and Roze's head turns this way and that, inspecting the paintings on the walls.

"Are you looking for something in particular?"

"Less than a minute before you disobey me, I see."

I snap my jaw shut, but then I hear a door open behind me. My breath hitches. "Roze—"

He looks over his shoulder, and then he grips my hand more tightly. "*Run.*"

We race down the hall, and pure panic rages in my veins. Roze is sprinting, but I struggle to keep up in my ridiculous shoes.

"Come on!" he urges me.

I kick the shoes off my feet, and now I'm barefoot, racing through the castle with him.

Heavy footsteps thunder behind us. I can't bring myself to turn around. I don't dare look back.

I have no idea if there is any logic to the path Roze is taking or if he is just as terrified as I am, choosing our direction at random. I've never run so fast in my life—my lungs are screaming but the fear in my head is louder as the guard's feet thunder behind me.

This is worse than killing him.

A great growl echoes behind me, rattling the crystal in the chandeliers overhead. A whimper of fear escapes my throat, and Roze pulls me faster down the hall.

I can hear him gaining on us, and I can't help it. I risk a glance over my shoulder.

The captain tears through the corridor behind us, his sword drawn, his eyes red and furious. The collar around his neck has loosened, revealing the gaping wound we left him, a crater filled with dried blood and the white glimpse of bone.

I beg my feet to run faster. Roze's breathing comes in heavy bursts as he pulls me.

But the guard is getting closer. He's nearly on our heels, and my heart fails. He grabs the hem of my skirt, and true terror lashes through me.

I cry out, stumble, and fall to the ground. The weight of the large man crawls up my legs, his bloody hands tearing at the back of my gown. I rip at the carpet with my nails, trying to scramble away. Ahead of me, Roze skids to a stop and turns back.

He draws a knife hidden up his sleeve and charges the guard—but then I feel the edge of a blade at my throat.

Roze freezes, his eyes glued to the guard's sword, which now rests against my larynx.

"*No—farther—*" The captain's voice is garbled, as though through a throat that's not quite reassembled.

Roze's gaze flits from me to the captain, his brows knit together.

The captain chuckles darkly in my ear. "*Re—venge,*" he growls, and I feel the keen sting of the blade beginning to slice through my skin as I take a breath, sure it will be my last as I watch horror dawn on Roze's face—

A feral screech echoes behind me.

Something strong and solid with the velocity of a falling star collides with the captain, and his body rolls off me. I stumble to my feet toward Roze and whirl around. And there, wings flapping, jaws growling menacingly, is Saint Waffles, ripping into the face of the guard with his claws. The little gargoyle roars and scrapes his talons, latching on to his shoulders with his hind legs, goring his face with his tusks. The guard screams, trying to wrestle Waffles away.

Roze seizes me by the elbow and pulls me to safety.

"*Go,*" he hisses, and we sprint down the hall again.

We round a corner, and he shouts, "I thought you locked Waffles in your room."

"I *left* him in my room, but he likes to come out to hunt at night."

"Good thing. He's a protective little bastard."

My heart squeezes. *You can eat my slippers all you want, Waffles*, I think.

Behind us, I hear Saint Waffles cry out as the captain roars. There's a sick *thump* and a small, gargoyle-ish whimper. *Waffles.*

I want to turn back, but there's no time. Roze pulls us through a door.

We're in some sort of sitting room in the nobles' quarters, but there are no other doors—a dead end.

Roze curses under his breath. There's nowhere to run. Nowhere to hide. Except . . .

I've never done it with someone else before, but with death chasing us, there's nothing left to lose. I grab Roze's arm.

"This way," I urge. Before Roze can protest, I pull him to a corner and push him against the wall, my hands on his chest.

"What—"

"Hush," I say, and I press my body into his, wrapping my arms around his waist.

And I let my shadows loose.

They burst from my skin like water through a dam, and I nearly cry with relief as they spill from me at last, blanketing me, encapsulating both of us in a cocoon of darkness.

There's no sound. There are only the shadows, slithering over our skin as Roze's chest heaves against mine. I'm grateful I can't see his face as I press my head to his chest and try to slow my breathing.

His body is stiff. His hands hover over my shoulders like he's afraid to touch me, and his heartbeat thunders in my ear, the only sound I can hear apart from his breathing and mine. I cling to that sign of life like an anchor.

After a few heartbeats like this, Roze slowly lowers his hands onto my shoulders. At first, I think he's going to push me away, but then his arms wrap around my shoulders, and he pulls me tighter to him. I ignore the wash of heat that goes through me even now. I can feel the hard planes of his chest and the strength in his arms as they hold me close.

Through my shadows, I see the guard crash into the room. He comes to a sudden halt, peering around the parlor. His eyes look so . . . dead. And yet, he's searching. He weaves through the space, looking behind furniture. I will my shadows to thicken. Hopefully, he won't look too carefully in our particularly dark corner, where Roze and I stand wrapped up in each other.

The captain's head takes a slow turn, his red-rimmed eyes scanning for movement. What reasoning capabilities do the undead have? What even *is* he?

There's no time to think about that. I need all my focus for my shadows, on releasing the pent-up fear, the anxiety, the rage that will keep us safe.

Obscure us.

Hide us.

Keep us secret.

I press myself into Roze until my body is flush with his, shoulder to thigh. I'm aware of every point of contact between us, like he's stamped on my skin.

"Sinclair," he breathes.

"*Shh*," I urge, keeping my eyes on the captain.

"*Sinclair*," he insists, desperate and angry. At what, I can't imagine. My hand slithers up his side and covers his mouth as I watch the captain look pointedly in our corner.

Roze struggles, trying to pull my hand away from his mouth.

He doesn't like to be touched.

A sting like acid bites my palm. I hiss as I pull my hand back, and the sound of it is enough for the captain to swing his head in our direction. I hold my breath, and I feel Roze hold his. My body trembles. I beg my shadows to stay solid.

He paces closer, moving slow as a predator, his eyes narrowed with malice. Blood pulses in the open wound of his throat, oozing down his neck. He's within an arm's reach, nostrils flaring, gazing into my shadows. Searching.

I'm still as death.

He lifts a large, meaty hand, reaching out in the darkness. It stretches toward us, closer, closer. His fingers are going to reach my shoulder. I brace myself.

Roze's arm wraps around my waist, jerking me silently farther into the corner, and the guard's hand closes around nothing.

He growls, a frustrated gleam in his eye. But then he turns away, huffing as he walks back through the door and away from us.

For a full minute I don't dare move away. I stay in the shadows with Roze, wrapped in their safety.

"Sinclair," he whispers. His breathing has turned more even, but there's still a tense clip in his voice. "Move."

I step away, pulling my shadows back with me. I'm shivering, still terrified. "What was *that*?" I ask.

Roze is pointedly not looking at me. "My mother's doing, surely. But I've never seen her resurrect the dead before."

"Not the guard," I say, studying his face. He keeps it stern, but there's something new and subtle in his expression—a secret. "When I put my hand on your mouth, you lurched. And then . . ."

It was like being stung. I glance down at those gloved hands.

"Why don't you like people touching you?"

Wariness lines the edge of his mouth. Now he's a moth caught in *my* web.

"Roze," I say carefully, stepping toward him. "Tell me what you're hiding."

His lips pinch together. "If I promise to tell you," he says, his voice gravelly, "will you wait until we get somewhere safe?"

I nod.

"Good," he says, regaining some of his composure. "We need to get back to Vandenberghe."

A high-pitched scream breaks through the dark.

"What was that?" I ask.

I whirl toward the hall, where the scream came from.

"Sinclair, wait—" Roze says, but I'm already sprinting from the room.

I know the captain is still out there, searching for us. Did he find another victim? I cannot help but think that someone is hurt or about to be, and it's my fault.

I hear Roze charge after me, but I don't slow down. More shouting echoes from the grand entrance hall. I round the corner, near a balcony. On the floor below, a smattering of people stand speaking in hushed, anxious tones.

"*Sinclair.*" Roze grabs my arm, and I jolt. His face is almost panicked. "We need to get out of here."

But I turn back to the crowd of people, instinct telling me that I *have* to know what's going on. I can't turn away from this. I jerk my arm free from Roze and go down a few steps. He calls my name again—a sibilant hiss from the shadows, where he stays.

There's an aching, prickling feeling in my head.

I just need to know . . .

A few paces down the stairs, I see a crowd of people before the parlor doors, all straining to get inside or peer through the doorframe. A moment later, Princess Belladonna shoves her way through the crowd. Her face is red and tearstained, her tiara is askew in uncommonly mussed hair, and her eyes are furious. Behind her, two grim-faced doctors emerge from the room followed by Sir Patrick Porcher, his ruddy face solemn as he meets the crowd.

"The Queen is dead," he announces, his voice booming off the walls. "Long live the Queen." Belladonna stops halfway across the room, and my chest pounds as I watch her pinch her lips and clench her fists at her sides, turning slowly to face the nobles.

I back up a step, feel the blood draining from my face. Because the last person who saw the Queen was . . .

A gloved hand claps over my mouth.

CHAPTER SIXTEEN

The coolness of Roze's gloves bites into my skin. He grabs my wrist with his other hand and twists it behind my back just to the point of pain. Then he comes close to whisper in my ear, and his icy breath caresses my cheek.

"*Do not* scream," he whispers in a voice that is entirely different from the one he used in the ballroom. Gone is Prince Charming. This isn't even the sarcastic prick I know from school. This is the Prince of Nightmares.

"*Do not* struggle," he continues. "And don't even think of alerting anyone to what you have just heard or the conclusion which you have surely just hastily drawn." He exhales a rattling breath that tickles my skin. With a voice like the edge of a knife, he says, "I will explain everything once we're back in Vandenberghe. Until then, you will be *silent*. You will be *still*. You will be *obedient*. Is that understood?"

Even though every instinct is screaming at me to run, to fight, to punch him again, I nod.

He carefully removes his hand from my mouth. I glare at him through the darkness. "Anything else, Your Highness?"

He grabs my jaw roughly, lifting my face close to his so that his breath is on my lips. "I told you to be *silent*. If you can't obey that order, I'll have to do something about that unruly tongue of yours, Sinclair."

His nose nearly brushes mine as he whispers the words into my mouth, the threat of them on his breath. The air between us is pure loathing, and my head feels heavy with it. Black dots speckle the edges of my vision.

I hate myself for ever dancing with him, ever smiling at him, ever looking at him with anything other than pure disdain.

Murderer.

Queen Killer.

When I don't reply, he smirks and says, "Good girl," and drops my face roughly. He grabs my arm and drags me behind him down the corridor.

There are a thousand things I want to scream at him all the way back to Berlaise House. The Queen is—was—awful. But we'd made a deal with her. We had a plan. Now he's made me complicit in yet another murder.

As we turn down the hall that leads to my room, I spot Saint Waffles sitting like a dutiful sentry outside my door. Relief floods me as he turns his head in my direction and bounds into my arms.

I make a sound between a laugh and a cry as his scaly skin rubs against mine and his cold nose sniffs my face for signs of injury.

"Good boy," I whisper. "Did the mean corpse hurt you?"

He whimpers, his lip tucked sadly under his fangs.

"Key, Sinclair," Roze demands, holding out a gloved hand.

I glare at him as I retrieve it from the hidden pockets of my skirt and shove it into his hand.

He's acting like he's completely unaware of how furious I am at him, the anger rolling off me as he unlocks the door to my room. I follow, and Saint Waffles gives him his attention for the first time. He drops from my arms as soon as we're in the room and turns on Roze, a low growl rattling from his little gargoyle throat.

Roze lowers his eyelids at Waffles. "Have you also decided I'm the enemy?"

I close the door and face Roze. "You've made yourself the enemy."

He sighs and pinches the bridge of his nose with those gloved fingers.

"For someone with such an impressive academic reputation, you do tend to jump to irrational conclusions."

"Don't do that," I snap. "Don't talk down to me. You *killed*—" I struggle to produce the words. "You killed—"

He cocked his head. "Killed whom?" he asks, coming closer. "Whom did I kill, little witch?"

The pure lethality in his eyes is evidence enough for me.

"You killed the Queen," I whisper, forcing myself not to break eye contact. I'm a witness to two of his murders, two of his acts of treason. He'll be executed, and so will I. If he doesn't get me killed first.

Roze steps away, shrugging off his coat and laying it on the chair next to my desk. "I told you what I was." He shrugs—actually *shrugs* at the idea. "She was going to kill you. Now you're safe."

"Is this a game for you?" I ask, folding my arms over my chest. "No, really. Is this fun? Do you get off on killing people or something?"

He turns toward me, the look in his eyes sharp as knives. "Do you imagine that I wanted to kill my mother?" He paces closer, backing me up until my thighs hit the edge of my bed. "There was no choice, Sinclair. It has been three days. We have found nothing. Another thorn is gone, and we're that much closer to death."

"Yours or mine?" I shoot back.

His gloved hand whips out and grabs my jaw. It's a violent move, but his grip is restrained. He brings his face close, silver eyes consuming me. "I killed my mother. I killed her. For *you*."

"I didn't ask you to," I breathe.

"You didn't have to," he says, and his expression is almost mournful. He releases my jaw, but he doesn't back away.

"I don't understand. Why make a bargain with her only to . . ." I can't finish my sentence.

"I want to know what happened to my father. So did my mother. I'm sure some part of her wanted to know if we might learn something she hadn't. But . . . one thing you should know about her—she always gets what she wants. And she wanted you dead. We've made no progress, and

I thought I might . . . plead for more time. But I suspected what it might lead to . . . what I might have to do. I was right. She refused."

He sweeps a hand through his hair, looking away for the first time. "My mother, as you know, cannot kill *meigas*. She needs me to work around her curse. But last night at dinner, when she played with your mind, I knew her power was growing. She wanted to frighten you." He looks back at me. "She gains power through fear. The more she is feared, the more powerful she becomes. Her plan was to gain enough strength that she could control me like a puppet . . . Then she'd have you disposed of—by my hand and against my will."

I suck in a breath. "So you killed her."

He nods. "So I killed her. Before she could force me to . . ."

"To kill me."

He swallows. "Yes."

I look down at my feet. "So . . . she's dead. And . . . we're free. From all of it."

He nods. "I believe so."

A breath breaks loose from my lungs, one I've been holding for three days, and I let myself fall back to sit on the bed.

We're silent for a long minute. I stare at my feet.

"How did you do it?"

"Do what?"

I swallow. "Kill her," I whisper. "You don't have a speck of blood on you."

He's a remarkably efficient assassin. I was too caught up in my own terror to reflect on it at the time, but the way he killed the guard in the sanctuary . . . He was quicker than quick, clean and calibrated. He moved like a shadow.

Roze studies me for a long moment, and I can see the thoughts stirring behind his eyes. A decision is being made. He turns and sits himself at my desk and flexes his hand, studying it as he speaks. "Did you wonder why my mother chose me to be her assassin? There's a reason she has *me* kill for her, when she could easily order one of her groveling guards to do it." As he speaks, he removes the glove, pulling at each finger one at a time. He does it slowly, deliberately, so I can watch every move. "I was not *born* the way my sisters were. At the end of the war, Castelle launched a surprise assault on my mother's home province, Septania. They burned it to the ground. Every home. Slaughtered every man, woman, and child. Burned my mother's family's estate, the monastery where she learned her magic.

"As you know, one of her abilities is a kind of . . . creation. When she saw what Castelle had done to her home, she poured out her grief and hatred for the Kingdom of Death on the land . . . and it made me."

I'm no longer breathing as I watch him pull his glove completely from his hand. Waffles is on his feet again, a low growl in his throat.

I watch Roze's face carefully. His lips form a thin line.

"I'm not . . . *real*, Sinclair. Not the way you are. I am an incarnation of her hatred." He looks up at me, a slow, sad smile spreading on his lips. "See? It's no wonder you loathe me. You really can't help it."

He lets his glove fall to the surface of the desk. "I know enough of magic to know that you're not supposed to make things like me. It goes against nature."

I stare at his bare hands. I haven't seen them before now—fingers that are long, pale, and elegant, like those of an artist, veins snaking down to his wrists and under his sleeve.

I look up to his face. Irises of shattered crystal have turned a dusty gray. I'm holding on to the post of my bed—I feel like if I let go, I'll shatter too.

"Do you want to know why I wear these gloves? Why I don't touch people?" he says, his voice low and dangerous.

I watch his jaw work, and I know he's deciding whether to tell me, whether it's worth it to bare this part of himself. And I'm honestly not sure if I want him to. This feels dangerous, like reaching into a serpent's nest, even if some masochistic part of me wants to.

"I'm cursed, Viola," he whispers.

I don't think I've ever heard him say my first name before. The way it

162

sounds in his voice when he's like this—raw and ruined—stirs something in me that makes me want to join him in the dark place he's in. To revel in it, hide away until the world is kinder.

"Cursed?" I repeat.

He nods. "Too real to be an illusion. Too illusory to be truly alive. So instead, I live a . . . half-life, not truly here, not truly not. Just pure hatred, made flesh."

My feet—and possibly my heart—carry me toward him before my mind catches up with what I'm doing. I stand before him, positioned between his knees where he sits at my desk. He looks up at me, his brows knit together.

"You're real," I whisper, like it's a secret. "You're as real as I am. Flesh and blood and bone. You're not your mother's hatred. You're your own."

I know it. Deeply and truly. Despite the evidence, he is not what he says he is.

Unexpectedly, he stands, so close that there's barely any space between us. He reaches a hand toward my cheek, and I think I might faint as he ghosts his bare fingers over my skin.

He leans close, and in his eyes, under his dark lashes, I see a boy who is lost.

"You don't understand," he says. His voice is perilous, and I have just an inkling that I may have made a grave mistake. "You see, this is how I kill them. My *touch* is poison. I carry daggers to make it quick, to make it merciful, but they aren't necessary. With my touch, I can kill any person, *meiga* or not, without leaving a single mark on their body. I could render you unconscious with a flick of my wrist."

He makes that exact motion, barely avoiding my cheek.

"If I were to do more . . . say, if I were to kiss you . . ."

I suck in a breath. His eyes are pinned to mine. I'm so afraid, I think I might sink to my knees. But there's another emotion there too—something warm and sticky and wicked that I won't name.

"You would die," he whispers.

A tremor passes through my entire body. A depraved thought occurs to me—that a death like that might be quite lovely, that a kiss like that might be worth the price.

I take a deep breath to regain my composure.

"But I touched you," I say. "I put my hand over your mouth. And a few days ago, when I punched you—"

He nods, still staring. "You're stronger than most, and *meigas* are harder to kill than others. That's how I really knew what you were. I guessed about the shadows, but when you touched me . . . When you hit me in the face that day in the Commons, I knew with absolute certainty."

I think back . . . to the bite in my palm as I silenced him with a hand, to the sting in my fist after my knuckles connected with his nose, to the heady, weightless feeling I get when he comes close.

My breathing shudders as I take his breath into my lungs.

Oh.

He leans in closer now, the tips of his shoes touching the tips of mine. "I wonder—"

His nose nearly brushes mine, and I dare myself to meet his gaze, to look back into his eyes, so dark they're almost charcoal. I can see every individual eyelash, every thought, every hesitation, and every reckless decision.

His lips brush mine, just barely. Immediately, my shadows break free from my fingertips, and darkness fills my blood. My vision goes fuzzy. I am swimming somewhere between reality and dreams, in the valley of the shadow of death.

Against my mouth he whispers, "How much of me could you handle before I took your life, Sinclair?"

CHAPTER SEVENTEEN

My knees buckle. I slump forward, and Roze catches me against him as I teeter on the edge of unconsciousness. Saint Waffles barks, and I jolt back to reality, stumbling away from the Prince and falling back on my bed. I'm breathing heavily, staring up at his imposing figure.

He almost knocked me unconscious, using that curse on his skin against me. *The bastard.*

"*Don't do that,*" I spit at him.

He blinks as though coming out of a dream himself. "I—" He bows his head.

I need to clear my mind. I need to *think.* And I know I can't do that in this room with Roze. He's a villain, and *I* am a fool.

I keep making this mistake, stumbling back into him like a moth drawn to candlelight before I remember that I can't trust him, that he's cruel and deadly. I come too close to him, mistaking this truce we have for safety. And then I get burned.

He killed the Queen.

He killed the Queen for you, my treacherous heart whispers.

But still. Things have gotten too complicated, the lines too blurred. I need to sort things out, and I can still feel the blood pounding in my ears after that . . . almost-kiss.

It's all completely overwhelming.

"If the Queen is dead," I say, sitting up and scooting far away from Roze. "Then . . . our temporary alliance is done, right? No more danger.

No need to keep up the ruse." I pull the Roquelart ring off my finger and look at it a moment before extending it to Roze, something tugging in my gut as I do.

My chin is tilted up, my expression cold. Roze eyes the ring. Then his gaze rises to mine, piercing and captivating.

He lifts a hand, and for a moment, I think he's going to take the ring back.

Instead, he unbuttons the cuff links on his left wrist. The silver roses fall to the floor with a dull clunk, and he rolls his sleeve up his forearm. He really has fantastic forearms—lean and long with prominent veins. It's a shame he keeps them shrouded beneath black clothing at all times.

He turns his forearm up, and I can feel both our hearts stop. There is the rose tattoo—its thorns sharp and sinister as ever.

"I—I don't understand," I whisper. "The Queen is dead. It should have disappeared, right? The countdown should have stopped."

Roze is staring down at his arm. He shakes his head, blinks, and wets his lips. "I—I thought it would."

My next breath is painfully long. "The guard," I say, "the one we killed. He . . . showed up at the fete after you killed her."

Roze nods.

"But that was her . . . that was her power."

"It was." He licks his lips. "Perhaps—I've underestimated my mother's power."

I lean back on the headboard to steady myself. For what feels like an eternity, I stare mindlessly at the wall while Roze gazes at the floor.

"What now?" I whisper finally.

He swallows. "What she really wants is my father's killer. If we can find that, maybe it will be enough."

I don't believe him, and I don't think he does either. The Queen killed all the *meigas* in Aragoa after the war while Alexandre was still by her side. She'll want me dead whether I deliver her husband's killer or not, especially now. But we have to find a reason to keep going, to keep fighting. We have to find a reason to not give up yet.

"We'll think of something," he whispers into the dark.

I don't respond.

He crosses the room to me, his black shoes all I can see until my chin is in his gloved hand and he's directing my gaze to his. Silver eyes bore into mine. "Sinclair, we'll think of something. I promise."

I choke on my fear. Because I'm sure he has already thought of something—his one sure way out of this. In the end, no matter what fragile truce we've come to, no matter what has passed between us in these short few days, he will sacrifice me to save himself. I'm not certain of much at the moment, but that I'm sure of.

I nod. "All right."

———

Ed looks like he's had quite a night. His hair and clothing have seen better days, and he smells like champagne and sex.

"What did you get yourself into?" I ask slyly as he stands in my doorway. Or slumps, I should say. He's still quite drunk.

"You mean who," he says with a smirk.

"Gross."

"I'll have you know I've ruined my reputation as a gentleman and left a lovely lady in bed alone tonight to see you initiated into the Grimmstones. You're welcome."

"I'm certain your reputation as a gentleman was already ruined."

He holds a hand to his chest as though shot, but then stumbles and falls flat on his ass on my floor, chuckling to himself.

"Am I going to have to carry you there?" I ask.

"Calm down. I'm fine."

Roze left a short while ago, and I let him believe I was going to bed. And then, as planned, Ed showed up to bring me to the Grimmstones' meeting in disguise. If everything goes according to plan, I'll be through the initiation before Roze realizes what's happened and can stop it, and once I'm in, I'm in—forever. I still don't know what this initiation will entail, and Ed is being ominously tight-lipped about it.

After he sorts himself out, he hands me a cloak and mask and tells me to follow him and to be quiet. He leads me to the library, to a dark alcove in a seldom-visited section, one story beneath the main floor. Here it is even darker than the rest of the school, windowless, and cold. I think we must be below the surface of the lake—there's a humid, earthy aroma to the air. A few simple gas lamps hang from hooks at the ends of shelves like watchmen, and at the end of the aisle, there's a small sculpture resting on a pedestal.

It looks like a girl, and in her hands, she holds scales, her pupilless eyes staring out at us like a divine judge.

"This is the entrance to what we call the Crypt," he says, and turns to me. "Last chance, Princess. Once you know our secrets, there's no going back. You're one of us."

"Lead the way," I say without hesitation. There isn't much left to lose anymore. Even the small chance of finding out more is worth any risk.

Ed turns toward the shelf behind the statue of the girl and runs his fingers along the books there. There's a volume on the far-right side that seems slightly less dusty than the others. He removes it and glances at me over his shoulder before he reaches into the bookshelf and points to something in the darkness.

I step toward him and peer into the darkness on the shelf. There, at the tip of his finger, is a small carved moth with a skull in its wings—the symbol of the Grimmstones.

"Brace yourself," Ed says, and presses his finger against the moth.

The wood gives way beneath his finger. The floor beneath us lurches. I sway, and both of us grab hold of the shelf for support. The bookcase and the floor slide forward. An opening appears behind the shelf, revealing a stone passage with a ceiling low enough that we'll both have to duck down to enter. There are no candles or lamps lighting the passage—it's a black void.

"That's the way?" I ask.

I can hear the smile in his voice as he says, "Oh, Sinclair, there's so much you don't know about this castle."

The bookcase shifts shut behind us and we are enveloped in darkness. I inhale a rattling breath. The air is cold here, and I wish I'd worn something under the cloak other than my sleeveless dress from the fete.

The passage goes on forever, taking odd turns and twists. I try to keep track of our path at first, but quickly give up. The darkness is all-consuming—I can't see my own nose in front of my face, so instead I follow the sound of Ed's footsteps just ahead of me.

We round a corner, and a gray, smoky light appears. We step through an arched doorway into a rotunda with an entire ceiling made of glass, the Mists undulating overhead. The floor has an intricate pattern etched into it—a labyrinth leading toward the center, where a group of cloaked figures stand. Waiting.

All their faces turn toward us as we enter, and my heart thunders against my chest as I wonder if I've made a horrible mistake in being here.

Ed stops before the labyrinth. "New initiate tonight, gents."

"We didn't discuss any new initiates." That's Roze's voice—the cloaked figure in the center. "We vet all new members together, Ed."

"You've been a bit busy, Your Prickliness. The boys and I discussed this one."

Roze glances around at the other masked figures. "You're all conspiring without me now?"

The rest don't reply, and Roze looks back at Ed . . . and then to me. I try not to fidget, silently begging him not to somehow sense me beneath the cloak, not to notice my female figure or see my hair poking out of my hood.

"Very well," he says carefully. "If you're all in agreement . . . we can proceed."

I hear Ed's quiet exhale of relief next to me. Then he leans toward me and whispers, "Look down." At my feet is the beginning of the labyrinth, the stone path snaking its way around the room. "Begin here. As you reach the words on the path, read them aloud. When you reach the center, you'll be in."

He leaves my side and joins the others. I take a deep breath and step onto the path. The labyrinth winds like a snake around the room, and I feel a bit foolish twisting all about while the Grimmstone Society silently watches me. But then I reach a large letter *N* carved into the stone on the outer edge of the labyrinth. I look around and notice other letters around the rim of its path.

Oh. The labyrinth is a compass.

Below the northern point are words that I read aloud.

"Bone for Determination, I yield thee," I whisper.

As soon as the words leave my lips, a mighty ache quakes through every bone in my body. I double over in pain, nearly falling to my knees.

A whimper escapes my throat, and I see one of the masked figures flinch. If I use my voice too loudly, Roze will surely know it's me.

Once the spots disappear from my vision, I take a deep breath and keep going.

Magic. This place has magic—it must have been created by *meigas*. How long ago? How many years before they were all wiped from the Kingdom?

I come to the eastern edge of the labyrinth, and below the letter *E* are more words. I brace myself this time before saying, "Blood for Ruthlessness, I yield thee."

My blood turns to lava, and I bite back a scream. I grit my teeth as the pain recedes and force myself onward.

When I reach the southern end, I don't let myself hesitate. Waiting will only make it worse.

"Breath for Fidelity, I yield thee."

My lungs fill with fire and a sensation like I'm drowning has my hands flying to my throat as I desperately try to inhale. I feel lightheaded and nearly stumble.

The breath abruptly returns to my lungs, and I can't help it. I gasp.

The figure that is Roze jerks forward, breaking ranks with the rest of the Grimmstones.

"Wait—who are you?" he demands.

"Initiates aren't allowed to speak on the labyrinth. You know that." That sounded like Fletcher.

I continue on, my legs now trembling, and I can feel Roze's eyes on me the entire time. I finally reach the western edge of the labyrinth.

"Bite for Ambition, I yield thee."

Pain like needles pierces my gums, pushing at my teeth. I'm certain for a moment that my teeth have all simultaneously fallen from my mouth. I clap a hand over my lips . . . and I scream. I couldn't hold back my voice if I wanted to, and I nearly stumble to my knees.

"*Sinclair!*" Roze's voice sounds furious. He nearly charges toward me, but one of them holds him back with a hand on his shoulder.

Roze turns, his attention now on the other Grimmstones. "Which one of you bastards brought her here?"

"It doesn't matter now. She's here. She has to finish," says a voice I don't recognize.

"No. No, this can't—she can't—"

"There are rules."

"*Damn the rules.*"

"Calm down, or we'll expel you from this meeting. She's almost done."

My eyes water, and I try to focus on breathing as the pain recedes. There's just one more stretch of the path, and I follow it to the center of the room where the robed figures stand. Roze moves toward me, but one of the larger boys holds him back as the figure I think is Ed (I've lost track) hands me a small scrap of paper and an elegant fountain pen.

"Write your dearest secret, but be careful. The Crypt will know if you're lying."

I stare down at the small scrap, still breathing heavily and shaking slightly from enduring the pain of the labyrinth.

My dearest secret. I'm not sure what I should write. Whatever it is, I certainly don't want Roze and the others to know about it. But who knows what the room will do if I'm not entirely honest? I set the pen to the paper and close my eyes. I think of Roze in my room just an hour ago, the fractured look in his eyes as he admitted his truth—that he isn't entirely real, that he's stuck between *is* and *isn't*, that he cannot touch a living soul.

And I scorned him for it. I condemned him for killing the Queen and holding me to this bargain . . . even though in doing so he saved my life.

He would hate me if he knew the truth. Of that, I'm certain.

I open my eyes and stare down at the paper. There is no way back. Only forward. And that means baring this truth I have tucked away in my soul.

I scrawl the words *I am afraid of myself*, fold the paper, and hand it to Ed.

He hands it to Roze, whose shoulders are slumped, like he's given up this fight. He slowly lets his cloak drop to the floor, removes one of his gloves, and places the paper in his bare hand. He closes his fist over it and brings it to his lips. I barely hear the words he whispers to it.

"When the darkness comes."

He pulls his face away, and in his palm the scrap of paper has transformed. The crease in the paper is now a small hairy body, and the flaps are wings. A moth.

It's large and beautiful—its muddy gray wings almost sparkle with magic. Roze holds its body between his thumb and forefinger and draws a needle from within his cloak.

He approaches me, and his eyes finally meet mine through the mask. A silent conversation passes between us in the course of a heartbeat.

You betrayed me.

I did it for you.

Let me protect you.

Let me save you.

It's too late for that.

"Remove your cloak," he says.

I don't know what's coming, but I obey, unclasping it at the neck and letting it fall to the ground. I'm still wearing the gown he bought me underneath. He breaks eye contact and lets his gaze travel over me. He paces around me, examining me, speaking in a low, contemplative tone. "We could do your hand—you do enough writing. But it's too conspicuous."

"Shoulder?" Ed suggests. "She's got an arm on her."

Roze glares at him through his mask and turns back to me. "Not shoulder. Back isn't quite right either." He circles me completely, looking me in the face. "If I had it my way, I'd do it right over that mouth of yours."

"Perhaps on her forehead. She's a braniac, isn't she?" the large boy suggests, chuckling.

Roze snorts. Then his eyes fall from my forehead, melting slowly over my face, my lips, down my throat, to where my chest is far more exposed in this dress than it normally is, my heart beating wildly just beneath my skin.

"Hold still," he murmurs.

He gently places the moth over my heart, outstretched across my breastbone. It struggles against his hold, its wriggling legs and fluttering wings tickling my skin.

Silver eyes flash up to mine. "This will hurt."

And without warning, he stabs the moth, driving the needle straight into my chest.

I gasp, convulsing slightly, and Roze's hand on my shoulder keeps me upright. He pushes the needle in, and I'm sure he's going to injure something important. I want to tell him to stop, that he could pierce my heart.

But then the needle disappears entirely beneath my skin, and Roze presses his gloved palm against my bare chest. I look down at his hand, feel the cool leather against my feverish flesh, and my heart slows. A new sense of calm overtakes me.

But it's more than calm.

It's . . . serenity.

Gently, he removes his hand, and I can't hold back a gasp.

In place of the moth wings is a tattoo, one that matches the one on Roze's neck—an enormous, beautiful moth with a skull on its body.

Gingerly, I reach up and touch it, almost expecting it to not be real.

"It's lovely," I say.

"Viola Sinclair," Roze says, his tone formal, "do you pledge yourself to the Grimmstone Society and its mission evermore?"

Forever is a long, long time. But I'm ready for this—the belonging, the power, the secrets. I'm a born keeper of them.

"I do," I say.

Roze's gaze bores into mine, shifting between my eyes. Then he nods.

"*Fiat tenebrae*. Let there be darkness."

"*Fiat tenebrae*," I repeat. "Let there be darkness."

"*Fiat tenebrae*," the others shout around us. "*Let there be darkness*."

The floor jolts beneath us, and I fall into Roze, clinging to his lapels. His hands go to my waist, steadying me. The ring of flooring surrounding the labyrinth in the rotunda moves, sliding away into a hidden alcove until we're standing on an island surrounded by a deep moat of darkness. And then in a blink, torches light all around, not just in the room, but in the pit.

I think there's something down there. I move to take a step closer, but Roze takes that moment to rip off his mask. His face is hard and cold as he hisses, "What have you done?"

I pull away from him, hands on my hips. "I will not be made to feel guilty after you kept me in the dark when clearly, being part of the Grimmstones is most likely what got your father killed. It's the only path forward." The other boys are removing their masks and robes, looking like they aren't sure whether to involve themselves in this argument. I whisper, "Remember what Professor Borges said—"

"Do you have any idea what you've gotten yourself into, Sinclair?"

"*Yes*, I do. Ed and I talked."

Roze's eyes flash toward Ed, who is now studying the domed ceiling with great interest. "Yes, well, I'll deal with him later." He looks back to me. "You've just painted a permanent target on your back." His eyes are burning. He's so enraged, he's almost shaking. "Not for one moment for the rest of your life will you be able to rest easy. You will *always* be in danger, *always* be a traitor in the Crown's eyes. As if being a *meiga* weren't bad enough."

"And what if I don't care?" I snap. "What if it's worth it? Ed said—"

"It's not Ed in here, love," Ed chimes in. "In here I'm known as Sailor." He points toward Fletcher. "I believe you know Squire." Fletcher nods toward me. Then Ed—*Sailor*—points to the others in turn. "And then there's Monk, Ranger, Major, Turnkey, Spinner, Sparrow, Rook, Weasel, Sculler, and—" He gestures grandly toward Roze, who scowls at him. "Reaper."

"Of course," I mutter, eyeing Roze.

"Speaking of which, you'll need a Grimmstone name as well. For secrecy and, you know, added mystery." He wiggles his eyebrows at me, and I roll my eyes.

"What about Damsel?" Rook suggests.

My face sours. "That's a little sexist."

"Personally, I like Princess," Ed says with a grin.

"*Not* Princess," Roze says definitively, arms crossed across his chest. "Something more subtle."

Fletcher rubs his chin. "Scrivener."

My face brightens. "I like that."

"Scrivener it is, then," Ed says.

Roze huffs. "She should not be here. You all know what's at stake, what we guard—"

"So this isn't about keeping me safe at all," I cut in, my frustration building. "You don't trust me."

"Reaper," Fletcher interrupts, "Sailor told us what she can do. A linguist who can actually translate ancient Aragoise? You know how valuable that would be to the Grimmstones."

Roze breathes fiercely through his nose. "I don't care."

Fletcher steps into Roze's space, lifting a threatening finger in his face. "You're not a prince here, Reaper. We're brothers. Equals. You took a vow to put the society *first*. And right now, the society needs *her*." Roze and Fletcher stare each other down for a long moment. "It's too late anyway," Fletcher says. "She's in, and now she can help us translate texts that have been lost for years."

"This is a good thing," Ed pipes up.

Roze glares at him. "Oh, I still haven't forgiven *you*, Sailor. We're going to have words."

"My life was in danger anyway," I say under my breath to Roze alone. "Seven thorns for seven days to kill me, remember? How is this a risk?"

He studies me, something burning behind those icy eyes. "I—we—would've found a way . . . without you becoming a part of this. You would've been free when all this is done. Now . . . it's a lifetime of living at the edge of a cliff, Sinclair."

He says we would've found a way without me joining the Grimmstones. I don't see how. Our time is ticking down, and we're no closer to finding a way to break the Queen's power than we were at the start. Our only clue is the little book, its runes that match those on the King's arm, and the words Professor Borges said to me—*with the King lie the answers, with the King lies salvation.*

"What is it the Grimmstones are hiding that's so important?" I ask.

Roze turns his attention to me, his expression finally softening. He extends a hand to me. "Let me show you."

He takes my hand and we move toward the edge of the pit, carefully peering over it into the chasm. My eyes widen. Swirling downward are shelves upon shelves of artifacts—scrolls, pottery, treasure, armor, and a thousand other glinting, beautiful, priceless things. This trove would definitely be worth killing for.

"The lost knowledge of Hivernia," Roze says. "The Grimmstone Society is nearly as ancient as Vandenberghe itself—around a thousand years old. No one quite knows who founded us, but lore says it was Oras, the first *meiga*, when they were a student." Roze shrugs. "It hardly matters. The point is, there have always been truths that are . . . inconvenient in certain circles. The society protects these truths, keeping them in this library."

He leads me down the stairs, and I say nothing as we descend the spiral steps that curve around the island in the center of the Crypt. The rest of the Grimmstones are already scattered throughout the pit, talking or examining various artifacts. There is so much to look at, but my attention snags on the very first shelf we pass. On it is a collection of delicate combs made of what looks like a pale blue stone.

"What are these?"

"They come from the Vielflus, an ancient culture that roamed the continent before the Holy Virtusian Empire." He leans close, whispering in my ear. "They're made of dragon bone."

I whirl toward him, our faces coming within an inch of each other as he smirks down at me. "*Dragons?*"

The seal on the book that Professor Borges gave me immediately springs to mind. But dragons are mythological. Nothing so large, so beastly could've ever existed, could it?

Roze chuckles, and the sound goes right to my toes. He whispers across my lips, "I told you we have secrets."

I swallow, looking back at the display. I study the delicate floral carvings on the nearest comb as I ask, "How do you find these things?"

He nudges my elbow, leading me on, farther down the steps. "Grimmstone alumni used to search for them before the Mists. It's always been the job of current Vandenberghe students to guard this trove and study it. We preserve this knowledge for a time when the Kingdom—and the world—is ready for the knowledge again, if ever."

I peer around the chasm. "The secrets contained here . . . they're that consequential?"

His eyes darken. "They would start wars and end empires. They would change the way you think about everything, Sinclair." A rush of fear and adventure washes through me. "That's why we have to protect them. That's why they're under threat. These days, the biggest threat to the collection has been my mother. She's been determined to purge the Kingdom of any mention of magic."

He guides me across a bridge. As we cross, I look over the edge and immediately wish I hadn't. The trench is so deep and so dark below that I can't see the bottom. Roze strides across without a problem, hands in his pockets, and approaches a small hallway hewn into the stone. Two rows of books, newer than the ancient items I've seen so far, line the walls.

"This is everything the Grimmstones managed to save on *meiga* magic before my mother had her little bonfire eighteen years ago," Roze says.

I enter the hall, mouth open in awe of the sheer number of books on magic. I don't even read the title before I seize a book off the shelf, letting its pages fall open in my arms. On the left side is an illustration of a *meiga* wielding magic with her arms lifted overhead, cupping the sun. On the other side is another *meiga* cradling a new moon in his arms. Complicated ancient Aragoise text surrounds them both.

Roze stands beside me, studying the shelf of books while I read.

"You have to know—" He clears his throat. "I want you to know that the Grimmstones are doing everything we can to protect suspected *meigas* from my mother." I look up from the book to find his eyes now earnest and set on my face. "We can't protect all of them. But when we can, we find them, and we hide them. It's been the main goal of the Grimmstones since I took over as leader." He smiles weakly. "We collect and protect secrets. Once, those secrets were treasures, now they're people."

I gape at him. All this time, Roze has been protecting *meigas*, using his public reputation as an arrogant, magic-hating royal as a shield. It's breathtakingly cunning, and I feel a slight twinge of guilt for having judged him so harshly in the past.

I exhale a rattling breath. "Doesn't your mother force you to kill *meigas*? Have you been saving them *and* killing them?"

He cringes, like my words are a physical blow. "That's why we try to find them before she does. Once she places a tattoo on my arm . . . there isn't much choice."

He looks so haunted as he says it. And I can see it all playing out in his mind—the way each murder feels like a personal failure, every touch of poisonous skin a reminder that if he'd been more cunning, he could've saved them. And they all die thinking he's the villain.

I put my hand gently on his arm. "It isn't your fault, Roze."

He grins mirthlessly. "Reaper."

"Hardly," I say. I huff a laugh as something occurs to me. "It's a bit like your name, isn't it? Is a rose at fault for having thorns if someone is thrown into its brambles? Your mother is the one doing the killing, even if you're her weapon."

He looks away from me, shifting uncomfortably, like he can't quite accept that answer. "Well, better to not be a rose, then."

I turn back to my book, but I make sure to mutter loud enough for him to hear, "I like your thorns."

They remind me of my own.

CHAPTER EIGHTEEN

I've found something.

The other Grimmstones have handed me text after text in ancient Aragoise, asking me to translate each one. I don't know how many the Crypt has—hundreds, maybe thousands. And while I'm translating, I'm searching anxiously for the words I think will lead Roze and me where we need to go next—words like: magic, Castelle, *meigas*, King Alexandre, armistice . . . peace . . . war. After hours of work, I'm staring at a manuscript—a fraction of a fraction of a manuscript, really. It's hardly bigger than the palm of my hand, and the coloring tells me that this particular piece of parchment was washed of its original text and reprinted at least once. The letters are faded, with ghosts of a previous text blurring their edges.

There are no indications of authorship, but my guess is that it must have been written by another *meiga* also searching for the *Book of Odds*, because in ancient Aragoise, it reads,

> *—A lifetime of searching did not yield Oras's book—*
> *—Yet I found that ancient answerer—*
> *—it showed me a portion of the Book of Odds in its crafty face—*

Something that was able to reveal the *Book of Odds*, but wasn't the *Book of Odds*? Below, almost too small to see, is the smallest emblem, and yet, it's unmistakable. A dragon, like in the crest of Castelle, same as on the book the professor gave me.

My hands tremble as I stare down at the paper. A half-hysterical chuckle escapes my throat. Roze notices my sudden excitement from where he's doing his own research across the room, and he comes to peer over my shoulder.

"They're connected, Roze," I whisper, showing him my translation. "Castelle, the *Book of Odds*, and your father's death. They're connected."

I feel his breath on my neck. "It seems they are."

I want to stay and research all night. I want to comb through the Crypt until I've found every last bit of possible evidence that could lead us to the *Book of Odds* or to some connection between King Alexandre and Castelle. And that's to say nothing of learning everything I can about my magic. I will sacrifice sleep and food. I'll live off tepid mushroom tea and the delicious smell of old parchment. With so little time left, what could be more important? We're so close to giving Roze an answer about his father's death. And once we do, this can all be over. Our bargain with the Queen will be complete.

But at nearly two in the morning, Roze convinces me to abandon my research for the night and return to Berlaise.

"It'll still be here in the morning, Sinclair," he drawls, dragging me away.

"Maybe your father found something in the Crypt," I tell him on the way back to Berlaise. Pieces of a puzzle are locking into place, an explanation forming in my mind as my pace quickens with my thoughts. "Something dangerous. What if he found the *Book of Odds*? I suppose it would still need to be translated. He'd need Professor Borges for that. But once it was, we'd be able to understand *all* the runes. And we'd know how they made the Mists vanish before—perhaps be able to do so again. At least that's the theory. So that begs the question, who benefits from keeping the Mists around? Who would want to keep Aragoa imprisoned like this and would silence your father to do it?"

"Are you going to pause for a response, or could I be adequately replaced with a houseplant for you to talk to?"

"Hush," I say, thinking aloud. "Castelle. It must be Castelle, Roze.

Who else could benefit from the state Aragoa is in? Which means there must be a spy. Someone inside the castle is loyal to Castelle." I look up at him with wide eyes. "Saints."

He blinks.

"I found a silver stake in the drawer of Professor Borges's desk. It had a dragon emblem carved into it—very similar to the one in the crest."

"And now she's disappeared," he says. His eyes go cold.

Guilt burns my chest as I realize what conclusion he's drawn. "We can't make assumptions," I say gently.

"You all but said she's a spy for Castelle."

"That's a *theory*. I know Professor Borges. She's been my mentor for years and has dedicated her life to finding out how to *vanquish* the Mists. It doesn't make sense for her to want to keep things as they are. And really—*her*, an assassin?" But as much as I try to give him reasons to doubt, the more it sinks in for me—Professor Borges is an obvious culprit. An answer, staring us in the face. We'd be fools not to pursue it.

Roze is staring off into the darkness of the hall, that familiar darkness in his eyes, like he can't even hear me. I can see the fury written on his features, the hunger for retribution.

I step toward him, and since I can't touch his face, I curl my fist in his shirt, drawing his attention back to me. Silver eyes meet mine.

"Promise me you're not going to hunt her down and do something awful. Not before we know more."

The cold anger in his face fractures just a bit. "Fine. I won't hurt her. But we do need to find her."

"Agreed."

I unbutton my dress, letting it crumple on the floor, and fall into bed without bothering to prepare for sleep. I'm somehow exhausted and wide awake at the same time, the residue of adrenaline from the dance, the Queen's death, and the Grimmstones still coursing through my system as I wrap myself in my covers and stare up at the canopy of my bed while

Waffles nuzzles into my hair, clearly relieved that I'm back under his supervision.

There will be so much to face in the morning. How many people know that Roze was the last person to see the Queen? If he's executed for it, will my neck be next?

He and I are twisted up together in this. As much as I would like to put distance between myself and Roze, the more I pull away, the closer he gets. Like a parasite. Like an obsession.

An obsession because, as I lie in my bed trying to fall asleep, I can't stop staring at the golden stars that speckle the canopy fabric of my bed, thinking about every moment with him—the heat in my bones, the residue of every brush of poisoned skin, a dark longing that I don't want to look at too closely.

Saints below, that almost-kiss . . . Even with the barest brush of skin, I could tell how soft his lips were, taste the desire on them. I clinch my eyes shut at the thought, trying to remember that I should be thinking about Kole as I fall asleep, not Roze. I need to remember that I loathe him . . . but I don't anymore, do I? That defense was shockingly, terrifyingly easy to crumple.

I am only now coming to terms with an uncomfortable fact—that Roze has occupied my thoughts for far longer than I want to admit. I once told myself that it was because he was cruel and horrible. But when I think about the time I've spent hating him and the passion with which I've hated, it doesn't make sense. My contempt is all tangled up in thoughts of the way his hair falls across his forehead, the proud bearing of his shoulders, and the heady feeling that overcomes me when he's near.

He'd loathe you all the more if he knew everything, my conscience whispers.

I wipe a hand over my face in the dark. I so badly want to talk to Cerise. Normally, she would be the one to force me to talk through my confused feelings. She's so good at getting me to talk about things—boys, stress, the awful years in the orphanage, my parents—when I would much rather talk about declensions and verb conjugations. Saints, I took that stubborn prying for granted. But I can't talk to her. The farther she is away from me, the safer she is.

With a huff, I throw back my coverlet, causing Waffles to grunt and kick in his sleep. Despite the late hour, I know sleep isn't going to come. My theory about Professor Borges is buzzing in my brain. I don't want it to be her . . . but we need answers. We've spent three days of seven. There are four thorns left. Four thorns before I—or Roze—or both of us—face certain death.

A knot forms in my throat, and I shut my eyes. I was so afraid Roze would sacrifice me to save himself. He killed his mother, and I was once more convinced he was the villain. But now . . . I can't stand the thought of *his* death. Not after everything—the things we've shared, the way he tried to protect me. I can't be responsible for his death.

I open my eyes and blink away wetness. I won't let myself lose it now—I have to stay focused. I reach over to my bedside table and retrieve the book Professor Borges gave me from the drawer—the Book of Castelle, I've decided to call it, after the very illegal dragon emblem on the front. I run my hand over the intertwined dragon and lion, following the turn of the dragon's tail. I flip open its pages, checking for the millionth time for any mark.

Blank. As expected.

I let it shut and hold it to my chest. What would someone want with a blank book? Unless . . .

Unless it's not really blank. Unless I just can't see what's written.

I sit up straight in bed. "I have to talk to Cerise," I say out loud to myself.

Charging out of bed, I slip on my robe and my slippers. Yes, involving her is risky, but she might be the only one who can help me, the only one who could save me, save Roze . . . It's worth the risk. Besides, no one wants Cerise dead. I'll ask her for this one favor. She'll be fine.

———

Moments later, I'm at Cerise's door, and I knock, quietly at first. There's no answer, so I knock louder. "Cerise?"

I hear a groan and a smattering of vulgarities from inside. Moments later, the door opens, and Cerise's tired eyes appear in the crack.

"Who izit?" she mumbles. "Oh. Hi." Her eyes are cold, but not as cold as I'd expected. I take it as a good sign.

"Hi," I say, offering a smile. "Listen, I know it's the middle of the night, but I really need to talk to you."

Her gaze turns frostier. "I'm still pretty irritated you lied to me."

I purse my lips. "You're right, but not about what you think I lied to you about."

The anger on her face is replaced with sleepy confusion. "Huh?"

"We need to talk," I say firmly. "There's something I need to tell you."

She frowns as she thinks, and I hear shuffling from inside her room.

"Do . . . do you have someone in there?" I ask, unable to hide the grin spreading on my face. "Is it Bianca?"

I try to peer over her shoulder. She moves in front of me to block my line of sight.

"Bianca?" I call, almost giggling.

Cerise closes the door behind her as she steps into the hall. "It's *not* Bianca. Now let's talk if you want to talk."

Cerise follows me to the common room, and before the last embers of the previous night's fire, I tell her . . . almost everything. I explain, at least, that I didn't lie about my feelings for Kole, and that I had to strike the sudden, unexpected deal with Roze to keep myself safe. But I can't tell her about the Grimmstone Society or that Roze killed the Queen. I don't know what he'd do if I betrayed him, but it's not just fear keeping me silent.

He killed the Queen for you.

A strange sense of loyalty has developed between the Prince and me.

When I'm done explaining, Cerise sits with her back to the hearth, elbows propped on her knees, staring up at the ceiling. "So he's forcing you into this fake engagement—"

185

"Not forcing me. I think—" I toy with my locket, studying the embers of the fire. "Roze isn't as bad as I thought. I think I've misjudged him for a long time."

"Misjudged him how?"

"I've realized that all that pride and cruelty . . . it's a sort of mask he wears. I keep catching him in moments when he's, well, kind. He protects the people he cares about, feels obligated to them, even at cost to himself."

She raises her eyebrows at me, studying me for a long moment. "Fucking Saints."

"What?"

She tosses her head back, chuckling at the ceiling. "You like him."

"I do not."

She snorts. "It's all right. I suppose he is pretty. For a boy."

"That . . . has nothing to do with anything."

Cerise barks a laugh as I fight back a blush. "Oh, stop it," I say, grabbing a pillow off the nearby armchair and throwing it at her far-too-gleeful face.

Of course, she catches it, grinning like a cat, and throws it right back at me, much harder than necessary. I, being the less coordinated of the two of us, am hit right in the face and topple backward.

"You ass," I say as she laughs, pushing myself upright. When we catch our breaths, I ask, "And it doesn't bother you? That I'm engaged to a Roquelart after what they did to your family?"

Cerise stills, her shoulders tightening. It's a familiar gesture—her body's response every time her dad's death is brought up. "You don't have much choice, do you?" she mutters.

"No," I say. "But even if I did, from what I've seen of the Roquelarts this week . . . They're not all the same, Cerise. The Queen controls her children like they're servants."

Cerise nods, a distant look in her eyes.

I draw the book that Professor Borges gave me from my robe pocket. "I need your help with something."

I hand it to her. She runs her hands over it, her long fingers caressing the intertwined dragon and lion, and I immediately want to snatch it back, like I'm afraid it will bite her if she gets too close.

"Why do you need my help with a book? Linguistics is your specialty," she says. But I know Cerise. She only needs her curiosity piqued.

"The pages are all blank, though. What if there's a hidden message? What if it's invisible ink or something?"

She narrows her eyes. "Does this have to do with whatever you and the Prince are up to?"

I think about lying, but with Cerise, I know I don't need to, even if I can't answer all her questions. She understands that much. "Yes."

She studies the cover. "You're not one to bend the rules, Vi. Anything with *this*"—she taps the symbol on the front—"is banned."

"I know."

She thinks for a moment, then grins. "All right, let's go."

"Where?"

"The laboratory, obviously."

———

After a few minutes of passing through the empty corridors of Vandenberghe in silence, Cerise decides to break it. "I snuck into your engagement party tonight."

"What?"

She glances at me, smirking. "You thought I was going to miss it because I don't have a fancy title?"

"Cerise," I chide. "You could've gotten in so much trouble."

"Says the girl walking around with this." She waves the book in the air. "Point is, I saw you with him"—for a moment, my heart stops, and I think she's about to tell me that she saw something she wasn't meant to, like the killing of the Queen or the two of us running from the captain—"when you were dancing." A sly grin spread across her face. "He's clearly infatuated with you."

I thank the Saints it's too dark for her to see my blush. "Believe me, he doesn't behave that way in private. He just knows how to charm the crowds."

I can't help wondering what Cerise saw to make her believe such a thing. What do Roze and I look like to the outside world?

"I don't know how I feel about him, honestly. I don't think I hate him, but I really thought I did," I say, almost accidentally, my inward thoughts spilling out before better judgment can stop me.

Her smile is knowing and crested with mischief. "There's a thin line between hatred and obsession. You've been toeing it for a while."

Finally, we enter the science wing, and Cerise flings open the door to her favorite room—the laboratory. It's perhaps the strangest room in the school, which is why she fits right in here, while the whole place makes me want to retreat to my books and tea in front of a cozy fire. The weirdness, the wildness, the adventure of it suits her perfectly.

Once we're inside, Cerise settles on a stool by a long table worn with the pockmarks of spills and burns. The wall behind her is strewn with peculiar objects—candlesticks; jars of congealed substances in every color imaginable; dark books with strange words on the worn bindings; a jar of eyeballs that look as though they might come from a frog or some other small, slimy creature; large, malignant tools with long blades and serrated edges; and a clay vase that looks suspiciously like an urn.

She takes a little gold magnifier from the table, the sort that fits in the eyelid without being held, wedges it onto her eye, and begins to inspect the book without mercy, running her fingers over the pages and bending the spine.

"Do you think . . . Could it be enchanted?" I ask.

Cerise glances at me apprehensively. I've almost forgotten that she hasn't witnessed the magic that I have in the last several days.

"I'm not going to look for the supernatural where the natural could be a reasonable explanation," she says.

She holds the book against the light of an oil lamp. I try not to cringe at her carelessness. I feel protective of it, and I try to tell myself it's because I've always treasured old, rare books, and not because it has begun to feel like a living thing to me.

When she passes it over the gas flame, its heat licking the pages, my shadows press at my fingers, and I have to bite my cheek to keep from snatching it from her.

But the flame doesn't harm it.

"Interesting," she mutters repeatedly as she works. "If it's invisible ink, it's not activated by heat."

She crosses the room to a cabinet and retrieves a mortar and pestle and then fishes out something that looks vaguely like a very rotten cabbage from a shelf of vegetables. She grounds the cabbage in the mortar, adds a clear substance, and then uses a brush to paint the liquid across a page.

"Nothing," she says with a frown. "Wait—"

The cabbage liquid disappears into the page, as though the book has swallowed it in one gulp.

We glance at each other, and Cerise grabs a few other vials off the table. She tries swiping various substances across different pages of the book— one a deep blue, another clear and pungent, and something a sallow umber color. They all vanish upon contact.

"Okay, this book might be magic," Cerise says.

Part of me doesn't want to believe it. Because if it *is* enchanted, then Professor Borges gave me an enchanted book from the Kingdom of Death just before I was sent to my execution. There's an explanation for that I haven't wanted to consider—that she was trying to incriminate me. It's too horrible to think that she may have had a hand in the Queen's attempt to murder me.

"The pages are just absorbing the liquid," Cerise says with a frown. She flips the pages back and forth, looking for stains or residue of the fluids. "It's almost like it . . ."

"Ate it," I finish.

We glance at each other. And I remember the strange weight of the book, its haunting presence.

"Why would the pages be blank?" Cerise wonders. "Did the book eat its own ink as well?"

Of course. "Cerise, try writing in it."

Cerise quickly finds a fountain pen and bottle of ink from the dusty clutter on the table. When she dips it in the ink and touches it to the page, the ink pools atop it for a moment, unmoving.

"Write something," I say.

Cerise dips the pen in the ink again and writes her name.

The letters stain the pages and make no sign of retreat.

"That's it," I say. "It only responds to ink. All other substances are washed away so that it isn't—"

But before I can say the word "ruined," the ink moves. It coalesces on the page and forms an angry splotch.

"All right, maybe not."

Cerise and I lean in closer. Then the ink separates again and forms letters.

"The heart is the dominion of evil," I read aloud. It's ancient Aragoise. The same text I translated for Professor Borges the night she gave me the book.

The ink coalesces again, forming an amorphous blotch once more, and this time, the blotch spreads across the book, multiplying until it covers the whole page. It turns the whole thing a bottomless black.

Intuition prickles on the back of my neck. I take a step back, pulling Cerise with me.

"What the—" she whispers.

The black ink rises from the page, bubbling to form the shape of something moving. It lifts from the page and twists into a writhing body.

We stumble backward into the shelves as a serpent, inky black and enormous, slithers from the spill. At full length, it is nearly as long as the table and its body is as wide as my calves. It rises before us, arching its neck, and opens its sleek, black jaws. It bares its fangs at us and utters a sharp, menacing hiss.

Cerise curses.

And I shout, *"Run!"*

The serpent strikes, crashing into the shelves behind us as we sprint for the door. Cerise's jars fall and clatter to the ground. The snake writhes angrily in the shards of broken bottles and slithers rapidly after us. I feel it snapping at my heels.

We nearly fall through the doorway, and I slam it shut behind us.

Cerise's hand is pressed to her chest as she curses again. "What the hell was that?"

I'm still holding tight to the doorknob, as though the snake could learn to turn it. I hear it hissing just on the other side, feeling the weight of its body still slamming into the door, begging to be let through.

"I think you made the book angry, Cerise," I say, and then realization dawns. "Oh Saints—"

"What?" Cerise asks, using the opposite wall for support.

"The book is still in there."

She lets her hand drop. "You must be joking."

"I *have* to get it back."

"Why?" Cerise asks. "It just launched a fucking *snake* at us."

"You don't have to come," I tell her.

She cringes. "I don't want you to go in alone, but . . . I really hate snakes." Her face is tinged green.

"And I really hate not having answers," I mutter as I turn the handle.

The snake is gone. Perhaps it has disappeared back into the pages.

Perhaps I'm not that lucky.

I slink inside and close the door behind me to keep Cerise safe, trapping myself in the room with whatever might be lurking there.

My slippers creak on the floorboards as I step toward the book lying open on the table, right where I left it. Waiting for me.

A sound freezes me in place—soft, like the sweep of a broom—and my skin chills.

Stay calm. You just need to get the book and get out.

I inch toward the book, the floorboards whining under my feet. There's the sound again, this time across the room. My heart starts to pound.

I reach a hand toward the book. I'm so close.

I catch a motion out of the corner of my eye. A black snout pokes out from the piles of books and bottles on the table. A forked tongue flickers.

I still. The snake and I are equidistant from the book, and, *Saints*, my chances of reaching it before it can lash out at my hand are slim. I could abandon this. I could leave the book. No one would know it was me who left it. But deep down, I know I can't. There's no turning back from the ill-fated quest Roze and I are now on. *I need it.*

So I reach. I'm trembling, shadows prickling behind my skin, and I think the snake can sense it, smelling my fear with its tongue flickering in the air.

I can see its slitted eyes—it's watching my hand with deadly focus, its head moving back and forth ever so slightly.

My fingers are nearly on the leather of the book. I can almost snatch it . . .

Something cool and waxy brushes against my ankle.

I jerk.

The serpent on the table strikes, and I scream. Searing pain burns on the flesh of my palm, and the snake's fangs are latched on to my hand. I tumble, the serpent's body flying in the air. He writhes and I try to throw him off as I fall, but he's latched on tightly. He's not letting me go.

I fall to the floor, knocking my hip and head painfully.

But then there's something beneath my back. And under my ankles.

Movement across the floor in all directions.

Quick.

Slithering.

I lift my head—black serpents rush me from every direction.

I thrash, waving my arm wildly to free it from the snake still on my hand. He wiggles angrily, wormlike, and bites down harder.

Cool, waxy bodies descend on me, covering me, touching me everywhere. A stab into my neck, and pain turns my vision white. Another sharp lance on my foot, and I struggle to breathe. Then another on my thigh, and my body goes rigid.

My shadows crash into the door of my mind like a battering ram, shoving at my fingers, begging to be let free, to burst from me, protect me.

No.

No, I can't.

Not now, when I'm so full of fear that it drowns me. If I let my shadows loose, I'll be lost in them. I might not ever find my way out of that darkness. I roll and struggle on the floor, screaming, nothing but panic clawing at my brain as they wrap around my ankles, tangle in my hair, coil around my neck.

I reach for the body of the snake that is still caught on my hand, and I rip it free, tearing the flesh of my palm as I do.

I'm desperate to get away. I stumble to my knees, but then I slip and fall again in the bodies. They hiss angrily, and another bites me in the thigh.

Another sting of pain in my shoulder.

There are more of them, multiplying by the second. My feet can't reach the floor through the mountain of snakes, and they wrap around my throat, my head. I can't see the room anymore, just the waxy feeling of black snakeskin against my face. Every part of me touches every part of them. Fangs lance into me over and over, and tears leak from my eyes as I choke and wail.

CALM.

CONTROL.

But my shadows don't care. They shatter my dam, bursting free, the darkness enveloping me, until—

I hear the thunder of feet on the floorboards. There's a bright light—a beacon. I look up and see Cerise standing over me with the gas lamp in her hand. She throws a pungent liquid on the pile, splashing it over the bodies.

"Viola, *run!*" she screams, reaching for me and grabbing me by the shirt.

Somehow her voice reaches me. My shadows snap back. I grab the book on the table and hobble as fast as I can toward the door, my legs already sluggish from poison. Cerise throws the gas lamp down. The pool of snakes erupts into an inferno, the hissing bodies wriggling in agony on the floor of the laboratory.

Cerise runs to me and grabs me by the arm. She hauls me through the door. "This is going to burn the whole lab down," she says as we watch the snakes go up in flames.

We can't let that happen. If the wrong person were to learn what we were up to tonight, it could mean losing everything. I know I shouldn't, but—

"No, it's not," I say. "Go outside. I'll be there in a minute."

She looks at me strangely but then nods, leaving the room and closing the door behind her.

I turn back toward the burning pile of snakes. Some wriggle free of the inferno, flames still licking their backs, and they slide under cabinets and beneath piles of disused crates and scrolls, quickly setting the edges aflame. The laboratory will burn within minutes if I don't act quickly.

I close my eyes and breathe. I have to be careful. I have to maintain some modicum of control . . . while also losing it.

I carefully lift the dam around my shadows.

Darkness spills from my fingers. Shadows crawl across the floor like tentacles until they reach the snakes.

Not too much, I beg. *Just enough.*

Calm.

Control.

With just a pinch of chaos.

Inch by inch, the shadows blanket the pile of black bodies along with the flame, smothering both. They roll across the room, wandering over everything, finding flaming snakes and crushing them.

Saints, it feels glorious—the destruction. Like the first breath of air when you're nearly drowned. I should pull back . . .

The shadows crawl up the walls, wafting over shelves, inking over windows. I feel powerful. I feel free.

Pull back, a small voice whispers.

Calm.

Contro—

I snuff the voice out like a candle, letting darkness flow from every pore, surrendering to it, relishing in it.

I don't know how I resisted this before now. It feels so *right*. It feels like coming home.

I am one with the darkness, one with everything that hungers and takes, that yearns and pines and devours.

The room is gone. There is only shadow.

Viola.

Viola.

Is that my name?

"Viola!" A hand grabs my forearm, yanking me back into reality so quickly that my stomach flips and my knees wobble. Two sharp brown eyes pierce mine. "Viola, can you hear me?"

My vision clears. *Cerise.* It's Cerise.

"Are you okay?" she says, a deep wrinkle between her brows. "It's over, Vi. You can stop."

I look around. The laboratory is in chaos, but it's otherwise fine. No signs of fire or cursed snakes.

"Viola, what's wrong?"

I turn back to Cerise. "N—nothing," I croak. My throat is raw, like I've been screaming for hours. But I'm not lying to her. There's nothing wrong—and that's just the problem.

I gave in to my shadows . . . and for the first time, I don't regret it.

THE FOURTH
DEADLY THORN

The Prince was hated by his family and all the Kingdom—a reminder of the death they had endured in war. He was as despised and cursed as ever a child was, even in a royal household that was already full of curses.

So, when the Queen threatened the Girl of Shadows—a curiosity that now occupied his every waking thought—there was no love in his heart to prevent him from doing a despicable thing to protect her.

He went to his mother and kissed her on the cheek.

The Queen fell down dead.

And the wicked Prince did not care.

But the Girl of Shadows, her heart still alive but brittle, made the mistake of offering it to the Prince. His fist around it was not gentle—he seized what he desired with a grip like death.

And the fragile heart shattered.

CHAPTER NINETEEN

"That was breathtakingly foolish of you," Roze growls the next morning.

We sit opposite each other at a long table in the dining hall. The hour is early, and the blackness of the Mists outside the tall lancet windows has barely grayed. Flickering candlelight dances on the polished surface of the table. I have little energy and even less patience.

"If you'd taken me with you—"

"You would have what? Poisoned a hundred snakes? Was I just supposed to know that the book was enchanted?"

The look he gives me could cut through iron. "You agreed to not go anywhere without me."

Roze looks exhausted. His uniform is still impeccable as always, and his hair is neatly coiffed, but his eyes are rimmed with lavender. He grinds his teeth as he watches me.

"I had to do *something*," I argue. "We're running out of time. What happens in three days, Roze?"

He licks his lower lip and glances away. "I don't know. The tattoo remains. Her death doesn't seem to have put an end to her power. Somehow, some part of her lives on."

His words sink into me like a knife to the stomach. I toy with the pleats of my skirt, my appetite for oat pottage suddenly completely absent.

"Sinclair—*Viola*." The use of my first name forces me to glance up, to meet the hard look in his eyes. "I'm going to keep you safe."

My eyes fall to the ring that's still on my finger as I rub my thumb over the family crest.

"And what about you? Who will keep you safe?"

"Don't worry about me."

I laugh bitterly. "You're used to that, aren't you? No one caring."

For a moment, he seems like he's about to say something, but then he stops and sips his tea.

"Don't go anywhere without me again, understood? *Anywhere*. You want to visit your friends in Marquet-Blanc, I'm with you. You want to go back to the Crypt, I'm with you. I don't care if it's a cup of tea in the middle of the night—"

I scoff. "And if I want to take a bath, you'll stand guard?"

He lifts his teacup to his lips. "Don't tempt me."

My face warms. Prick.

He lowers his cup to the saucer, and I notice that the liquid is solid black. I stir my tea delicately. "You drink your tea straight?" I ask.

"Naturally," he says. "As though I'd pollute it with cream or sweetener."

"The stronger the better," I agree.

"Absolutely."

He watches me over the rim of his cup, taking another sip. His leg is folded elegantly over the other. A paragon of aristocratic snobbery. We sip our tea in silence, and it is tolerable if not companionable.

Until a guard rushes toward us. He slows as he approaches, stiff backed, like he's afraid Roze might bite him. "Your Highness," he says, "The Queen—"

Roze waves him off. "I was informed of the Queen's death."

The guard shakes his head. "Sir, your *sister*, the Queen, has requested your presence in the throne room immediately."

I meet Roze's eyes, and I know we're both thinking the same thing— whatever Belladonna has to say won't bode well for either of us.

———

"I've been thinking about what I said to you about your parents," Roze says as we make our way to the throne room, surrounded by guards. "I suppose the gentlemanly thing to do would be to apologize."

I hadn't had time to think about his stinging words about my family—honestly, there have been far more important things to worry about. "Is this what constitutes an apology for you?"

"I didn't mean to cause you pain."

I raise an eyebrow.

He sighs. "I said what I did about your parents because you should know that you don't need them. You don't need anyone."

"Don't tell me what I need."

He rolls his eyes. "They're two miserable people who abandoned their child because they didn't understand her."

He stops in the middle of the hall, and the guards halt around us—his way of reminding them that though they may be escorting us to the throne room by the Queen's orders, he is still their Prince. He controls them.

"But I do," he says, inclining his head toward me. He says it loudly enough for the guards to hear. None of them react—it's their job not to—but I know that this is another display of power. He is letting them all know what I am to him.

What he's pretending I am to him.

I have to remember that—it's a convenient ruse, but a ruse all the same. With the Queen gone, we don't have to continue the engagement for her sake, but it gives us an excuse to stay close, to continue working together to break the power of the rose tattoo.

Roze lowers his voice to a whisper. "I just want you to know . . . I understand."

His eyes navigate mine—shards of crystal smoke that seem to say, *You and I are alone here together.*

And a lurid desire takes shape in my heart, a thought so vile that my better judgment recoils from it—what it might be like to wrap myself in

Roze's world, his hate-filled existence, a pair of vipers in a nest, embracing the darkness and striking all who challenge us.

I have to look away from him and shake myself to keep from dwelling on it.

He says nothing, studying me for another moment. The guards stand at attention, waiting for the royal to signal that they may continue.

I only breathe again when Roze turns away from me. The first guard enters before us and bows in the direction of the throne.

"His Royal Highness, Prince Roze, and Miss Viola Sinclair," he announces.

And we step inside. The room is shrouded in darkness—the chandeliers overhead do little except to cast everything in an eerie glow, creating shadows in odd places.

Two thrones overlook the room in the center of a raised platform, guarded in front by a great gold lion. One throne is for the belated King, and one is for the Queen, dead not a day. Belladonna is in that seat, hands hanging loosely over the arms, back and neck rigid as we approach. On either side of the thrones, Roze's other sisters sit in five matching chairs arranged in two lines.

They're a beautiful and deadly bunch—that serpentine look that is definitely a family trait evident in the tilt of their heads, the stillness of their bodies, the sharpness of their eyes. Queen Belladonna's gaze latches on to mine, and I immediately freeze.

Because her eyes are black orbs—no whites—pools of night so thick that they eat up all the surrounding lights.

I blink, and they're normal again.

Is this another one of the Queen's illusions? How could she possibly be able to torture me like this from beyond the grave?

Belladonna's red-painted lips turn into a frown—I've been so terrified that I forgot to curtsy. I stumble into one, and I don't miss the shadow of amusement that passes over Belladonna's face.

But Roze . . . he doesn't bow.

"Brother," she says. Her voice is sharp, on the edge of rage. I glance up at Roze from my supplicant position, but his head is held high, staring down his nose at his sister.

"Hello, sisters," he croons.

Belladonna's red smile widens. "I suppose I can't expect any manners from *you*. You were always more mongrel than prince."

The sisters smile as one.

That's not how I would describe him at all. I can't imagine how anyone can look at Roze, at his perfectly styled hair, his elegant clothing, his superior demeanor, and not see a prince.

"You aren't in mourning attire," Roze observes. Each one of them is dressed in the same hue of deep red, hems pooling at their feet like six identical puddles of blood. "Good to know how little the death of a family member means to the lot of you."

Queen Belladonna's knuckles grip the armrests of the throne. Roze is an expert at getting under anyone's skin. Prince of making himself a problem.

Belladonna's lips pinch together so that they look like a bloody slash across her white face.

"A guard is missing. Would you know anything about that?"

"I do not. My, isn't that concerning?"

The sisters narrow their eyes simultaneously, and goose bumps rise on my arms. There is something so unnatural about them.

Belladonna taps the throne with a long finger. "You haven't asked," she says, "how our mother died."

No emotion crosses his face. "How?"

Belladonna bares her teeth. "Brutally."

Brutally. What does that mean? What did Roze do?

You've always known he was a monster. Just like you.

"Brutally?" Roze asks, his eyes narrowed.

"The body is barely recognizable," Belladonna says.

"It was *her*," exclaims Wisteria. She glares bitterly at me.

"What?" I say. "I never—"

"What would Viola have against our mother?" Roze asks.

"I don't trust her," Wisteria says. "Some cavern girl that we never even saw before this week, and now suddenly we're throwing her parties and welcoming her into our family?"

"We're betrothed," Roze answers.

"And that's another thing," says Oleandra. "You've never shown any interest in marriage before, and now suddenly you don't leave her sight."

I hate that they're talking about me as though I'm not here. I have a sinking feeling that I know where this is headed.

"You did something to him," Narcissa accuses me with a familiar cruel sneer on her face. She almost sounds like she admires me.

"Narcissa," Roze warns.

"She can speak for herself, can't she?" Narcissa asks.

"I can," I say, lacing strength into my voice. If I want to stay alive, I have to look like I belong.

"Then answer this question, Miss Sinclair," says Belladonna. "Are you a *meiga*?"

My blood runs cold.

"Of course she isn't," Roze lies.

"I didn't ask you, Roze. I asked *her*," Belladonna says.

My breath falters and my fingertips begin to itch with my shadows. This isn't right, and it isn't fair. I've done nothing but hide my shadows from the public eye, hold them back, dutifully and painfully.

I consider my next words carefully. "The late Queen killed all the *meigas* after the war. None remain."

"Perhaps she missed one," Azalea hisses.

"And perhaps," says Belladonna, "her death is Viola Sinclair's retribution." That clownish smile returns to her face.

There is no more hiding. Now it's time to fight.

"Strange that the Queen should have such a quarrel with the *meigas* when she was one herself," I say.

Their smiles all drop at once. The throne room is silent except for Roze's sharp breaths next to me.

"What did you say?" Belladonna says, but her eyes aren't on me—they're on her brother. "*You*. How dare—"

"Viola is my betrothed."

"She's not *family*."

"She might as well be."

"I did *not* kill the Queen," I interrupt. "Nor am I a part of any plot against the Crown."

"You haven't answered the question," Belladonna says. "Are you or are you not a *meiga*?"

"I—"

"*Stop*," Roze says, and Belladonna's eyes flash. For a moment I think she'll come down off her throne and strike him. But to my amazement, she listens. Roze takes a deep breath. "Sister," he says to Belladonna. "May we speak with you privately?"

Belladonna's lips pinch in anger for a long moment while my heart thunders in my chest before they twist into a saccharine smile. "Of course," she croons. "I intended to visit my mother's body. Perhaps you'll accompany me."

CHAPTER TWENTY

The catacombs snake beneath the castle for what feels like miles below the earth. It's damp and cold, and the chill eats at my skin through my Vandenberghe sweater. There are no gas lamps either—our path is lit by a single candle, carried by Belladonna.

I don't know why Roze wanted to speak with her alone. Perhaps he was just delaying my condemnation as a *meiga*. It hadn't occurred to me that having Belladonna as Queen might speed up my execution, not delay it.

We pass a tunnel leading farther downward, its stairs spiraling into black. An echoing scream breaks through the air from that void—the sound of a man being tortured. I jump back, and Roze grabs hold of my arm as I do.

"Dungeons," he whispers to me, and my stomach roils.

We approach a grate at the end of our tunnel. A man sits on a stool, his cloak wrapped around him, hood up so we can't see his face—like a wraith. When Belladonna steps forward, he bows his head slightly.

"Take me to the late Queen," she orders. The tomb keeper silently stands, retrieves a torch from the wall, and unlocks a latticed door. Belladonna turns her head back to us and smiles. I can't help but feel like we're walking into a trap.

The air beyond the gate is cold and thick and the walls leak with a substance too dark to be purely water. It's so damp that we must be passing beneath the lake that chokes the castle walls. I wrap myself tightly in my sweater and move subconsciously closer to Roze. We pass a threshold into a larger chamber, and Belladonna stops.

"This," she says coldly, "is where Mother dumped the bodies of the *meigas*."

My mouth parts. "I thought they were thrown into the lake."

That was how the Crown handled all traitors. Most corpses are burned since the Mists came—it's the cleanest way to say farewell when we can't keep graveyards. They are not kept here in the belly of the Castle.

Belladonna's eyes darken. "She had use of them."

For what?

As we enter the chamber, the distinct presence of death hangs in the air. The ceilings are several stories high, the walls piled with bodies. Some are old, clearly from the first purge of *meigas* eighteen years ago. Others are clearly not.

Roze curses beside me, taking a deep breath and closing his eyes. Saints—he must've been the one to kill most of these people. I grab his elbow, clenching reassuringly. We just need to make it through the chamber. But Belladonna is moving painstakingly slow.

The whole room has a strange, sick smell—bodies being left to rot and grow ripe with bacteria in the humid air. One on the wall closest to me is just bones, but there's still a lance through its chest cavity, broken off at the ends and left in the corpse's chest.

Another is newer—some of its naked flesh remains, hanging from a rib cage in strips. But the way its abdomen is shaped is strange.

I squint my eyes, peer closer . . .

And yelp as a rat's nose pokes out of the folds of stomach. I cover my mouth, nausea burning my throat. Something cool touches my wrist.

I jerk, thinking of the rat's tail, before I realize that it's Roze's gloved hand. He squeezes my wrist and gives me an unreadable look—either he means it to be comforting, or he's warning me to keep my composure. Maybe it's both.

When we're through the chamber, the tension in my chest barely eases. We cross through several more halls before Belladonna halts before a black iron gate. Above it on the wall, the royal family crest—the same that is on my ring—glimmers in the torchlight. The royal crypt.

Belladonna glances back, her red gown like a strange beacon in the dark. "I'll take it from here, keeper."

He gives her a swift nod, the hood of his cloak obscuring his face. "Yes, Majesty." He gives Roze and me a look of pure loathing as he passes. And then he's gone.

We're alone with Belladonna now.

"Just a little farther," the new Queen says.

We follow her through the gate and into the chamber—the darkest part of the catacombs yet. The light is so meager that I can only see into the alcoves where bodies lie an arm's length away. These are wrapped in grave clothes, mummified with dignity, unlike the *meigas* in the other chamber.

"Our mother is dead," Belladonna says without looking at either of us. "The Queen was murdered. You both understand that such a thing can't take place without consequences."

"Viola doesn't need to be involved," Roze says.

Belladonna whirls around, charging at Roze, her face lit fiendishly by the light of the torch—and there are tears staining her face. "I *know* it was you," she bites. "*You* and *her*, and if I thought I could get away with having your head severed from your body, Roze, I would do it."

Roze's nose wrinkles as he stares down at his sister. "Tears, Bella? Really? I'd have thought you'd be glad to finally get out from under Mother's thumb."

"She's our mother."

"She was a monster, and you know it." His familiar cruel smile appears. "You hated her. Just admit it—you *loathed* her for what she did to you. What she made you into."

Belladonna pales.

"You think I didn't notice? That I was so self-involved I wasn't paying attention to what she was doing? She relished torturing you, keeping you under her thumb until you were so broken from fear and rage that you were just like her—"

Fast as an asp, Belladonna strikes. At first, I think she's struck Roze with her bare palm—a deadly act—but when he groans and turns his face back toward her, there's a bloody slash across his cheek. I glance down at her hand—she's hidden a thin, sharp pin between her fingers.

"She's the *Queen*," Belladonna hisses, full of rage.

"She *was* the Queen," Roze corrects, his face stolid.

Belladonna laughs—manic and humorless, and the sound of it raises gooseflesh along my arms. "You idiot. You think this is over because you destroyed her body? She made sure something tethered her magic to the waking world in case something like this should happen. Without a body, her magic doesn't dissipate—she's simply no longer restrained by a corporeal form. Don't you see? You've only set her *free*." A deep frown sets on Roze's face as Belladonna continues. "There *is* no end to this, Roze, not until she has everything she wants. You can't escape her—her will, her power. What she wants, she gets." She shakes her head. "You have no idea what you've done."

She turns away and continues down the hall. Finally, she halts before an alcove. There, in the rectangular space carved from the ancient stone walls, is a body covered in a thick shroud. A mortsafe encases it; Belladonna draws a little silver key from her pocket, and the iron cage groans as she unlocks it.

Why would she need to cage the body?

She turns to us, the light of the candle distorting her face. The Book of Castelle is in my pocket, and suddenly I'm very aware of its presence, like it's calling to me.

"Brace yourselves," Belladonna says, slow and wicked. "She's quite gruesome." She sets the candle on the ledge of the stone box and reaches for the shroud, peeling it back to reveal the face of the dead Queen.

The breath is sucked from my lungs. This is nothing, *nothing* like what the guard looked like when Roze and I killed him.

Saints below.

Her once lovely face is mostly intact, but the rest of her is mutilated. A pile of meat. A few recognizable pieces litter the mound of red-and-black flesh. A fingernail. A spindly foot, several of the toes broken at odd angles. Her chest is an open cavity, the organs completely missing as though she was mauled, consumed.

Bile climbs my throat as I stare at the body. I think if I try to speak, I'll surely vomit. Beside me, Roze is stiff, and I'm afraid of what I'll see if I look at his face.

Could Roze have done this? I had struggled to accept that he'd killed his mother in cold blood, had excused it as necessary—an act meant to protect me. But *this*. This is the work of a monster.

"Roze," I whisper.

Belladonna takes a step toward me, and Roze doesn't move—he seems frozen in the spot, his eyes glued to the husk of his mother's body.

I back up a step, and Belladonna stalks toward me, a new rage lighting her eyes. I feel sluggish. My limbs are numb and heavy. She reaches out a delicate hand and lifts my chin so that I'm looking her in the eyes.

Her irises are the same color as Roze's, but they're also altogether different. I see in them a deep hunger, something feral and dark and inhuman. I think she would eat my heart out if I gave her a chance.

"Let's be clear," she says. She's no longer speaking like a queen; she speaks like a fiend. "I know what you are, and I hold you responsible not only for the death of your Queen, but the King as well."

"Viola didn't do this," Roze argues, stepping in front of me.

"Then tell me, brother dear," Belladonna hisses. "How it is that she became *this*." She thrusts a pointer finger toward the corpse, untempered rage in her eyes as she glares at Roze.

I suck in a shallow breath. There's such a look of hatred and knowing on her face. This isn't really about accusing *me*—Belladonna believes Roze did this. She's goading him into a confession by blaming me.

He narrows his eyes at his sister. "You know the strength of our

210

mother's powers. You don't think it's beyond her to mutilate her own flesh to strengthen hatred of *meigas*?"

"You're suggesting our Queen was killed by her own hand?"

"I'm suggesting death benefits her more than life ever did."

Belladonna's eyes coldly scan Roze's as I hold a breath. That piercing gaze of hers seems to discern everything, and I don't believe for a moment that she thinks Roze is blameless.

"There will need to be a scapegoat for her death," the new Queen whispers. "Already the nobles are crying out for justice. They're testing me—seeing if I'll be as merciless with *meigas* as Mother was. They want a Queen with a heart of iron and a fist of fire." Her eyes flash to mine. "The people will have their vengeance for their lost Queen, or they will rebel. And I will not let the throne fall because of the inconvenience of sentiment or truth."

Roze's hand shoots out, grabbing me by the arm and pulling me behind his body, as though he can protect me from Belladonna's wrath by blocking me from her sight. "If you grant her clemency, I'll continue to work as your assassin, just as I did for Mother."

I can only see the side of his face from where I stand—his jaw set and his eyes steely. My heart beats erratically.

Belladonna's glare sharpens. "If you want to save your bride, Roze, you'll have to offer something better than promises you don't intend to keep."

"I'll do it," he says. "You know I'm useful. I'll kill whoever you want."

"And if I want *you* dead?" she sneers, but it sounds less like malice and more like resentment.

He laughs. "Then I wish you luck. Who exactly do you think would be able to handle such a task?"

Belladonna glares at her brother and he meets the steel in her stare with his own.

"You cannot hide her forever." Belladonna turns to me. "You should know, *meiga*, that I will defend my sisters and my Kingdom against *any* threat. Whether she's betrothed to my brother or not."

"Bella, *please*," Roze pleads.

Her eyes set on him, and I can see, for just a flash, the desperation, the sadness, the fear in them. "You have no idea what we're up against, Roze," she whispers. "For years, I've . . . done my best to shield our sisters, you, the Kingdom. But our mother . . ." Her shoulders suddenly jerk strangely, and her eyes fly around the room, glancing into the shadows. She turns back to Roze and leans close. "Listen carefully, you damned idiot, or we'll all be forfeit. Abandon this ridiculous quest with *her*"—she motions toward me—"and use whatever wretched magic is in that awful skin of yours to *hide*—"

A strange scraping sound fills the chamber, coming from all directions—and then I hear a low groan, like an animal in pain.

Belladonna's face pales. "No," she whispers. "*No, no, no*—"

"What have you done, Bella?" Roze says, gripping me harder by the arm.

Bones fall from the alcoves, tumbling into piles on the stone floor. Half-decayed bodies crash downward, some bloated with marbled flesh, others with ancient leathery skin stretched taut over skeletons. They crash into heaps on the ground.

And then the heaps move.

They stand, one by one, the royal dead. Partially eaten torsos, skulls with half the skin still attached, entrails dragging on the dirt behind them. They all stalk toward us, the vengeful dead, the royals who want me to join them in the afterlife.

"Bella, *stop this*," Roze yells. His face is bloodless. I imagine that his poison doesn't work on those already dead.

Belladonna is on her knees now, her eyes full of terror. "I can't."

Behind her, the mound of gore that was once the Queen's body moves. It wriggles, wet spots illuminated by the flicker of candlelight. Coalescing, rearranging, smearing blood over stone in dark streaks, the Queen lifts herself from her resting place. There's not enough of her body left for her to stand on, so instead she floats like a specter. Bones and flesh hang in shreds from her half-broken rib cage. What must've once been her heart dangles on strings of viscera. Her breasts are naked and lashed open, blood and yellowish nerves hanging loosely from her chest.

Bile rises in my throat. Trembling head to toe, I want to scream, I want to cry.

Calm!

Control!

Her face is lovely and bloodless white. She opens her eyes with difficulty, like they've been dried shut, but when she does, her gaze finds mine immediately.

"*Shadow girl,*" she snarls.

The dead Queen lunges for my face, mouth open wide, teeth bared. Her bony fingers latch onto my head, digging in painfully, knocking us both backward as my eyes lock with her bloodshot ones. And when they do, just as Belladonna's did in the throne room, her pupils grow and consume the rest of her eyes until they are all black, and she is pulling me in, in, in to that darkness.

"Viola!" Roze bellows.

Before the world turns black, I catch a glimpse of the little gray ghost boy standing over me, watching with cold eyes.

Bloody Annie.

Bloody Annie.

Bloody Annie.

CHAPTER TWENTY-ONE

This is what swimming must be like.

A strange floating sensation rocks my entire body. A dull roar fills my ears. I force my eyes open, and I'm not in water at all. I'm in a forest, though I've only ever seen one in paintings. Oak trees, tall and dark, tower over me, and the air smells wild and foreign, full of pollen and earth and all things alive. There are no such smells in the castle of Aragoa.

I blink and sit up. I'm lying on a patch of earth beneath a towering oak, and I can see moonlight through the branches overhead.

Moonlight.

I've never seen the moon—only its dim luminescence through the Mists.

Everything here is dreamlike, sleepy. But if this is a dream, it's more vivid than any I've ever had. How do I feel the chill of the December air? How do I hear the chirp of crickets and the distant call of owls?

I look back down from the moon, and ahead there's a clearing in the trees.

And in the middle stands a figure, covered in a white cloth. It's completely still, like it just snapped into existence moments ago. I clamber to my feet and take a step toward it. I'm startled at the realness of the slight squash of the earth, the feel of twigs breaking beneath my feet.

The figure doesn't move.

The shroud is old—its edges are tattered and gray, like a white sheet that has been washed too many times.

I should turn back, but the rational, self-preserving part of my brain is asleep. And the part that thrives on darkness? That part is wide awake.

I take a step into the clearing, and all sound ceases—the whisper of the breeze and the vibrato of insects have gone completely silent.

My insides twist, but my feet move as if controlled by some higher force. I take another step closer, blades of grass brushing feather-light against my legs. I can see the cover moving slightly, as though blown by a breeze that isn't there. The figure hasn't moved.

I'm meant to remove that cover. I know it in my bones. Like I know my shadows. Like I know my own darkness.

And yet, I know that when I do, something in me will fracture. There is no going back. This is the final breath.

Finally, I'm within reach. I stretch out a trembling hand, and my fingertips brush the fabric . . .

The figure moves, and I jerk my hand back.

It's just a small blooming movement, like whatever is beneath it has taken a deep breath.

I reach out again. Fear has me by the throat.

This is inevitable.

It always has been.

I curl my fingers around the cover. I pull, and it flutters to the ground.

I have only a moment to take in the face before me, the face that I *knew*, somewhere deep inside me, I would see. The frightened and pale face of the little boy, the ghost that has haunted my every step for weeks. *My brother.*

And he whispers, his voice more real than ever, *"Bloody Annie. Bloody Annie. Bloody Annie."*

Tears burn in my eyes as I look into his deep brown ones. Without knowing exactly what I mean, I beg, "Please."

His face contorts, a look of consuming rage taking over his small features. There's not even time to take a breath—he leaps at me. I gasp and fall back as he latches on to my face with sharp fingernails. We topple to the ground as he tears at my hair, my face, my neck with jagged nails.

I'm screaming.

I'm crying.

No, those aren't my cries. I force my eyes open. My brother is crying. The sound of it is like listening to my own soul crack open. My heart is breaking—it's *breaking*, and I know I will never recover even as he shreds my skin with nails like knives, and I try in vain to shove him off me.

Tears slip free from my eyes.

End me. I would deserve it.

And I stop fighting. My arms fall back on the grass, and I let my baby brother tear into me as I look up at the moon.

What a lovely way to die. Under the moon with the grass beneath my back.

More tears spill down my cheeks. No, that's blood. It won't be long.

But then two hands wrap around my baby brother's throat.

"*No!*" I scream. But his eyes bulge as the hands wrap tighter, cutting off his oxygen.

"*Let him go!*"

For the first time in my life, when I call on my shadows, beg them to come forth, they don't. *Now* they fail me. When I need them most.

It's not Roze I hate. It's not Queen Maria or Belladonna or the princesses—it's my shadows. The disease that is my lifeblood, that I can't cut away. No cure, save death.

The hands grip harder, pressing into my brother's trachea, and I watch the life drain from his face for the second time. And then I see—those hands are covered in black leather gloves.

Night edges my vision.

The last thing I see before surrendering to the darkness is my brother's face, sad and betrayed—my final accusation. But then it twists, the skin moving around the skull like liquid flesh, bubbling and re-forming until the face I'm staring at is completely different.

The dead Queen.

And she's laughing.

"Hello, Annie."

THE FIFTH
DEADLY THORN

The Prince and the Shadow Girl thought they had escaped the Queen, but she had grown more dreadful than either of them knew. Her magic no longer depended on a mortal body of flesh and blood and bone, and without its constraints, she could execute her revenge unhindered by its mortality, haunting the Shadow Girl's every waking moment.

The Queen's six hateful daughters were determined to slay the girl in their mother's name. So the Prince did another wicked thing—he feigned the girl's death and brought his sister, the new Queen, a false heart. And he locked his Shadow Girl away in a tower, where she would be safe forever, alone in the darkness, with only his despicable self for company.

CHAPTER TWENTY-TWO

I open my eyes the next morning to the dim light of my room. The stars that speckle my bed canopy are blurred as I gaze up at them, and it takes several seconds for me to realize that I am *not* in a forest, that I *am* alive, that my heart *is* beating.

My face feels wet and cold—I'm crying. When did I start crying?

But then my grief is broken by a slobbery tongue slurping up my tears.

"Waffles," I mutter, reaching up to nuzzle his little scaly head. I scratch him behind the ear, and he responds with a whimper, laying his little head on my shoulder. I curl my face into his leathery skin.

"What happened?" I wonder aloud. My throat is rough with disuse.

"I've been wondering the same thing."

I lurch, twisting my head toward Roze's voice. He sits in a chair by my bed, his long legs propped up on one of the four posters, his head resting thoughtfully on his fist.

"*Roze.*" I can't ignore the relief that spreads through me at the sight of him nor the undeniable truth that I'm glad to see him.

I'm *glad* to see Roze Roquelart.

"In fact," Roze continues. "That's exactly what I was going to ask you."

His silver eyes are shadowed with violet, and the pallor of his skin is haunted, wrung thin.

I sit up in the bed and wrap my arms around my knees. I don't want to tell him about what I just saw—a vision? A dream? A nightmare? No,

I know better than that. This was one of Queen Maria's illusions, which means I really should tell him.

"I don't know," I say truthfully. "One minute we were in the tomb, and then . . . I saw things."

"What things?"

I take a breath. My chest feels uncomfortably tight, and I fiddle with my locket to calm myself. "I was in a forest. I saw my brother." Now I can't help the tears that are leaking from the corners of my eyes. I feel exposed and raw, but I force myself to keep going.

"I've been seeing his ghost for weeks, everywhere I go. I tried to ignore him, but he was in this dream—vision—whatever—and he was more real than ever. He attacked me. I thought I was going to die. But then I saw hands wrap around his throat—*your* hands. And then his face turned into your mother's."

Roze is silent for a moment, his face expressionless—not a glimmer of empathy. Silently, he lowers his legs to the floor and sits on the edge of my mattress. I'm not looking at him, but I can feel him watching me. Saints, I wish he would look away.

"Tell me what happened to your brother."

I can't look at him. Instead, I stare down at Saint Waffles on my quilt, who gives me a sad look that seems to say, *You should tell him.*

I can't. Not even Cerise or Kole knows this.

"Sinclair?" he says. I don't look up. My heart has a thick adamantine fortress around it. I will not lower the bridge for Roze.

"Viola." My eyes jump to his. Gone is that bored, austere expression of his. In its place is something almost tender, still edged in poison and the bite of winter, but gentle, nonetheless. I once read a tale of a man who killed his horse and climbed inside its carcass to keep warm in a blizzard. That feels like the sort of solace Roze offers me now—terrible, bloody comfort.

When I open my lips, it's like jumping from a cliff. I know there are rocks at the bottom, and I'm trusting the boy with the poisoned hands and the broken heart to catch me.

"I killed him," I whisper.

I watch Roze carefully, but his face doesn't change.

No fear.

No judgment.

Instead, he nods, as though it's the most normal thing to say in the world. But this is the boy who just killed his own mother and hasn't shown an ounce of regret.

"How did it happen?" he asks.

That's the worst part of it, and I almost stop myself from telling him. But there's a tear in my careful armor, and the truth feels like it's being ripped from me.

"We were very small. He tried to steal my locket." I lift it up to show him.

He comes close, peering at it. "May I?" he asks.

I nod, and he takes it in his hand, flipping it over, examining it. The short chain is still around my neck—he's close enough for me to smell spice and cold. What would it be like if he closed that locket in his fist and yanked me closer? I internally shake myself. I shouldn't be thinking like that right now.

He looks up. "What do you have inside it?" he asks.

"It doesn't open. Or at least, I've never been able to get it open. I've had it for as long as I can remember." I take the locket back from him. "I was very possessive of it when I was little. My brother was just a baby, and one day he wanted to play with it. He didn't know any better—to him it was just a pretty thing he wanted to hold. But I wouldn't give it to him. I remember him screaming and hitting me. I was angry, and . . . I wanted to hurt him. I remember that feeling—that I wanted to hurt my little brother. And then . . . there was just darkness." I look down at my locket. "I woke up, and my brother was dead."

Roze swallows, the moth tattoo on his throat bobbing. "Your shadows— they can kill."

I nod.

"My middle name is Annette, and I went by Annie when I was little.

I've been hearing his ghost say my name—*bloody Annie*. Then your mother called me that in the vision." I choke on my next words. "That's who I am. Bloody Annie."

There it is. The reason he should hate me, fear me, regret me.

"I didn't mean to," I whisper, my vision blurring as I stare down at the locket. "I swear by the Saints. I didn't mean to kill him."

Roze laughs, and I peek up at him, horrified. "Of course you didn't," he says. There's a quiet gleam in those crystalline eyes of his. "You were a child."

I stare at him as he reaches a hand up. Leather cools my face as he sweeps a strand of hair behind my ear.

"It was an accident, Sinclair. You had power you couldn't control. I can relate."

I don't want to believe him. Claiming innocence feels like a betrayal of the small, truly innocent life I took. Isn't the appearance of my brother's vengeful ghost evidence of my guilt?

Roze's eyes darken. "Is that why they got rid of you? Because you killed your brother?"

I nod, dreamlike, incapable of words.

"Bastards," he mutters. His hand is still on my face. He clears away a tear with his gloved thumb. "What happened isn't your fault. What you are isn't your fault."

He goes quiet, and after a moment, I realize I have as well. My tears have ceased, and I stare back at him like I'm in a trance.

"I think I've been looking for you my whole life," he whispers. He says it like a secret that has slipped through the cracks, like he didn't mean to voice it out loud. But now it's out there, hanging in the air around us.

My breath stops in my lungs. Something snaps taut between us— something soul-deep and penetrating.

"You killed your mother," I say. I'm not sure if I'm trying to convince myself that he's evil or relishing in the idea that he is *like* me, that we are two halves of the same rotten soul.

"Yes," he says—frankly, no shame.

I lean closer. "You did it for me."

I see him swallow, and the sense of power it gives me is heady, addicting.

"Yes," he whispers, low and gruff and desperate.

His gaze flits over my face, finally settling on my mouth. "Viola," he says, enunciating each syllable with what could be disgust or reverence, "I want to kiss you."

I suck in a breath, and my eyes fall to his mouth, to those lips made for sneering and spitting insults, the lips that would kill me in an instant.

"But you can't," I say. "Because you're cursed."

A ghost of a smile passes over his lips.

"Because I'm cursed," he agrees. A gloved thumb moves from my cheek to my mouth, brushing across my lower lip.

Something warm and liquid fills my belly as I stare at his mouth while he caresses mine.

"You're going to need to stop that," he says.

"Stop what?"

"Looking at me like that," he says. "Before I do something very stupid."

I don't want to stop. But a whine breaks through the tension. Saint Waffles puts his head on my knee, staring up at me with morose eyes.

I lean back from Roze, deliberately putting distance between us, and he drops my chin. I'm grateful for it, but I also hate it. I'm so tired of self-control.

He clears his throat. "There's something else," he says. "I want you to know that what you saw in the tomb . . ." The image of the brutalized body of his mother burns in my mind. "I didn't do that to her. I only kissed her on the cheek. It was painless. Like falling asleep. What was done to her . . ." He takes a deep breath, and there's something in the shiver of his mouth that makes me think he didn't *entirely* hate his mother. "What was done to her must have been done after I left her body."

I can sense a fork in my path—to trust the tortured Prince who has saved my life on multiple counts at this point . . . or distrust the Huntsman whose arm is still marked with the price on my life. It's unclear which path will prove treacherous, but perhaps it's time to put a little more faith in my heart than my head.

"I believe you," I say. "But what does that mean?"

"It's possible it was my mother's own doing, like I told Belladonna. But perhaps my sisters wanted you to think it was me. They wanted you to fear me."

I almost smile. "I already fear you."

It's the truth. I can't stop being afraid of him, or of myself. But I'm starting to think that there's something lovely about fear.

"Maybe they want to brand *meigas* as brutal killers," I suggest.

He nods in agreement.

Looking around at my dormitory, I ask, "How did I get back here?"

"Your shadows flooded the catacombs." He shakes his head disbelievingly. "It was . . . utter darkness. I've never seen anything like it. But it subdued my mother's power enough in the moment that I was able to get to you. I brought you here."

"And Belladonna?"

The corner of his lip twitches. "Alive."

"Thank you," I say. "You keep saving my life."

"I'd appreciate it if you didn't need constant saving," he says sourly. He's returning to our game of hate—resentment is easier to swallow than longing.

"We have two days, Roze," I say. The hopelessness of it hits me suddenly. *Two days.* And we're no closer to figuring out how to defeat the Queen, how to stop the clock. We still have no idea what answers the King might hold. There is some hidden thread connecting all of this. I can feel it, but I just can't see it.

Both of our eyes inadvertently fall to his forearm, where the tattoo is hidden beneath his sleeve.

"We need to learn what the Book of Castelle has to do with this," I say. "Maybe we could go back to the Crypt—"

"You're not going anywhere," Roze says.

I cross my arms. "And why not?"

The look on his face promises violence. The prince has retreated; the assassin has returned. "My mother's spirit is alive and well, and more hell-bent than ever on sending you to an early grave. Without a body or a throne, she no longer cares about the opinion of the Court—she won't let politics or decorum stand in the way of killing you. My sister is too terrified to stand against her—she'll do her bidding, and she has an army of guards at their command. And Belladonna has issued her first command as Queen—until my mother's supposed killer is caught, she's confining the entire Kingdom to their residences."

"Why?"

"They're looking for *you*." He eyes the door warily. "They've already begun to search homes. Belladonna has spread the news that you're a *meiga* and a traitor to the Crown and has threatened to imprison anyone suspected of aiding you or possessing magic themselves."

"She's going to punish people . . . because she blames me for the King's death and you for the Queen's?"

He nods. "I believe my sisters are trying to draw you to them. They think you're too noble to let other people suffer in your place." Then he glares at me. "But before you go marching into Belladonna's arms under some misguided notion of martyrdom, I'll remind you that my family *hates* all *meigas* who aren't my mother. Belladonna will kill them whether you walk into her trap or not."

I let out a shuddering breath. "What do we do?"

The look in his eyes could melt steel. "We keep you hidden."

"So I can't leave my room?"

"Actually, I'm going to insist that you do. I only brought you back here so you could gather a few items."

"And where exactly am I going?"

"Somewhere safe, where you will remain."

I glare up at him. "How am I supposed to find anything on the book if I'm under lock and key?"

"We'll figure something out. But you'll do it in hiding. No more late-night experiments with Cerise. No more traipsing about the library. I'm going to take you somewhere they can never find you, and you're going to stay there as long as is necessary for your survival."

I scoff. "How am I supposed to survive that and not go insane?"

He smiles cruelly. "You'll have my delectable company for entertainment, of course."

CHAPTER TWENTY-THREE

The Grimmstones protect their own. Sculler and Spinner lead Roze and me through the castle, watching for guards at every turn.

The halls of Vandenberghe are silent and empty of the usual bustle. At the glass bridge, Ed is waiting for us, and for once, his expression is serious.

"You have a clear path to the passage," he says. "I've taken care of the guards in that wing. You shouldn't have any trouble." His eyes soften as he looks at me. "Godspeed, Scrivener."

As Roze and I cross the bridge, I mutter to him, "Why is everyone treating me like I'm a hero for having my life threatened?"

"Don't underestimate the importance of symbols, darling," he says, keeping his hand on my elbow.

Roze and I creep silently through the doorway to the main castle. He carries my bag, laden with a few clothes and more than a few books, on his shoulder while I carry Saint Waffles under my arm. More than once on our way through the castle, we have to hide behind a tapestry or shut ourselves in a closet when we think we hear footsteps, but Ed has done his work well. They don't come near us.

Belladonna has shut down the entire Kingdom to find me, and I still don't understand her level of hatred for me. I can't be the only *meiga* in the Kingdom whom the Queen missed when she executed the rest, the only baby with power hiding in her veins.

No one ever reveals their powers, of course, but there are always suspects—the kitchen maid whose pies are too delicious to be natural, the schoolyard boy whose aim with rocks always manages to meet his enemies, the old man with the wizened eyes and a knack for taking the winnings during card games. Those whose talents are too suspicious tend to disappear.

But the refrain that's been playing in my mind for days now is *why me?* Why was I singled out to take the fall for the death of the King? The only clue I possess is the blank book weighing down my sweater pocket.

Roze leads us into a gallery. Every inch of the walls is covered in works by the masters—dark, romantic landscapes, portraits of kings and nobles, a few baroque works with their macabre depictions of gruesome murders. I can't believe Roze grew up with unhindered access to such pieces, like they're just part of the furniture.

He approaches a portrait on the far end of the room of a woman standing on the moors, her black mourning dress whirling around her. He runs his gloved hand along the edge of the gold frame until it catches. He does something with his fingers that I can't see, and a moment later, I hear a soft click. The portrait swings open, and a dark hall appears beyond it. He stands back and grins at me.

"After you," he says.

I stare at him. "What is this?"

"Did you think I became an accomplished assassin without having a few secrets?"

I lower my lids. "You're nothing but secrets."

He smiles charmingly, and I look away, trying to ignore the way my belly flips and the memory of his thumb on my lip as he told me he wanted to kiss me.

It's reckless to think about it. It'll come to nothing. His very skin is poison . . . but that doesn't seem to be enough to stop my imagination.

I take a step into the tunnel, and when Roze closes the portrait behind us, we are enveloped in darkness.

I feel his hand on my elbow. "Follow me," he says, his lips close to my ear.

His fingers trail down my arm until he clasps my hand in his. He leads on, pulling me behind him, though there is no light to speak of. Saint Waffles, the cowardly thing, whimpers softly in my arms.

"It's all right, Waffles," I whisper to him, but I'm not sure if it is. The hair is raised on my arms.

I stumble, and Roze catches me by the arm. "We need to be quiet in here, Sinclair," he whispers. "Take care that you're not heard through the walls."

"You haven't told me where you're leading me," I say testily.

His grip on my hand tightens. "Somewhere safe," he says. "Now, no more questions. And keep up."

His tone is cutting, but he keeps his hand in mine, helping me navigate the darkness. We walk in silence, his hand occasionally trailing up my arm, and what's meant as a comforting caress sets my blood on fire. And before I can help it, I imagine him making those same motions *without* gloves, with nothing separating his skin from mine. With those long, elegant fingers trailing everywhere, running over every area of sensitive skin, light as feathers, until I'm burning.

I want to stop him right here. I want to beg him to push me up against the wall the way he did outside his bedroom, to hold my jaw in his grip like he did after killing the Queen. I want him to do dangerous things to me in the dark, where we can pretend that it's possible.

Saints, what's wrong with me?

We walk for what feels like hours, and I completely lose track of the turns he's taken, helplessly lost in my own imagination. There's no way I'll be able to find my way back after this. We begin climbing stairs curved into a spiral—we must be in a tower.

The steps seem endless. My ribs are aching and I'm sweating through my shirt when a light finally appears around the bend, a flicker that illuminates the darkness, and I almost cry with relief. Roze's tall silhouette is now visible as we reach a landing at the top, and I realize the light is coming from under a door.

He retrieves a small silver key from his pocket and opens the door, glancing back over his shoulder at me before pulling me through—he hasn't let go of my hand for a moment.

The room is octagonal, its ceiling hatched with wooden rafters as though its builders forgot to finish this part of the castle. The rest of it is plain, unornamented stone, which is a sharp contrast to the collection of dark, stately furniture strewn about the room. A large bed rests against one wall, draped in a thick coverlet of deep green with black and silver embroidery threading through it. It looks so comfortable that I immediately want to sink into it, to fall asleep and forget all my waking nightmares. A black, lacquered desk is against another wall, bottles of ink neatly organized atop it. There is a sizable bookshelf, filled with thick volumes, and on a bench beside it are more books in neat stacks, as though the shelf had run out of room. Before a hearth filled with ashes of a recent fire, an overstuffed chair and ostentatious chaise rest atop a rug that I'm sure is precious enough that it *should* be on display in some other part of the castle, not squirreled away at the top of a tower. Almost like it was stolen. I don't even have to ask whom this room belongs to.

And before the only window rests a pianoforte, sheets of music spread on its stand. It's a beautiful instrument, dark and gleaming, exactly like its owner.

"Welcome," the Prince says, strolling into the room and throwing himself down on the chaise. The fabric is a dark green threaded with black roses—like his name. He looks like a painting draped atop it, and I have to look away.

I don't dare step farther into this room. The whole place leaves me dizzy, as though Roze's poison has seeped through every inch of it.

"What is this?" I ask.

"This is my room. I rarely use the one in Berlaise. For one thing, it can't fit a piano."

"We're nowhere near the royal residences."

"No. I have my own rooms there as well. I'm occasionally required to visit to keep up appearances, but this is where I spend most of my time, away from meddlesome courtiers—not to mention my sisters."

Roze feels so separate from his family that he cannot bring himself to live near them. But he doesn't live in the school with the rest of us either.

An outcast. Belonging nowhere. Alone. Like me.

No, not like you. No one is like you, a small voice whispers in my mind.

I stare down at my hand, letting my shadows blacken my fingertips. "Who knows about this place?"

"No one."

"Not even Fletcher or Ed?"

He snorts. "Like I would trust Ed with this knowledge."

Waffles, tired of being carried, has started squirming in my arms. I release him, and he immediately flaps over to the nearest piece of furniture and begins a sniff inspection of the entire room.

"You want me to hide here?" I ask Roze as he watches Waffles probe his belongings for any sign of danger . . . or perhaps snacks.

"What I want has very little to do with anything lately. Right now, this is the safest place for you."

Silence hangs between us. The air feels charged now that we're holed in here together. I frown. "But how will we investigate the book if I'm confined to this tower?"

"Make a list of anything you need. I'll bring you whatever I can—from the Crypt, from the Roquelart library—anything."

"I can't know what might be useful unless I can *see* what's there."

"Not an option."

"But—"

"You're in too much danger to leave this room."

"I'll wear a disguise."

"*No.*"

I make a frustrated noise in the back of my throat. Roze is not a researcher. If he does this without me, he'll use those knives he keeps strapped to his chest to find answers, not books. He'll reach the wrong conclusions.

He snorts. "Please, Sinclair. You're as conspicuous as a peacock in a petticoat. Tell me what you need, and I'll bring you what I can."

I huff in annoyance. "If there's anything in the Crypt with runes or with the dragon of Castelle, I need to see it. And perhaps some books on magic. I don't even know how to start parsing the enchantment on the book."

Roze nods.

I take a deep breath. "Well . . . where am I supposed to sleep?" I ask, and immediately realize that there are few things worse that I could have said.

He quirks an eyebrow at me, and the heat in my cheeks worsens. I curl a loose band of hair around my finger to occupy my hands.

"You may sleep where you like. Take the bed—I don't sleep much, and I don't mind the chaise." He backs away, crossing to the pianoforte. "Make yourself comfortable. You're welcome to the bookshelf. I'm sure you're itching to peruse it."

Without looking at me again, he sits at the piano and lifts the lid over the keys. And then he does something entirely unexpected—he takes off his gloves. He tugs the leather off slowly, revealing long, pale fingers. I note again how elegant and lovely they are, like the hands of an artist. My visions from the journey up here return with a vengeance as I think about those hands fisted in my hair, sliding down my chest, gliding up my thighs till they're gripping my hips.

I realize I'm staring and shake myself. I've never felt like *this* before, this burning. Not for Kole. Not for anyone. And my stomach sours at the thought that it's all a waste, because nothing is possible with him. I need to accept that and move on, or the pain will be unbearable.

I cross to the bookshelf and nearly stumble as he starts to play. I turn to watch over his shoulder. The song . . .

It's soft and haunting. His face as he plays is reverent, peaceful—the first I've seen of this expression from him. His eyes are closed, like he's praying. My gaze falls to his fingers as they kiss the keys. I wonder if the poison from his hands is leaving its mark on the piano. It's a wonder that skin so dangerous can create something so beautiful.

His body moves with the music while he plays, rocking forward and backward. I, on the other hand, am frozen. Entranced. I could die to the sound of his melody washing over me.

And gazing at those elegant fingers that kill with their touch, I realize what I should have known days ago . . . Something has begun in me that I can't stop.

CHAPTER TWENTY-FOUR

Roze leaves with the promise to return with research materials for me.

"And that's *all* you'll be doing while you're gone? Finding the books I need?" I ask with a raised eyebrow.

"No," he says, his tone clipped as he straps his knives to his arm.

"And what else does this little excursion entail?"

He dons his jacket and straightens his lapels before simply answering, "Hunting."

And then he's gone. And I'm left feeling utterly useless while I wait for his return, hopefully with an armful of research. Every hour, every minute feels unfathomably precious now. But with the whole castle confined to personal quarters, all the guards searching for *meigas*, for *me*, there isn't much that can be done about it.

I can try to sleep, even if it isn't dark yet. I've been restless all week, and I may as well catch up now and spend the night researching when Roze returns. I approach Roze's bed, spreading a palm over the thick coverlet, and imagine the Prince sleeping there in comfort and luxury.

He said he doesn't sleep much. With a life like his, I suppose no one would.

But . . . to sleep on Roze's bed . . . I don't know if I can bring myself to lie under his covers, to wrap myself in the sheets that he sleeps in. I'm not sure if it's even advisable for my health. Will they have traces of the poison that leaches from his skin on them? Will I fall into death in the night and simply not wake up?

I climb on top of the coverlet and force myself to lie down, stiff as a board at first. But whether by poison or exhaustion or the scent of winter and apples on the fabric, I soon close my eyes and let the darkness take me.

But my sleep is fitful, and my dreams are full of my baby brother's face. I see hands around his neck and then feel them around my own. And for the first time in years, along with the ever-constant feeling of guilt, grief crawls its way inside my chest, and I dream of my brother's hand in mine and the way he smiled while we played.

I wake gasping with a coil of nausea in my gut, covered in cool sweat. I reach up to wipe it from my face and realize that there are tears there too. I pull my legs in tightly and wrap my arms around my knees. The naked truth is that I'm trapped, and I hate it. I've never felt more exposed for what I am.

A danger.

A menace.

Isn't that my fear? That this is why the Queen wants me dead? Because she *knows* what I'm capable of. Because I'm a threat—to the Prince, to the royal family, to everyone.

I will *always* be a threat.

It's not lost on me how similar my shadows and Roze's curse are. But unlike me, he has control of his curse. He wears those gloves and touches no one. He might be trapped, but at least he hasn't killed anyone without intending to.

I *cannot* just sit here and let my mind wander down dark paths while I wait for Roze to return. I need to *do* something. With a frustrated huff, I swing my legs over the side of the bed and cross to the bookshelf.

The titles are surprising. Art and poetry. Tragic plays. Epic poems. I suppose I shouldn't be shocked—as a member of Berlaise House, Roze's studies focus on the arts. I always thought it strange that a person who seemed so . . . inhuman . . . loved the humanities. I used to wonder if he'd chosen Berlaise because he didn't quite understand people and thought that maybe some time in the arts would help him figure out how to be human—wrap his cold mind around things like empathy, friendship, love. Now I know better. I've seen behind his mask.

My eye catches on a small black book. It looks familiar—its spine is worn and free of markings. I pull it from the shelf and flip it open. Inside I find poetry—precise, complex sonnets on each page—the book of poetry that Roze took from the library.

I flip through the pages, and the book falls open to a page marked with a black silk ribbon.

A ribbon that looks hauntingly familiar.

I hold it between two fingers, my mouth falling open. Immediately I know the truth, but my heart somehow can't believe it. This is *my* ribbon— the one I lost that day Roze introduced me to his family and took my hair down in the hall. *He kept it.*

I stare at it, at the frayed edge that I know well. He *kept* it . . . and hid it in a book of poetry.

I think I've been waiting for you my whole life.

A strange mixture of hope and anxiety wells within me. I look down at the page that he has left the ribbon in as a marker.

I nearly drop the book.

Because I recognize this sonnet, particularly the first line.

The heart is the dominion of evil.

My hand is shaking. Like I'm in a dream, I replace the ribbon and return the book to the shelf, as though I can unsee what I have seen.

That sentence was the one that appeared in the book when Cerise and I took it to the laboratory, the sentence that Professor Borges said I'd mistranslated in a way that was too *wooden* just before sending me to be executed.

Roze knows something that I don't. Now I am sure of it.

And there's another thing I am sure of—I need answers. I can't stay in this tower a moment longer. If Roze wanted to keep me safe and seques- tered in his tower . . . Well, he shouldn't have hidden information from me. So I will use my shadows in the only way they've ever served me—to keep me hidden.

It's ridiculous, really. My life and Roze's are threatened, and yet I'm most afraid of running into my parents. But I can't let fear hold me back any longer—I *need* to find Professor Borges. She may be aligned with Castelle, but I won't know until I can speak with her myself. If Roze finds her, he'll show no mercy to the person he thinks is responsible for his father's death—which is why I need to reach her first.

I've already tried searching her office. The next logical step is to look for her where the Queen and her guard are least likely to venture—the caverns. It's also, unfortunately, the last place I want to be. But if finding her means risking seeing my parents, then so be it.

I follow Roze's secret passages with Waffles at my feet, running my hands along the dusty stone wall, looking for one of his exit points. The air is cold, and it seeps through my socks and my sweater. Winter is particularly harsh this year, and it feels like an omen. I nearly sigh with relief when my fingers touch the canvas. I push on the painting and it opens for me, revealing a dark hall on the other side.

No light illuminates the gallery. I allow my shadows to shroud me as I creep through the halls, pausing before each corner, listening for the footsteps of soldiers. There are close calls—a guard turns a corner, and I almost think he sees me before I dash into an alcove and cover myself in shadows. Near the entrance to the servants' quarters, several guards are on patrol, but Waffles is able to make a commotion down an opposite hall—it sounds like he might've attacked a suit of armor—sending them all running toward the noise and away from me, and I slip into the kitchens.

The way into the caverns is odd—a result of a hurried, makeshift solution to thousands of people being stuck together in a castle that was never meant to hold so many. Off the kitchen are storerooms, dark and cool places for keeping vegetables and the rare portions of meat we eat, and these wind into dripping, dark passageways. Stone and mortar give way to the irregular texture of rock—I have to run my hand along the way and tread lightly to keep from stumbling. I should've stolen a candle before coming.

Waffles bounds up behind me, having shaken off the guards, just as the passage widens into a great cavern, a massive open space with stalactites littering the ceiling. Gas lamps are hung from hooks along the wall, and tables are arranged around the room—a sort of common area for the hundreds living in the mountain.

I take a deep breath, inhaling the familiar taste of cool, coppery air, and I realize that it has been *years* since I last came this way. I have no reason to revisit the orphanage or my parents.

I pull my sweater tightly around myself and head toward the first of many halls leading to residences. I have no idea where the professor might be, but I don't have much time. The whole castle is looking for *me*, and it won't be long before the guards search for me here.

The first hall leads to nothing, except the pale faces of common folk scowling at me when I knock on their doors. Some of them I recognize from childhood.

They know me. They know the guards are searching for me, and they could turn me in. I suppose it depends on whether they still think of me as one of them even while I'm wearing Roze's ring.

In the second hall I round a corner and hear the echo of a child's laughter. A girl no taller than my waist runs past me, a fistful of small bones in her hand. I smile, remembering the games we would play with chicken bones in the orphanage—drop them in a pile and see if you can pull one free without moving the others. We made do just fine without real toys.

"Come back, you!" a familiar voice shouts, and my heart skips a beat.

A moment later, Kole jogs around a corner, face flushed, and his eyes land on me.

"Viola," he says breathlessly.

He's manipulating you, whispers Roze's voice in my head.

"Hi," I say. "What are you doing here?"

He looks to the right and left and steps close to me, almost like he's trying to hide me from sight. "I should ask *you* that. When they locked down the castle, I decided I'd rather be here with my family than shut up in Marquet-Blanc." He points to the little girl now clambering over a rock formation. "That's my niece."

"Oh."

"What are you doing here?" he repeats. His eyes look slightly panicked as they scan my face. "The things they're saying, Vi—"

"I know," I say. "They aren't true."

He sighs and runs a hand through his hair. "We need to talk. Let's get you out of the open."

He leads me down a side passage to an alcove used for storage. A few crates are stacked in a corner with what looks to be a supply of soap rations and rags.

"I'm looking for Professor Borges," I say, not wanting to waste any time. "It's important. Have you seen her down here?"

Kole shakes his head. "Can't say I have."

My shoulders slump. "I thought she might be staying with family. She's been missing from Vandenberghe for days." I shake my head. "I have to keep looking, even if I knock on every door."

"Is this about that book you showed me?"

I look up at him. His hands are on his hips, and his jaw is clenched—he's worried. "Yes."

Kole shakes his head. "I know you said it was important, but is it really that important right *now*? Viola, they're saying you killed the Queen. They're saying you're a *meiga*." He exhales a shaky breath.

I hesitate, biting my lip. I study Kole's face—his peat-green eyes that have always been so full of compassion and curiosity.

He's never given me a reason not to trust him.

And I need people I can trust, now more than ever.

"I need to tell you something," I start, fiddling with the sleeve of my sweater. "I didn't kill the Queen. But it's true . . . I am a *meiga*, Kole."

I catch the moment the truth hits him, his pupils narrowing slightly, his nostrils flaring. He freezes for a moment and then takes a deep breath. "Okay . . ."

"I know I should have told you earlier. I was just so afraid. I've kept it to myself for years because I didn't know what you'd think, and I was scared. But now things have gone so horribly wrong—"

He leans a hand against the wall to steady himself. "Okay. Okay," he says. "Does the Prince know?"

I nod.

He looks back down at the floor and shakes his head. "Saints, it all makes sense. How did I not guess it?"

He still isn't looking at me.

"Kole," I say, taking a tentative step forward. I reach out a hand to place it on his shoulder . . .

And he flinches.

"Kole?"

He bends over, dropping his head into his hands.

"What's wrong?" I ask.

"How could you do this to me, Vi?"

Something drops in my stomach.

"Do what?"

His breathing turns heavy. "They're hunting down *meigas* as we speak. They're looking for you everywhere. What am I supposed to do now?"

I take a step back. "You can help me find Professor Borges. She can help."

His eyes are set on the floor, his face blank.

"Kole, look at me."

"What do you want me to say, Viola?"

I choke. "That you'll help me. Say that we'll figure this out together."

"You're a *meiga*."

"We're not what the Crown says we are. We're not evil."

"It doesn't *matter*," he hisses, standing up straight.

I take another step back. "Why are you angry at me?"

"Why am I angry? I have to decide whether to turn you over to the guard or risk being tried for treason myself, and you want to know why I'm angry?"

Ice slides down my back.

He finally meets my gaze, and when he does, there is only fear and fury in his eyes. I know with sudden certainty—he doesn't see his friend anymore. He sees a threat.

Roze's words ring in my head. *Men like him discard people as soon as they fail to prove themselves useful.*

And suddenly, the guise that I've been wearing with Kole for months shatters around me. I am unmasked, and it's too late to pull myself back.

"What's wrong with you?" I bark. "We're *friends*."

"And yet, you've been keeping this from me this whole time."

"Because I was *afraid*. And it turns out I had good reason to be." I glare at him with a venom that I haven't felt for anyone, even for Roze.

An expression forms on Kole's features that I've never seen before—bitterness and hatred. It turns his handsome face ugly. "What were you hoping I'd do now? Tell you it was all going to be all right, that it doesn't matter to me what you are? Maybe you were hoping I'd tell you that I've had feelings for you for ages, that I'd love you no matter what."

His words are like a slap. Blood drains from my face.

He narrows his eyes at me. "Yeah, I've noticed. You're really damn obvious, Viola."

"I didn't— I haven't— I didn't expect anything—"

"It doesn't matter. I was going to tell you I didn't feel the same way, but I was hesitating because I didn't want to hurt our friendship. But now?" He shakes his head and curses again. "I can't believe you're doing this to me."

I snap. "*I'm* doing this to *you*?" Waffles starts to growl at my feet and shadows pour from my fingertips, and I don't even think to stop them. "My life is in danger, Kole. My *life*. All I did was turn to a friend, and now you're acting like—like my mere existence is some great insult to you."

He shakes his head, looking at me with something like . . . disgust. "You're not stupid, Viola. You have to know what you are. The fact that you thought you and I could—" An unmistakable shudder tremors through his body, and a feeling worse than death unfurls in my heart.

He's afraid of me.

He's disgusted by me.

The pain in my heart is real, visceral. Shattering.

"I just wanted your help," I mutter. My voice is small and pathetic. The way he's looking at me is like I should have known. Like I'm being presumptuous by daring to have feelings for him.

I am nothing.

My magic has made me worse than nothing.

A disease. A menace.

Darkness starts to cloud my vision and my heart. Waffles yips to get my attention, but I barely hear him. I don't even notice my shadows beginning to flow freely from my fingertips as my mind fills with memories— the disgust on my parents' faces when my shadows first appeared, so similar to Kole's expression now; my mother's heartbreak as she held my brother's limp body; my father's rage. *My fault. My ugliness. My evil.*

The absurd urge to tear open my own flesh and rip my shadows out with my bare hands consumes me. But instead, they burst from me like water breaking a dam, and I scream. I fall to my knees, barely cognizant of my surroundings, but I know my shadows are *everywhere*, and I don't care. I'm so tired—of holding back, pretending not to feel, hiding.

Tears fall down my cheeks, not just for Kole, but for my parents, for my brother, for every hateful word ever spoken against what I am, for a lifetime of pain that I've borne like a soldier. I'm breaking. I can't carry the burden anymore.

The pounding of footsteps breaks through my thoughts. I swing my head toward the hall just as a pair of men round the corner. My shadows instantly spring back to me, hiding beneath my flesh. *But they saw.* I'm sure they saw them. The men blink like they aren't quite sure of themselves.

"Are you all right, Miss?" one of them says, holding a light up high to see my face. His clothing tells me he's a commoner, like me. "We heard a—"

He stops dead. His eyes are no longer on me—they're set several feet away. And when I follow the track of his gaze . . .

Oh Saints.

Kole is on the ground. His body lies at an odd, twisted angle, skin pale as ash, almost bluish, and his eyes . . . his eyes stare right at me, fixed on me but not seeing me.

"Is—is that boy dead?" the other man asks.

I don't answer. I've lost my voice. My ears are ringing.

No. No, no, NO.

One of them approaches, inspects him, looks for a pulse. He doesn't need to say aloud what all three of us already know.

He turns toward me slowly, eyes narrowed. "What happened?"

I choke. Words won't come.

This isn't happening. This can't be happening.

"Why's he all twisted like that?" says the other man, taking a step backward.

More footsteps. Several more people enter the hall.

"What's going on?"

"Who screamed?"

"Oh my Saints, is he—"

And then I hear the words that break me out of my trance. One of the first two men says, "I thought I saw . . . I wasn't sure, but . . . now the boy's dead, and . . ."

"*Stop blabbering.* What did you see?"

His eyes find mine. "It was her. She—she had this darkness coming from her. It was everywhere. And then the boy was dead."

Silence resounds as every face in the hall turns toward me. Waffles nips at my shin, urging me to get up.

Go, I urge myself. *Get out NOW!*

Then I'm running. I shove people aside, sprinting for the exit to the castle, not registering faces. Waffles flaps behind me, growling and gnashing at anyone who gets too close. My tears are cold against my cheeks as I run at a full sprint.

I don't slow down until I reach the safety of Roze's tower, and I lock myself inside.

CHAPTER TWENTY-FIVE

At least Roze looks as bad as I feel.

He returns to the tower sometime after I do—I'm not sure how long. Time seems to have turned funny. I might've waited for him for five minutes or five hours. Either way, I spent the entire time staring at the wall, the memory of Kole's dead eyes plaguing my brain.

Roze leans against the doorframe, his skin pale and clothes rumpled. And he's covered in blood.

"I've taken care of our undead guard problem," he says. He sidles over to his desk, and I notice a slight limp in his step. He draws a flask from a drawer, and I don't want to ask what's in it as he takes a long swig. He hunches over his desk, breathing deeply.

"What did you do?" I ask, thinking of the professor. Did he find her before me?

"Belladonna believes you're dead," he says, and turns to me. His gaze meets mine, but his eyes are distant—the cold indifference of a born killer. Saints, how I wish I could do that—kill and feel nothing. But then again, Roze excels at masking his true feelings.

"What happened with the undead guard?"

He lowers his head. "When my mother commanded me to kill you, she asked for your heart as proof of your death. I put the guard's heart in a box, gave it to Belladonna, and told her it was yours. Removing the guard's heart seems to have stopped him."

I wrap my sweater tightly around myself. "And Belladonna believes you?"

He pauses. "Bella is cunning. I don't know whether she believed me. But regardless, she's put the supposed heart of the Queen's killer on display in the grand entrance."

My stomach sours.

"What about your mother?"

"My mother's spirit is with Belladonna. My hope was that she would be convinced as well, that she would consider my orders fulfilled and the magic binding the tattoo would be broken."

I glance at his covered arm, the sleeve speckled with dark blood. "But?"

He sighs. "The tattoo remains."

I swallow. Every time hope is dashed it feels like the fall of a blunt axe on my neck—*our* necks. Swing after painful swing until death finally decides to claim us.

We both look at the floor without really looking at it. Roze steadies himself with a hand against the chair by his desk, and it's only then that I realize his gloves are off, long fingers wrapped around the chair back. The fingers of a musician, fingers still caked in blood.

I imagine those fingers on my cheek, on my neck, tangled in my hair . . .

"I can't do this," I murmur. I'm not sure what I'm referring to.

He pulls his gloves from his pocket, tugging them back over his fingers. I think I'm relieved. I was staring at those fingers the way one watches a snake swallow a mouse, fascinated and scandalized.

"What can't you do?" he says. His tone is low with exhaustion.

Of all the things I feel like I can't do right now, I choose the simplest. "I can't stay in this tower, waiting for our time to run out."

He grimaces, but there's a fracture of empathy in his eyes. "You step outside this room, and she'll find you. The guards are everywhere. My mother's power can reach you anywhere."

I clench and unclench my fists. "I never wanted my powers. All I've ever wanted is to learn and to do something with my life that matters, that . . ."

That makes up for what I did.

Tears burn my eyes. Shadows press at my fingertips, and I beg them both to go away. Roze is watching me closely, like he's just now trying to decipher what I am.

"You don't owe the Kingdom anything," he says. "No matter what happened."

I shake my head. He's wrong. I owe it everything. I know what my shadows are capable of. Now more than ever.

He crosses the room to me. I try not to look at him—my captor, my savior. But he puts a gloved hand under my chin and lifts my eyes to his.

"I *will* get you your life back," he says. His voice is low and strained. "I promise. You deserve to exist without fear."

I almost falter. I almost fall into him. It would be so easy. I feel raw and exposed, like a wound, and I want to wrap myself up in Roze to stop the bleeding. I want to plunge so deeply into him—his body, his words, his soul—that I forget the boundaries between us, that I lose all sense of me and him, and we just become *us*.

My voice comes out a reedy whisper, "What if I *am* something to fear?"

He shakes his head as he scans my face. His breath is close enough to make my head feel fuzzy. The scent of him—spice, winter, apples, and something else that I now realize is the scent of his poison. He's dangerous in the loveliest way. Elegant peril.

"If their peace is disturbed by your existence," he says, "then they never deserved peace."

His words spear me, break me like a battering ram. Because he's *wrong*.

"I left the tower," I admit.

He blinks. "*What?*"

"I needed to find Professor Borges, so I went down to the caverns—"

"*Viola.*"

"I told Kole that I'm a *meiga*."

Roze stares. "You told . . . Kole Belcamp . . . about your magic."

I bite my lip. "Yes, and—"

"Did he hurt you?"

"No."

His eyes flash. "Lucky him. If he had, I'd wrap his intestines around his neck and shove them down his throat until he choked and died on his own entrails." He sweeps away from me back toward the bookshelf. "And I'm not in the mood for another mess."

I cringe, even if a part of me longs for that protection. "You hate him that much?"

"I didn't give a damn about him before. Now he knows your secret. Now, he's a threat."

I close my eyes. I've cried them dry. Now they just burn. "Roze," I whisper, letting the words leak from me like ink into water, like poison into wine. "I killed him."

He stops, his hand caught midair where he'd been about to skim the spine of a book. The back of his head is still—no indication of any emotion, any reaction whatsoever. I stare at his snowy locks, desperately wishing I could read his mind through them.

"So," he says in a voice low and careful, "not a threat, then."

It's a joke that lands like a punch to my stomach. "Please don't—"

"How did you do it?" He turns, and his face is cold—not judgmental, not sympathetic or approving, just stoic.

"I didn't mean to."

He snorts. "Obviously."

For some reason, that makes me bristle. "You don't think I could? If I really had to?"

He falls casually into his armchair, looking up at me with that aristocratic expression that makes him look especially punchable. "Darling, I think you'd put your own head in the guillotine if you thought it'd make someone else's life easier. That's just the problem."

"You're *wrong*," I screech, the conviction of my words straining my already raw throat. Every cell in my body feels wide awake, and shadows swirl around my fingertips.

He raises an eyebrow. "A little killer, are you?"

"Meigas *are dangerous. Look what I did to my brother!*" I shout. Darkness swirls around my fists, streaming to my ankles in dark tendrils.

Roze doesn't balk, even as the shadows pool at his ankles, licking at the hem of his pants. "You were a child. It was an accident."

"That doesn't make me any less of a monster," I spit. I feel like a monster now. Like I might grow claws and teeth at any moment and become the darkness itself.

"It does." He stands from his chair, buttons his bloody jacket, and takes a step toward me—a show of trust, or possibly a death wish. "I've lived my whole life with a mother who is a *real* monster. Believe me, Viola, it does." I stare at him through my grief and rage, and the expression on his face is soft. Unguarded. I take a deep breath, and my shadows begin to taper.

"I don't want these powers," I whisper—my silent wish since childhood.

"I know," he whispers back, like we're children sharing a schoolyard secret. "Neither do I."

He reaches toward me, takes my face in both his gloved hands, and leans his head toward mine, like he wants to touch our foreheads together . . . but of course, he can't. "You're no monster, Viola," he whispers, quicksilver eyes piercing the darkness in mine. "Although," he says with a smirk, "as someone who's been on the receiving end of your right hook, you are rather vicious."

My lips twinge upward of their own accord.

For a long, quiet moment, we stand there. I grip his forearms while he holds my face, fabric separating true touch. But for now, it's enough. It's as much comfort as either of us will get.

Eventually I pull back and wipe my eyes on my sweater sleeve. Looking for a way to change the subject, I ask, "If your mother was such a monster, how did your father survive her?"

Roze takes a step back, slides his hands into his pockets, and shrugs. "I think Mother might have been kind once. But apparently, that was before I was . . . created. I don't remember it. I believe their relationship was at least cordial in the beginning."

"But it wasn't love."

Roze frowns, turning toward his desk, and begins to remove his blood-stained outer clothing. "A form of it. Although perhaps there are better words. Theirs was an arranged marriage. For my father, I'd say he . . . esteemed Mother, at least at first. But mostly he agreed to marry her because she was the princess of a small kingdom that had thus far refused to assimilate into Aragoa, and it gave us an advantage in the war for them to marry. But Mother . . . for her I'd call it an obsession."

I lift my eyebrows. "Obsession?"

He nods. "She was a formidable woman. She *always* got what she wanted, except with my father. She never quite had *all* his attention, and it drove her mad. She went to greater and greater lengths to please him, and the more she pursued, the more he pulled away. She became parasitic, eating away at everything he was, his very will to live, until he was . . . Well, I'm sure you remember what your King was like in his final months."

I do. He'd attended fewer and fewer public appearances, always looking wan and distant, like his body was there, but his mind was somewhere else.

I study Roze. "And which are you more like? Your mother or your father?"

He freezes, then slowly looks over his shoulder at me, a hard glint in his eye. "What do you think, Sinclair? Do I look like someone who will settle for anything less than having everything I want?"

I swallow, but I've spent enough time around Roze now to know how to see through his intimidation. I step toward him, and he watches me carefully. "I think you're neither. I think you'd rather lay your own life down than slowly leach the life from someone you claim to love."

I reach out and take his hand. He stares down at our joined hands in surprise, the dark leather contrasted against my skin.

"You're nothing like your mother," I whisper. "And you're better than them both."

Roze sleeps on the chaise, and I settle into the bed after he assures me with a sly grin that his sheets won't kill me. It feels strange to be in his bed. I imagine him lying in the black silk at night, always alone, always in the dark.

Any discomfort I had about sleeping there vanishes when I tuck myself in. This bed is *exquisite*, more comfortable than anything I've ever slept on before. That's not saying much—I moved from my bed at the orphanage to the one in Berlaise House. It's soft and cool and it envelops me like a cocoon.

From my place under the covers, I watch as Roze readies himself for sleep, undoing the buttons of his shirt.

I shouldn't look.

It's rude.

But I do anyway. I bite my lip, feeling my cheeks burn at the sight of his pale chest and the taut leather straps still securing a myriad of knives over his sleeves. There must not be an ounce of fat on him, all of him hard ridges and planes. He reminds me of the knives he has bound to his body— solid, silver, sharp . . . absolutely lethal. The body of an assassin.

He turns his face suddenly toward me where I'm tucked under the covers, and a devilish grin spreads across his face. "Should I wear something more modest, Sinclair? Your blush is up to your hairline."

I glare at him from beneath the covers. "I was just imagining what it would be like to strangle you with those leather straps."

He throws his head back and laughs—airy and aristocratic. He crosses to the chaise and drawls, "I could make a joke about breath play, but I don't want to offend your virginal ears."

I blush down to my toes and hide my face in the blankets up to my eyeballs. "How did you know?"

"What, that you're a virgin?" He throws himself down, long legs draping off the edges of the chaise. "I didn't until you just confirmed it. It was a well-informed guess."

"You're a prick."

He chuckles lightly. "There's no shame in it, Sinclair."

I've spent my teen years throwing myself into academia partly to avoid my tangled feelings about relationships and intimacy. Thoughts of romance—of sex—bring up a knotted mess of emotions—longing to be finally, fully wanted but fearing that my shadows will keep anyone from coming too close.

Better to keep such desires to myself and in the dark, where they belong.

"Are you not a virgin? You can't touch people."

He shrugs. "True. But I've found creative ways around that." He cocks an eyebrow and winks. "The gloves help."

The blood drains from my face. He barks a laugh at my expression and settles himself farther back onto the chaise.

Moments later, he murmurs into the dark, "Good night, darling."

Three little words, but I replay the sound of them over and over in my head as I fall asleep.

THE SIXTH
DEADLY THORN

So the Prince hid the girl away in his lonely tower, but his clever schemes did not thwart the wicked Queen. Still she lurked in the dark castle halls, finding new and devilish ways to unleash her nightmares, waiting for that moment when the Prince and the Shadow Girl were too wrapped in each other to see her coming strike.

And the most nightmarish of all the Queen's weapons were not the specters she spun with her magic, but the very lies that the Shadow Girl and her Prince whispered to each other in the dark. They wove their hearts together with threads of deceit, and the Queen laid her trap with the tangle of them, that they might be caught together in a web of their own making.

CHAPTER TWENTY-SIX

Dim light filters through the Mists over the piano in the morning. I curl into Waffles and soak up the warmth in a bed so comfortable I could die.

Roze has gone somewhere, so I languish in bed for a few minutes, thinking.

We have until sundown tomorrow. A day and a little more left.

That's all the time we have, and I wonder if Roze has started to feel as I have—that this is all hopeless, that we are running from something bigger than both of us, that it can't be outrun or outsmarted.

Eventually, I sit up and push my feet into Roze's slippers. I love that he has slippers—even if they're the most elegant, dark slippers I could imagine existing. The thought of owning anything for simply its coziness goes against everything I know about him, but Roze is complex, like the flower he's named for. There are layers upon layers to pluck like petals, each time discovering something new. Perhaps that's part of the reason I'm warming to him. I like complexities, and he's a puzzle I could solve forever.

I'm stoking the fire when he opens the door carrying a teapot and a small package under his arm.

A smile breaks on my face, but he stops abruptly in the doorway. Roze's eyebrows shoot toward his hairline as he glances me over.

Oh. I'd completely forgotten that I'd tossed my skirt aside just before crawling into bed the night before. My shirt is barely long enough to cover my rear.

"Sorry," I say, retrieving my skirt from where I hung it over a chair.

He recovers and smirks. "By all means, don't clothe yourself on my account, Sinclair."

I glare at him while I pull on my skirt.

He busies himself with pouring tea while I make myself decent. In a few minutes, he's set two cups of dark tea and a plate of pastries from that box on the small table before the fire.

Saint Waffles leaps up on the chaise and rests his head on my lap. I glance at Roze to see if he'll disapprove of Waffles being on his fancy furniture, but he says nothing as he leans back in his armchair, one elegant leg crossed over the other while he sips his tea. He's dressed more casually this morning—slacks and a sweater of dark gray instead of his usual black. Every inch a prince.

"There are two thorns now," he says. My heart sinks all over again at the reminder. One will disappear at sundown tonight. The other, at sundown tomorrow—the moment Roze's time to execute me expires, and his life will be forfeit.

Roze brushes his pants leg. "What I still don't understand is why my mother is so determined to have *your* life. You're hardly the only *meiga* to exist. This bloodlust she has for you doesn't make sense."

I bite my cheek, organizing the information we have in my head. "Your father was a Grimmstone. He wanted the war with Castelle to end, at least when he was younger. Now he's dead. And your mother wants me dead. I'm one of the only people who might be able to find and translate the *Book of Odds*, which will rid us of the Mists and free us from the castle."

"You're suggesting there's some truth my mother doesn't want discovered if the Mists fall, that it might have to do with Castelle and the war."

I shrug. "Professor Borges was the only person capable of learning how to translate that book. If she's disappeared and your mother wants me dead as well—" I look up at him.

He nods, his eyes hard. "We keep you alive, and we find Professor Borges."

I exhale deeply, meeting his gaze. "This is bigger than our survival. If I'm right, the Kingdom's survival depends on this."

Roze says, "I'll search for the professor. You stay in the tower and go through the materials I brought you. Try to find out what my mother knows." He glances out the window at the swirling Mists. "Find out what will happen when the Mists fall."

I eye the stacks of books and manuscripts on his desk, and though I'm itching to get my hands on them—

"I'm going with you."

"You most certainly are not."

I huff. "I have to speak with her myself." And Roze can't go alone. I need to be there to shield her from him. He would drag her before Belladonna, and I can't let that fate befall my mentor, whether she's a traitor or not. "She gave me the book. I need to know why. Let me come with you. I'm just as capable of keeping myself hidden as you are with my shadows."

"My sister isn't nearly as determined to see *my* head on a platter—"

"Are you sure about that?"

He sighs, smoothing a hand over his hair. "I think it's very likely that Professor Borges collaborated with my mother to have you killed."

I pause. Then a manic laugh escapes my throat. "That's ridiculous. I *know* Professor Borges," I argue.

"You *think* you know her."

"That's rather condescending. Besides, we thought Professor Borges was allied with Castelle. She can't be allied with Castelle and your mother."

"I'm trying to keep you alive, Sinclair."

"Oh, it's *Sinclair* now, is it? Last night it was Viola."

"Last night you weren't so irritating."

I cross my arms. "You know, for a moment, I forgot how awful you are."

"Your first mistake," he says. He wipes his mouth with a napkin and stands. "The whole Kingdom is searching for you, darling. And what's worse, after what happened to Belcamp, everyone knows why. I don't trust a soul outside this door with you unless they have a death moth inked on their skin." He crosses to the door.

"Where are you going?" I ask.

"To the other Grimmstones, and I will find Professor Borges and speak to her," he says. "You're right that we need to question her, but you're not leaving this tower."

"You *need* my help," I object.

"No, Sinclair. I need you to stay out of sight." He opens the door. "Don't leave."

"Wait, *Roze*—" I rush forward, but he slams it in my face.

I try the handle, but then I hear the click of a key in the lock.

The bastard locked me in.

"*Roze!*" I screech. I jiggle the lock furiously and kick the door. "Roze, come back here and let me out!"

There's no response.

I bang my fist on the door. "*Roze!*"

Still fuming, I drop onto the piano bench, glaring at the gold doorknob and imagining all the things I'll scream at Roze when he returns.

Maybe I'll say nothing. Maybe I'll just punch him in the nose again.

I fidget with the hem of my skirt, chewing on the edge of my tongue. It's torture—sitting here while he takes all the risk. The best I can do is throw myself into research with a vengeance.

With the King lie the answers.
With the King lies salvation.
The heart is the dominion of evil.

He and that strange sonnet are the key to stopping the Queen. I know it in my bones, and I need to know what the poem means, why it appeared in the book, and why Roze has it marked in a book of sonnets.

My gaze wanders to the window beside the piano. Through the Mists, I can barely make out the tops of adjacent towers around Roze's.

And then something catches my eye.

Below Roze's tower, at the edge of the lake, is a turret with a domed roof of glass. I recognize that dome.

Going to the window, I press my hands up against the glass. My view is hazy through the Mists, but I squint my eyes, and then I'm certain—I'm looking at the Crypt, the home of the Grimmstones. It just barely juts from the water, surrounded by windowless stone walls, hidden from view from either the shore or castle windows—all except this one. It's barely visible through the Mists.

Secretive. Like Roze. Prince of Secrets.

A dark shape on the stone catches my eye. Wiping condensation from the window with the sleeve of my sweater, I squint harder, forcing my eyes to focus.

My breath catches. A Hivernian rune is carved into the stone surrounding the dome, one of the four on the cover of the Book of Castelle. And there—another. And two more on the other side. The runes make a complete circle. I run to the bedside table where I left the book. Sure enough, the runes match those that circle the seal of the entwined dragon and lion.

So the Book of Castelle and the Grimmstones are connected. Why? The answers must lie in the Crypt.

I glance toward the door. I have to get out of here. We're running out of time, and I can't sit on this information until Roze returns. I doubt Roze has a key to the door hidden somewhere, but maybe there's something I can pick the lock with. If only I had Kole's key that can open anything.

I pull open the drawers of his desk and find only scrap paper full of scribbled musical scores and a few fountain pens, nothing I can use on the lock. I sigh, pivoting to a different idea. What if there's another way out? Roze *is* known for his hidden passages.

I set about investigating the room, making more of a mess than is *absolutely* necessary. I'm being petty, throwing pillows aside, tossing back sheets, scattering books on the floor after checking inside each one, but it serves Roze right. He locked me in here, after all, and I've had about enough of having my life tempered by others' expectations.

After thoroughly dismantling the room, I've found *nothing*, and I flop back on the bed, stripped of its sheets, annoyed and sweating. I refuse to be consoled by the obnoxious softness of the mattress.

Now I'm furious at him. Everything about him is rich and sleek and perfect—like a snake.

I study the headboard beside me as I lie there, glaring at its carved, mahogany perfection. The stain is so dark it's nearly black, and the scrollwork is exquisite. Delicate little leaves and, of course, roses are strung on spiny vines netting the entire thing. In the center is a framed face of some sort of fiend, its mouth twisted into an odd smile. Its eyes are oddly deep and seem to watch me no matter which way I turn my head. In fact, they're too deep.

I sit up in the bed and crawl closer to the face. I extend a shaking hand toward it, inserting a finger into the eyeholes, half expecting something to bite me or else snatch my soul into the afterlife.

But instead, I touch wood, and it gives way. A mechanism clicks, and a seam in the headboard cracks open. My breath is shaky as I push on the face, and it opens onto a dark tunnel.

The tunnel before me is black as night and so narrow that my torso would barely be able to fit through.

I look over my shoulder at Roze's destroyed room, at Waffles lying flat on his back, soundly asleep before the hearth, and then turn back to stare into the tunnel, like the mouth of some waiting monster, faced with a choice I very much do *not* want to make. I could just stay in the tower and wait for Roze to return. My secret is out—the whole Kingdom knows I'm a *meiga*. They believe I'm dangerous . . . and they're right.

But then I think about the two thorns left on Roze's arm. I think of the feel of leather sliding across my cheek and the hope in his voice— *we'll think of something*. It's enough to make me push myself into the space.

It's terribly dark, like a blanket of shadows. I'm forced to lift myself up on my elbows, my shoulder jutting painfully into the low ceiling. I scramble forward on my forearms, my feet dragging behind me on dusty stone. I feel my feet drag over the lip of the headboard, and I'm fully inside the tunnel.

I'm just starting to get my bearings when the headboard door slams shut behind me.

I gasp, inhaling dust into my mouth, and I cough.

No no no.

I try to crane my head around to see the door, but even if I did have enough room to peer over my shoulder, it's too dark. I can't see anything. My shadows slam against my mental walls that hold them back, curling around my fingertips as panic rises in my throat.

Calm.

Stay calm.

Shuffling backward, I try to kick at the headboard with my shoe. It doesn't budge. I try again, this time kicking harder, but the headboard is sealed tight. There's no room for me to turn around.

I take a deep breath and lay my head on the stony floor.

It's fine.

No way out but forward.

I push myself on my elbows, crawling an inch at a time. The darkness is so thick that my eyes are blown wide. All I have are the feel of the stones under my fingers to claw my way forward.

Before long I'm breathing heavily. The air is stale. I wonder how long it's been since this passage has been used.

Not much longer, and I'm cursing the brashness that led me to crawl into this hole. Wouldn't it have made more sense to wait for Roze?

A lot of good it'll do me now.

One arm in front of the other, legs dragging behind me, knees scraping on the stone. The tunnel begins to slope downward. I hope desperately that I'm going down into the castle.

There are forks in the passages, and I guess at random which will lead me to an exit, keeping track of my path in my head. *Left. Left. Right. Left. Middle. Right. Left.*

But after an hour of not finding a way out, I'm beginning to question this whole endeavor. I should crawl back . . . return to the tower, wait for Roze, and bang on the headboard until he hears me.

But when I begin scooting my way back through the passages, there are turns that I don't remember. I was so careful to map my path, but none of it makes sense now.

I try to retrace my crawling, moving back down the passage and starting over, but I find myself in another unfamiliar passage. And yet . . . they all seem the same. Pitch black. Cold. Too small for my body.

It's like the passages have rearranged themselves while I've been crawling. I should be able to sense which way is up—that will lead me to the tower. But each time I try to climb higher, I find myself crawling deeper down, like the world has been turned on its head.

I'm not sure how long I crawl, each tunnel no taller than I can lift my head, no broader than my shoulders. Or how far. The minutes melt into hours, and I know . . . I'm completely lost.

There is only the sound of my breathing as I see nothing and think of everything. I have nothing to do with my time except reflect on what has led me here and keep crawling.

At some point, the stone turns damp and freezing.

At some point, the skin of my elbows and legs goes numb.

At some point, my fingers turn bloody as they scrape on the stones, and I stop feeling the pain.

At some point, I begin talking to myself.

Sometimes I laugh.

Sometimes I cry.

Has it been hours or days?

I roll on my back to rest. I think I fall asleep. Maybe this happens several times—I forget.

My throat is so dry it hurts. I wonder if a far-future excavation will reveal the bones of a teenage girl in the stone walls of the castle of Aragoa. I can appreciate the irony. Earlier this week, I buried a man in the floor.

Still I crawl on. The passage begins to narrow, and the small amount of room that I'd had to lift myself is gone. I pull myself forward. The tunnel is so small that I can't bend my elbow. I reach my arms out in front of me and scrape forward by the tips of my fingers, dragging my body against the stone until the ceiling presses against my back and the floor squashes my breasts . . . until I struggle to breathe. The walls on either side press into my shoulders.

It's no use. It's time to give up. I know I can't go on. I know it would be foolish to call attention to my presence in the wall—the whole Kingdom is searching for me. But my throat is raw, and my body has reached its breaking point. I'm lost and so tired, so tired.

I pound my fist against the side of the passage, but my body is weaker than I expected. My pounding barely makes a sound.

"*Hello?*" I shout, my voice coming out raw and weak. "Help me! Someone help!"

Is Roze already up in the tower, wondering where I've gone, furious scowl on his face? That's if years haven't passed since I entered the darkness of the tunnel. Time feels like a fuzzy, useless thing now.

Perhaps it's easier to give up.

I stop pounding on the wall.

I just need a minute to rest.

I lay my head against the cool stone and close my eyes.

In a hazy state of half consciousness, I contemplate several things.

First, that in my relatively short life, there are few things I'm genuinely proud of. I have spent each and every moment since my brother died living in fear. I wish I'd been braver.

Second, that I don't hate Roze. In fact, what I do feel for him is warm, wild, and desperate—something like a fever. I don't hate it.

Third, that I don't want to die.

———

There's a soft scraping sound in the tunnel—too close. My eyes fly open, and I freeze. Something furry brushes against my leg.

I twitch and shriek, banging my leg painfully against the side of the tunnel.

I can still feel it there. Something is moving, curling around my leg, around the back of my knee with a featherlight touch.

I scream and thrash against it, shoving myself forward into the impossibly small space. I keep moving, but its small body curls around me, scraping and hissing softly with small, sharp feet. There's nowhere left to go, and I can't get away from it. *I can't get away.*

"Help! Someone, help me!" I shout, jerking my legs violently trying to crush the thing, kicking over and over. But it climbs higher, scraping and scampering, curling up my thigh.

I thrash forward, turning my head to the side so that it will fit in the narrow space of the tunnel. I stretch forward into the blackness. I kick my feet mercilessly.

But it's climbing high up my leg, under my skirt, against my inner thigh.

I scrape the stone ahead of me. My fingernails are now bloody shards. The walls press in so painfully that I'm surely about to dislocate a shoulder.

The creature hisses angrily. I feel its claws climb higher, reaching the tender skin between my legs. Something brushes against my underwear.

I scream—the sort of scream that haunts castles this old. I scream and scrape and flail. My shadows shoot from me—

The wall beside me trembles. I freeze, fear and hope vibrating side by side in my chest like a tuning fork. And then light breaks through the wall, spraying my eyes with dust and rock. I don't care. I shove my hands through the opening, pulling myself forward and away from whatever is trying to gnaw into my skin.

I tumble out onto the floor, still thrashing madly, the feeling of little feet littering my skin everywhere as I swat my hands all over my body, trying to get it off.

Someone grabs hold of my wrists, and I look up. And Professor Borges's perplexed face peers back at me.

CHAPTER TWENTY-SEVEN

Professor Borges blinks, her eyes wide behind her spectacles. "Miss Sinclair?"

I try to speak, and it comes out as a cough and then a sob.

The professor tuts. "Dear, what happened?" she reaches down to help me to my feet, gently brushing me off and looking me over.

"It's a long story." I struggle to get the words loose. My head is pounding.

Her brow wrinkles as she inspects me, and then she glances down the hall behind me.

"As I'm sure you know, the castle is locked down." Her lips pinch together as though she's locked in indecision. "The kitchens aren't far. Let's get you cleaned up and find you a nice cup of tea."

I'm too weak to form a coherent thought, and I slump against her as she loops her arm through my elbow and leads me down the hall.

My vision rocks, and the lights from the gas lamps are blurred as we pass them. The pain in my head is beginning to recede.

"Professor, where have you been?" I ask, nearly sobbing. "I've been looking everywhere—"

"I'm sure you have, dear. And I'm sorry. The truth is, I've been in hiding."

"Hiding?"

"Yes. It's more complicated than I can explain right now, and you're in no state to absorb it anyway. Suffice it to say that I knew things were about to go sour. I fled."

My head is fuzzy, and I resolve to not ask any more questions until the spots disappear from my vision.

"I don't recognize this part of the castle," I say weakly.

"Never mind that, dear. I'll explain everything. Save your voice."

She leads me through a door into a kitchen. It's large enough for a team of cooks, and I wonder if this kitchen cooks for nobles, perhaps even the royal family.

Her bony hand still grips my elbow as she pulls me toward a long table and sets me down on a stool. She lights a candle and puts the kettle on the stove while I stare at the floor and gather my thoughts and stop the trembling in my limbs.

"Thank you," I say, "for rescuing me. I don't—"

I can't finish the sentence. I'm not ready to put into words the doom that was going through my mind in the passage. Not yet.

"Just, thank you," I finish.

She peers at me over her shoulder, her mouth set grimly. "You are very lucky I was close by. I heard a scream from the walls, and I was sure I was being haunted." She chuckles to herself, like it's an absurd thought. If she only knew.

"How did you break into the wall?" I ask. Professor Borges is skin and skeleton. I can't imagine her being able to break through stone.

Her hands falter as she reaches for two teacups on a shelf. Her shoulders stiffen, and she keeps her back to me.

"Professor?"

She reaches into her pocket and draws out a small cloth bag. "I've taken to carrying my good tea leaves around in my pocket. One never knows when emergencies such as this one will arise, no?"

I simply stare at her, and after a moment she looks away, fiddling with the strings on her bag of tea leaves rather than looking at me.

"Professor," I say with more force, "are you a *meiga*?"

It's a theory I've kept private from Roze. Maybe it was more a hope than a theory—that my mentor gave me a magic book because she's like me. It's an incredibly risky thing to ask—but the manacles of fear shattered somewhere in the dark walls of the castle. I'm not interested in easy lies; I want truth.

Her fingers go still. And then she slowly unties the bag of tea leaves. Her hand shakes as she starts spooning them into a diffuser.

"You should know better than to ask such questions, Viola. These are strange times."

"Please," I say, desperation edging my voice. "Professor, why did you give me that book? You knew it was magic, didn't you?"

She says nothing as she pours the hot water into the teacups and drops a diffuser into each. The cup and saucer rattle in her hand as she extends it to me. I take it from her and see she's given me a lovely little diffuser. The orb is the shape of a small golden apple. Amber liquid streams from the small diamond-shaped holes in its body, staining the water.

"What you've guessed is true," she says.

My head snaps up to look at her. Pale moonlight, barely piercing the Mists outside the high windows, washes half her face in white. She looks so frightened.

"I promise I won't tell anyone," I whisper. I hesitate before what I'm about to say. My secrets are deadly and precious, but hasn't she extended her trust in telling me her own? And there is a small part of me that hopes that having another *meiga* to confide in will mean I'm not so alone with my power. And I might even have found someone who can teach me to control it. "I'm . . . Professor, I think you know what I am."

She grimaces, sympathy in the creases around her eyes. "Drink your tea, Viola."

Perhaps now isn't the right time to discuss such things. I nod and take a long sip.

Oh heavens.

It's *delightful*. After the horrors of the passage in the wall, I'm sure there's nothing that could have been better for my body or soul.

"There are two types of *meigas*—the light and the dark," she begins.

267

"I am a light *meiga*. I have the ability to create, to divine, to reveal, and to unify. I can bring things into being that are not. When I imagine a thing, it *becomes*. I knew to hide before this recent chaos started because I saw it before it was."

I gape at her. "That's incredible." I had no clue that such power could exist in a *meiga*. If only I could have had training. What would I be able to do with my shadows?

She doesn't reply, and she won't quite meet my eyes. Instead, she keeps her gaze on my teacup.

"Professor, I need to know—why did you give me the book?" I say, anticipation bubbling inside me. "What do the runes mean? What do they have to do with the King?"

I need to ask her about her possible connection to Castelle, but I don't want to make an enemy out of her with that accusation. Not yet.

Her lips pinch, like she's reluctantly amused. "So many questions. You've been through something harrowing, Miss Sinclair, and still, you cannot quiet your mind."

I'm not sure if it's a reproof or a compliment.

I take a deep sip from my cup, and I can feel the steaming liquid travel all the way down to my belly, its warmth soothing the rawness in my throat. The spiced flavor reminds me achingly of Roze. I take another deep sip, breathing in the steam as I do. I'm not sure I've ever had a cup of tea this wonderful, but perhaps it's just what I've been through, that this cup is offering the comfort I desperately need.

"Viola," she says.

I blink, my eyes flying to my professor's face.

She pushes her glasses up her nose. "Where is the book?"

My fingers feel oddly numb.

"Prince Roze has it," I say. True enough. It's in his room, but I'm not about to reveal the existence of Roze's tower to anyone.

She nods. "Good."

The professor is quiet for a moment, and I expect her to begin answering my questions about the book. Instead, she says, "Perhaps it's time to surrender."

"What?" I look up.

Her eyes are soft and sympathetic. "There may not be a way out of this. And if you don't allow things to take their course—think of what will happen to the Prince."

"But Professor . . . she'll kill me."

Professor Borges stares at me, giving no response. Her face is strangely calm, and I have trouble focusing on it.

But . . . I can't say the thought hasn't occurred to me. Tomorrow at sundown, Roze will be out of time. And I have no reason to think the book will even help. Roze's life is at stake because he's protecting mine. I could surrender to Belladonna, make things easy on Roze. Maybe that's the best gift I can give him for all he's done for me . . . all he is to me.

But I remember that feeling I had in the walls of the castle when everything was so dark and hopeless. I want to live.

"Drink," the professor says, nodding to my tea.

I obey greedily.

"I feel sorry for Roze," I say. "I wish . . . He's been through enough as it is. Now he has to choose between his life and mine."

"Roze?"

I look up at her.

The professor's look is chiding. "You know better than to drop his title, Viola. He may be your fiancé, but he is also a Prince of Aragoa."

I blink. "He . . . let me . . . call him by . . . his name." I feel breathless. The room is warm, and I feel so tired. I want to fall asleep and never wake up. The flame of the candle blurs strangely.

"How presumptuous of you to heed him on that matter," she says, taking a sip of her own tea.

I squint at my professor. Her words aren't making sense to me, and I can't put my finger on why.

"Where is he?" she asks.

"I—what?" My thoughts are turning hazy.

"This is important, Viola. Focus. *Where is Roze?*"

I try to focus on the professor's face. "Why aren't *you* using his title?"

Numbness burns my lips and throat. My hands begin to tingle.

The professor doesn't answer my question. Instead, a smile spreads on her lips. "Answer the question, Viola."

I try. But I can't remember how to speak.

My arm shakes as I try to lift my cup to my lips. It suddenly feels incredibly heavy.

It slips from my grip.

And shatters on the ground.

The world sways.

The tea—

The tea—

It's—

It's wrong

It's delicious

It tastes

like winter

and hope

and

poison.

I slide from my stool, and the pain as my hip and shoulder collide with the ground is a distant echo. In my clouded vision, I see the little gold apple diffuser rolling in a splash of spilled tea. The professor's feet step toward me.

"Your heart is your weakness, Viola. And I will have it, no matter what you've done to my son."

The world vanishes.

CHAPTER TWENTY-EIGHT

I hear mumbling. Two voices—one low and cold, the other like hellfire. My eyelids are heavy, and there's a sharp pain like a knife in my stomach.

"What were you thinking?"

"I'm trying to—"

"If you'd asked *me*, I'd have told you it wouldn't have worked to lock her away."

"I didn't know if I could trust you."

"*I'm* her best friend. You two can't even decide if you want to claw each other's eyes out or bury your tongues down each other's throats."

"Careful, Crémant. I'm not in a forgiving mood."

"I cower in fear."

Gingerly, with no small amount of pain, I sit up and pry my eyes open. Roze and Cerise stop bickering immediately. Roze takes a step toward me, but Cerise elbows him out of the way and rushes to my side, putting a hand on my forehead.

"How do you feel?" she asks. Her expression is more worried than I've ever seen her.

"Horrible," I try to say, but my throat produces a dry cough instead. Cerise hands me a glass of water, and I take several large gulps before I try to speak again.

"What happened?" I ask.

"You were poisoned," Roze says. He drags a chair over to the side of the chaise and plops himself down in it. He rests his crossed feet up on the edge of the chaise beside my shoulder.

"Waffles came and got me," Cerise says. "I found you unconscious and covered in spilled tea."

At the mention of his name, Saint Waffles grunts from the end of the chaise, resting his scaly head on my shin and looking balefully up at me. "I'm all right, Waffles."

I wonder how he could have possibly escaped the room. But I remember there are times when he's broken out of my room when I'd sworn I left the door locked. Gargoyles certainly are strange, mischievous little creatures.

Roze breaks in. "She couldn't carry you by herself. It was lucky she was able to find me."

Cerise glares at him. "Oh yes, so lucky. Tell me, how much do you know about poisons, Your Highness? She wouldn't be breathing right now if I hadn't been there."

Roze gives me a chastening look. "Speaking of which, what were you thinking, drinking something someone else gave you? From now on, the only food or drink you can trust is what I've tested first."

"Or me," Cerise amends, but Roze gives her a look like he doesn't want to allow it. "I gave you an antidote," Cerise says. "But it'll be a while before you're back to normal. Who gave you that tea?"

I lean my head back on the cushion and stare at the ceiling. "It was the Queen. She was disguised as Professor Borges," I say. I'm sure of it. Though my brain was addled at the time, her final words to me still ring in my head. She called Roze her son.

"Belladonna?" Cerise asks.

"No, Queen Maria."

Cerise's dark brows twist. "The *dead* Queen?"

"It's complicated. She's not . . . entirely dead." I wipe a hand down my face and make eye contact with Roze. "How was she able to poison me? I thought you said she couldn't harm me directly?"

He works his jaw thoughtfully. "She didn't. She offered you tea. You drank it."

I narrow my eyes at him. "That's quite a loophole."

"Magic can be impish that way. You need to be more wary of the gifts you accept."

"You're saying this is *my* fault?"

"I'm saying everything comes at a price, darling."

Cerise raises her eyebrows as she watches this exchange, and I try not to read into her expression. When she looks at me, she says, "I thought you knew—Professor Borges was arrested. She's been locked up in the dungeons."

Both Roze and I turn our attention to her.

"Why? How do you know?" Roze asks.

"She's not the only one. It's like some sort of inquisition down there. People in the caverns are being arrested on the smallest suspicion of being a *meiga*."

It's started. Belladonna is doing the Queen's dirty work—throwing people in the dungeons in an attempt to root me out.

I meet Cerise's eyes, realizing that I haven't faced her since Kole's death, since the whole Kingdom found out what I was, how dangerous I was. She must have heard—there were so many witnesses.

"I know what you're thinking," she says, "and none of this was your fault."

I want to snuff her words out like a flame, suffocate them with shadows the way I did Kole. "How can you say that? I killed our friend, Cerise."

"It was an accident."

"*It doesn't matter.* And now all these other people are being locked up on my account—"

Roze groans theatrically. "Don't blame yourself for my mother's insanity, Sinclair. Listening to your self-flagellation, as heroic as it may seem, is exhausting, and I've just carried you up too many flights of stairs to entertain it."

I meet his gaze, about to snap back at him, but his eyes pierce mine, prying me open, laying bare all the guilt I feel. He drops his feet to the floor and leans in close to me, his lips close enough that I can almost taste the poison. "And in case you get any ideas about avenging those unfortunate souls down in the dungeons, let me make something perfectly clear—you are not to leave this tower again."

I bite down on my tongue, glaring back into his silver eyes. As soon as Cerise is gone, I'm going to let him know *exactly* how I feel about being locked in this tower. It was one thing after Kole, but not even getting lost in the castle walls and being poisoned by the Queen has made me forget that Roze has been lying to me. I can't allow him to keep me here while both our lives are in his hands.

"Thank you for your assistance, Crémant," Roze says, turning to Cerise. "You're no longer needed. You can return to Marquet-Blanc House."

Cerise narrows her eyes at him. "Like hell."

I take her hand, and her gaze swings toward mine. I squeeze her hand, give her a hard look that says everything I don't want to say in front of Roze. "It's all right," I say. "I'm fine. You can go now."

She frowns, but she turns to Roze and says, "Keep her hydrated and resting, Roquelart. No food till morning, and only small amounts after that."

Roze nods.

Cerise stands, but she grips my hand harder. I know she doesn't *want* to leave, but I need to figure this out with Roze. And there are parts of this that even Cerise can't know.

"Thanks for saving my life," I say, managing a smile.

She smirks. "You handle my snakes, and I'll handle your poison."

"You handled the snakes too. But, deal."

Cerise turns to leave and says over her shoulder, "Take care of her, Highness. Anything happens to her, I'll kill you myself."

I brace myself for Roze's retort, but to my shock he says, "You have my word."

I glance at him, and he's looking at Cerise with utter conviction.

Cerise holds his stare for another moment and nods. She spares me one last glance before she passes through the doorway and latches the door behind her—I pray it won't be the last time I see her.

With Cerise gone, I whip my head toward Roze, ignoring the pounding in my head, the pain in my stomach. "You have some explaining to do."

He lifts an eyebrow.

I stand on wobbly feet and retrieve the book of poetry from the bookshelf. Sitting back down on the chaise, I shove it in his face. "What is this?"

He gives me a flat look. "A book. Obviously."

"Don't be cute."

He leans back. "You'll have to specify your complaint, Sinclair. I took a book of poems from the library. I committed no crime."

"You marked it with my ribbon." The words feel thick in my throat. I open the book on my lap, pointing to the particular line that has haunted me for six days. "That's a translation of the line in the Book of Castelle—the line written in ancient Aragoise. You don't know ancient Aragoise."

He shrugs. "I know a little—part of my early royal education. Not as well as you, admittedly."

"Roze—"

"Fine," he says, and sighs. "I searched the professor's office days ago, same as you. And I stole your exam."

I blink at him, letting my gaze fall back to the poem, back to those words. "Why?"

"Frankly, I didn't believe that Borges is innocent. I wanted to get my hands on anything that connected the two of you."

I'm annoyed that that makes sense. As much as I want to believe in Professor Borges's innocence, I can't help but see the logic in what he's saying. "Why didn't you tell me?"

"Why did you feign a fainting spell so you could sneak away to her office by yourself?"

Touché.

My eyes land on the fire, flickering peacefully. Either Roze or Cerise must've lit it to keep me warm while I was unconscious. "We might've been more effective if we'd trusted one another."

"A little late for that, darling," he murmurs, offering a sly grin that I'm in no mood to return.

We've both lied and schemed our way through this week, but despite that, I have grown to trust him—not to tell the truth, not to refrain from violence or forgive his enemies, but to do what's necessary to protect those he cares for. And . . . maybe I've become one of those people.

"Why did you take my ribbon?" I whisper, not meeting his eyes.

He's quiet for a long, precious moment. "Isn't it obvious?"

My heart staggers. "You hate me."

It's both a fact and a challenge.

"I never hated you."

I raise my eyebrows at him. "No?"

"My feelings for you have always been . . . complicated." He sighs. "Most of the time I wasn't sure what I felt for you . . . only that I . . . *felt*."

I watch him closely as he picks a bit of imaginary lint off his trousers.

"And frankly, that separates you from everyone else. I grew up so used to feeling nothing, not really caring for anyone except myself. You . . . intrigued me." He folds his fingers together in his lap and cocks his head at me. "You showed up at Vandenberghe one day, arms full of books, derision on your lips, and I was stricken." He smiles at me—that smile could level kingdoms. "Such a strange, deplorable, lovely creature, Viola Sinclair."

I stop breathing. After a beat, the Prince looks away, his eyes falling to the book of poetry. He takes it from my lap, his gloved fingers brushing the tops of my thighs. Even through layers of fabric, the touch causes goose bumps to spread over my legs.

Luckily he seems—or at least acts—unaware of his effect on me. His finger runs along the first stanza of the poem. "Look at the meter, the rhythm of it, like a song. The syllable with the greatest meaning on the upbeat. It's a masterpiece." He recites the sonnet, but not the translated version. He's memorized it in ancient Aragoise.

It's . . . beautiful. The words roll off his tongue like wine. I want to scoop them up and taste them for myself. Maybe kiss them off his poisonous lips.

When he's done, I'm breathing heavier than before. "Why did you memorize it?"

"I like to memorize poetry." He meets my eyes. "And this seemed like an important one."

I break eye contact simply because I can't stand to look at him anymore. "We have to figure out what this means."

I lift myself from the chaise, cross to his desk, and pull a scrap piece of paper from his desk drawer. I jot the words of the sonnet in ancient Aragoise and stare at them, hands braced on the table. They seem like poetic gibberish to me. But . . .

What if there was a mistranslation?

What had Professor Borges told me just days ago, when we talked about this exact sentence on my exam? Wooden—that's what she'd called my translation.

I double-check it. But the meaning is clear—the book's translation matches mine, and it's sound.

The heart is the dominion of evil.

"Any luck?" Roze asks me over my shoulder.

"No."

I growl in disappointment. I fold the piece of paper and tuck it into the pocket of my skirt. But when I take my hands away from where I'd been bracing them on the table, the sudden movement causes my vision to spot.

The world starts to go sideways, and suddenly, Roze's arms are under mine, holding me up. As easily as if I were a rag doll, he lifts me into his arms and carries me back to the chaise, setting me down gently. "I believe Crémant's explicit instructions were to rest."

"I'm sorry," I mutter as he adjusts a pillow under my head. "We just have to solve this."

"Saints, you were poisoned, Sinclair. You're no good to anyone if you don't recover."

He sits down, this time on the edge of the chaise, and we're silent for a long moment. All that has happened settles between us as I stare up at the ceiling. My head is clearing—the antidote is working.

"Roze?"

"Hmm?" He's staring into the fire, not looking at me.

"How are we supposed to fight power like this?" I look at him pleadingly. "We have a day left. How can we—"

"Don't," he says abruptly. His eyes are steel. "Not yet."

I choke. "Maybe it's time I turn myself over to Belladonna."

He pauses. Then laughs. It's the same cold, cruel laugh that I spent the better part of my time at Vandenberghe hating. But it hits my ears differently now. I recognize that what I thought was coldness was actually loneliness, and what I thought was cruelty was actually pain. "You're not going to do that."

"Are we back to this again?" I say testily. "Don't try to control me."

"Can you even walk yet, Sinclair? How do you plan to turn yourself in?"

I frown down at my still-weak legs, realizing he has a point.

"We're not there yet," he says. "We have time."

"Till sundown tomorrow."

He smirks. "Eons."

He stands, removing his jacket. "I suppose I'd better clean up your mess," he says, putting his hands on his hips and surveying the room.

"Sorry," I mutter. "I might've taken out my anger on your room."

He peers around the room darkly. "I suppose I deserve it."

Roze reassembles the room while I rest. He's bending down to reach under the bed, when he curses. He stands, holding a black slipper in his hand—a slipper that is gnawed to bits.

"You feral beast!" He marches over to where Waffles lounges on his armchair and waves the slipper in his face. "I'll have you stuffed!"

Waffles opens his mouth, panting, his wrinkled lips pulled into a clear smile, and I laugh, unable to help myself. The sound seems to break Roze. The rage melts from his face, and he lightly scratches Waffles's head and hands him the slipper. "Have at it, you. It's ruined anyway."

He continues to tidy the room. I don't mention again what hangs over us like a dark cloud—the last thorn will disappear from Roze's tattoo tomorrow at sundown. This is our last night.

When the bed is made, Roze wordlessly pulls his sweater over his head, loosens his tie, and flings himself onto one of the overstuffed chairs.

"You should get some sleep," he mutters as he situates his arm under his head. "You still need to recover."

I feel much better now—all my dizziness is gone and my stomach is back to normal. I move toward the bed, but something stops me, my hand stilling on the silk sheets. Roze and I have admitted some things and omitted others, but I can't help the feeling that I don't want to go into whatever tomorrow brings with regrets.

"Roze . . . do you . . . do you want to sleep in the bed?"

He opens his eyes just a sliver and peers up at me. His face betrays nothing, but his chest rises a little more rapidly. A tremble of fear that I don't altogether hate spreads to my toes.

"I don't think that's a good idea."

Well.

Now I'm offended.

"And why not?"

He stands up in one fluid motion, taking a single step toward me. "Because I can't touch you," he says. "And if we're getting in that bed, I'm going to want to."

I swallow, but I tilt my chin up at him and put my hands on my hips. "Even if you could, you're presuming that I would let you."

"And that's not on your mind?" he says with a sardonic tone, a little tilt on his lips.

"I didn't ask you to sleep *with* me. *Next* to me," I argue. "Look, neither of us knows what will happen tomorrow. I just . . ." *I want to be close to you.* I can't seem to make myself say the words.

But he cocks his head, like the same thought has occurred to him. Wordlessly, he crosses to the bed, and together we slip between the covers. He folds his hands behind his head and stares up at the ceiling.

"There, Sinclair," he says. "You've gotten me into bed. I suppose you're happy now."

"Oh please," I say, nestling into my pillow. "I'm doing you a favor. That chaise isn't nearly as comfortable."

He smiles, and it's half-cocky, half-genuine. He turns his head toward me, his smile faltering, and reaches out with a gloved hand to brush a loose curl behind my ear. My whole body freezes as I stare back into those crystalline eyes.

The smirk is gone. His expression is sober, soft, almost . . . anguished. My eyes are locked with his—I couldn't look away if I wanted to.

He's beautiful. That's always been undeniable. But I'd always thought of his beauty as more of an objective thing. Now, fear no longer rules me, and I can see the truth. It's not just the sharp edges of his jaw and cheekbones, the shadows in his eyes, the perfect bow of his sinful lips—it's that when I look at him, I see all my pain, all the despair of living a life of self-loathing, reflected in his face.

His life is the echo of mine, and in him I've found what I've been looking for my entire life—understanding.

I want him.

It's undeniable now.

But it's also not possible. He's deadly, and I shouldn't play with poison. I should look away from those despairing eyes right now and go to sleep.

Then again, maybe Roze is right, and I'm not really interested in rule following, in good behavior. If I'm a moth and he's a flame, I want to burn.

I glance away from him, biting my lip. "So?" I say, forcing my voice to be light and teasing. "Now we're in bed. Do you want to touch me?"

His eyes darken and he mutters, low and rough, "Yes."

"But you can't."

"No."

"Because it would kill me."

"Yes."

"Hmm." I scoot close to him, resting my head on his pillow till I can feel his breath on my face, move my body into his till there's just a hair of separation between us. "But this is fine," I whisper against his lips. "This isn't touching."

His breath quickens. "Wicked thing."

His voice is playful, but his face is hard as he looks at me. He lifts a gloved hand to my face and gently traces it over my cheek, my brow, my jaw, like he's trying to memorize the shape of me.

"I would have married you, you know," he whispers.

My heart stops. I want to respond, but what is there even to say to a declaration like that?

Roze doesn't seem to notice. He continues to trace the contours of my face as though he hasn't just devastated me.

"I tried not to think about it, to imagine it. But then, when I put my ring on your finger . . ."

He picks up my hand, still wearing the Roquelart ring, and toys with my fingers. We both stare at the ring, gleaming in the light of the fire.

"I put my ring on your finger, and I felt . . . monstrous. Possessive. Like if I ever saw another's ring on your hand, I'd rip it off and make them choke on it."

My lip twitches. "So violent."

"Always." His eyes flash to mine, cutting and bright.

Something melts deep in my belly at the look in his eyes. My breath is coming out in short shudders. This is dangerous. Definitely inadvisable. But I can't stop.

"What would it be like?" I whisper. "If we were married."

He shifts slightly closer, weaving his gloved fingers between mine. His thumb gently strokes my hand while his eyes are still on my face.

"I despise big weddings," he says.

"Me too."

"Though I suppose I'd have to marry you in the cathedral. Tradition—you know."

"That would be awkward, with what we did to the Captain of the Guard there."

He snorts. "I think it'd be rather fitting, holding hands and declaring our vows to one another over his grave. Murder and lies brought us together, after all."

I laugh, hiding my face in the pillow.

His eyelids lower—the gray of his irises darkening to a deep slate beneath long, black lashes. "But I'd have you long before that."

My heart skips a beat as I peek back up at him. "Oh?"

He nods and releases my hand, moving it back to my face. He draws a line over my cheek, then down my jaw, my throat, my collarbone. Gooseflesh spreads down my body, and my eyes flutter shut.

"I'd have you tonight," he says. "I'd have my hands on every inch of your body until I'd memorized it, until I knew it well enough to wring pleasure from you with my eyes closed."

I can't breathe. "Rather confident of you," I say.

"Not confident"—I feel his cool breath on my lips as his hand skates lower, over the swell of my breasts, coming to rest at my waist and gripping me firmly there—"just very dedicated to seeing what expressions you make when you come undone."

A sound between a sob and a moan escapes my lips. "Roze—"

"Saints, I love it when you say my name like that." His hand comes up to grip me on the back of my neck, his thumb caressing my cheek. I open my eyes to see him watching me earnestly, pleadingly. "Let me, Viola. I can't touch you—not with my skin. But—" He swallows. "Let me give you what I can."

His thumb strokes my jaw suggestively.

I want to give in, but it doesn't seem fair. He's had so much taken from him, his skin an ever-constant barrier between him and everyone else. "I want all of you, Roze," I say. "No gloves or anything else between us."

He swallows thickly. "I know, darling. Believe me, I know. But let's take what we can."

"I suppose—*oh*."

My words are stolen from my lips, because he drops his head, and then his lips are trailing down my front, over my shirt. Those gloved hands hold my waist, gliding up my sides. And when his lips meet the peak of my breast, my eyes flutter shut and my hands grip his shoulders, holding on like he's my anchor in torrid waters.

Roze gasps through his teeth and jerks back suddenly.

"Wh—what?" I ask breathlessly.

"Your arm nearly brushed my face. You didn't notice?"

"No." I'm still dazed. All he's done is kiss me, and only through the cotton barrier of my shirt. And yet, I'm already unraveling.

Roze frowns, scanning my body, the bed. "Let me bind your hands."

"B—bind my hands?" I repeat breathlessly.

He smiles, and I get the sense that he's almost trying not to laugh at me. "So that you don't accidentally touch me, Sinclair."

"Oh. Right. Sure."

He moves his knees to either side of my hips and lifts himself until he's kneeling over me, caging me between his legs. He unbuttons the top of his shirt and then loosens his tie and yanks it off in one quick motion.

"What are you doing?" I'm not sure how undressing himself could possibly help.

"You ask too many questions," he says, and the faintest, most wicked glimmer of a smile twists his lips.

I make an indignant sound. "Maybe I'll badger you the whole time just to spite you."

He smiles, and—*Saints*, it's charming. Perfect teeth and dimples on full display. "You can try. I like a challenge."

He seizes my wrists with one gloved hand and holds them together in front of me. He grips the end of his tie in his teeth as he wraps the other end around my wrists and ties it off in a tight knot. When he's done, he checks that it's secure, then pushes my bound hands down, resting them on the pillow over my head.

I'm fascinated by the whole scene, my eyes as shackled to him as my hands are. My whole body is on fire—every nerve ending on edge, and I want to both wiggle and hold completely still.

"No touching, Sinclair," he says, raising his dark brows at me.

The hand not holding my wrists sweeps down my arm, his touch featherlight, raising goose bumps along the path he's carving, until he reaches my jaw. He grabs it in his hands and turns my head so that I'm looking straight into his eyes.

"You're sure?" he says.

"Yes," I breathe, and that's all the permission he needs.

CHAPTER TWENTY-NINE

His hand trails from my jaw down my throat and over my breastbone. My heart thunders as he slides his palm down, popping buttons free as he goes. Then his hand goes lower, pushing down my skirt and my undergarments with it, running his hand down my thighs, until my legs are free. Slowly, so slowly, he moves his hand back up my stomach and gently brushes both sides of my shirt to the side, and finally, I'm bare before him.

"Viola." He whispers my name like a last rite.

His hand rests on the center of my stomach, like he can hold me here, keep me here forever.

But we both know that's a fantasy.

We both know time is not on our side.

My heart thunders in my chest as he looks down at me, perusing my body, consuming me, devouring me. It's so blatantly indecent, the way he's looking at me, that my face burns, even as heat pools in my stomach.

And then his eyes flash up to mine. My breath stops. I've seen so many emotions in those eyes before—rage, mirth, indifference, even tenderness. But I have *never* seen the look in them now. His irises are dark silver, shadowed beneath his long lashes—and in them is only pure, raw hunger.

I'm afraid, I think. *And I love it.*

He lowers himself onto my body, and I can feel the weight of him— the glorious weight of him—as he moves both hands now, down my torso, over my ribs.

His fingers are wonderous.

And for a moment, there's a grievous ache in my heart to feel them—the realness of them. Those long, lovely musician's hands on my bare skin.

I can feel his cool breath over my heart, his lips so close, hovering just above skin as he explores, as he learns what my body will do for him. My wrists tug at the knotted tie as I ache to run my fingers through his snowy white hair, to feel the shape of his shoulders.

I shove the thought from my mind—it'll do no good. Roze is right. It's time to take what we can. This is all life is willing to give us, and I think we're both ready to stop fighting it.

We will burn our way to destruction, a great blaze of anarchy, wrapped up together to the last.

His hands move lower, slowly and gently, giving me time to prepare, and to burn. I want to urge him to hurry up, because if he doesn't touch me soon, I might scream.

And then he does.

His fingers barely graze my center, and a whimper escapes my throat. Roze's breath is heavy, shuddering.

"Please," I say, and I don't even know what I'm asking for. Please touch me. Please let me go. Please make this last forever.

"Viola," he whispers, like it's poetry. His hand is on the side of my face again and I open my eyes to look back at him. "Whatever you want," he says. "Anything."

My hands curl into fists. I want to touch him. But I can't. So instead, I take this. I lift my tied hands and grab hold of his shirt with my fingers, pulling him close until his lips hover just above mine. "Everything," I breathe against his mouth. "I want everything."

He exhales, breath blading over my lips. "Thank the fucking Saints."

And then he touches me. Lightly at first, until I'm gasping into his mouth. And then he's doing things I can't name, and my mind goes blissfully blank, every worry and question and fear dissolving into nothing in light of *this* feeling, *this* moment, here with him, where I belong.

The cool bite of leather gloves against my burning flesh is better than anything I've ever felt. Is this what it's like? Is this what Cerise was telling me I'm missing? Or is this more?

Because I feel like I'm falling over an edge, and I'll never climb back up. I know that no matter what happens tomorrow, after this I will divide my life in two. Before Roze Roquelart. And after Roze Roquelart.

His fingers move faster, precise and firm, and I lose control of my body. I crack, shatter, fall to pieces, and I'm left feeling rent and loose.

What was it he said? That he was dedicated to seeing my face as I came undone?

Well . . .

I am undone.

When I finally open my eyes, there's something wild in Roze's. His pale face is flushed, and his breath is harsh. A lock of his hair falls from his face, hanging between us. In one swift movement he loosens my bonds and my hands are freed.

"You. Are. A miracle," he says. "More wonderful than stars."

The urge to reach up and stroke his cheek is so strong. "Roze—"

He gives me a sad smile and shakes his head. "No. It's all right. It's enough."

I grab hold of his shirt, touching what I can. "It doesn't have to be. Let me."

It's all I need to say for him to catch my meaning, but he freezes. "Viola . . . no one has ever—"

"It's all right," I say.

I reach up to his hands where they're now holding him up on either side of my head, and I lace my fingers through his.

He lets me pull the gloves from his hands, and when I slip them onto mine, I relish the warmth of him, even if it does make me a little lightheaded, the residue of poison painting my palms.

He shuts his eyes as I run my hands over him, his head hanging over me. When my hands linger too close to his waistband, a low groan escapes his lips. "You're torturing me, darling. You know that."

"Sorry," I mutter. The truth is, I don't know what I'm doing. I only know that I want him to have everything, to give to him everything he's given me, to pull him as close to real intimacy, to a normal life, as he's ever been.

He chuckles lightly. "I didn't say I hated it."

I bite my lip. "I'm just scared."

His eyes open, his gaze locking with mine. "Viola Sinclair, lion of Vandenberghe, afraid? Ridiculous."

With one hand, he undoes the fastening to his pants. "Relax. I'll teach you."

And then he's showing me how to touch him, his hand over mine. It's strange and clumsy and wonderful. I'm nervous the whole way through, but I keep my focus on his face. His eyes are closed, his expression a mix of desperation and tranquility, and I try to memorize his face like this, brutally elegant and *mine*.

Then everything turns feverish, reckless, burning.

Sweat breaks on his forehead, and his eyes burst open. "Eyes on me, darling," he says. "Always on me."

I meet his gaze, boring into me as we move together. He isn't touching my body, and yet, I feel like I'm being excavated, hollowed out, taken by that ravenous look in his eyes alone.

He breaks, shuddering, and drops his weight on me. I feel his breath on my bare shoulder as I wrap my arms around him.

Cerise was right when she said that there were fine lines between hatred and wanting. But those words were all wrong.

Before, I didn't hate Roze—I *loathed* him.

And now?

I don't want Roze—I *crave* him.

Like I could gnaw my own arm off to get to him. Tear his leather gloves from his hands and swallow him whole, fingers first—his punishment and my satisfaction. A cruel, selfish, indulgent death.

After a few minutes he lifts himself up and looks in my eyes again. Something passes between us—something neither of us can quite put words to.

"I would die to touch you," he says.

I pinch my lips together. My throat thickens, and I try to not let the emotion show on my face. I run my fingers through his hair, his gloves on my hands. "Stolen moments. It'll be enough."

It has to be enough to have him just for now. Just like this.

I close my eyes, and Roze shifts back to his side of the bed.

My thoughts fade to black, and while I sleep my dreams are full of fear and longing, desire for what I can't have alloyed with the relief of finally being held and not feared.

But in the morning, Roze is gone.

THE SEVENTH
DEADLY THORN

It came to be that the dreadful Prince was as scheming as his mother. Though the Shadow Girl was clever, she was not as conniving as he. And though she was dreadful, she was not as despicable as he. With that devilish spirit he stole for her what she could not take for herself—time, which she believed deep in her heart that she did not deserve.

But being clever, she did not accept the Prince's gift, but learned to scheme and connive and be just as despicable.

So the girl finally learned the depths of her own darkness and loved it.

CHAPTER THIRTY

I would never toss Waffles from a tower window, but I *would* daydream about it, especially if he, like this morning, is growling incessantly after I've had far too little sleep. The Mists are still pitch black outside when I wake with my face sticking to the sheets—it must be an hour or two before dawn. My head is drumming again, and it takes a minute of me staring listlessly into the embers dying in the fire to remember what happened last night.

Roze.

My heart stutters as I reach out for him—but the bed is empty, and his side of it is cold.

Groaning, I pull myself to sitting and push my hair back from my face. "Roze?"

I look around, and my eyes fall on the side table . . . where the Book of Castelle lies open. And a single rose rests atop it. I swing my legs over the side of the bed and approach the rose on the table. It's a gorgeous bloom, a deep, rich red—the color of twisted desire.

Gingerly, I pick it up, feel the sharpness of the thorns on the pads of my fingers. Beneath it, there's a letter written on parchment, laid atop the book. I recognize Roze's handwriting—an elegant, curling scrawl, obnoxiously grandiose even for a prince.

Viola,

By the time you recover enough to read this letter, I'll be several hours gone. I'm sure you'll be furious that I've left, but pace yourself—your anger will be much worse before this letter is done.

Consider this my confession. I've kept certain truths from you, which were neither advisable, nor convenient, to share until now.

Also, I didn't want to. As you've pointed out on numerous occasions, I can be rather self-serving. Even if you would accept an apology for my deceit—and we both know you wouldn't—I would not offer one. But I will apologize for how this news will reach you—from a letter and not from my lips.

When my mother ordered me to kill you, I tried, I truly did. I concocted all sorts of plans for your demise—most of them involving my poisoned skin on yours. But no matter how much I attempted to muster the same hatred in my heart that my mother bears for you, it was overcome by something else—another emotion, which I won't burden you by naming.

So I contrived a new plan. Since her murder, my mother no longer cares for the formalities of Court. She wants dominion, to rule with complete control—more a cruel goddess than a queen. She has been gaining strength, the Kingdom's fear feeding her magic. Now there is only one thing my mother desires more than your death—power. And I plan to give it to her.

She made a dreadful mistake when she created me, one that has caused her to both love and resent me all my life. In a fit of grief, she poured her magic into the earth, forming me and losing that portion of her magic to me in the process. In exchange for your safety, I plan to offer her that magic back, giving her the power she craves.

To my grave misfortune, I cannot live without that magic, since it is the very thing that created me. So, I'm afraid this is goodbye, darling.

Lest you get it into that clever head of yours to try to stop me,
I'll tell you that by the time you read this letter it will be too late.
It will be done before the sun rises.

Viola, you are free, and as it turns out, that is all I want.
Believe me, I'm as surprised as you are.

Yours, always,
Roze

I stare down at the letter, Roze's words ringing in my ears.

The rose is still in my hand. It's my last reminder of him—this thorny, wilting thing, lovely but dead.

He tricked me. And I'm in too much shock to even be angry.

Just a few days ago I was afraid Roze would decide to kill me to save himself. Now he's offering his life for mine. It's more than anyone's ever done for me—a devastating gift. He refused to give a name to what this is in his letter, but I know. I feel it too. And I won't let him offer himself to the Queen for me, not when he's spent his whole life at her mercy.

I grip the rose tightly, not caring that the thorns pierce my palm as I squeeze my eyes shut and let tears roll down my cheeks.

Roze said it was too late, but he didn't count on Saint Waffles waking me so early. I might have enough time to stop him. I have to try.

I drop the rose on the book, ready to bolt from the room, but then my eye catches on a red, angry blotch on the open Book of Castelle before me—drops of my own blood that have fallen on its pages from the rose's thorns. My blood is . . . vibrating, full of life.

I lean closer, watching the blood form a single word, written in curling script.

Hello.

I cock my head to the side. Hello?

I move Saint Waffles off his snoozing place on the chair so that I can sit before the book. Tentatively, I pick up one of Roze's fountain pens and write—

Hello?

For several agonizing seconds, nothing happens while my knee shakes under the table. Then more words appear, this time in ancient Aragoise.

The heart is the dominion of evil.

That damned poem again. It seems to be the only thing the book wants to say. I sit up and study the words again. Is there some deeper meaning to them that I'm meant to understand? The translation is correct, but no translation is perfect. *Your translations are too wooden.*

Fine, I can be flexible. There's a lesser-known translation of the word that's been rendered "dominion"—*kingdom*. I write a new sentence in the book, inserting "kingdom" in place of "dominion."

The heart is the kingdom of evil.

My ink drains onto the page, and the book doesn't respond. If I get this wrong, will those snakes burst from the pages again?

I bite the end of the pen. Heart. What could it mean that the heart *is* the kingdom? That doesn't make much sense. But I look at the original language.

The Aragoan word for "heart" does phonetically sound similar to another word—Castelle. They share a similar root. Could that be a coincidence when the Kingdom of Death's symbol is on the cover? I try replacing the word.

Castelle is the kingdom of evil.

That makes sense. The ink sinks into the page. The book is silent.

I frown. Everyone knows that Castelle is evil. But . . . I assumed that this book originated in Castelle, if its symbol was on the cover. It wouldn't consider itself evil. My mind ventures back to Sir Patrick's lecture, to everything he told us about the Kingdom of Death.

The pen drops from my mouth.

What was it Sir Patrick told us about *meigas* in Castelle? They use a darker, more sinister magic. I turn my trembling palm upward, staring down at it. *Darker. More sinister.*

There's one word that I haven't tested in the translation, only because it so often means *evil*. But in some very rare cases, it can mean . . . I scrawl the new translation quickly across the page.

Castelle is the kingdom of shadows.

The *meigas* there, who betrayed Aragoa, who destroyed so much—they were like me. They had my magic. Dark and sinister shadow magic. Magic that destroys.

In seconds, a new text appears.

Who is this?

My heart stops. As I stare down at the words, I quickly write back, *I'll ask you the same question.*

My name is León.

León. As in *King* León of Castelle? A block of text appears on the page, each line coming faster as though the writer was scribbling furiously.

There are only two people who have the ability to access this book, myself and one other, and you are not him. I don't know what trickery you have involved yourself in to be able to speak with me, but you have committed a grave error in attempting to impersonate a king.

Impersonate a king? I write back quickly. *I didn't impersonate anyone.*

A pause.

What is your name?

I hesitate. I don't know if I should trust this book, but . . . *With the King lie the answers. With the King lies salvation.* What if Professor Borges wasn't referring to King Alexandre, but to King León? She gave me this book. She must've known who it would give me access to.

I put my pen to the page but hesitate again. This is the King of Castelle—sworn enemy of Aragoa, of Roze's family, of everything I know and everyone I love. He sent the Mists. He's singularly responsible for the deaths of thousands. Professor Borges wanted me to have this book, but if she *is* a spy for Castelle, can she be trusted?

Without closing the book entirely, I turn to the cover so that I can run my fingers over the embossed dragon and lion intertwined there. I've stared at it countless times over the last seven days, but for the first time, I'm seeing something I hadn't before. The way they're curled together, claws digging into the other . . . it doesn't seem like the fight to the death that it once did. It almost looks like the embrace of a friend or a lover. Opening the book again, I write—

Viola

The King pauses for a long time again.

Viola Sinclair?

Panic rises in my gut. *How do you know my name?*

The next reply comes quickly. *I gave it to you.*

A rock drops in my stomach as I stare down at those words.

You have access to this book because you bear my blood. It recognizes my blood and the blood of Alexandre of Aragoa. If you are able to access it, if you are Viola Sinclair, then you are my daughter.

I want to beg him to stop. I drop the pen, backing up from the book, because this is all too much. But his words keep flowing, despite the thundering of my heart.

In the war, your mother and I sent you to Aragoa to keep you safe from the growing dangers of our Kingdom. Alexandre promised he would keep you safe. We found a family willing to take you in, give you their name, and keep your identity a secret. We placed you safely in their care before the Mists fell, before everything changed.

The air freezes around me. My ears ring as I stare down at the words. My family—the one that abandoned me—they were just a surrogate. My brother's cherubic face flashes in my mind, the brother who I loved more than my own life. He wasn't my blood. *That's* why my parents dropped me in the orphanage when he died. I was a stranger from a foreign, dangerous land. And I'd killed their only child.

More words form on the page.

You have a locket that you've kept since birth, yes?

With a shaking hand, I write back,

Yes

And have you ever been able to open it?

No

I thought not, he replies. *Just as with this journal, it is activated by the blood of our family line. With your blood, the locket will open.*

I blink, staring at his words for a moment. I almost don't want to take him up on his challenge, because if he's telling the truth . . . But I have to know. Even if reality is difficult to swallow, even if nothing is ever the same again, the truth is always better than a lie.

I press my thumb against a thorn of Roze's rose again and swipe it over my locket. It effortlessly pops open, and my breath catches when I see a small dragon on a coat of arms inside—just like the one on the silver stake.

As I hold it, King León writes,

It is the symbol of our House, he says. *I gave you that locket the day you were born, dear one.*

And what about the lion? I write back. *The book has a lion wrapped around a dragon on the front.*

The intertwined lion and dragon, he says, *is the symbol of a kingdom that never came to be—Aragoa and Castelle together, a single unified kingdom spanning the Hivernian Peninsula. It was our dream—mine and Alexandre's.*

I flip the cover of the book to look at the symbol again—the embrace of unity, not division—peace, not war.

I write, *How was it possible you and Alexandre were friends, with your countries at war?*

There's a brief pause, then his reply comes, like his pen is resting between sentences while he's thinking how best to tell the story.

I met Alexandre in the Forest of Avenc in my youth. I was hunting game, and I believe he was looking to escape his father for a few moments, when we happened upon each other in the woods. In those days the war was raging its hottest, and our fathers were at their war camps nearby. My upbringing taught me that I should hate him, that though I was just a boy, I should have slain him then and there—my sworn enemy. I would have been a hero to my people, and my father would have been endlessly pleased. But I was shocked by his appearance. He and I were both so young, not even old enough to attend Vandenberghe yet. I'd been taught that Aragoans are creatures of pure evil, barely human. But Alex . . . He looked anything but. Golden hair and eyes so blue, they reminded me of the wild sea off the cliffs of my Kingdom.

He stared at me across the glade while I held my bow. And when I didn't raise it against him, he nodded to me and disappeared. At that time, nobles of both Kingdoms attended Vandenberghe on the condition of nonviolence within its walls, as they both laid claim to its origins and renown. Alexandre and I were both in Berlaise House. We had a zealous academic rivalry, but it gave way eventually to friendship. And given time and many late-night talks before the common room fire, friendship turned to love. We spoke at length about peace, about a new world where Aragoan and Castellian ideologies could coexist, about a unified Hivernian Peninsula. Where our fathers were conquerors, Alex and I were dreamers.

When we left school, we knew we would not see each other until we'd swayed our separate Courts toward our dream of peace. So we created two books, using our magic, to communicate—the one you write in and the one I write in.

I loved Alexandre, more than I ever loved any woman. Even more than your mother, I'm sorry to tell you. He was my water and sunshine. I knew I would never be the same after him. Meeting him was like seeing the sun for the first time after spending my entire life in darkness.

My hand covers my mouth as I stare down at the page. The Princes of Aragoa and Castelle were involved in a treasonous affair while their nations waged war. It's more than enough reason for any number of people to want them both dead. They were going to stop the war. They were going to put aside ideology in favor of unity, something that would have made many people very angry.

There's so much I need to ask him. I write, *Are you a* meiga?

Yes, he replies. *Of a different kind than what is common in Aragoa. There is so much you don't understand about the war. Alexandre told me how the story was twisted. Maria . . . she has always been vindictive.*

I don't understand. What was twisted?

León's response comes slowly, like he's considering carefully how to explain his next words.

There are two sides to meiga *magic—the dark and the light. Once they coexisted, balanced and entwined. But as the war intensified, both Kingdoms began using* meigas *loyal to their side against the other. Our family favored the dark while Aragoa favored the light, and as hate grew between our Kingdoms, so did separation between dark and light magic. We encouraged our* meigas *to push their magic to greater and greater heights, gaining power we never thought possible—terrible power, costly power. The light* meigas *in Aragoa did the same.*

Shadow magic is, at its root, destruction and death. Soon, without light, the land became death itself. Death on its own was never something to fear, but without light magic to balance the darkness, death consumed Castelle. The realm of the dead was rising to meet us, and we were quickly being separated from all that was living, separated from the rest of the world. Your mother and I wanted to give you a chance to escape that death, we wanted to give you a chance at life, *even if it was in our enemy Kingdom.*

I breathe deeply, staring at his words. What does he mean, that death consumed Castelle? I want to ask, but I haven't forgotten how little time I have left. Instead, I write, *Queen Maria is a* meiga. *She's growing more and more powerful, and she's trying to have me killed.*

If she wants you dead, then it is likely she's discovered who you are, he replies. *Your royal heritage. Light* meigas *have ways of discovering the truth, revealing what has been hidden.*

She wasn't told?

No. It was deemed best to keep Maria in the dark. I'm afraid Maria's hatred of you has little to do with you and much more to do with events that took place before you were born.

Alex and I . . . we were both Crown Princes, expected to carry on our family lines, and therefore were required to marry women of noble birth. When we were young, we fooled ourselves into thinking we could be together. Alex, ever the dreamer, believed in our dream for far longer than I did, and I, fool that I am, let him believe.

Even while we were planning for our future unified kingdom, I didn't share my concerns with Alex—that there would still need to be an heir, that there would be feuds over bloodlines that would fracture our newborn kingdom. Unlike Alex, I had served as a soldier, had seen the horrors of war, had seen the hatred that already ran so deeply between dark and light meigas. *I didn't want more bloodshed.*

It was our final night together, and Alex had no idea. We swore that night that our love would endure anything, until death ripped us apart. All the while Alex didn't know that I would be gone before sunup, that the next day I would sign a betrothal agreement to your mother—a princess of Gault, whom I'd never met.

I didn't know my father planned to break the armistice that night. He'd never been in favor of it—visions of Castelle's glorious reign over the entire peninsula clouded his regard for the lives of his own people, certainly for those of Aragoa, who by then was far weaker than us. We had the might of the shadow meigas, *and their magic was quickly consuming the light.*

That next day, while I signed away any hope of a future with Alex, my father broke the armistice and the war was reignited before sunset. Alex and I never saw each other again.

With a lump in my throat, I write, *So you betrayed him.*

Yes.

I take a deep breath, absorbing this information. *What does that have to do with the Queen?*

With our kingdoms at war again, Alex's father had his sights set on the small coastal Kingdom of Septania, which had thus far refused to assimilate into Aragoa. Its port would grant Aragoa pivotal access to Castelle, and perhaps more importantly, it was home to House of Lucia, an ancient priory for light meigas. Maria, the Septania princess, was a gifted student there. I believe Alexandre wooed her and led her to believe he had more of his heart to offer than he did.

They were wed and had children before your mother and I were even married. Alex and I did not speak in those days, but I believe he was angry and bitter about my betrayal. He used Maria as a tool for his revenge against me. Her heart was the casualty.

Biting my lip, I write back, *And what did you do?*

I was consumed with wrath. Not jealousy—I knew there was no love between them, at least not from Alex. But I couldn't believe what Alexandre had done. The acquisition of Septania threatened to destroy Castelle. Thus far, it had been our fathers' war. Now it was ours, and this was his shot across the bow. I knew I had no choice but to respond. So I took a naval fleet and laid siege to Septania, attacking in the dead of night. I burned Maria's kingdom to the ground. It was an act of grief and hatred.

I suck in a shallow breath, remembering what Roze told me about his own birth—that his mother's kingdom had been destroyed, that it was her grief and hatred, spilled into the earth, that sprouted him from the ground.

I am not proud of my actions in those days. Love and war do not mix, dear one.

No kidding.

As I understand it, Maria sank deeper into bitterness and hate as every attempt at gaining Alexandre's affections failed. She blamed the fall of her home not only on me and Castelle, but on all shadow meigas.

304

Alexandre still hid me for you, I write. *You didn't always hate each other?*

He pauses before writing back. *I don't think we could ever truly hate one another. We loved each other too strongly, and sometimes that has destructive effects. It's true that we didn't speak for a long time after the siege on Septania, but when I begged Alex for his help to save my child, he answered. The bond between us was deep enough for him to do that much. I don't think Alex ever forgave me, but eventually he did deign to speak with me again, through these books. He was always more gracious than I.*

He assured me that you'd be safe, that you'd be allowed to train with your magic in secret. We sent a trusted dark meiga *with you to watch over you and to teach you when you were ready.*

I blink at those words. I write, *Before Queen Maria, I never knew another* meiga.

King León's response is slow, his words careful. *We sent one of our most powerful* meigas *with you. Ona Borges.*

I blink down at the words. I should have guessed it—it's so obvious. The professor disappeared just as the recent danger for *meigas* really began. Her office was always full of those outlandish objects . . . *She never told me,* I write.

Again, his response is delayed.

Then when she returns to Castelle, she'll answer for her failure.

I don't know why Professor Borges didn't tell me who she was or what awaits her in Castelle if she ever escapes Queen Maria, but there are more important things right now.

How can I stop the Queen? Does she have a weakness?

His words come hurriedly. *If Maria is after your life, you are in dire straits, dear one. She is formidable. A light* meiga's *power is always anchored to an object in their possession. It would be something important, but not an object that just anyone can access. Do you know of such an item?*

My heart thunders against my ribs. I know *exactly* which item the Queen would use to anchor her power.

She has a mirror.

Then destroy it, he says.

I bite my cheek as I write back, *I don't know if I can.*

If the mirror is enchanted, it surely can't be as easy as breaking it. Queen Maria would never leave her power so vulnerable.

He replies, *I know the power you have, Viola. Don't pretend you don't know exactly what you're capable of.*

I gulp. I need to make him understand. What the Queen has become— she's more force than human, a living nightmare. But . . . have I not also become a living nightmare? Are my shadows not also something to fear?
No. I can't think like that, not after what happened to my brother. I bite my lip before writing back.

I can't always control my shadows—they're dangerous.

Even writing it down feels like I'm revealing a secret. But when I read King León's words, they're like an arrow through my heart and steel in my bones.

Then be dangerous.

CHAPTER THIRTY-ONE

My footsteps are quick and quiet as I make my way to Vandenberghe, my mind clear for the first time in a week. Saint Waffles's little feet pound on the stone behind me—he refused to be left behind in the tower.

First, I need the Grimmstones.

As I enter Habert House, I have no idea which room is Fletcher's, but there's candlelight flickering in one of the private study rooms. I follow it on intuition, and sure enough, I find him bending over a large text, his eyes focused and a crease between his brows.

"Late night or early morning?" I say.

His head snaps up, and he blinks. "Scrivener."

I smile grimly. "I need your help."

Minutes later, we've woken Ed. He rubs his eyes in a chair in the Habert common room, Waffles hopping up onto his lap like they're good friends.

"All right, Princess," Ed says. "Why am I awake at this Saintsless hour?"

I take a deep breath.

"Roze has done something," I say, looking pleadingly at their sleepy eyes. "If we don't stop him before sunup, something terrible is going to happen to him."

I thought I could do this. I thought I could get the next words out. But they turn to ash on my tongue.

"What's he done?" Fletcher asks.

I take a deep breath, readying myself to trust them with my deepest secrets. "I'm a *meiga*. Queen Maria's spirit is still alive, and she wants me dead. Roze is making a bargain with her to save me. He's forfeiting his life so that his mother can regain the power she lost when she created him, on the condition that she lets me live."

They both stare. Ed speaks first, cursing colorfully, and runs a hand through his hair.

"Please," I say, leaning forward, "we don't have much time. I need you two to find Roze. Do whatever you have to to stop him."

Fletcher sets his jaw. "We'll find him."

"I can't come with you. There's something else I have to do," I say. "I can't tell you what, and I'm sorry. But trust me, it's necessary to save Roze."

"We'll do our best," Ed says. He stands and puts a hand on my shoulder. "Stay safe, Princess. Roze would kill us if something happened to you."

I steel myself against the ache in my heart. "Thank you."

Ed squeezes my shoulder, his face grim for once. "*Fiat tenebrae.*"

I nod. "Let there be darkness."

"Roze fucking Roquelart, making a mess for the rest of us to clean up, as usual."

Cerise grumbles as she pulls on her boots and tucks her night shirt into her pants, but I don't miss how quickly she agreed to help me. Perhaps I should be more afraid to involve my best friend, but I can't push her away any longer. I need her. Guilt is a knot in my chest, but I have to ignore it.

Cerise pulls on her trench coat as we march down the hall. "It's cold as death out here. Where are we going?"

"You said Professor Borges is in the dungeons?"

Cerise nods. "That's what I heard."

"Do you think there's any way we can get her out?"

Cerise clenches her jaw. "I don't know. The dungeon cells are supposed to be nearly impenetrable."

I sigh. "So that won't work. Maybe we can sneak in. If I could just speak to her—"

Then Cerise stops, grabbing my arm. "Viola, Kole had that special key thing."

A rock sinks in my stomach. "Cerise, we can't—"

"We have to."

"No."

"Why not?"

I balk. "What do you mean, why not? I—I killed him, Cerise. I can't just take his things like he's not dead because of me."

She puts both hands on my shoulders. "This will work. It won't change what happened to Kole, but it will help you save Roze."

I bite my lip, not meeting her eye as nausea roils in my stomach. I glance at the window, though, the Mists still swirling black. Dawn is coming. There's no time for my guilt.

"All right."

CHAPTER THIRTY-TWO

I let Cerise do the digging around in Kole's room in Marquet-Blanc House while I stand guard outside with Waffles. I can't stand to be in his bedroom, to see his things, smell his scent. I have to keep going, and if I face those things, the guilt might make me vomit. After a few minutes, she returns smiling, holding the little golden key.

We stop by Professor Borges's office in the halls by the library, and Cerise doesn't question me when I take the silver stake with the crest of Castelle. Afterward we're silent as we cross the glass bridge and sneak past the guards into the main castle.

My heart thumps wildly, but I feel strangely disconnected from my body as we descend into the dungeons, like all this is just a nightmare.

The dungeons are deep beneath the castle, down that horrible, unlit staircase that Roze and I passed in the catacombs. The walls are cave-like, stalactites dripping cold water from the ceiling, all of it cast in the dim light of a candelabra Cerise snatched from the main castle on our way down. Waffles has gone very quiet, his little head lowered like he expects danger around every corner.

As we poke our heads around the corner of a hall, there's a guard sitting on a stool by the entrance to those dungeons.

"How are we going to get past him?" I ask.

"What did you bring me for?" Cerise says, offering a grin. She's trying to break the tension, pull me back to earth. I'm too far gone for that. She draws a little vial out of her bag.

"*Don't* poison him," I say.

"I'm just going to drug him. Calm down," she says, ripping the tail of her shirt and dousing it with the liquid. Without another word she saunters around the corner. The guard looks up, the surly old face of someone who doesn't like his quiet to be interrupted.

"Morning," Cerise says in a singsong voice.

"Who—"

Swift as wind, she kicks his stool out from under him and he tumbles to the floor. She grabs him by the collar before he can react and shoves the cloth over his mouth. He coughs and struggles, but she holds his head steady. In moments, his eyes are lolling. Cerise drops him unceremoniously onto the floor, and his head cracks sickeningly. Saints below. I really hope he wakes up with nothing worse than a concussion.

"I should have been much more frightened of you before now," I say, coming around the corner.

Cerise chuckles as we enter the dungeon halls. "Never trust a chemist."

The natural alcoves of the cave have been utilized for cells. Bars sometimes cover openings barely wide enough for a human to crawl through. I hear the dripping of water and the echoes of weeping throughout the space, so hauntingly distant that I'm not sure if they're human or ghost.

All the cells are occupied. *All* of them. I don't stop to make eye contact with a single prisoner. How many of them are suspected of being *meigas*? If I look at them, I might break, and right now, I need to be unbreakable.

Finally, we see a huddled figure with long, bushy hair in one of the cells.

"Professor?"

The professor's salt-and-pepper head pops up. No longer is she the pillar of authority and intelligence that I know. She looks frail and small, like she's been in the prison for several days.

"Miss Sinclair," she says, her voice wispy and deep. "I would ask what you're doing here, but I'm no fool." She stumbles to her feet, and her legs shake. I wonder if they've fed her, or at least given her water. Her face looks waxen, like she might have been sweating through a fever.

"You know, don't you?" she says.

"I'm more interested in what *you* know. I want to get you out of here, but we don't have a lot of time right now. I know you've been keeping secrets, and I need to know what they are."

She frowns, emphasizing the lines around her mouth and eyes. The candlelight casts strange shadows across her face.

"I know that you are the daughter of King León and Queen Isabel of Castelle." She approaches the bars, and her spindly fingers curl around them. Her eyes are looking at me with an odd intensity, a glow in her irises.

Cerise's eyes go wide, looking between Borges and me, but my gaze is set on the professor.

"But you kept that from me. Weren't you supposed to train me to use my power years ago?"

The professor's eyes narrow. "You were always cared for. Kept alive."

I swallow thickly. "You had orders, and you failed to fulfill them. Why?"

"It would have put your life in unnecessary danger. We're in an enemy kingdom, dear."

"*Unnecessary danger*," I repeat. "I was already in danger. The Queen tried to have me killed, and if I knew what I was—" I want to say that she doesn't know what it would have meant to me, to know that I wasn't an outcast, that I was different for a reason. Someone somewhere *loved* me. "If I'd known what I was, I could have been prepared."

I could've stopped all of it. I could've prevented so many deaths. I could've caged the monster.

The professor purses her lips. "I did what I could. When I suspected that you might be in danger from the Queen, I stole that book from the King's personal library. I gave you all the information you needed to discover who you were."

312

"You could have simply told me what the book was and how it worked," I retort. "Instead, you left me to figure it out on my own. Did you know they planned to kill me? Were you just going to let it happen?"

Her face hardens as she takes a step back from the bars. "There wasn't *time*. We had minutes. You wanted me to tell you that you were the heir to the Castellian throne just before handing you off to the guard? I know what your shadows can do when you can't control your emotions, Viola."

"Hold on. The heir to the—" Cerise starts. But I interrupt her.

"So you hid your treachery from me because you were afraid of what I'd do to you?"

Rage burns within me. The same shadows she feared press at my fingertips. I *hate* them, and the more I hate them, the more they come.

"Whoa, breathe, Viola," Cerise whispers.

She's right. I close my eyes.

Calm.

Control.

I open my eyes, set them on the professor, and see that she's nearly as furious as I am—face white and shaking. "The King asked too much of me. I served in a *war*—I saw my friends die by my side. And then he asks me to come *here*, to enemy territory, while the Mists were closing in, because he wants his daughter kept away from court. As though I didn't have a home. As though I didn't have family.

"But then I took the job at Vandenberghe, and I found a new life, one that was, for once, peaceful. So no, when the time came, I did not want to tell you the truth or train you. I wanted things to stay as they were. I much preferred for you to grow up naive about your identity, to study language and contribute with your mind, not your power . . ." She tips her head forward. "And I think you did as well. Tell me you wouldn't have been content, absorbed in books and runes for the rest of your life."

"It wasn't your *choice*," I growl, my voice rising above a whisper. "I deserved the truth."

"I was imprisoned for your sake," she hisses.

"We all make sacrifices," I retort bitterly.

313

"I fought for your father for years. Now you're going to accuse me of disloyalty when you're gallivanting around with the Roquelart boy? I've heard what's been happening between you two while I've been wasting in his father's dungeons." Her eyes fall to the ring still on my finger. "Roque trash." She says it with a sneer on her face, and I recognize the hate for Aragoa and all it represents in her mind. This is exactly what my father and King Alexandre were trying to end.

"The Prince isn't my enemy," I say. "I haven't made up my mind about you, though. I'm going to try to let you out, but only so you can help us. Maybe my father will be more forgiving if you make the right choice now."

I finally break eye contact with her and examine the lock on the cell— these locks are notoriously impossible to pick. I've never seen anything like it—a round orb without markings or any discernable keyhole. I'd never be able to pick it, and it was pure luck that we were able to find Kole's key. I turn it over and over in my hand until I finally feel a slight catch beneath the pad of my finger.

"Cerise, can you bring the light closer?"

She does, the flames flickering prettily on the metal. And then I spot it—the smallest of holes in the very bottom, hardly bigger than a speck.

"Hold this still," I say, letting Cerise cradle the lock while I finagle Kole's key. It has a number of bars that expand from the center, all in various sizes. I find the smallest one and insert it into the hole—it barely fits.

I twist it, the lock clicks loose, and I release a breath.

The door whines as I pull it open, and Professor Borges steps stoically out of her cell. I intentionally do not turn my back to her.

"What do you require of me?" she says, holding her chin high.

"Queen Maria has a mirror. You're going to help us destroy it," I say. "The Queen is using her power to terrorize us. But you know more about her magic than anyone, don't you?"

"I've taken a special interest in the powers of the Queen, yes." She folds her arms in front of her imperiously. "But I can't just wave and make her terrors go away. I'll need certain things—"

"Certain things like this?" I reach into my pocket and withdraw the small silver stake.

She gapes. "How on earth did you get into my office?"

"I'm good with locks."

The professor huffs. "Yes, you'll need that to destroy the mirror and break her connection to her magic. It cannot withstand contact with pure silver. Now, I would thank you for releasing me, but since your existence is the reason I was arrested to begin with—"

"Good," I say, cutting her off. "Then let's go."

I push the professor ahead, letting her lead the way. Every moment we waste is a moment closer to sunup, when Roze will be out of time.

As we pass by the cells leading to the entrance, I glance sideways at Cerise and notice she's giving me a strange, bewildered look.

"What?"

"Vi . . . you're some sort of princess?"

I shrug.

Her face is a little awed, a little amused. "Well. I'll have to practice my curtsy."

"Shut up."

CHAPTER THIRTY-THREE

We creep up the monstrous curving staircases, the grand chandeliers hanging overhead, surrounded by the sheer splendor of the Kingdom that sees me as its enemy. I belong to another.

"Queen Maria's mirror is in her chambers," I whisper to Cerise and Professor Borges as we navigate the halls. "We can only hope they didn't move it after her death."

"The silver stake might be useful, should we run into anything the Queen has concocted to terrorize us," the professor says.

"Then Viola should have it," Cerise says.

The professor's eyes sharpen. She clearly doesn't think I should be the one handling her things, and actually, I happen to agree. I hand the stake to Cerise.

"*No,*" she says, holding up her hands. "Viola, you take it."

"I have my shadows."

"And the gargoyle," Professor Borges adds.

It seems like an odd comment to make. "Oh. Yes, I guess that's true." I glance down at Saint Waffles, trotting beside us.

The professor raises her eyebrows. "Your parents sent him with you to Aragoa for your protection. Didn't you notice how peculiarly loyal he is?"

I look down at Waffles's squat form, and he looks back up at me, his mouth panting and eyes smiling. "I thought that was just his personality."

Professor Borges scoffs. "Gargoyles are fearsome beings—creatures of pure night trained to protect their human companions from all manner of evil. They will slaughter enemies, reduce a threat to shreds of flesh and bone in moments if they sense any danger."

Waffles's tongue lolls sloppily out of his mouth.

"He's terrifying," Cerise says.

The professor bristles. "*Don't* underestimate a gargoyle, girl. It'll be a mistake you never forget."

"All right," I say. "I have Waffles and my shadows. Cerise, you take the silver."

She grumbles but takes the stake from me.

"Good. Now keep up."

I glance out the casement windows as we sprint past them. The Mists are still black—no sign of the sun. It's little consolation.

———

I'm breathless, and there's a sharp pain in my ribs as we climb into the upper castle, toward the royal residences. I round a corner, expecting us to find ourselves in the hall that leads to the Queen's chambers, and I am met with a sight that is completely wrong, but familiar—the hall outside the throne room.

I jog to a halt, Cerise and Waffles beside me and the professor lagging behind. This hall is larger than the others, with a grand ceiling painted with the faces of the saints among clouds and beams of glorious sunlight. I can barely make it out with the chandeliers lit so dimly, turning what must have been an awe-inspiring piece into something vaguely ominous.

"This is wrong," I say. "We must've gotten turned around."

The professor tuts. "You've led us to the throne room. I thought you knew where you were going."

I shake my head. "I was sure this was the way, I just—"

My words lodge in my throat as I turn. On the other end of the hall, the way we *just* came, is a dead end.

"What the hell?" Cerise mutters, looking back and forth between both ends of the hall. "What's happening? Where's the hall?"

"It's the Queen," I whisper. I cross back to the end of the hall we just came from.

It's an illusion, I think confidently. *Just like the faceless guards. Just like the beetles in my soup.*

I reach out a hand toward the wall, begging my palm to fall through it like smoke. But instead, my palm smacks into dark, embroidered wallpaper, the feel of thread beneath my fingers entirely real.

"Impossible," Professor Borges breathes. "This is magic I've never seen."

I swallow. "She's getting stronger."

She feeds on fear. And even at that thought, panic seizes my chest. I close my eyes and take a deep breath, palm still flat against the wall.

Calm.

Control.

I will *not* feed her power.

I turn on my heel toward Cerise and Borges, looking around at the room the Queen has created from the hall we were just in. No doors. Save one. "All right. There's only one way forward."

I take a step toward the doors to the throne room, but Cerise stops me with a hand on my elbow. "Aren't we falling into a trap?"

"Yes," Professor Borges says, arms crossed. "You're playing right into her hands."

"We don't have a choice."

I reach toward the doors and hesitate when my hand touches the cool gold handle. I release one more steadying breath and push open the door.

The throne room is pitch black. There are no windows here, and the candelabra lights just a few feet ahead of us. The lush scarlet carpet silences our footsteps as we pad farther into the room. My shadows beg to be set free, ready to lash out at a moment's notice. We tread farther into the darkness, and the flickering candlelight reveals the thrones and the princesses' empty chairs beside them.

"No one's here," I whisper.

The words barely leave my lips when a low, soft growl reaches my ears. A growl that definitely does not belong to Waffles. My heart jumps into my throat as I turn in its direction—toward the darkness behind the thrones.

"What was that?" Cerise asks.

"We should go," Professor Borges says. "*Now.*"

We turn and rush toward the door. The professor gets there first, reaches for the handle . . . and it's gone. The door has transformed into a solid wall. And I can just barely hear the faintest sound—scratching and whimpering on the other side.

"Waffles is trapped outside," I say. "The Queen's shut us in."

Another rumbling growl rattles across the floor. I scan the darkness behind the throne. My breath is still. I think I can see something moving in the shadows, but that could be just a trick of my eyes.

But then it's unmistakable. A shape moves in the dark behind the Queen's throne. The light of the candles catches on something. An enormous paw. Wild yellow eyes meet mine.

A roar, loud enough to split eardrums, slices toward me, and it leaps. Teeth and claws lunge for me.

I run, hurtling for Cerise as a great, dark lion collides with the floor behind me. It bounds off the door and leaps again, and I barely duck in time before it flies over my head.

"*Cerise!*" I scream.

On the other side of the room, Professor Borges is flat against the wall, eyes wide in terror.

Cerise grabs me around the waist and holds the stake out against the lion. Why couldn't the professor have had a *sword* of silver?

The lion whirls around, and Cerise and I stumble onto the dais behind the thrones. They'll do nothing to barricade us from the beast.

"Viola," Cerise says, and she points up. I glance upward—above is a baldachin, a surface of solid gold and draping fabric that canopies the throne. She grabs me by the arm and throws me toward the column supporting the baldachin. The lion paces closer to us, and I quickly climb the column, using the curtain to hoist myself up.

I reach down to my friend.

"Cerise."

She glances up to me and grabs my hand. The lion leaps, and I heave her up. The beast's great paw catches Cerise on her foot, and she cries out as I pull her onto the surface of the baldachin. I tug her under her arms and pull her to safety.

Below us, the lion growls and paces on the dais. It's only now that I realize it has a gold sheen to it—and that the lion statue that stands guard before the throne is missing. I look to where Professor Borges is against the wall. She's cowering, visibly shaking, and she's taken hold of a marble bust to protect herself.

I can barely see the shape of her in the darkness. I try to spot the beast beneath us, but it seems to have crept back into the darkness.

"We need to get to the professor before it attacks her," I tell Cerise.

She cringes. "We can't just sit up here and wait for that thing to go away?"

"No."

"Would it be so bad if it ate her? She was horrible to you."

I give her a chastening look, and she sighs. "Fine."

I creep toward the back of the baldachin. I don't see the beast anywhere. I listen intently for a moment—no breathing, no low growl. It can't have just disappeared, can it?

I slip down behind the curtain as silently as I can. The walls are covered in thick drapes, and there's nearly a foot of space for me to walk behind them, obscured in darkness.

Cerise slides down behind me and stifles a groan as she lands on her bloody foot. "What are you doing?" I hiss.

"Protecting you."

"You're injured."

"I don't care."

I want to argue with her that this is no time to be noble, but we have so little time. "Stay here," I command. "I'll get the professor."

She glares but nods, and I turn down the pathway. I'm careful not to brush the curtains, not to give away any sort of movement. It's so dark that I can't see past my own nose here. I can't *hear* anything either.

Then, a shriek from nearby—the professor. I hear the running of feet, the ripping of claws across carpet, and then silence. I try to quiet my breathing, to make myself utterly invisible.

I'm not sure if I should keep going or if I should turn back. And then I hear something—breathing. Close.

I freeze and press myself into the wall behind me. There's a faint sound, like the thud of paws on plush carpet. I bite the inside of my cheek, not daring to breathe, begging my heart not to beat too loudly.

I glance down, and I can see the shadows of its enormous paws in the candlelight—just outside the curtain. Can it smell me?

I press my head back into the wall and hold in a whimper.

And that's when I feel something sticky drip onto my shoulder. I shift my arms, feel the wall under my fingertips. The whole wall is covered in a thick, dripping liquid. I try to pull my arms away without making any sudden movements. The muck covering the walls pulls against them painfully. It's like honey, but thicker, stickier.

I'm trapped.

Another scraping sound—closer.

My heart races, pounding painfully against my ribs. My breaths are coming in sharp bursts, and my shadows itch like mad against my fingertips.

A low, deep growl—right outside the curtain. Inches from my stomach, the lion presses its nose into the fabric, pushing against it. He's sniffing—I can hear it. The shape of his head in the curtain inches closer. I don't dare breathe.

No. No. Not yet.

A sharp whistle rings across the room. The lion's head pulls back immediately. And it roars—a sound that rattles my bones. And then it bounds away.

The sticky substance releases me, and I fall forward, tumbling through the curtain. But the lion is preoccupied and doesn't see me. There, across

321

the space are Cerise and the professor. Cerise is holding the silver stake, her eyes proud and angry as she faces the lion.

It prowls closer, bent low.

"What are you doing?" hisses Professor Borges.

"I'm saving the damn princess," Cerise says. And then she slashes threateningly at the lion. It lurches back and growls furiously, baring its golden teeth.

And behind them, without any warning, the door to the room rematerializes, handle intact.

The professor sees it, her eyes widening slightly. She glances between me and the lion. The world slows as realization dawns—I know what she plans to do.

She rushes for the door. It bursts open for her, and then the professor is gone.

She's abandoned us.

But at that same moment, Saint Waffles bounds into the room, a truly ferocious roar almost too big for his small body ripping from his chest as he launches himself at the lion.

To my amazement, the lion cowers, hunching its shoulders and backing away. Waffles shows no mercy. His wings launch him into the air, and he comes down at the lion with all four sets of claws bared, his tusks aimed right for the lion's throat.

The lion reels backward, swatting at Waffles in the air. Then it seems to think better of its decision to fight rather than flee. It ducks beneath Waffles as it dashes through the door behind the professor. I can hear its heavy paws pound away through the hall—the exits must have reappeared.

Waffles sends it off with a final roar of warning before landing at my feet. I breathe deeply, trying desperately to regain control of my breathing, and turn to Cerise.

"Why did you do that?" I nearly shriek. I feel the tears threatening to burst from me. I want to shake her.

"You're going to make it through this, Viola," she says, breathing as heavily as I am. "Only you can stop the Queen. I'm going to make sure *you* make it through this."

I pinch my lips together, and then I pull her into a fierce hug. "Thank you," I say. "But never do that again."

CHAPTER THIRTY-FOUR

The Queen's power has grown—the halls are not the way I remember, like someone has taken the castle apart and rearranged it. It takes far too long to find our way.

"Listen," I say as we climb a staircase that I *think* will lead us toward the Queen's rooms. "If something else attacks us, I may have to try to use my shadows. If that happens, you have to run. They're dangerous, and I can't control them."

Cerise nods. "Sure thing, Your Highness."

"Please don't start calling me that."

She grins at me devilishly, like she has no intention of obeying that particular order.

"So, are you going to tell me what's going on with you and Bianca?" I pant as we climb further stairs, eager to pay her back for her teasing and to distract myself from the task at hand.

"Nothing's going on," Cerise says, keeping pace with Waffles beside me.

I glance sideways at her, ready to call her bluff, but then I catch the anxious set of her jaw. "What is it?"

Cerise sighs, glancing sideways at me. "It wasn't Bianca in my room the other night. It was Belladonna."

I stop dead in my tracks. *"Belladonna?"*

She grabs my elbow and pulls me farther down the hall. We can't stop our search, even for this. "We slept together after the All Hallows Eve masquerade. She was that girl in the swan mask, remember?"

"But . . ." I don't need to say my thoughts aloud—that she hates the Roquelarts. She judged me so harshly for being with Roze in the beginning.

"I know, I know," she growls, stuffing a hand in her pocket. "At the ball, I didn't realize it was her behind the mask at first. I tried to write it off as a stupid mistake, but I couldn't stop thinking about her. Anyway, that's part of why I crashed your engagement party. I wanted to see her again. I *had* to."

"And here I thought you were there to see me."

She elbows me in the side, and I almost manage to smile, but my guilty conscience squashes the impulse. *You killed someone*, it whispers.

"Belladonna is . . . intense," I say as we pass down another hall.

Cerise snorts. "Yeah. I like it." She glances up at a painting of a robust Roquelart king holding a musket, his foot proudly propped on the body of a bear. "It's sort of like you said. Not all the Roquelarts are the same, and Belladonna . . . I know she seems nasty. But you have to realize it's all a mask."

I think back to her pouring wine on my lap. "Could've fooled me."

Cerise shakes her head. "It's how she deals with having Queen Maria for a mother. She keeps everyone at arm's length, but she does more to protect Roze and her sisters than you can imagine. She takes the brunt of her mother's torture so that they don't have to. No one sees it. So yeah, it makes her a little *intense*."

I remember the fear in Belladonna's eyes in the catacombs, the look of a beaten dog, and the way she warned Roze about the Queen, how she tried to save him. Somewhere beneath that exterior of pure poison, Belladonna cares about her sisters, about Roze. What exactly has Queen Maria put her through? What does it mean to be the Crown Princess in such a kingdom, where the Queen unleashes pure terrors? Does she save the worst of her terrors for her eldest daughter?

We have to be getting closer to the Queen's room—the halls here are untouched, but the search is still taking far too long. As we ascend the stairs into the darkness, I think about Roze and what he might be enduring at his mother's hands—I don't want to think my darkest thoughts, that it might already be too late.

But León was right—it's time to stop being afraid. It's time to be a thing to fear.

None of the lamps are lit in the halls of the royal residences. All we have is the dim, blue predawn light that manages to pierce the Mists outside the windows. As we creep down thickly carpeted corridors, a pungent smell fills the air. I struggle to place it at first, but it gets stronger as we continue. The smell is twisted and slightly . . . off. Like sour milk. Like bog water.

"Vi," Cerise whispers.

"I smell it," I say. We turn down the hall toward what I think are the bedrooms and stop.

Because the floor ahead is completely covered in a thick layer of water. It's putrid, a deep green-black, and bubbling toward us, slowly covering the last of the floor. Cerise, Waffles, and I back away from it, not letting the foul water touch our feet. And then I see something break the surface of the water.

Waffles starts to growl.

The thing rises from the water—

Its shoulder appears first. Then a head—bald, slimy, and hairless with lake muck hanging from its scalp in long ropes. It lifts an arm, distended at an odd angle, and rises up on its haunches. It's shaped like a human, but its limbs are too long for its body. Its bony form, with translucent, grayish skin, slick with slime, rises over the water like a wraith.

"Cerise—"

I back up half a step, a breath away from running. But in that breath, it scurries toward us, fast as a spider. I scream and scramble away from it, stumbling on the carpet. It catches me around the ankle, and its sharp, spindly fingers claw at my calves. Cerise shrieks and grabs my arm, but then she slips in the murky water too. Waffles roars and gnashes at the creature, but it slips from Waffles's jaws easily.

The thing lifts its head, and I nearly let go of Cerise's hand from fright. Its face is human-shaped. But it has no eyes or nose. Just an enormous, smiling mouth. The monster hisses, opening its great mouth to reveal teeth like long, sharp needles. It reaches out its claws and grabs Cerise by the ankles, dragging her toward it.

"*No*," I scream, and I dive for Cerise. I grab her by the wrists and pull, but I can't find purchase on the floor.

Cerise is screaming, and I try to yank her free, but the thing's grip is sticky and sure.

"*Viola*," Cerise screeches, "your shadows!"

The creature is backing up, pulling Cerise toward the water. Her ankles slip beneath the surface.

"I could hurt you!" I shout back to her.

Cerise's face is wild and terrified. The thing tugs her harder, dragging her farther into the bog, and she sputters and chokes on the putrid water as she tries to kick it away. I dig my heels into the slippery carpet, but there's no traction. Waffles grabs me by my collar with his mouth and tries to tug us both free. I'm flailing in the water, splashing, sputtering, struggling to hold on.

I pull Cerise toward me, wrapping my arms under her shoulders. The thing screeches and without warning releases Cerise. It disappears into the water. Cerise falls onto me. I don't dare let go. Not even for a moment.

"*Let's move!*" I yell, trying to yank her to her feet.

"Viola," she says, and the tone of her voice has me freezing. She's staring at the water with wide eyes.

I look down, and my stomach sinks. All around us, the water moves, small bubbles popping to the surface. Something else is in the water.

"Go," she whispers. "*Now!*"

We sprint for dry ground. Just as we do, the surface bursts open and hands, dozens of slimy, clawed hands, grasp for us. Waffles takes flight, snapping at the creatures from above. But there are far too many. I can feel their claws scraping against my shins, grabbing my ankles under the water, but I throw myself forward onto the dry carpet, kicking mercilessly at the *things* under the water.

"*Viola!*"

One of them has Cerise around the waist, and in a breath, her slick hand slips from mine.

She stumbles in the water, eyeless faces emerging from all around her. The hands tear at her clothes, raking her legs, grabbing at her coat. I lunge toward her, grabbing her extended hand. Waffles flaps toward me, grabbing me by my collar again and pulling me away from Cerise.

"*No,*" I yell at him. "*We can't leave her!*"

Several of the monsters are half out of the water now, their bony torsos and mouths full of needle teeth exposed, biting and scratching Cerise.

I pull with all my might, clasping her hand with both of mine. But our hands are slick, and I can feel hers slipping from me.

I glance around for anything, *anything,* that might be of help, and my eyes land on a suit of armor nearby.

"Hold on," I shout to her and let go of her hand. As soon as I do, she splashes into the water. The creatures claw at her, and she swings her fists wildly at them, kicking and shoving them back into the murky water.

Waffles finally releases me as I clamber toward the suit of armor and grab the sword held in the knight's hands.

"Cerise!" I toss it in the air, and it lands beside her in the water.

She snatches it, pushes to her feet, and slashes at the monsters. Her teeth are gritted as she roars at them, swinging her sword and cutting into hands and faces.

The sword is dull, but it's enough that the creatures hiss and cower. More emerge from the water, trying to find a way to get close to the girl furiously brandishing her weapon.

"Viola, *go!*" she yells over the monsters' screeching. Reaching into her pocket with one hand and hacking at the monsters with her sword with the other, she retrieves the silver stake and tosses it toward me.

"I'm not leaving you!" I shout back. I bend down and grab the stake from the soggy carpet.

"Don't be stupid! They want you, not me! Get out of here—I can handle this!"

My eyes flit between her and the creatures. Their grayish blood is now staining the water from where Cerise has sliced into them. I don't want to leave her.

But Roze.

Cerise fearlessly swings her sword and then looks back at me. *"Now!"* she screams. "I'll never forgive you if you let the damned Queen win."

And I think about what she said about Belladonna, about the Queen's power over her, and I know—this is Cerise's battle to fight too, her sacrifice to make.

I force myself to turn away from my friend and sprint down the hall.

Cerise's cries of fury follow me as I run.

CHAPTER THIRTY-FIVE

It's just me and my gargoyle now.

And I think . . . maybe it was always going to be this way.

In the end, I am always alone.

The halls are silent as the grave. I study the night outside the windows at the end of the foyer, so tall they make me think of sentries standing guard over the royal family. The Mists have shifted from pitch black to a dark, moody gray, and a lump forms in my throat.

I have so little time.

I'm cold. My skin is numb and clammy, and I'm half drenched from the bog water. My body is exhausted. I don't know how much more fight I have in me. My legs are sluggish, and my arms are heavy. I want to find Roze and stop this, but I've been living for seven days in a state of near terror, always running, always hiding.

I'm so tired of hiding.

A sad, distant sound interrupts my thoughts, and I stumble. *A violin.* The sound is so melancholic, whining like a dying animal.

I glance at Waffles, and he returns my apprehensive look.

I force my thoughts elsewhere, keep the fear at bay, and make my legs move, sluggish as they are. But then the sound of the violin grows louder. Closer.

My breath catches in my throat, my whole body seizing up. Then the violin's song shifts, turning from sad and slow to strained, desperate, frantic. It fills my mind and my bones, and the hair on my arms stands on end.

I run.

There's a door at the end of the hall, and I fly through it without thinking, my heart and my mind moving too fast for my legs. I crash through room after room, giving no heed to whatever might be behind each door. All I know is that I need to get away from the sound of the violin, chasing me through these halls.

The pace of the music increases, becoming shriller and more frantic. My heart feels like it might fall out of my chest. Tears stream from my face as I crash through doors, my aching feet tearing at the carpet. The sound comes closer. It's at my back.

Something seizes my throat, like a noose, and yanks. I fall backward, hitting my hip hard on the ground, and the noose drags me, fast as wind, backward into the dark hallway. I try to scream, but the invisible noose is tight around my neck, crushing my throat, cutting off my air.

Waffles bounds after me, running as fast as his feet can carry him, but I'm moving too fast, the carpets burning my face and hands. My vision speckles and the sound of the violin is in my ears, surrounding me, in me.

I will not die like this, at the hands of the Queen's nightmares. *I will live.*

And suddenly, the violin's song goes silent. The tug around my neck stops, and I'm still on the floor.

My heart starts to slow, and I peek through my arms, wrapped around my head. I'm . . . I'm in the Queen's bedroom.

A moment later Waffles collides with me, sniffing around my face, nudging my shoulder.

"I'm all right," I mumble, not sure if it's the truth.

Pushing myself gingerly to my feet, I take in the room. It looks untouched from when Roze and I were here days ago—covered in dying flowers and dust.

And in the opposite corner—the magic mirror.

I take a step toward the mirror, keeping my eye on its black depths. Do I simply drive the stake into the glass? Can it be that simple? I approach the mirror again and gaze at my own reflection. Odd. I'd thought the mirror hadn't shown my reflection before, not until I asked it a question.

I take the stake from where I'd stowed it safely in my pocket, approaching the surface of the mirror cautiously. I stare back at my reflection, and it has every hair on my body standing on end. The mirror seems completely ordinary. If I passed it in a hall, I wouldn't even notice that it was enchanted.

Slowly, like I'm afraid the mirror will sense its impending doom, I lift my hand. I allow myself one deep breath and then bring the stake down like an axe on its glassy surface.

Silver against glass screeches as the stake slips down the surface, and my fist collides painfully with the glass. I drop the stake and cradle my hand.

"Ouch," I mutter, shaking it. Saint Waffles growls, and I glare at the mirror. "So. Not that easy."

I pick up the stake and bite my lip, studying the mirror again.

"It *is* a magic mirror, isn't it?" I say to Waffles. "Maybe the trick to destroying it lies in knowing how to use it."

The mirror is the tether for the Queen's power, so logically, destroying it would weaken the Queen's power, cutting her ability to focus it, to channel it. If I can't break it, what if I just *un*-tether her power? I am a *meiga*, after all. What if there's a way to take the mirror as my own tether—steal it from the Queen?

I step closer to my reflection, staring hard into its depths.

"Magic Mirror," I say, "show me your secrets."

Nothing.

My reflection stares back at me, mirroring my slight frown.

I crinkle my brows together and move my hand in front of the mirror. As expected, the reflection moves with me. I jump once, and it jumps with me. I look up into my own face and frown.

And the reflection smiles.

I tumble back and trip over the rug, falling to the floor. Waffles skitters backward, growling.

My reflection stays standing, towering over me. That devilish smile grows wider, and slowly, it lifts a leg and steps through the frame.

I scramble away, my back hitting the foot of the bed. The reflection steps toward me, completely outside the mirror. Saint Waffles throws himself between me and my reflection, but it pays him no mind as it lowers itself until it's squatting before me. He tries to snap at it, but his jaws pass right through it, like it's made of smoke.

It holds out a hand in front of itself, and I flinch. But then a teacup and saucer appear in its outstretched hand. It lifts the teacup to its lips and sips. "My, aren't you pathetic?"

I stare back. This has to be another one of the Queen's illusions.

The reflection sets its cup back on its saucer and sniffs. "I've been waiting for you to show up again, you know."

My heart is still pounding in my ears, and I stare back at my own face.

The reflection shrugs. It's such an oddly human gesture. "What are you?" I ask.

The reflection looks at me like I'm an idiot and points behind it to the mirror.

"You're . . . a mirror?"

The reflection scoffs. "I'm *the* Mirror. I hold all the answers—past, present, and future. Whatever you wish to know, I can tell you, as long as you ask the right questions."

I take a deep breath. "Did the Queen create you?" Is it something like Roze, flesh and magic, human and not?

Its hand strikes, gripping me by my throat, surprisingly solid. "I'm something worse," it hisses. Its hand around my neck is surely real, closing over my windpipe, crushing my larynx. But when Waffles leaps at it, teeth bared and claws out, he passes right through it again.

But what the Mirror hasn't seen is the stake hidden in my hand, that I'd slipped under my thigh as I fell moments ago. Gripping the stake in my white-knuckled fist, I swing it sharply up into the Mirror's ribs.

Its eyes—*my* eyes—go wide. Its hold on my throat goes slack, and I sink back, coughing. Regaining my breath, I turn my head to watch the reflection stare down at the stake lodged between its ribs, its chest jerking and twisting oddly, its form shimmering like a light about to flicker out.

"The crest of Castelle," it heaves. Then its narrowed eyes land on mine, and it hisses, "What are you?"

"M—my name is Viola. Viola Sinclair."

Its head tilts. "No."

I swallow. Apparently that wasn't the answer it was looking for. "I am the daughter of King León of Castelle," I whisper, the words feeling strange on my tongue.

The Mirror makes a peculiar hissing sound in its throat. "Get this *thing* out of me."

"No."

"Get it *out*, wretched girl!" Its eyes are alight with rage—its teeth are bared. "I am a power older and stronger and stranger than you'll ever understand. You don't know what you've done."

"You're the Queen's tether for her magic. I came here to cut off her power at its source," I snap.

Something shifts in the Mirror's eyes. It shifts back, moving in an inhuman way, more like light than a living being. "You came to sever the Queen's power?"

"Yes."

The Mirror closes its eyes, almost as though in prayer, and when it opens them, the fury is gone from its expression. "Remove the silver from my side, little witch, and I will help you."

I furrow my brow warily. "Why?"

The Mirror hisses again. "Because the Queen has trapped me here like a slave, and I have served her relentlessly for decades." It lowers its head, my own curls falling over its eyes. "I am a being of revelation and truth. A life as the personal puppet of a deranged light *meiga* is well beneath me."

I let my gaze fall to the stake in its side. I shouldn't trust it. The plan was to destroy it. "Help me how?"

It growls in frustration. "You've already broken my tether to the Queen. But my own magic is being kept at bay while the silver stays lodged inside me. Remove it, and I will teach you anything you wish to know."

This is a bad idea. Logically, I should walk away. Or I should drive the stake deeper, until the Mirror stops shimmering and disappears completely. But . . .

"What sort of things could you teach me?"

A slow smile spreads on its face—my smile. "Anything."

Anything. What could I ask that would help me save Roze? What might this being know about the Queen? How to kill her? How to fight her magic? How to break the curse of the seven thorns?

Without giving it another thought, I reach up, seize the stake, and with a swift yank, dislodge it from the Mirror's side.

It groans as though in deep pain, its eyes going glassy for a moment. It sinks to its knees, and a perfect replica of my own school skirt pools around its legs.

It utters another aching sigh, lifts a hand, and a teacup and saucer appear in its grip. "All right, then. Ask your questions," it says, taking a sip.

"Questions?"

It rolls its eyes vexedly. "I can't give you an answer without a question, now, can I?"

I swallow and ask, "You'll answer any question?"

"Any question that has an answer."

"How do I kill her?" I can't help but think that if Roze had asked the question, he'd sound cold and threatening. I sound more afraid than fearsome.

The Mirror wags one of my own fingers at me. "That's not the question you need."

I frustratedly rub my eyes.

It leans forward. "You need to know what *you* are and what *she* is."

"What does that mean?"

The Mirror's smile is full of cruelty and self-satisfaction. "You are the same, and yet not. You are both the whole and the part."

Why did I think this would be easy? Of course the Mirror won't give straightforward answers. "You're saying we're the same . . . because we're both *meigas*. But how are we different?"

Setting her teacup aside, she leans forward, resting her arms—*my arms*—on her knees. "You are two sides of the same coin. The Queen is a light *meiga*. She wields the powers of creation, revelation, and unification."

"I knew that already."

The Mirror acts as though she doesn't hear me. "*You*, however . . ." That cruel smile returns. "You are different. I haven't met one of you in quite some time. Little Shadow Girl, a dark *meiga*, from the Kingdom of Darkness itself. You wield the power of destruction, obfuscation, and separation. All things dark and dividing."

Something tightens in my chest. Sir Patrick's lecture from days ago comes roaring back to me. "Is dark magic evil?" I ask.

"Do you think you're evil, girl?"

I don't have an answer to that question.

The mirror licks her teeth. "Evil is relative. Are the stars evil because they dwell in darkness? Humans use them to navigate and mark their seasons. Is the sun good because it brings light? It scorches the land with its heat."

I frown. "I've never seen either."

The Mirror's grin reveals all its teeth. "Yet."

"My shadows kill people," I whisper, the sick feeling that's been with me since the caverns twisting in my stomach. Kole, my brother . . . how can their deaths ever not be evil? At the very least, they were horrible, horrible accidents and all my fault. They didn't deserve to die. "You said my power is destruction. How is that not evil?" I ask, staring at my hands, pale in the light.

"It depends on what you destroy, now, doesn't it?"

I swallow, staring back into my own eyes. Could the Mirror be right? Is it possible that I've made my shadows into a twisted force of fear and self-loathing? Maybe I'm truly the monster the Queen thinks I am—but it takes a monster to kill a monster.

Like and unlike. The same and not.

My father told me to be dangerous. Maybe I can be dangerous and still be something good.

"How do I do it?"

The Mirror's eyes gleam. "That answer lies in something you've been searching for for a very long time. And a great many questions will be answered by it."

Something sparks in my mind. "Where is the *Book of Odds*?"

It bares all my teeth in a catlike grin. "*Now* you're asking the interesting questions. It is far beyond these castle walls."

I deflate. "Then how can I know what to do?"

"I have seen it." It taps its forehead. "In here. I will show you what you need to see."

"Show me," I urge.

As soon as the words leave my lips, something solid lodges in my esophagus, and I choke. Coughing, I reach into my mouth, bending over until something mushy and damp falls from my throat onto the floor. A wad of parchment paper.

"You couldn't have just handed it to me?"

The Mirror only smiles.

I unfold the soggy paper in my lap. My breath shakes as I smooth it out and realize what I'm touching. Even if it's the Mirror's reproduction— this is the actual text of the *Book of Odds*. No one has seen it in eons. And it's covered in Hivernian runes.

I want to curse the professor for being such a coward as I peer down at the runes. This is translation work far above my skill level, but still I piece together a few clauses as well as I can.

"This is an account of the first time the Mists came," I whisper.

The Mirror is silent as my fingers trail down the page, picking apart sentences where I can.

"The power that creates is the power that destroys," I translate. "In the end, after all our efforts were in vain, the devastation undid itself . . ."

My eyes scan the page until they land on an illustration. An Ouroboros—a serpent consuming its own tail.

I look up, meeting my own eyes in the Mirror's. "I have one more question."

The Mirror's eyes light with excitement. "Yes?"

"Mirror . . . who sent the Mists?"

The Mirror grins viciously.

CHAPTER THIRTY-SIX

The sky has turned to dark ash. The sun is coming, and I am running.

I will find the Queen and stop Roze from offering himself. The Mirror is gone—the Queen's power is untethered, unfocused, crippled. I know now that I can face her—that whatever untrained power rests in my bones has to be enough. I only need to find her.

I have no idea where the Queen might be, where Roze might be. The castle is *enormous*, and that's to say nothing of Vandenberghe across the glass bridge. They could be anywhere.

Annie.

I freeze. Ice slides down my back. *No.* I thought this was over with—that this waking nightmare ended after I had that vision of the woods. Slowly, I turn to face the direction I came.

There, half-obscured in the darkness of the hall, is the ghostly image of my little brother. He looks almost solid now, halfway between ghost and boy. His precious face stares at me with dead, unfeeling eyes.

Backing up a step, I whisper, "What do you want?"

Annie.

His mouth moves as he says it, but the sound seems to come from everywhere and from inside me, his childlike voice ringing through my very soul.

"Please," I choke. "I can't—not now."

I need to help Roze. I don't have time for another delay.

ANNIE.

My brother's voice is insistent, his little eyes wide now.

"*I'm sorry*," I plead. "I'm sorry for what I did to you. *Please*, I have to go." I back up another step. I turn to leave, and his voice cuts through the darkness once more.

"He's in the auditorium." This time his voice is natural, human. My heart skips a beat and I look back at him. His face is pale, but more solid than ever. His chest rises and falls like he's truly breathing. "Tell him the truth, Annie. Tell him everything."

My face feels numb. For several moments I don't respond.

"*Annie—*"

"Okay." I'm not sure what makes me say it—whether it's because I know I want Roze to know me, everything I've learned about myself, everything I've been through, or because I can't say no to my brother when it feels like I'm looking at the real him for the first time since I was small.

My little brother smiles at me—a smile that I can barely remember from long ago. "Sorry I took your locket." The note of sadness in his voice is unmistakable. "Bye, Annie." And then he's gone—vanished like he was never there.

I blink several times, and Waffles whimpers at my feet, staring up at me. Somehow it was easier to deal with seeing my brother's face when I thought of him as a ghost haunting me, but whatever this was, it wasn't meant to scare me. Seeing him—it was torture. It was healing.

I scrub away stray moisture in my eyes and take a deep breath. "Come on, Waffles," I say, and I continue my descent down the winding passages of the castle, now with a direction—Moody Hall, the auditorium of Vandenberghe.

I sprint through the halls of the school, Waffles at my heels, flying past stained glass and Corinthian columns, looking for any sign of the Queen's spirit or Roze.

But when I pass the dining hall, I freeze. Breakfast has started. Some students are out of bed, nursing cups of tea and oat toast in their seats. Except . . . they aren't moving.

I step closer, but don't dare step inside. It's like time is suspended. Eyes are open, but they don't blink. Tea is half poured, hanging in the air over empty cups. I look down and notice—for the first time—black, thorned vines creeping along the ground. They trail in the corners, crawling over seats, winding up over furniture, and twisting around students' legs.

Once, all the Queen cared about was maintaining control and the respect of her people. She relished the formality of Court—the etiquette, the balls, the fashions. Now she's a wild thing, the power within her consuming her. I remember what King León said about magic being driven to greater and greater heights, how without the dark, the light becomes sick, and vice versa. Whoever Queen Maria once was, she is something entirely else now.

I follow the vines with my eyes—they're growing toward me, their source somewhere deeper in the castle.

I force myself to turn away from the dining hall, away from the students caught up in the Queen's magic, and follow the path of the vines. They grow thicker as I move down the hall, occasionally punctuated by roses of such a deep red that they're almost black. Waffles begins to hunch his shoulders, a low growl in his throat.

Soon, I struggle to step through the vines and have to climb on top of them. The thorns tear at my shins and skirt. Finally, we reach their source— Moody Hall, the auditorium where I have spent countless hours for schoolwide events. The doors are gone, ripped away by vines as thick as my legs, those sinister roses blooming everywhere. I peer around the arched doorway, and air freezes in my lungs.

Every inch of the room is covered in briars, snaking over chairs, clinging to chandeliers, ripping through the banners of each house and covering the crest of the school that hangs above the stage. The floor is so thick with them that it's hardly visible. And of course, it's all spotted with roses of deep blackish red. I sat in the auditorium's worn, wooden seats my first day at Vandenberghe, so in awe of the school and its history that I could almost cry. And now the hall is covered in the Queen's strange growth, a monstrous garden, barely recognizable.

There's no sign of anyone, but this is certainly where the vines are coming from. I take careful steps inside, Waffles flying close to my shoulder. There's something on the wall, between the high windows. It's small—hardly visible—but it can't be roses. It's a pale cream color, mostly obscured by branches.

I climb over several huge vines to get a better look, reach up to grab hold of the branches on the wall, pull myself up until my face is level with—

I fall back, a scream caught in my throat, landing painfully on a thorny branch. My stomach roils—there, barely visible through the vines, is Ed's face.

His eyes are closed, skin pale, and blood is trickling down his forehead and from his mouth. The vines hold his body against the wall, leaving just his face visible.

And then I notice the others. My eyes pass over the rest of the wall, and I make out each one of them, almost completely obscured in growth—the rest of the Grimmstones.

Are they dead? No, no they can't be.

Saints, I told them to find Roze. I sent them here. This is *my* fault.

A woman's voice, eldritch and echoing, breaks the silence. *"Miss Sinclair."*

The Queen.

Her voice, unmistakable in its coldness, says my name like it's a sin. But I don't see her anywhere.

"I'm here for Roze," I call. The fear doesn't control me anymore—it's a part of me now. "Where is he?"

"My son is safe from *you*," she says, the sound coming from everywhere all at once.

A movement by the stage catches my eye. I squint. A pool of water begins to billow from the floor like from a spring, pitch black, a void. A head emerges from the pool, then a pair of shoulders.

Belladonna.

She rises from it like she's suspended, her hair long and stringy, her eyes sunken and red-rimmed. She looks up toward me and grins, cruel and inhuman.

My breath hitches. What happened to her? She looks so different from just a day ago—like she's several days dead.

She tilts her head up, and for a second, I know I'm looking into the eyes of the daughter, not the mother. Her eyes are wild and desperate, and her mouth forms a word that her voice doesn't produce—*Help*.

Then her head snaps back. And slowly, she lowers her gaze to me. This time, when she speaks, the Queen's voice is back. "Hello, Miss Sinclair," she says.

Waffles charges, his claws tearing through thorny vines as he attacks, launching himself into the air toward her.

Belladonna merely raises an eyebrow. "Enough of you, foul creature."

She waves, and I hear a heartbreaking, world-ending whimper, and Saint Waffles's form freezes midair. His eyes are open, his mouth frozen in a snarl, his teeth and claws bared.

He falls to the ground, thumping on the steps. She's turned him to stone.

Waffles.

Rage wells within me. "You're going to regret that," I snarl.

I'm the other side of the coin, the equal to the Queen's power. I have the secret of the *Book of Odds* now, the secret to end the Mists, end *her*. I just need to figure out how I can do it without hurting the Grimmstones or—Saints help me—Belladonna. And I need to find Roze.

I glance out the windows. The sky is still a deep ashen gray—the sun hasn't risen. There's still time. There *has* to still be time.

"My power has allowed me to do unspeakable things," the Queen says through Belladonna, stepping out of the pool and sauntering toward me. The vines don't obstruct her path—she passes through them like water. I back up a step unconsciously, and she observes the hands that don't belong to her, the hands that she controls, like she's trying on a body. "But my daughter serves me willingly. All my children do. Even the wretched Prince."

"Where is he?" I spit.

"You want to see him?" says the same voice, but from a different direction. To my left, Princess Wisteria emerges from a second pool of water like a marionette. Her eyes are just as deep and bloodshot as her sister's, glazed over like she's been through something harrowing. She too speaks with the dead Queen's voice. "Fair warning—he's looking rather wan. Finally, he appears as weak on the outside as he's always been on the inside."

A giggle echoes through the room, and I twist to my right as another princess emerges from a pool of water—Oleandra.

"Oh, poor little Viola," she says in the Queen's voice. "How you've underestimated the hopelessness of your situation."

I won't let her sway me. I won't let her break me.

I am the darkness. My magic destroys. And I will destroy the Queen.

Belladonna takes a step closer to me. "Your very *existence* threatens my Kingdom, my family, my home."

I shake my head. "All I wanted was to be left alone. It's you who made me your enemy."

Belladonna surveys me with a bored expression. "Oh? And you've been so innocent, have you?"

A chorus of strained giggles erupts as princesses spring up all over the room, popping up from pools of water like corrupted daisies. Hemlock, Narcissa, and Azalea.

I spin in place, but there's no way I can stand without turning my back to one of them. I'm so terrified that I'm angry. My shadows tremble within me like a cloak of darkness.

Belladonna smiles. "Perhaps you need a reminder." She snaps her fingers.

The room disappears, winking into blackness like someone blew out a candle. And then a completely different scene materializes before me.

There is my mother, sitting in a chair, my baby brother on her lap. She's shelling nuts into a basket, one of her usual tasks she did for the community in the caverns, and she hums softly to herself, rocking my brother while she works. The song is a distant memory. A lullaby. I remember her singing it to me as a child. She opens her mouth to sing aloud, my brother gazing up at her face adoringly.

But the words are different.

Hush, my darling, hush,
Oh-la-lee-la-lay
Hush, my darling, hush,
Or Bloody Annie will take thee away.

Her eyes snap up to mine, and the look in them is like a knife through my heart. Tears welling, eyes burning. It's the look she gave me the day she and my father sent me away.

The day I killed my brother.

Old grief seizes my chest, a stone crushing my heart.

And then the scene disappears. I'm in the Berlaise common room, everything awash in pink light. Kole is tinkering with his little golden tools on the sofa next to me, and everything is warm and wonderful. But then he looks up at me, the light catching the gold in his green eyes, the metal rims of his glasses.

"I thought we were friends, Viola," he says. "Why . . . did you do this to me? Why did I deserve this?"

You didn't, my heart screams. *You were mean and awful to me. But you're just a stupid boy. You didn't deserve to die.*

He stares at me with a look of such sadness, such disappointment, that I feel my heart shatter all over again, and grief is a living, angry thing in my stomach. I want to tear it out of me.

But then the scene fades, and I'm in Roze's tower. He's there with me, near the piano by the window. His face is grim, but his eyes shimmer as he lifts his hands—his gloves are gone, and somehow I know that the poison is too. Roze slides warm fingers over my cheeks till his hands are caught up in my hair, and a shiver passes through my body. He leans forward till his forehead rests on mine and we're sharing breath. I grab him by the wrists just to have an anchor.

I don't dare close my eyes. I'm afraid he'll disappear like the others. And right now, he's tender and unafraid, and he can *touch me.*

Not real, a voice calls in the distance.

But I'm not listening. I lean forward—

"I know what you did, Viola," he whispers.

And then my skin starts to burn. I fall to my knees, but his grip on me tightens, my neck blistering beneath his touch, my vision spotting black and white.

"I know what you did."

No.

Not real.

Shadows shoot from me like arrows, and for a moment everything is black. When my vision clears, I see Moody Hall again, covered in vines, and Roze's sisters staring at me with abject horror and hatred.

I don't understand why until I see the ring of dead, dark vines circling me, and I realize—I've killed them. My shadows broke through the hold of the Queen's magic on me.

I glare up at Belladonna. "Where is Roze?"

I can feel her mother's ire through her eyes, but for a moment Belladonna's own expression flashes through—sad, desperate.

"It's too late anyway," she says, although she seems uncertain. "You want to see him? Fine."

She snaps her fingers. And Roze materializes before me.

He lies on his back on the floor. His gloves are gone, revealing those pale pianist hands, and his sleeves are rolled up to the elbows. The tattoo of the rose is on full display. There's one thorn left, and it's fading.

"Roze," I choke.

He opens his eyes wearily, and they find mine. He seems weak, like he's waning too. His mouth opens barely, like he's trying to speak but can't.

I look back up at Belladonna.

"Let him go, or I'll destroy you," I hiss, my shadows forcing their way out of my hands and winding around my fingers like snakes.

As one, the sisters smile. "His bargain is nearly done. His spirit is already fading. Strike me now, and you destroy your Prince as well."

No, no, there has to still be time.

All the sisters are watching me with a disturbingly similar gleeful expression on each of their faces.

"I'll make a trade," I say again to the dead Queen's spirit. "My life for Roze's."

Roze's eyes shoot up to mine, full of hard rage. *"Viola,"* he croaks. A chill skitters over my skin at the weakness in his voice.

Azalea says in the Queen's voice, "Do you really think I would let Roze get away with his rebellion?" The sisters step closer as one. Their eyes turn dark and condemning. Furious. "You've been so clever in how you've gotten your claws into him. He was willing to give his life for yours. But then again, he's never known what's best for him. Roze was disloyal. There are consequences for that."

I shake my head. "He doesn't deserve this."

Her expression is soft, almost . . . sympathetic. It's so disturbing on a face possessed that I don't breathe as she says, "Oh dear. You've fallen for him, haven't you?"

She exchanges glances with the other sisters, all possessed with the same spirit. "Didn't he tell you what he is?"

That he isn't *real.* That he was created, not born.

"I don't care," I say. I will fight for him. He deserves to exist.

"A *terrible*, unforgivable mistake," she hisses. "I created Roze by accident—consumed as I was by grief after Castelle destroyed my home, I let my emotions overcome me." Belladonna tilts her head back, looking down on me in an expression that is purely Queen Maria. "My magic is light. It is born of logic and control. It creates. But there is the other way— the wicked way. Emotion and pain beget the dark magic. It destroys. When I created Roze, I created something using dark magic. I . . . melded . . . the two ways." She turns her gaze on Roze, a look of pure disgust on her face. "Such an act is obscene. Roze is a poisoned prince. A life that takes life. An abomination."

At that word, Roze closes his eyes, as if accepting the truth of that condemnation.

"I told you I would do whatever it took to protect my family, Miss Sinclair. If that should include taking back the power I foolishly gave Roze all those years ago, then so be it. He has endangered us all by protecting *you*."

"You're the danger, not me," I growl. "Why don't you tell the truth— that *you* are the reason we're all trapped in this castle. *You* sent the Mists. *You murdered your own people*."

The Queen's lips pinch in fury. Roze manages to open his eyes and stare at the possessed face of his sister.

"Fine," she snaps. "I created the Mists. I was tortured with grief, full of righteous rage against Castelle, and the Mists were made. And yes, the people paid the price—hardly an anomaly in the war games of rival kingdoms. But look what they have done—they kept the *filth* of Castelle away from Aragoa for nearly two decades, thank the Saints."

I shake my head. "Any way you paint it, you are a liar and a traitor. You've killed thousands. Single-handedly. And you've been deceiving everyone about it for years."

"You are not one to lecture me on truth. Time to confess, Miss Sinclair."

My face pales.

"Don't be coy, dear," Wisteria says, her voice motherly and chiding. "All I ask for is honesty. You know it's the least I deserve after all you've done." She tilts her head like she's studying me. "*Honesty*, Miss Sinclair. With your Prince . . . and yourself. I'm giving you a last chance at redemption."

When I say nothing, she exhales through her nose resignedly. "He hears it from your lips or mine. It's your choice."

Belladonna charges forward and grabs Roze by his hair, pulling his head back against her legs. She pulls a dagger from her waist and rests it on the long column of his throat, against the moth tattoo. "Perhaps it should be the last thing he hears."

Her hand on his head lazily threads through his hair, petting him. His eyes, however, are glued on mine.

I meet his gaze, steel myself. "King León of Castelle is my father. That's what the book was hiding," I say. "I don't belong here."

His smile is small and incredulous. Fire sparks in his eyes despite the knife at his throat. "Of course," he croaks. "How could I not see it—you terrible, lovely thing." His smile broadens, looking down his nose at me. His eyes are softer than I've ever seen them. "Hello, Princess."

I can't look away from those quicksilver eyes.

"Roze—"

The dagger tightens on his neck, and he winces. "You're still not telling the truth," Hemlock says with a strange twist to her neck, baring her teeth.

"Hiding things again," Oleandra adds.

"Keeping your secrets and trapping the Prince in your snare," says Narcissa.

My eyes snap away from Roze as I watch them speak. They take another step forward.

"*Tell the truth,*" they say together. Their voices echo against the towering ceiling of the hall.

I shake my head. *No.*

"Viola?" Roze says. There's hesitation in his voice. I nearly flinch at the sound of it.

I can't look at him. I can't. My whole body trembles as I hold my shadows at bay. My veins have turned black with their presence, like they're trying to press their way through my skin.

Belladonna clenches her fists and shouts, "*Tell him.* Tell my son the truth, little *witch.*" She spits the words. Full of hatred.

Hatred I deserve.

Tears break free from my eyes. "I'm sorry. I'm so sorry, Roze."

His face turns wary, genuine fear in those eyes of shattered glass.

I can hardly see through the tears that blur my vision. I deserve this, like I deserve the horrors of the Mirror and the Queen's torturous visions, like I deserve what happened to Kole and my brother and everything the Queen has unleashed on me.

They are all judgments. For what I am.

This is justice.

I want to tell him. I beg my lips to work, but when I open them, they make no sound. My knees go weak. Roze wrenches himself from Belladonna's grasp, knocks aside the dagger, and lunges across the floor to catch me, holding me up, handling me like I am some fragile thing to be protected—not a monster, not a creature of darkness.

He sinks to the floor with me, his arms firm around my shoulders. I am consumed with no other thought except that I don't deserve him. I thought he was a wicked and cursed thing, like me . . . but he isn't. He may not be kind, but he is good—the sort of person who trades lives with someone with whom they used to trade insults.

He has a type of darkness, but nothing like my own.

He draws a handkerchief from his pocket and uses it so that he can lift my chin without touching my skin.

"Viola," he whispers.

I can't look at him.

I lift my eyes instead to the cinquefoil window at the end of the hall, towering over our heads. The Mists turn a dusty rose color—the sunrise.

"Roze," I say. My throat is raw and rasping from crying. "I killed your father."

CHAPTER THIRTY-SEVEN

Six Weeks Earlier

It was All Hallows Eve—a time for dark things, some would say, but in the Kingdom of Aragoa, it was an excuse to wear a mask and pretend to be someone or something else for a night.

The King and Queen hosted a masquerade ball, and the whole Kingdom was invited. The revel occupied every ballroom and banquet hall in the lower castle. Nobles and people from the caverns bumped shoulders, stumbling and tossing back glasses of deep red wine, which was all the more disturbing when no one looked human—bodies adorned in elaborate dress, their heads donned to look like dark crows, emerald-eyed foxes, and all manner of creatures tusked and tailed, warted and whiskered.

There was a charge in the air, like the night was spelled for misfortune. I could first sense it when the King and Queen took their customary dance to officially open the ball. She in her mask of a white lioness, and he in the mask of a lion, meant to be a matching pair. But the King stumbled through the dance, clearly drunk, not looking in the Queen's face once. It was embarrassing to watch, honestly. And when it was over, he left the masquerade quickly, apparently considering his duties fulfilled for the evening.

The Queen's mood soured after that, and it hung over the revelry like a thundercloud as she sat seething on her throne. I actually empathized with her at the time.

After an hour or two, Cerise was terribly drunk as well, laughing hysterically in her tiger mask, dressed in an elegant navy suit and dancing with anyone she could grab hold of. I'd spent most of the evening watching over her, making sure she didn't do something she would regret the next morning.

I wasn't interested in drinking and dancing, not when the only person I wanted to dance with was taking his studies too seriously to participate. I wanted to be in the library with Kole, Waffles on my lap, book in hand, but instead I was at the masquerade, trying to avoid small talk.

"It's getting late," I told Cerise around midnight, when the party was becoming so raucous I was seriously concerned about getting back to our dormitories in one piece.

But Cerise's eyes were glazed over as she watched a group of noble-born girls in pretty dresses laughing together. In the center of their brood, a girl in a pure white dress stood like a queen holding court. I didn't recognize Princess Belladonna behind the white feathers of her swan mask, and neither did Cerise.

And then their eyes met. Even over the noise of the crowd, I could hear the hitch in Cerise's breathing.

Without looking at me, she handed her wine to me and said, "It's no use, mother dear. I cannot finish my weaving. You may blame Aphrodite, soft as she is." She grinned devilishly at the swan-masked girl.

Knowing what I know now, I wish I could have warned her just how perilous it can be to fall in love with a Roquelart.

"You can't quote poetry at me to get out of leaving," I complained, following her as she stumbled toward the noble girls.

"I think I can—you love linguistics. Words are your weakness." And then she waved me off, determined to go flirt as she stumbled into the crowd.

I sighed. I supposed I should stand guard while Cerise made a fool of herself. I found a step to sit on and pulled a book out of the pocket of my dress.

"You of all people would bring a book to a party," drawled a voice over me.

My stomach clenched, and I looked up. Prince Roze stood over me, wearing the most elegant suit I'd ever seen—all black, gold stitching of roses and thorns winding up the lapels and the tie. His face was covered in a mask like a stag with devilish prongs twisting up from his head, but I could still see the unmistakable sneer on his lips.

"Is my reading disturbing Your Highness's evening?" I snapped.

"Why did you even come if you're just going to sit in the corner and read—" He snatched up my book.

"Hey—"

"*Tales of the Brothers Grimm*," he read. "My, your tastes are macabre, aren't they?"

I glared at him. "Don't you have anyone else to bother? I'm sure there's some half-drunk nitwit duchess waiting for your attention."

"Jealous, Sinclair?"

I snorted. "Give me back my book." I made a grab for it, but he held it high over my head. "Are you five years old?"

"What will you give me for it?" he crooned.

"How about I resist the urge to strangle you?"

"So violent," he said with a devilish smirk. "I like it."

My cheeks burned. "Give. It. Back."

"Beg."

My blood lit on fire. This was so like him. Prick.

"Come now, Sinclair," he taunted. "It can't be that difficult to offer your Prince some deference. Just a little respect. That's all I ask."

I stepped close, my face an inch from his. I could feel his breath on my lips. "The day I beg you for anything is the day I die."

He continued to smile at me. "Maybe *I* should beg. Would you like that, Sinclair? Me on my knees before you?"

Something hot and confusing shot through my body. I *had* to get away from him.

"Fine. Keep it," I muttered, weaving as much disdain as possible into my words. "Maybe you'll actually learn something."

I heard him chuckle behind me as I stormed out of the ballroom. I stomped through several halls, just wanting space to take a breath. There were so many bodies around that the normally frigid castle was warm. I'd started to sweat through my dress. The lights and the sounds were overwhelming.

I walked until I'd calmed down, my pace slowing as I found empty halls. I would check back in with Cerise in a few minutes—see if she was ready to leave, or if she'd found someone she'd rather go home with. In the meantime, I studied the architecture and the paintings that adorned the walls. Every room in this part of the castle was the definition of extravagance—wallpaper with embroidery so thick it stood inches off the walls, vases of hand-painted porcelain, murals painted by masters that stretched across every ceiling. The whole castle was a work of art, and I found it far more interesting than the party anyway. I wandered for longer than I realized, exploring the beauty of it.

Eventually, I opened a door to what I thought was another gallery and was surprised to find that it was a balcony, now closed in with glass, Mists pressing against the panes. I almost turned back when I heard voices. But then I stopped dead in my tracks.

One of the voices was unmistakable—Roze. I quietly crept behind a column.

"What could possibly be your reason for this?"

"That is not for you to question." My brows rose. That was the voice of the Queen.

"She's no one. What's she done to you that you would ask this of me?"

"You are at my *command*—"

Roze sighed deeply. "I'm tired."

"I don't care how weary your drinking and lazing about in that ridiculous school makes you. You *will* follow my orders."

"I—"

"*That* is my final word, Prince."

Roze was silent. A moment later, the Queen's figure came into view, and I shrank back into the shadows of the colonnade. She swept through the door leading back into the castle.

I peered around the edge of the column. Roze Roquelart's back was to me, hunched over the balcony's edge, hands gripped on the railing. His back heaved deeply, almost as though . . . he were crying.

It broke him to be his mother's knife in the dark. I realize now that this was the moment she first commanded him to kill me, that the disobedience that would follow was what led to that infernal tattoo being magicked onto his arm.

He was so trapped, in this life of pain and isolation. Who wouldn't become cruel in those circumstances? Who wouldn't embrace the role of the sadistic murderer his mother wanted him to be, just to survive?

He turned and stepped away from the balcony, and I was so lost in thought that I didn't react quickly enough. He lifted his head and spotted me among the shadows.

"*You*," he growled, voice like pure venom. "Get out."

"I—"

"*Get out!*" he roared.

I whirled toward the door and rushed back into the castle. Roze and I had a rivalry, a mutual dislike of each other, but he'd always been cold, aloof. Never had he spoken to me like *that*, with pure fury. Even now, I'm unsure whether it was embarrassment that made him shout me away . . . or if he was trying to protect me from himself.

I raced down a hallway, paying little attention to where I was going. Finally, I found a dark, desolate place. I slid to the floor against the wall and buried my head in my knees.

I tried to catch my breath.

But then a soft scraping noise sounded from the end of the hall.

I jerked my head up.

The hall was dark, but there was a figure at the end of it. A person—tall, swaying gently like a phantom. I remained frozen where I sat, unable to move as it came closer.

And then it came into the light—*the King*.

I supposed King Alexandre had once been handsome—his hair was still golden, his frame still tall and proud, adorned tonight in black finery. But his flaxen locks were disheveled and thin, his eyes red-rimmed with enormous dark circles sinking them into his head.

He was pacing the hall, his steps uneven and frantic. "Bones and blood, bones and blood. What else? What else?"

He leaned against the wall, breathing heavily for a moment, and then his eyes lifted.

He spotted me.

"What are you doing here?" he growled.

"I—I—" I stuttered. How did one address the King? I muddled through a curtsy, but it only made the King sneer at me. "I'm sorry, Your Majesty," I said.

I started to leave the hallway.

"Stop," he commanded.

I obeyed, but I could feel my heartbeat in my throat. The King was clearly drunk out of his mind, and there was nothing good that could come from an encounter with a man of power in a dark hallway.

"Sir?" I said, keeping my tone formal.

"Who are you?" he asked.

I blinked. "My name is Viola Sinclair."

"Sinclair," he hissed. His lips formed a tight line. There was anger in his face that I didn't understand, like I'd offended him somehow. I'd never encountered him in my life, but now he was looking at me like he hated my very existence.

"Brown hair. Curly. Like your mother," he murmured, almost to himself. "But your face is your father's. Yes, I can see it—in the nose and cheeks—"

I stammered, confused. The woman I thought of as my mother had yellow hair. Certainly, neither of the people I thought were my parents knew the King.

But now I know that Alexandre was remembering his love, my father, a king with hair like night whose face I'd never known.

"Too long," he murmured. "Damnable Mists . . . too long. And it's my fault."

"Sir?" I was no longer certain that he was even in his right mind.

"Too long . . . my *people* . . . my fault . . . too damned *weak* . . ."

"Should I go find someone?"

"*No!*" he barked, and wiped a hand over his mouth. "No." He took a step forward. "You and I are fine . . . right here."

Apprehension roiled in my gut. His breaths were so labored—he seemed on the verge of collapse.

"Listen to me carefully, girl. You can't trust her."

"Sir?"

"*My wife*," he spat. His face was beet red, his eyes watering. Had he taken something? "*My damn wife.*"

I opened and then closed my mouth, having no clue how to respond.

"I know what you are," he said, lowering his voice. "I know what you do. You—you can stop it."

This is the moment I should have run.

I know now what he meant. He knew who I was the moment he heard my name, the moment he remembered in his addled state what he and León had hidden up their sleeves. A daughter. A dark *meiga*. A power equal to the Queen.

"Your Majesty, I don't—"

He careened forward, an inexplicable look of fury on his face. The King grabbed the skirt of my dress, curled an arm around my waist, and slammed me into the wall.

"*The darkness*," he cried. His eyes were pure fury, and I wasn't even sure if he was actually seeing me or some hallucination. There had always been rumors that the King was half mad.

"*Don't you see, girl? It's* her*! It's her that's doing this to me. She wants it*

357

all. The whole rotting Kingdom." He was nearly crying. "*I can't stop—I'm not strong enough—*" And then he dissolved into tears.

"Sir—" I said, trying my best to sound comforting, but still full of fear. My shadows already ached to be set free.

"*YOU!*" he shouted, snapping his attention back to me and slamming me back into the wall. He held my arms by my sides, shaking me, and I whimpered, tears of fear beginning to slip down my cheeks.

"*The darkness,*" he growled again. There was so much hatred in his eyes, but something else too. Grief. "*You can stop it. You. You. Before she—*" His face turned ashen gray as he stared at me, and his eyes—a thin sheen of white covered them.

"Beast of darkness. Death dressed as innocence. *Set the darkness free.*"

"Please stop," I begged through tears. Shadows pushed from my fingers, curling around my hands.

"Stop holding back! You can stop this! You can save our Kingdom! *You!*"

Alexandre roared, throwing himself at me and shoving his fist against my windpipe. I choked. My vision spotted, and in moments, my lungs burned. I kicked my feet out uselessly against him, clawed at his arm with my nails. Nothing broke the adamantine grip he had on me.

Black started to blur the edges of my vision. He was killing me. I was going to die.

Alone. In a dark hall. At the hands of the mad King.

Unless . . .

As soon as the thought was born, my shadows took it as permission. As soon as the fear for my life took hold, they burst from me like a dark inferno.

I wasn't even sure how far they reached, how much they filled that dark hallway.

Instantly, I was surrounded by night, and I fainted. When I woke, the King's body was next to me, his silver eyes staring at me. And I knew that the killer in me wasn't gone.

CHAPTER THIRTY-EIGHT

"Please," I beg Roze. "I didn't mean to—I'm so sorry."

He stares at me. His arms are still around my waist, but I get the feeling that he's hardly aware of them.

A hand creeps onto his shoulder. I startle—I hadn't even seen Belladonna approach. She glowers down at me.

"I am sorry, Roze," she says in the Queen's voice. Her words are comforting, but her voice is cold. "You cannot really be to blame for being drawn in by her. She has dark magic, after all. The darkest—a true daughter of Castelle. Your father recognized it, and she killed him."

"*I didn't mean to.*" I nearly scream it, taking a step back from Roze. It's the cry that I've been desperate to make since it happened, since I've been hiding from the truth.

"Is that the same excuse you use for the trail of bodies you've left in your path?" the Queen sneers through Oleandra. The sisters are closing us in.

I shake my head, desperate. "It's not like that." I look at Roze pleadingly. "Roze, our fathers . . . they loved each other. They wanted to end the war—"

A hand strikes my face, Belladonna's talon-like nails biting into my skin, and I yelp in pain, crumpling to the ground more from shame than anything.

"*Be silent!*" she roars. "You are a murderer, a liar, and a traitor. You have brought a blight of death on our Kingdom, and I will hear no more of the poison that comes from your lips."

Tears fall freely now—my shame exposed in front of Roze and his cruel family. The sisters come closer and the briars around us thicken. "You have destroyed *lives*, Viola Sinclair. You have murdered and deceived since you came to this Kingdom," she sneers.

"It was an accident," I plead weakly, even as darkness creeps into my heart. Even as the shame becomes nearly unbearable.

"It's what you *are*," the dead Queen's voice spits. "Deplorable, depraved thing. You can't help but murder. It's in your nature."

She turns toward Roze. "She'd have killed you too, Prince. Eventually. She destroys everyone around her."

He doesn't say anything to his mother. He only stares at me, his face still frozen in shock, white as bone. "All this time . . . You said you were helping me find who killed my father."

Hot tears are still spilling down my cheeks. "I hoped . . . hoped I could find some other explanation." I think of Professor Borges. "Without anyone else being killed."

"You lied to me," he croaks.

"No," I say, my heart aching. "I didn't lie. But I couldn't tell you the truth."

"I *loved* him," the Queen screams. "I loved Alexandre, and *your* father is the reason he never returned that love. Never loved our daughters. And *you* are the reason he's dead." There is genuine grief on Belladonna's face, screwed into the expression of her mother's spirit.

Anguish, real and visceral, burns on her face. *I* caused that pain. *I* am the cause of so much pain. Kole. My brother. The King.

The Queen is right.

I am the villain of this story.

I am the monster.

I screw my eyes shut.

But I hear Roze approach. He's no longer paying attention to his mother. Instead, his eyes are on me, where I'm crumpled like a coward on the ground. Slowly, he kneels before me. He lifts his hand as though he wants to touch my face before he realizes that his hands are still bare. Instead, he grips my shoulders.

"*Viola*," he whispers. His face is so broken, so determined. I choke on a sob. His voice is tender, and I don't deserve it.

Roze heaves a breath, his own voice cracking with emotion. "Viola Sinclair, there is nothing wrong with you," he says. "I know your darkness. From the moment I saw it, I couldn't get enough of it. I wanted to wrap myself in it. Get drunk on it every night." He leans closer, his cool, poisoned breath brushing my lips. "You're a thing to be feared. And you need not apologize."

Staring back into Roze's eyes, I remember the words of my father.

Then be dangerous.

I am done keeping my shadows tethered. I am done with fear.

Shadows drip from my hands. Not a rush this time, just a slow unfurling. It's like breathing for the first time, not a gulp of air, but a clear, true breath. Soon, shadows surround me. They wrap me in a tight shell, a cocoon of black, filling every pore, baptizing every inch of me until they are me and I am them.

I let them fall away until they form a cape, a crown, and two swords of pure darkness.

There is belonging in the shadows.

There is salvation in death.

And something lovely and steady in pain.

And I realize, with sudden, breathtaking clarity—*This is who I am*, who I was always meant to be.

A thing of darkness. A true child of my kingdom.

To be free of the Queen's darkness, I will embrace my own.

I stand, and Roze stands with me. My chin is tilted high, proud and unafraid of myself for the first time. And his face is spread in a wicked grin.

"What have you done, Roze?" the Queen whispers through Belladonna's mouth. "You are a traitor. Your father—if your father saw this—"

361

Her voice is strained and hysterical. All the princesses' eyes are wide with fury. "Castelle has brought our Kingdom to its knees."

Roze advances on Belladonna. My stomach twists in fear as he comes within an inch of her face. "It was you, Mother dearest, who taught me to love no one and nothing." He sneers. "You raised me on destruction and hatred, so that I could only be drawn to someone like her."

A sour expression crosses the Princess's face. "You still choose her—after what she's done, what she could do to you?"

His grin broadens. "You made me this twisted thing. It's because of her darkness that I find her irresistible. Besides, what evil of hers could ever come close to the destruction that your"—he eyes the overgrown brambles—"*goodness* has wrought?"

Belladonna's face twists in rage. "*Traitor.* I should have taken back my power sooner." Suddenly her eyes flare bright white. She opens her mouth unnaturally wide and shrieks—a sound so inhuman that it sends a chill through the room. She launches herself at Roze, levitating off the ground and flying through the air with her white gown billowing around her. She stretches out her hand, and great thorny vines whip toward us from every direction.

I don't think. I act. On instinct. On fear. On love.

Shadows erupt from me, colliding like a tidal wave with the vines, with Belladonna. Her screech is immediately silenced. The vines fall flat and dead to the ground while Roze and I remain safe in a cocoon of night.

I let my shadows flow freely from me, relishing them. They feel different than ever before—moldable, submissive. They don't overcome me. I overcome *them*.

I hold my hands out at my sides, moving my fingers, feeling my power. I clench my fists, and the shadows back toward me. When they clear, Roze stands beside me, unharmed, staring at me with a look of admiration and delight. Belladonna lies on the ground, her face white and trembling. When her eyes meet mine, I know I'm looking at Roze's sister, not the possessing spirit of the dead Queen.

"Is she gone?" I ask Belladonna.

Her lip trembles. She looks more frightened than I've ever seen her. "What have you done?" she rasps.

Suddenly pools of water form around the feet of the other princesses, billowing up around the hems of their dresses. They sink into the floor.

And then they are gone.

Roze looks back at me, the expression on his face a question. I stare back at him, holding my breath. My skin prickles. It's too silent, the disappearance of the princesses too quick.

There's a clap of thunder, and every lamp in the room flickers out at once. The Queen's voice is suddenly everywhere, and Roze and I turn our backs to each other, searching for the source of it.

"What have you done to my magic?" the Queen's voice cries from the walls, the ceiling, the air around us.

"I've broken your Mirror," I call out, steeling my spine, holding my shadows like whips in my hands. "If you want to destroy us, you'll have to do it on equal footing, with magic as untethered and unpredictable as mine."

For a moment, the darkness is quiet. Then the Queen's voice whispers in my ear, "So be it."

Lightning flashes, piercing the darkness of the room. And in the silhouette of the tall windows, I see a spindly, hulking shape, tall enough to reach the ceiling of the hall, standing over us.

"Roze," I whisper.

He turns toward it, and I grab hold of his sleeve. It lifts one massive leg toward us and screeches, a sound halfway between a bird of prey and the roar of a lion, so loud that the chandeliers that hang overhead rattle.

Oh Saints.

"Roze!"

He grabs me and pulls me away just as a massive leg slices down on us, piercing the marble.

Roze grabs for me, taking my arm in his hand, and pulls me toward the door.

"Wait!" I scream. *"Waffles!"* I release Roze's hand and fly toward where

I can still see his little stony form beside the stage. I have no idea if he can be fixed, if what's been done can be reversed, but I know I'm not going to leave him here.

"*Viola!*" Roze shouts, and I hear a shriek as the monster jabs a leg into the stone near him.

I reach Waffles just as the creature notices me again. I scoop him into my arms and am met by the broad side of a vine, swept into my back by the monster. I cry out as thorns pierce me, and I stumble to the ground.

I hear a low moan, not far away. Belladonna is still on the ground, shielding herself with her arms and curled into a ball. I rush toward her, clambering over briars.

"Belladonna," I call as I reach her.

She lifts her head, and my stomach twists. Her face is stained with tears and blood.

"*Go,*" I urge her, lifting her to her feet.

"What?" She looks at me dazedly. "Why are you helping me?"

"Because Aragoa needs its Queen."

She stares at me, something piercing and meaningful passing between us. Then her eyes fall to Waffles in my arms.

"Give me your gargoyle."

"What?"

"I can fix him. I'm a light *meiga*. I can undo whatever my mother did to him." At the look of shock on my face, she adds, "Didn't you wonder how I knew what was going on between you and my brother? I have the power of insight."

I shake my head and shove Waffles into her arms. There's little time to take in this information. "Take care of him," I urge her. "And . . . Cerise."

She looks at me sharply and nods. Then I nearly shove her in front of me toward the door. I don't watch to see if she makes it through—I run, instead, toward Roze.

He leaps over the seats of Moody Hall, dodging the great monster's legs, while it spins and spits at him. He looks up just as I reach him, and he grabs hold of my arm.

"We need to let the Mists inside," I shout at him.

He heaves down lungfuls of air, stumbling over seats. "What?"

"The Mirror showed me the *Book of Odds*. The Mists are the only thing that will stop your mother."

"But they'll kill everyone."

I shove him just in time to spare us both from being skewered by a massive, hairy leg. We scramble back toward each other, and I take hold of his arm. "The *Book of Odds* said that last time the Mists came, 'the devastation undid itself.' Your mother's magic is like an Ouroboros—it can only destroy itself." I grab his arm and run down the steps toward the stage as the monster swipes a huge leg past us. "The Mists can destroy her," I pant, "because they're *her* magic. We keep the Mists contained to this room, and once she's gone, they'll be gone."

"You're sure?"

"Well, no, but it's my working hypothesis—"

We spring away from the monster as another clap of thunder and lightning bursts outside. I don't see Belladonna, and I hope she made it through. Another leg, black and covered in spines, crashes down in front of us, ripping through the old stones of Vandenberghe, and we crash to the ground. I barely notice the fresh tears in the skin of my knees and arms.

"We need more than a hypothesis right now, Sinclair," Roze shouts.

"You'll just have to make do, because that's all I've got."

We sprint in the other direction, tearing down the stairs, crawling over vines toward the stage. I can't even see the shape of the thing overhead—the room is too dark. But I can hear it turning in place, tracking us. Its body is so big that it can hardly move in the room without bumping the walls.

It hisses, the sound of it crawling across my skin.

Roze grabs my arm and pulls me back just as another leg comes down in front of me. The marble cracks, and I fall on the shattered stone, crying out as rubble slices into my calf.

"*Up!*" Roze yells. "Keep moving!"

I grab his elbow, and we run down an aisle of chairs.

"Why can't you use your shadows?" he shouts over the roar of the monster.

"I can, but I told you—her magic has to destroy itself. That's what the book said."

"You killed those vines—"

"But not *her.*"

The Mists have turned black outside; the wind is howling. Thunder rattles the buttresses, and lightning flashes again—

I get a glimpse of the monster. Its head is black and hairy with eight massive eye sockets each filled with serrated teeth.

The mouths gnash at us, spit spilling from the lids. A cry of terror escapes me, and Roze grips me tighter.

It stabs at us again, one leg after the other as we skip over chairs, trying not to lose each other in the darkness.

There is no running from it.

"Then how do we get to the Mists?" Roze hollers.

"Hold on—"

I glance up at the thing as we run. I let my shadows free, and they rage from me. The fear of everything I have seen since the moment the King attacked me bursts from me, pouring out of me, emptying me of every ounce of bitterness and spite . . .

My shadows bite at the spider's legs, wrapping around them. It hisses angrily, tumbling backward and crashing into the stone wall of the hall. The wall crumples, ancient stones flying into the night.

I strike.

A spear of solid shadow flies from my outstretched hand—pure, controlled fear and fury. It flies through the hole in the castle wall, pierces the invisible magical barrier created by light *meigas* so long ago, and in a spray of starlight, an enormous gash opens to the night air that allows the Mists to flood through.

In a twisted waterfall, the poison seizes everything it can reach. It finds the monster first, curling around it, choking it. The spider struggles, its long legs flailing so that Roze and I have to duck, flattening ourselves to the floor. The vines and briars grow black and brittle, the roses withering and dying.

"Come help me with the Grimmstones!" I shout, turning away from the threat overhead.

Even as the Mists billow toward us, we rush for Ed, Fletcher, and the rest. The boys blink awake as the Queen's power weakens. Roze and I tear the vines from them and push them toward the great doors of Moody Hall, still dodging the thrashing legs of the spider.

"*Come on*," I shout, grabbing Fletcher by the wrist and coaxing him to move faster as he stumbles sluggishly over dead branches.

I reach the doors and push the boys through one by one. Roze has Sculler by the collar and practically throws him through the doorway. "Now you!" he shouts.

"What?"

"*Go*, Viola!" His hand is on the great wooden door, ready to slam it shut.

"You—" A stone of dread drops in my stomach. "You're not coming?"

His eyes are dark and steely as he says through panting breaths, "If you're right, I am my mother's creation. Her power lies within me. While I live, so does she."

With a feeling like ice in my veins, I realize—Roze plans to die.

I look up—I can no longer see the ceiling at all. It's full of the dark haze of the Mists. They're now sweeping down the walls, crawling across the floor.

"Viola, *go*!"

But I'm not listening to him. Instead, my mind is whirring, trying to find any way out of this for him, because I can't—I *can't*—leave him to die. I watch the Mists twist and crawl, my hands absentmindedly fiddling with my locket—*my locket*. Of course.

I look back at him. "You're not doing this alone." I charge toward him and slam the door shut behind me, closing both of us in the hall with the Mists and the spirit of the Queen.

Horror fills Roze's face. "Don't do this to me. Don't make me responsible for—"

"*Roze.*" I grab his arm and yank him aside, just as a great, hairy leg strikes out of the cloud of Mists, crashing into the stone archway around us.

We bolt as stone falls over our heads. I aim for the corner of the room, still free of the Mists. I'm nearly there when my foot catches on a vine. My ankle twists painfully, and I tumble to the floor.

"*Viola!*"

The Mists are filling the hall, black as death, coming toward us like a great, malevolent cloud.

There is nowhere left to run.

Roze crawls toward me on his elbows. His face is sweaty, his eyes tired and wild, and he throws himself on top of me. He grips my shoulders, head bent and buried in my shoulder. He's trying to protect me from the Mists . . . but also from himself, from the poison on his skin.

And it is that moment that I realize what has been staring me in the face all along.

"Roze," I whisper in his ear, and gently, I move my fingers closer to the collar of his shirt. The cloud of Mists undulates closer. Gently, still fearfully, I let my fingers brush the warm skin of his neck, and I immediately feel weightless and foggy. I hear him hiss—a sound of protest and pleasure.

He pulls back enough to look at me. "Viola . . ."

He thinks I have given up. That I beg for death.

He's right.

But not in the way he thinks.

I release my shadows from my fingers. They wrap around Roze's neck

368

like a collar, daring to creep up into his snow-white hair, beneath the collar of his shirt. They are an extension of me, and somehow I can almost feel the muscles of his back, the strength of his shoulders. It's like I'm melting, and I can't tell if it's from the poison or because I want to wrap myself up in him, bury myself in him like a coffin, let him take my mind, my body, my soul, straight to the grave.

"Roze," I answer him, lacing my voice with meaning, looking at him with confidence—the same confidence as the day that I punched him—so that he will know to trust me. "Kill me," I whisper.

Roze's eyes narrow as he thinks.

"Trust me, and *kill me*," I plead. The Mists are nearly on top of us now, ready to swallow us whole.

And then the corner of his lips lifts, his eyes glinting with affection. "Always," he mutters. And he kisses me.

CHAPTER THIRTY-NINE

I'm not thinking about death as I kiss him—not his, and not mine. For once, I think of nothing . . . and feel everything. There's an inward fracturing, every defense obliterated by ferocious, demanding desire as Roze kisses me, and I have a moment to register the softness of his lips, the hunger in the way he presses them to mine. There is nothing tender here. This is the kiss of a man who has been touch starved for a lifetime. Cursed with lovelessness. He kisses me like he will never have enough. Like I am the answer to every despicable desire of his heart.

He cradles the back of my neck, his fingers weaving into my hair.

I move my hands from his neck to wrap around his back, snaking my shadows everywhere.

This is no longer about escape, it's about being found, and taking what is ours—world be damned.

His lips move against mine, devouring me, and I claw at him, pulling him closer.

I let my shadows ensconce him. Like a moth in a cocoon, I bury him. Like a viper swallowing a mouse, I take him.

Like my brother. Like Kole. Like his father. With the last dregs of my life, I take his.

And then we are both falling. Me by his lips, and him by my darkness.

I am first struck by the smell of grass and heather. Then, the warmth on my face like butter and liquid joy, which means . . .

I open my eyes. And I laugh—full chested and free.

Roze breathes deeply on top of me. "What could possibly be so funny?"

I shove his shoulder lightly. "Roll over, you buffoon. It's the *sun*."

Roze rolls off me, and though I miss his closeness, the look on his face when he opens his eyes is priceless. His face cracks into a grin I have never seen—a smile that shows me that he has dimples when he truly smiles, that he would have been a torturously adorable child had he ever been allowed freedom or fun.

And his eyes. It is only in the sunlight that I can now see them clearly—not silver, but pale blue.

He catches me looking at him when he turns his head.

"Viola," he says, his voice soft. He reaches toward me, and then stops, his hand freezing in the air. That familiar restraint crosses his face. But then it vanishes. Fingers bare, he reaches toward me and brushes his knuckles along my cheek.

Death has no power here.

Because death has all the power here.

"I don't understand," he says.

I don't answer right away. I want to be sure. This was my greatest gamble, but the clues were all there.

I sit upright as well and take in our surroundings. The neighboring woods are thick with powerful oaks, twisting every which way as though they've had all the room in the world to grow whatever way they thought best. There are bees, gliding from flower to flower, happy with the simple work of their existence.

A wild laugh escapes me. "We're in Castelle, Roze."

He sits up with me. "The Kingdom of Death." He shakes his head disbelievingly.

I strain the tall grass through my fingers, feeling its warmth. "My father said death started to infect the land of Castelle when too much dark magic was used here. So much so that it became death itself. It *became* the afterlife. I guessed that we would be taken here—to my father's Kingdom."

But never did I think death could be so lovely. Everything here is bright and sharp, like I've been dreaming for a very long time and have only just woken up.

"For us to be truly rid of my mother, I needed to die—the abomination."

My heart aches. "You've always been more than that, Roze. If you were just your mother's awful power, you'd be gone now." I reach out and take his hand. "But you're not. You're here."

He stares back at me with such warmth and wonder that I think I might burst. "I'm here."

For a long moment, or possibly a lifetime, we are silent, both content to sit there in the sun.

He leans back, hands behind his head, and gazes up at the sky.

"Not that I'm in any rush—this all seems rather pleasant—but if we're dead, how are we going to get back?"

"It won't stay the Kingdom of Death. It's already starting. The land is healing." I pull a small yellow flower between my fingers, studying it in wonder. "We've broken the Queen's hold on Aragoa, allowing dark and light to coexist the way they were meant to, the way León and Alexandre wanted them to. It's going to heal Aragoa, Roze," I whisper. "Castelle too, I think. Everything will be balanced again." I close my eyes, taking a deep, slow breath. I silently promise myself to never breathe stale cavern air again.

"Viola, look." Roze is pointing to the tops of the trees. In the far distance rise charcoal-black mountains, and ensconced among them, its dark twisting spires piercing the sky, is a castle.

"Well," he says with a quiet laugh. "Welcome home, Princess."

EPILOGUE

And so, the Prince of Nightmares and the Girl of Shadows found themselves in the very place from which they'd run for seven long days—the realm of Death Itself. And to their amazement, this was not a defeat, but a victory.

For the Kingdom of Death was not a gruesome place of sorrow and despair, but a realm where lost things were found, where the Shadow Girl could return to her true home, and the Prince could be free of his mother's torment.

Here, the Queen had no power over the Shadow Girl and her Prince.

Here, the cursed Prince could touch and love her.

And she could glory in her darkness.

ACKNOWLEDGMENTS

Seven Deadly Thorns, my firstborn book baby, wouldn't have been possible without a kingdom of people.

Endless gratitude to Camille Kellogg, who forced me, screaming like a toddler, to make my world-building make sense. Every vibes writer needs a logical editor. Thank you for showering me with encouragement and making this book the best version of itself.

Thank you to my agent, Caitlin Blasdell, for copious editorial notes, timely wisdom, and tireless championing of this book. Thank you for choosing to believe in this project and in me as an author. I couldn't have a better advocate.

Thank you to Alex Antscherl for your kind guidance, for your hard work, and for always being a joy to work with.

Enormous appreciation to the entire Bloomsbury team for your relentless hard work and for making this process such a positive one for a new author.

Thank you to Teagan White for the absolutely breathtaking illustrations. Nothing else could have captured the darkly lovely mood of this book so well.

Thanks to my beta readers: Rebecca F. Kenney, Caitlin Foley, and Cay Leytham. Your feedback got me from an ugly first draft to something resembling a query-able novel.

To my writer friends and the online writing community—everyone who commented on a pitch, who laughed bitterly with me about the perils of this industry, who hyped me up during dark days. This book is yours.

Thank you to my friends and the Tea and Tarts book club. Your unparalleled taste in books drives my writing. Thank you for supporting me and for salivating over every new piece of book art I had to show you.

Thanks to my kiddos for keeping me humble. You're right, it's not that cool to have a book published. I'll get you your chocolate milk now.

Thank you, Waffles, the best of Frenchies, for your obvious contributions. No thank you for barking at my feet while I was trying to write.

Lastly, thank you to the readers who love a white-haired book boyfriend, whose favorite color is morally gray, who'd gladly spend their days getting lost in a haunted castle. I write for you.